Dedalus European Classics
General Editor: Mike Mitch

The Dedalus
Meyrink Reader

The Dedalus
Meyrink Reader

Edited & Translated by

Mike Mitchell

Dedalus

Dedalus would like to thank The Austrian Federal Ministry of Education, Arts and Culture for its assistance in producing this book.

Published in the UK by Dedalus Limited,
24-26, St Judith's Lane, Sawtry, Cambs, PE28 5XE
email: info@ dedalusbooks.com
www.dedalusbooks.com

ISBN 978 1 903517 85 7

Dedalus is distributed in the USA by SCB Distributors,
15608 South New Century Drive, Gardena, CA 90248
email: info@scbdistributors.com   web: www.scbdistributors.com

Dedalus is distributed in Australia by Peribo Pty Ltd.
58, Beaumont Road, Mount Kuring-gai, N.S.W. 2080
email: info@peribo.com.au

First published by Dedalus in 2010
The Dedalus Meyrink Reader copyright © Mike Mitchell 2010

The right of Mike Mitchell to be identified as the editor & translator of this work has been asserted by him in accordance with the Copyright, Designs and Patents Act, 1988.

Printed in Finland by Bookwell
Typeset by Marie Lane

A C.I.P. listing for this book is available on request.

Contents

* All translations are by Mike Mitchell unless otherwise stated.

The Editor

For many years an academic with a special interest in Austrian literature and culture, Mike Mitchell has been a freelance literary translator since 1995. He is one of Dedalus's editorial directors and is responsible for the Dedalus translation programme.

He has published over fifty translations from German and French, including Gustav Meyrink's five novels and *The Dedalus Book of Austrian Fantasy*. His translation of Rosendorfer's *Letters Back to Ancient China* won the 1998 Schlegel-Tieck Translation Prize after he had been shortlisted in previous years for his translations of *Stephanie* by Herbert Rosendorfer and *The Golem* by Gustav Meyrink.

His translations have been shortlisted three times for The Oxford Weidenfeld Translation Prize: *Simplicissimus* by Johann Grimmelshausen in 1999, *The Other Side* by Alfred Kubin in 2000 and *The Bells of Bruges* by Georges Rodenbach in 2008.

His biography of Gustav Meyrink: *Vivo: The Life of Gustav Meyrink* was published by Dedalus in November 2008. He has recently edited and translated *The Dedalus Meyrink Reader.*

Foreword

The Dedalus Meyrink Reader contains both material that has not previously been published in English and extracts from works that have already appeared in English. The new material comprises the stories from the anthology *Fledermäuse (Bats)*, apart from 'Meister Leonhard', which is contained in *The Dedalus Book of Austrian Fantasy: 1890-2000*, 'The Clockmaker', a chapter from the unfinished novel *The Alchemist's House* and three autobiographical articles. *Fledermäuse*, published in 1916, signifies a move away from the style of Meyrink's early stories, with their emphasis on the satirical, the grotesque and the macabre, to a more intense engagement with the occult; some also reflect his response to the horrors of the First World War.

The autobiographical articles were written in the later 1920s, though 'The Pilot', unpublished in Meyrink's lifetime, was probably written in 1930/31. The longest of these pieces, 'The Transformation of the Blood' goes into great detail about Meyrink's lifelong preoccupation with esoteric knowledge, especially yoga.

These articles are followed by extracts from Meyrink's five novels, as well as four stories from his earlier period, which were collected in *Des deutschen Spießers Wunderhorn* (*The German Bourgeois' Magic Horn*, 1913).

Part 1

Cricket Magic

'Well?' the men asked with one voice when Professor Goclenius entered, walking faster than usual and looking noticeably distraught, 'Well, did they release the letters? — Is Skoper already on his way back to Europe? — How is he? — Have his collections come as well?' The questions all came at once.

'Only this here,' the Professor said. Beside the bundle of letters he put on the table, he placed a small jar containing a whitish dead insect the size of a stag beetle. 'The Chinese ambassador himself handed it over. He said it had arrived today, having for some reason come via Denmark.'

'I fear he's heard bad news about poor old Skoper,' a clean-shaven man whispered behind his hand to the man sitting next to him, an elderly scholar with flowing locks who — both prepared specimens for the Science Museum — had pushed his spectacles up onto his forehead and was examining the insect with keen interest.

It was a strange room where the six men, all specialists in entomology, were sitting. There was a musty smell of camphor and sandalwood, which only served to intensify the exotically macabre atmosphere created by the porcupine fish hanging from the ceiling — goggle-eyed, like the cut-off heads of a ghostly audience — by the garishly painted red and white demon masks of savage island tribes, by the ostrich eggs, hyraxes, narwhal tusks, contorted monkeys' bodies and all the other grotesque shapes from distant zones.

Hanging on the walls above worm-eaten brown cupboards that had a somewhat monastic look, in the putrid evening light pouring in from the overgrown museum garden through the potbellied barred window, were faded, larger-than-life pictures of bark beetles and mole crickets, lovingly framed in gold like revered ancestral portraits.

Crooking its arm invitingly, an embarrassed smile playing round its goitrous nose and circular, glassy eyes, the museum assistant's top hat on its head and dry snakeskins dangling round it, a sloth leant forward from its corner, perfectly aping an ancient village schoolmaster being photographed for the first time.

Its tail disappearing in the distant shadows of the corridor and its vital parts, following a request from the minister of education, in the course of being varnished, the pride of the institute, a forty-foot-long crocodile, stared in through the connecting door with its perfidious feline gaze.

Professor Goclenius had sat down, untied the string round the bundle of letters and glanced through the first lines, muttering to himself.

'It's dated from Bhutan, 1 July 1914 — that is four weeks before the war broke out — so it must have taken more than a year to get here,' he said to the assembled group. 'Our old colleague, Johannes Skoper, writes:

I will give a full account of the wealth of specimens I have found on my long journey from the Chinese border, through Assam, to the so far unexplored country of Bhutan in my next report. Today I just want to describe briefly the bizarre circumstances surrounding the discovery of a hitherto unknown white cricket — Professor Goclenius pointed to the insect in the jar — which the shamans use for their superstitious practices. It is called Phak, which is also an insulting name for anything resembling a European or other person of white race.

One morning I heard from some Lamaist pilgrims, who were heading for Lhasa, that not far from my campsite was a very high dugpa — one of those satanic priests feared throughout Tibet. They can be recognised by their scarlet caps and claim to be direct descendants of the demon of the fly agaric. However that may be, the dugpas are said to belong to the ancient Tibetan religion of the Bhons, of which we know as good as nothing, and to be descended from a foreign race, the origins of which are lost in the mists of time. This dugpa, the pilgrims told me, whirling their little prayer wheels in superstitious awe, was a Samtsheh Mitshebat, that is a being that can no longer be described as human with the power to 'bind and loose', a being, to put it briefly, with the capacity to see time and space for the illusions they are and for whom, therefore, nothing was impossible here on earth. There were, I was told, two ways to climb the steps leading beyond humanity: one, the 'path of light', leading to union with the Buddha, and a second one taking the opposite direction, the 'path of the left hand', to which only a born dugpa knew the entrance, a spiritual path full of horror and dread. Although very infrequent, they went on, such 'born' dugpas were to be found in all parts of the world and, strangely enough, were almost always the children of especially pious people.

'It is as if the Lord of Darkness had grafted a scion onto the tree of saintliness,' the pilgrim who told me this said. 'There is only one way by which one can tell that a child is spiritually part of the clan of dugpas: if the whorl of hair on the crown of its head goes from left to right instead of from right to left.'

I immediately expressed the wish — purely out of curiosity — to meet this dugpa, but my guide, himself from East Tibet, resisted the idea stubbornly. It was all nonsense, there were no dugpas at all in Bhutan, he kept shouting, and anyway a dugpa, especially a Samtsheh Mitshebat, would never reveal his arts to a white man.

The man's dogged resistance made me all the more suspicious and after hours of argument that went to and fro I got him to admit that he was a member of the Bhon religion himself and knew very well — from the reddish colour of the fumes the soil gave off, he tried to tell me — that there was an 'initiate' dugpa living in the vicinity.

'But he'll never reveal his arts to you,' was his constant refrain.

'Why ever not?' I finally asked.

'Because he will refuse to accept responsibility.'

'What responsibility?" I insisted.

'The disruption he created in the realm of causes would mean he would once more be caught up in the maelstrom of reincarnation, if not something even worse.'

I was keen to learn more about the mysterious Bhon religion, so I asked, 'According to your faith, does a human have a soul?'

'Yes and no.'

'How do you mean?'

In answer the Tibetan plucked a blade of grass and made a knot in it. 'Has the blade of grass a knot now?'

'Yes.'

He undid the knot. 'And now?'

'Not any more.'

'In just the same way a human has a soul and has no soul,' he said simply.

I tried a different way of getting a clear idea of his views. 'Fine,' I said, 'let's assume you fell off that narrow mountain pass we crossed recently' — it wasn't more than a foot wide — 'would your soul have lived on or not?'

'I wouldn't have fallen off.'

Trying another tack, I pointed at my revolver and said, 'If I were to shoot you dead, would you live on or not?'

'You can't shoot me dead.'

'Yes I can.'

'Try it, then.'

I'll do nothing of the sort, I thought, a fine mess that would leave me in, wandering round these boundless highlands without a guide. He seemed to be able to read my thoughts and gave a scornful grin. I remained silent for a while.

He suddenly went on: 'It's just that you can't "will" anything to happen,' he said. 'Behind your will there are wishes, some you're aware of and others you're not, but both are stronger than you are.'

'So what is the soul according to your faith,' I asked, irritated. 'Have I a soul, for example?'

'Yes.'

'And will my soul live on after I die?'

'No.'

'But you think yours will live on after you die?'

'Yes. Because I have a name.'

'What do you mean, a name? I've got a name too.'

'Yes, but you don't know your true name, so you don't possess it. What you think of as your name is just an empty word that your parents thought up. You forget it when you sleep. I don't forget my name when I sleep.'

'But when you're dead you won't know it any more,' I objected.

'No. But the Master will know it and not forget it, and when he calls it, I will rise again. But only me, not anyone else, for only I have my name, no one else has it. What you call your name you share with many others — just like dogs,' he muttered contemptuously to himself. I could understand what he said, but didn't show it.

'What do you understand by the "Master"?' I asked with apparent casualness.

'The Samtsheh Mitshebat.'

'The one near here?'

'Yes, but the one nearby is only his reflection. The one he really is, is everywhere. He can also be nowhere if he wills it.'

'So he can make himself invisible?' I couldn't repress a smile. 'You mean now he's inside the universe, now outside? Now he's there, now he isn't?'

'But a name's only there when it's spoken and not there when it's not spoken,' the Tibetan countered.

'And can you, for example, become a "Master" as well?'

'Yes.'

'So then there'll be two Masters, eh?'

Inwardly I was jubilant. To be honest I was fed up with the fellow's intellectual arrogance and now I'd caught him out, I thought my next question would have been: if one of the masters wants to make the sun shine and the other wants it to rain, who'll win? I was, therefore, all the more nonplussed by his strange answer: 'If I am the Master, then I am the Samtsheh Mitshebat. Or do you think there can be two things that are completely alike, without them being one and the same thing?'

'But there would still be two of you, not just the one. If I were to meet the pair of you, I would meet two people, not one,' I objected.

The Tibetan bent down and searched among the piles of calcspar crystals lying around until he found a particularly transparent one and handed it to me, saying mockingly, 'Hold that in front of your eye and look at the tree over there. You can see two of them, can't you? But does that mean it's two trees?'

I couldn't think of an immediate answer and, anyway, I would have found it difficult to pursue a reasoned discussion of such a complex subject in Mongolian, which we were speaking, so I let him enjoy his little victory. Inwardly, however, I could not overcome my astonishment at the mental agility of this semi-savage with his slanting Mongol eyes and filthy sheepskin coat. There is something strange about these highland Asians, outwardly they look like animals, but once they open up their minds to you, a philosopher appears.

I returned to the starting point of our whole conversation. 'So you think the dugpa wouldn't reveal his arts to me because he refuses to accept the responsibility?'

'That's right, he wouldn't.'

'But what if I were to accept the responsibility?'

For the first time since I'd known him, the Tibetan lost his composure. He could scarcely control the agitation which animated his features. His expression wavered between inexplicable, savage cruelty and gloating malice. During our many months together we had confronted all kinds of extreme danger, we had traversed terrifying abysses on swaying bridges of bamboo not more than a foot wide that froze the blood in my veins, we had almost died of thirst crossing deserts, but never had he lost his inner calm, not even for a moment. And now? What could it be that had sent him into such turmoil? I could almost see the thoughts buzzing round and round in his head.

'Take me to the dugpa,' I said insistently, 'you'll be well rewarded.'

'I'll think about it,' he answered after some reflection.

In the middle of the night he woke me in my tent. He was ready to do it, he said.

He'd saddled two of our shaggy Mongol horses, that aren't much bigger than large dogs, and we rode off into the dark. The men in my caravan were lying, fast asleep, round the glowing embers of the fire.

Hours passed without a word being said between us. The characteristic musky smell given off by the Tibetan steppes on July nights and the monotonous swish of the broom as the horses' legs swept through it was almost overpowering; to stay awake I had to keep my eyes fixed on the stars which, in these savage highlands, have a blazing, flickering quality, like burning scraps of paper. They have a disturbing influence, filling one with unease.

When dawn crept over the mountain tops, I noticed that the Tibetan's eyes were wide open and permanently fixed, without blinking, on a point in the sky. He was, I could tell, in a trance.

Did he know the place where the dugpa was staying so well that he didn't need to look where he was going? I asked several times without getting a reply. Finally he spoke, his voice slurred, as if he were asleep: 'He draws me to him, just as a lodestone attracts iron.'

We didn't even stop for lunch, without a word he kept spurring his horse on. I had to eat the few pieces of dried goat's meat I had with me in the saddle.

Towards evening we came round the foot of a bare hill and stopped by one of those fantastic tents that are sometimes to be seen in Bhutan. They are black, pointed at the top, hexagonal below, with the sides curled up at the bottom. Supported by tall poles, they look like giant spiders with their bellies on the ground.

I had expected to meet a grubby shaman with matted hair and beard, one of those crazy or epileptic creatures that are frequently to be found among the Mongols and Tungus. They drug themselves with a decoction of the fly agaric mushroom and see imaginary spirits or utter incomprehensible prophecies. Instead, the man standing before me — motionless — was a good six foot tall, strikingly slender in build, clean shaven, with an olive-greenish sheen to his complexion, a colour I've never previously seen on the face of a living man, and eyes that were slanting and unnaturally far apart — a racial type completely unknown to me. His lips, like the skin of his face perfectly smooth as if made of porcelain, were bright red, razor-thin and so curved, especially where they rose up high at the corners in what seemed like a pitiless frozen smile, that they looked as if they'd been painted on.

I couldn't take my eyes off the dugpa, not for a long time; thinking back to it, I'm tempted to say that I felt like a child, breathless with horror at the sight of a fearful mask suddenly emerging from the darkness.

On his head the dugpa had a close-fitting scarlet cap with no brim; otherwise he was entirely clothed in a costly sable fur dyed orange which came down to his ankles.

There were no words spoken between him and my guide, but I assume they communicated by secret gestures for, without asking what I wanted, the dugpa turned to me and said, unprompted, that he was ready to show me whatever I wanted, but I had to agree to accept all the responsibility, even if I did not know what that entailed.

I — naturally — immediately expressed my readiness.

As a token of that he demanded I touch the ground with my left hand.

I did so.

Without another word he set off in front of us and we followed for a short distance until he told us to sit down. We squatted by a small mound resembling a table.

Did I have a white cloth?

In vain I looked through my pockets, but all I could find was a faded old folding map of Europe in the lining of my coat — it must have been hidden there all the time I was travelling round Asia. I spread it out between us and explained to the dugpa that it showed the place where I came from.

He exchanged a quick glance with my guide and once more the Tibetan's face was briefly suffused with the expression full of hatred and malice that had struck me the previous evening.

Would I like to see cricket magic?

I nodded. It was immediately clear to me what was to come, a well-known trick, luring insects out of the ground by whistling or something like that.

And I wasn't wrong. With a little silver bell these shamans carry hidden about their person the dugpa made a soft, metallic chirping noise and immediately a mass of crickets came swarming out of their holes in the ground and crawled up onto the faded map.

More and more.

Countless insects.

I was starting to get annoyed, having endured a tedious ride for a trivial display I'd seen often enough in China, but then I realised that what I was seeing was ample compensation for all the discomfort: the crickets were not just a hitherto unrecorded species — which was interesting enough in itself — but their behaviour was highly unusual. Scarcely had they crawled onto the map than they started running round and round aimlessly in circles, then they formed into groups which surveyed each other suspiciously. Suddenly a rainbow of light appeared in the middle of the map — it came from a prism the dugpa was holding up to the sun, as I quickly established — and within a few seconds the hitherto peaceful crickets had turned into a mass of insect bodies tearing each other apart in the most horrible way. It was such a revolting sight, I prefer not to describe it. The buzzing of the thousands upon thousands of wings produced a high humming note which went right through me, a shrill mixture of fiendish hatred and mortal anguish I shall never be able to forget.

I commanded the dugpa to put an end to it immediately. Having already returned the prism to its pocket, he simply shrugged his shoulders.

In vain I tried to force the crickets apart with a stick; the blind frenzy of killing was unstoppable. New hordes kept arriving and the foul, wriggling mass grew bigger and bigger until it was the height of a man. As far as the eye could see, the ground was teeming with maddened insects. A whitish swarm, squashed together, pressing towards the middle, impelled by just the one thought: kill, kill, kill.

Some of the crickets that fell off the pile were so seriously maimed they couldn't crawl back up and tore themselves to pieces with their pincers. At times the humming note was so loud and so horribly shrill that I felt I couldn't stand it any longer and put my hands over my ears.

Finally, thank God, the insects grew fewer and fewer, the swarms crawling out of the earth seemed to get thinner and eventually stopped entirely.

'What's he doing now?' I asked my guide, when I saw that the dugpa was showing no sign of moving. Instead he seemed to be making great efforts to concentrate his thoughts on something. He had drawn up his top lip so that I could clearly see his sharpened teeth. They were pitch black, presumably from the betel chewing that is customary here.

'He is binding and loosing,' I heard the Tibetan reply.

Despite the fact that I kept telling myself that it was only insects that had died there, I felt completely drained and close to fainting, so that his voice sounded as if it came from far away: 'He is binding and loosing.'

I didn't understand what he meant by that and I still don't understand today. Nothing more worth mentioning happened, but I continued to sit there, perhaps for hours, why I couldn't say. I had lost the will to stand up, that's the only way I can describe it.

Gradually the sun sank and the clouds and countryside all around took on that improbably lurid red and orange colour familiar to all those who have been to Tibet. To give an impression, the only comparison is the crudely painted walls of the menageries of travelling circuses in Europe.

I could not get the words 'He is binding and loosing' out of my mind, little by little they built up into fearful imaginings: the twitching heap of crickets turned into millions of dying soldiers. I was so weighed down with an immense, mysterious feeling of responsibility I could hardly breathe, and what made it all the more tormenting was the fact that I looked in vain for the cause.

Then it seemed as if the dugpa had suddenly disappeared, to be replaced by a repulsive statue, all scarlet and olive green, of the Tibetan God of War. I fought against it until my eyes could fix on the real world again, but it did not seem real enough to me: the fumes rising from the ground, the jagged icy peaks of the mountains soaring above the distant horizon, the dugpa with his red cap, myself in my half European, half Tibetan clothes, the black tent with the spider's legs — all that could surely not be real. Reality, imagination, vision? What was truth, what was illusion? And the abyss that kept yawning in my thoughts whenever the choking fear of the incomprehensible, terrible feeling of responsibility welled up inside me once more!

Later, much later, on the journey back, the incident grew in my memory like some rampant poisonous plant which I couldn't pull up, try as I would.

At night, when I can't get to sleep, a dreadful suspicion of what 'He is binding and loosing' might mean slowly starts to dawn on me. I try to stifle it, just as you try to smother a fire that has broken out, to stop it being spelt out explicitly. But it's no use resisting, in my mind's eye I can see reddish vapour rising from from the heap of dead crickets and forming banks of cloud which, darkening the sky like the grim harbingers of the monsoon, are pouring westwards.

And now, as I write this, once more I'm overcome with — with —

'The letter appears to break off at that point,' Professor Goclenius said. 'And unfortunately it is now my sad duty to tell you what I learnt at the Chinese embassy about the unexpected death of our dear colleague, so far away in Asia ...' The professor got no farther, he was interrupted by a loud cry: 'Incredible! The cricket's still alive! After a whole year! Incredible! Catch it. It's flying away.' The men were all shouting at once. The scholar with the flowing locks had opened the little jar and shaken the apparently dead insect out.

The next moment the cricket had flown out of the window into the garden.

The entomologists were in such a hurry to catch it, they almost knocked Demetrius, the old museum attendant, flat on his back as he came in to light the lamp.

Shaking his head, the old man watched them prancing around

outside with their butterfly nets. Then he looked up at the evening sky and muttered, 'What strange shapes the clouds have during these terrible days of war. There's one there that looks just like a man with a green face and a red cap. If his eyes weren't so far apart it could almost be a human being. It's enough to make a man superstitious after all these years.'

How Dr Job Paupersum gave his Daughter Red Roses

Sitting motionless and staring into space late one night in the sumptuous *Café Stefanie* in Munich was an old man of the most remarkable appearance. The threadbare tie, that had taken on a life of its own, and the massive domed forehead with hair flowing down to the back of his neck indicated a distinguished scholar.

The old gentleman possessed little in the way of worldly goods, apart from a sparse silver Vandyke, which, from its source among seven warts on his chin, just reached down to that point of his waistcoat where unworldly thinkers generally have a button missing.

If truth be told, that was the sum total of his worldly possessions. When, therefore, the snappily dressed professional gentleman with the pince-nez and black waxed moustache at the corner table diagonally opposite, who up to that point had devoured a portion of cold salmon, lifting each mouthful to his lips on the point of his knife (each time a diamond the size of a cherry glinted on his elegantly extended little finger) and now and then casting protuberantly searching glances in his direction — when, therefore, this gentleman wiped his lips, stood up, crossed the almost empty café, bowed and said, 'Would you be interested in a game of chess, sir? At one mark per game, perhaps?' Paupersum's reaction was all the more eager.

Vivid phantasmagoria of all kinds of opulence and indulgence appeared before the scholar's mind's eye and even as an inner voice whispered, 'God must have sent me this chump,' his lips were already commanding the waiter, who had just come bustling up and set off, as was his wont, a range of faults in the electric light bulbs, 'Julius! A chessboard. '

'If I'm not mistaken, it's Dr Paupersum I have the pleasure of addressing?' was the opening conversational gambit of the professional gentleman with the waxed moustache.

'Job ... yes, er, yes, Job Paupersum,' the scholar admitted abstractedly, for he was spellbound by the magnificence of the whopping great emerald, in the shape of a car headlamp, on the tie-pin adorning the throat of his opponent. Only the arrival of the chessboard released him from the spell and in no time at all the pieces were set up, the loose knights fixed with spittle and the missing castle replaced by a bent matchstick.

After his third move the professional gentleman divested himself of his pince-nez, adopted the classical thinker's pose and fell into brooding lucubration.

'He must be trying to find the most stupid move on the board. I can't think why else he's taking so long,' Paupersum muttered to himself, staring absent-mindedly at the lady in lurid green silk, the only other living being in the room apart from himself and the professional gentleman, who was sitting in solitary splendour on the sofa, like the goddess on the front page of *Over Land and Sea*, attacking a plate of cream horns, her cool woman's heart secure behind a hundred pounds of fat.

'I give up,' the gentleman with the emerald headlamp finally announced, pushed the pieces together, produced a gold case from somewhere inside his jacket, fished out a visiting card and handed it to Paupersum, who read:

Zenon Savanievski

Impresario for Freak Shows

'Hmm. Yeees. Hmm — for freaks hmm — for freaks.' For a while Paupersum kept repeating the word vacuously, then, his mind on building up capital, he raised his voice and asked, 'But don't you fancy a few more games?'

'Certainly. Of course. As many as you like,' the professional gentleman said politely, 'but shouldn't we discuss some more lucrative business first?'

'Some more — *more* lucrative business?' the scholar exclaimed, faint wrinkles of suspicion appearing at the corners of his eyes.

'I happen to have heard —' the impresario went on, ordering with graphic gestures a bottle of wine and one glass from the waiter, '— quite by chance I happen to have heard that despite your eminence as a scientist you have no position at the moment?'

'Oh yes I have. I spend the day wrapping comforts for the troops and putting stamps on them.'

'And that keeps body and soul together?'

'Only insofar as licking the stamps provides a certain amount of carbohydrates for my organism.'

'But then why don't you make use of your knowledge of languages instead? As an interpreter in a prisoner-of-war camp, for example?'

'Because I've only learnt Old Korean, regional variants of Spanish, Urdu, three Eskimo languages together with a few dozen dialects of Swahili and at the moment we are unfortunately not at war with those peoples.'

'Serves you right for not learning French, Russian, English and Serbian,' the impresario muttered.

'If I had, it would just mean the war would have broken out with the Eskimos instead of the French,' the scholar objected.

'Really? Hmm.'

'Yes, my dear sir, there's no hmm about it, that's the way things are.'

'Personally, in your situation, Herr Doktor, I'd have tried to place articles on the war with some newspaper or other. All made up, of course, you wouldn't have to leave your study.'

'I've tried that,' the old man wailed, 'reports from the front, concise and factual, touchingly simple in tone, but —'

'Are you crazy?' the impresario broke in. 'Reports from the front concise and simple in tone?! When you write reports from the front you pull out *all* the stops. You should have —'

Dr Paupersum dismissed his advice with a wave of the hand. 'I've tried everything humanly possible. When it was impossible to find a publisher for my book *On the Probable Use of Sand for Blotting in Prehistoric China*, an exhaustive four-volume treatment of the subject, I turned to chemistry' simply watching the other man drink the wine loosened Dr Paupersum's tongue — 'and quickly invented a new way of hardening steel...'

'Well that must have brought in the money!' the impresario exclaimed.

'No. A manufacturer I showed my invention advised me not to bother patenting it (later on he patented it himself). He said you could only earn money with small inventions that didn't attract your colleagues' notice and arouse their envy. I took his advice and invented the famous folding confirmation chalice with automatic rising bottom to make it easier for the Methodist missionaries to convert savage tribes.'

'And?'

'I was sent to prison for two years for blasphemy.'

'Go on, Herr Doktor,' the impresario said encouragingly, 'this is all fascinating.'

'Oh, I could go on for days about hopes that came to nothing. For example, in order to get a scholarship a well-known patron of science had announced, I spent several years studying in the Museum of Ethnology. The result was a book that attracted a great deal of attention: *How, According to the Shape of the Palate in Peruvian Mummies, the Incas Would Probably have Pronounced the Word Huitzitopochtli, if the Word had been Current in Peru instead of in Mexico.*'

'And were you awarded the scholarship?'

'No. The patron of science told me — this was before the war — that at the moment he was short of money. Moreover, he was a pacifist and had to save up because the most important thing was to consolidate Germany's good relations with France in order to preserve the humanitarian work and ideals that had been established at such great effort.'

'But then when the war broke out you'd have prospects of getting the scholarship?'

'No. He said said that now he had to save more than ever so he could make his own small contribution to making sure the old enemy was vanquished for good.'

'Well, I'm sure your luck'll be in once the war's over, Herr Doktor.'

'No. Then he'll say he really has to save so that all the humanitarian work and ideals, that have been destroyed, can be built up again and good relations between the nations can be re-established once more.'

The impresario thought for a long while, then asked in sympathetic tones, 'How is it you've never shot yourself?'

'Shot myself? To earn money?'

'No, no. I mean … er, well … I mean it's remarkable that you've never lost heart, that you keep going back into the fray.'

At once Paupersum became restless. A fearful flicker animated his expression, which up to that point had been fixed, as if carved from wood. A similar wild glint, a look of agony, of profound, mute hopelessness, can be seen in the eyes of frightened animals on the edge of the cliff, with their pursuers behind them, before they plunge into the abyss so as not to fall into the hands of their tormentors. Twitching, as if with repressed sobs, his skinny fingers scrabbled round on the table, seeming to look for something to hold on to. The crease running from his nose to his mouth suddenly lengthened and stiffened, twisting his lips as if he were fighting against paralysis. He swallowed a few times.

'Ah, now I know,' — the words came haltingly, as if he had to struggle to stop himself slurring them — 'now I know, you're selling insurance. I've spent half my life trying to avoid meeting someone like you.' (In vain the impresario tried to interrupt, and raised both his hands and eyebrows in protest.) 'You're implying I should take out insurance and then find some way of killing myself so that — yes, so that my child at least can live and won't have to starve to death with me. Don't say anything. Do you think I don't know that nothing can be kept secret from you people? You've dug invisible passages from house to house and you peer, beady-eyed, into the rooms where there's money to be made, so that you know everything about us: where a child's been born, how many pennies this or that man has in his purse, whether he's thinking of getting married or going on a dangerous journey. You keep tabs on us and you sell each other our addresses. And you, you look into my heart and read the thought that has been eating away at me for ten long years. Do you think I'm such a miserable egoist that I wouldn't have long since taken out insurance and shot myself for my daughter's sake — off my own bat and without any of you, who intend to cheat us and cheat your own company, who cheat here, there and everywhere, telling me how to do it so that nothing would come out? Do you think I don't know that when … when the deed's done you'd be off in a flash to tell them — for another cut, of course: "It's a case of suicide, you don't need to pay out." Do you think I can't see — as everyone can — my dear daughter's hands getting whiter and whiter and more transparent with every day that passes, do you think I don't know what it means when she has dry, feverish lips and coughs during the night? Even if I were a scoundrel like you people, in order to buy medicine and nourishing food I'd have long since… But I know what would happen, the money would never be paid out and… and then… no, no, it doesn't bear thinking about!'

Again the impresario tried to interrupt to allay the suspicion he was an insurance broker, but his courage failed him when the scholar clenched his fist threateningly.

After a series of gesticulations which were totally incomprehensible, Dr Paupersum muttered, 'No, I must consider some other way of finding help,' — it was clearly the end of a train of thought that had been going through his mind — 'the business with the Ambras giants, for example.'

'The Ambras giants! That's it! That's what I wanted to ask you about.' Now there was no stopping the impresario. 'What is this business with the Ambras giants? I know you once wrote an article about them. But why aren't you drinking, Herr Doktor? Julius, quick, another glass.'

Immediately Dr Paupersum was once more the scholar.

'The Ambras giants,' he said in a voice now devoid of emotion, 'were misshapen people with immense hands and feet. The only place they occurred was the Tyrolean village of Ambras, which suggested it was a very rare form of disease caused by a pathogen which would only be found in that one place, since it obviously didn't thrive elsewhere. But I was the first person to prove that the pathogen was to be found in a local spring, which in the meantime has almost dried up. Certain experiments I carried out indicate that I could prove this by using myself as a guinea pig; within a few months my own body — despite my advanced age — would show similar and even more extreme malformations.'

'Such as?' the impresario asked eagerly.

'My nose would undoubtedly grow longer by eight or nine inches and start to resemble a trunk, perhaps somewhat like that of the South American capybara, my ears would expand to the size of plates, and in three months at most my hands would be the size of an average palm leaf (lodoicea sechellarum), whilst my feet would unfortunately scarcely exceed the dimensions of the lid of a 100-litre barrel. My theoretical calculations concerning the expected bulbous growths on the knees, in the manner of the Central European bracket fungus, are still in progress so I cannot absolutely guarantee —'

'Enough, enough! You're the man for me,' the impresario broke in breathlessly. 'No, please don't interrupt. To put it in a nutshell: are you willing to carry out the experiment on yourself if I guarantee you a yearly income of half a million, with an advance of a few thousand — well, let's say… let's say five hundred marks?'

Dr Paupersum was struck dumb. He closed his eyes. Five hundred marks! Was there that much money in the world?

For a few minutes he visualised himself transformed into an antediluvian monstrosity with a long trunk; already he could hear a negro, in the gaudy attire of a fairground barker, bawling out at a sweaty, beer-sodden crowd, 'Roll up, roll up, ladies an' gen'lmen! Only a measly ten pfennigs to see the most 'ideous monster of the century!' Then he saw his darling daughter, restored to health, dressed in white silk, blissfully kneeling at the altar, the bridal wreath round her hair, the whole church radiant with light, the statue of the Virgin resplendent… and… and… suddenly his heart stood still for a moment: he would have to hide behind a pillar, he couldn't kiss

31

his daughter again, couldn't even let her see him in the distance to give her his blessing from afar, he, the most repulsive being in the whole wide world. If he did, he would scare the bridegroom away! From now on he would have to be a creature of the dusk, avoiding the light, carefully keeping himself hidden by day. But what did that matter? Not a jot if only his daughter could once more be healthy. And happy! And rich! He fell into a silent ecstasy. Five hundred marks! Five hundred marks!

The impresario, interpreting the long silence as indicating that Paupersum couldn't make up his mind, started to deploy all his powers of persuasion: 'Listen to me, Herr Doktor. Don't say "no". That would be turning your back on Fortune when she's smiling on you. Your whole life has taken a wrong direction. Why? You've crammed your head full of learning. Learning's a load of nonsense. Look at me. Have I ever bothered with learning? That's something for people who're born rich — and they don't really need it. A man should be humble and, well, what you might call stupid, then Nature will look kindly on him. After all, Nature's stupid too. Did you ever see a stupid man going bankrupt? You should have worked on the talents your Good Fairy gave you at birth. Or have you perhaps never looked in a mirror? A man with your appearance — even now, without having tasted the Ambras drinking water — could have been making a decent living as a clown for years. My God, the signs Mother Nature gives are so obvious even a child can understand them. Or are you perhaps afraid that as a freak you'd have no friends to talk to? I can tell I've put together a sizeable ensemble — and all people from the top drawer. There's an old gentleman, for example, who was born with no arms or legs. I'm going to exhibit him to Her Majesty the Queen of Italy as a Belgian infant who's been mutilated by the German generals.'

Dr Paupersum had only taken in the last couple of sentences. 'What's all this nonsense?' he snapped. 'First you say he's an old gentleman, then you're going to exhibit him as a Belgian infant!'

'That only increases the attraction!' the impresario countered. 'I simply tell them he aged so rapidly out of horror at having to watch his mother being eaten alive by a Prussian uhlan.'

'Yes, well, if you say so,' said Dr Paupersum cautiously, disconcerted by the impresario's quick-wittedness. 'But tell me one thing: how do you propose to exhibit me before I've got a trunk, feet like dustbin lids and so on?'

'Nothing simpler. I'll smuggle you to Paris via Switzerland on a false passport. There you'll be put in a cage where you'll have to roar like a bull every five minutes and eat a few live grass snakes three times a day — don't worry, we'll manage, it just sounds a bit revolting. Then in the evening we'll put on a special show: an actor masquerading as an explorer will demonstrate how he captured you with his lasso in the Berlin jungle. And outside there'll be a poster with: "Genuine German Professor! Guaranteed!" After all, that's the truth, I won't have anything to do with fraud. "Live for the first time in France!" And so on. My friend d'Annunzio will be happy to compose the text, he'll give it the right poetic pizzazz.'

'But what if the war should be over by then?' Paupersum objected. 'With my bad luck…'

The impresario smiled. 'Don't you worry, Herr Doktor, the day will never come when a Frenchman won't believe anything that's to the detriment of the Germans. Not in a thousand years.'

Was that an earthquake? No, it was just the trainee waiter dropping a tin tray full of glasses as a musical prelude to his night shift.

Somewhat flustered, Dr Paupersum looked round the café. The goddess from *Over Land and Sea* had disappeared. Her place on the sofa had been taken by an incorrigible theatre critic who, mentally panning a premiere that was to take place in a week's time, licked his forefinger to pick up a few breadcrumbs off the table and chewed them up with his front teeth, giving a good imitation of a polecat as he did so.

It gradually dawned on Dr Paupersum that he was sitting with his back to the rest of the café and had presumably been doing so all the time, so he must have seen everything he had just experienced in the large wall mirror, from which his own face was now staring at him

33

pensively. The snappily dressed gentleman was still there too and he really was eating cold salmon — with his knife, of course — but he was sitting right over there in the corner, not at Paupersum's table.

'How did I come to be in the Café Stefanie?' he asked himself.

He couldn't remember.

Then he slowly worked it out: 'It comes from starving all the time and then seeing other people eating salmon and drinking wine with it. My self split in two for a while, it's not unknown and perfectly natural. Suddenly it's as if we're among the audience in the theatre and performing on the stage at the same time. And the roles we play are made out of the things we've read and heard and — secretly — hoped. Oh, yes, hope is a cruel playwright indeed! We imagine conversations we think we're having, we see ourselves make gestures until the outside world grows thin and everything around us takes on different, delusory forms. We don't think the words and phrases that come out of our brain in the way they usually do; they come wrapped in observations and explanations, as in a short story. A strange thing, this "self". Sometimes it falls apart like a bundle of sticks when you untie the string...' Again Dr Paupersum found his lips were murmuring, 'How did I come to be in the Café Stefanie?'

Suddenly all his brooding vanished as a cry of delight swept through him. 'But I've won a mark at chess! A whole mark! Now my daughter will get well again. Quick, a bottle of red wine, and some milk and —"

Wild with excitement, he searched through his pockets. As he did so his eye fell on the black armband round his sleeve and at once he remembered the awful, naked truth: his daughter had died during the night.

He clasped his head in his hands. Yes, died. Now he knew how he came to be in the café — he had come from the graveyard, from the funeral. They had buried her that afternoon. Hastily, soullessly, sullenly. Because it had rained so hard.

And then he had wandered round the streets, for hours on end, gritting his teeth, desperately listening to the clatter of his heels and counting, counting, from one to a hundred, then starting again, to stop himself going mad from the idea that his feet might unwittingly take him back home, back to his bare room with the pauper's bed where she had died and which was now empty. Somehow or other he must have ended up here. Somehow or other.

He clutched the edge of the table to stop himself collapsing. Disjointed words and phrases kept popping up in his scholarly mind: 'Hmm, yes, I should have... blood... transfusions. I should have transferred blood to her from my veins... blood from my veins...' he repeated mechanically a few times. Then a sudden thought gave him a start: 'But I can't leave my child all by herself, out there in the wet night.' He wanted to scream it out loud, but all that came was a low whimper.

Another thought jolted him: 'Roses, a bouquet of roses, that was her last wish. I won a mark at chess, so at least I can buy her a bouquet of roses.' He rummaged through his pockets again and dashed out, hatless, into the darkness, in pursuit of one last, faint will-o-the-wisp.

The next morning they found him on his daughter's grave. Dead. His hands thrust deep into the earth. He had slashed his wrists and his blood had trickled down to the girl sleeping below.

His pale face shone proudly with the peace that can never be disturbed by hope again.

Amadeus Knödlseder, the Incorrigible Bearded Vulture

'Out of the way, Knödlseder,' Andreas Humplmeier, the Bavarian golden eagle, said, snatching the piece of meat the keeper was holding invitingly through the bars.

'Bastard!' the bearded vulture croaked, beside himself with fury. He was well advanced in years and had already grown short-sighted during his long period in captivity; all he could do was fly up onto his perch and send a thin jet of spittle in the direction of his tormentor.

It was like water off a duck's back to Humplmeier. Keeping his head well out of range in the corner, he devoured the meat, just putting up his tail feathers in a gesture of contempt. 'Come on, then, if you want a good thrashing,' he mocked.

It was the third time Amadeus Knödlseder had had to go without his dinner. 'Things can't carry on like this,' he muttered, closing his eyes to shut out the sneering grin of the marabou stork in the adjoining cage who was sitting motionless in a corner, supposedly 'giving thanks to God' — an occupation which, as a sacred bird, he felt it incumbent upon himself to pursue tirelessly.

'Things can't carry on like this.' Knödlseder went over the events of the past week. At first even he had had to laugh at the eagle's typically Bavarian sense of humour. One instance in particular stuck in his mind: two haughty, pigeon-chested types, strutting like stiff-legged storks, had been put in the next cage and the golden eagle had cried out, 'Hey, what the hell's that? What are you supposed to be?'

'We're demoiselle cranes,' came the answer.

'Oh, how very naice,' the eagle replied in a prissy voice. 'And what're they, when they're at home?'

'Anthropoides virgo.'

'Virgo? Well I never! I believe you, thousands wouldn't,' the eagle said, to general hilarity.

But Amadeus Knödlseder himself had soon become the butt of the vulgar bird's coarse mockery. Once, for example, he'd hatched a plot with a raven, with whom the vulture had got on very well until then. They'd pinched a red rubber tube from a pram, which the nursemaid had carelessly left too close to the bars of the cage, then placed it in the food trough. Humplmeier had jerked his thumb at it and said, 'There's a sausage for you, Maddy.' And he — Knödlseder, the royal bearded vulture, who until then had been unanimously esteemed as the crowning glory of the zoo — had believed him, had flown with the tube onto his perch, grasped it in his claws and pulled and pulled at it with his beak until he was quite long and thin himself. Then the elastic material had suddenly snapped and he'd fallen over on his back, twisting his neck horribly. Knödlseder automatically rubbed the spot; it still hurt. Again he was seized with fury, but he controlled himself so as not to give the marabou the satisfaction of schadenfreude. He shot him a quick glance. No, the obnoxious fellow hadn't noticed, he was still sitting in his corner 'giving thanks to God'.

'Tonight I escape,' was the decision the bearded vulture came to after turning the alternatives over in his mind for a while. 'Better freedom and all the worries about where the next meal's coming from than one more day in the company of these base creatures.' A brief check confirmed that the trapdoor in the roof of the cage still opened easily — the hinges were rusted through, a secret he'd been aware of for some time.

He looked at his pocket watch. Nine o'clock. It would soon be getting dark.

He waited an hour, then, without making a sound, packed his suitcase: one nightshirt, three handkerchiefs (he held them up to his eye; A. K. embroidered on them? Yes, they were his), his well-thumbed hymn-book with the four-leaf clover in it and then — a melancholy tear moistened his eyelids — his dear old truss which, painted in bright colours to look like a cobra, his mother had given him as a toy for Easter shortly before humans had taken him from the nest. Yes, that was everything. He locked the case and hid the key in his crop.

He decided to have a short sleep before setting off, but hardly had he put his head under his wing than he was startled by a clatter. He listened. It was nothing important, just the marabou stork who was secretly addicted to gambling. At night, when all was quiet, he would play 'odds or evens' against himself in the moonlight. He played it by swallowing a pile of pebbles then spitting some of them out: if there was an odd number, he'd won. The vulture watched for a while, highly delighted to see the stork lose one game after another. But then another noise — from the artificial cement tree with which the cage was embellished — drew his attention. It was a low voice whispering, 'Pst, pst, Herr Knödlseder.'

'Yes, what is it?' the vulture replied in an equally quiet voice, gliding down silently from his perch.

It was a hedgehog. He too was Bavarian born and bred but, in contrast to the odious eagle, he was a plain, simple fellow who abhorred coarse practical jokes.

'You're going to escape,' the hedgehog said, with a nod at his packed suitcase. For a moment the vulture wondered whether, to be safe, he ought to wring the little animal's neck, but the honest creature's frank, open expression was disarming. 'Know your way round Munich at all?'

'No,' the vulture admitted, somewhat disconcerted.

'There you are. I can give you a few tips. First of all, head off left round the corner soon as you get out, then take a right. You'll see when you get there. And after that,' — the hedgehog shook a pinch of snuff from his snuff box onto the back of his paw and took it with a loud sniff — 'and after that just keep straight on till you come to an oasis of peace, we call it Daglfing. You'll have to ask again there. Bon voyage, as they say, Herr Knödlseder.' And with that the hedgehog went off.

Everything had gone well. Before dawn began to break Amadeus Knödlseder, quickly swapping his own shabby braces and hat with the embroidered, edelweiss-bedecked articles belonging to the eagle, who was snoring away like a steam engine on his perch, cautiously opened the trapdoor and launched himself up into the air, clutching his little suitcase in his left claw. The noise did wake the marabou stork, but he didn't see anything for, still drowsy with sleep, he'd immediately gone into his corner to give thanks to God.

'Flat as a pancake,' the vulture muttered as he flew through the rosy dawn over the dreaming city, 'and just about as interesting. To think it calls itself the city of art.'

Soon he had reached the delightful purlieus of Daglfing and, hot from the unaccustomed exertion, descended in order to purchase a pint of beer.

He strolled in leisurely fashion round the deserted streets. Nowhere was there a bar open that early. The only exception was a shop, Barbara Mutschelknaus's 'emporium'. For a while the vulture inspected the motley collection of goods in the window, then an idea suddenly occurred to him. Making his mind up at once, he reached for the door handle.

There was one thing that had been bothering him during the night: how was he gong to keep body and soul together? By hunting? A short-sighted old bird like me? he asked himself.

Hmm. Or establish a guano factory? But the prerequisite for that was food, lots of food. Nothing comes of nothing. But now he had conceived a different plan. He went into the shop.

'Jesus, Joseph and Mary, what an 'orrible beast!' old Frau Mutschelknaus screeched at the sight of her unusual early customer. But she soon calmed down when Amadeus Knödlseder gave her cheeks a friendly pat and intimated, in elegant German, that, in order to complete his wardrobe, he intended to make substantial purchases, above all of brightly coloured ties of all shapes and sizes. Captivated by the vulture's jovial manner, the old woman soon had the counter covered in mountains of the most magnificent neckties.

And 'Sir' took the lot without demur and had them packed in a large cardboard box. He selected just one bright scarlet tie for himself and asked her to tie it round his long, bare neck, all the time giving her fiery glances and warbling seductively:

> One burning kiss from those cherry lips
> Reminds me of
> The rosy blush of dawn —
> Tally-ho, tally-ho, tally-ho!

'There, that suits you down to the ground,' said the old woman, tickled pink, when the tie was neatly knotted. 'Makes you look like' — a real fancy man, she almost said — 'like a proper gen'lman, it does.'

'And may I trouble you for a glass of water, dear lady,' the vulture begged in dulcet tones.

Charmed out of her usual suspiciousness, the old woman hurried off into the rear quarters of her establishment, but hardly was she out of sight than Amadeus Knödlseder grabbed the cardboard box, darted out of the shop without paying and the next minute was soaring up into the heavens. He was soon pursued by a flood of shrill curses from the despoiled entrepreneuse, but the malefactor, with not the slightest twinge of conscience, sailed on through the empyrean, his suitcase in his left claw, the cardboard box in his right.

It was only late in the afternoon — the departing rays of the setting sun were already preparing to kiss the glowing Alpine peaks goodnight — that he descended once more. As the balmy air of his native mountains caressed his cheeks, he revelled in the magnificent views.

The plaintive song of the shepherd boys floated up from verdant pastures to vertiginous, icy peaks, charmingly interwoven with the silvery tones of the homeward-bound herds.

Guided by the natural instinct of a denizen of the skies, Amadeus Knödlseder was delighted to see that fortune had smiled on him and led him to a prosperous little marmot town.

True, as soon as he appeared the inhabitants made for the safety of their homes and locked their doors, but when they saw that Knödlseder did not tear an ancient hamster — a corn merchant who had never been able to run away fast enough — limb from limb, asking him instead for a light and enquiring about lodgings, their fear quickly subsided.

'You're not from around here, to go by your dialect,' he remarked affably once the hamster, quivering so much he could hardly speak, had given him the information he sought.

'No, no,' the old corn merchant stammered.

'You're from the south?'

'No. From — from Prague.'

'Aha. Of the Mosaic persuasion then, I presume?' the vulture enquired with a grin and a wink.

The hamster, afraid it might be a Russian he was facing, immediately denied it. 'Me? Me? How can you say that, Herr Vulture! Jewish? Me? On the contrary, for ten years I was shabbes goy for a family that, though Jewish, was poor.'

Knödlseder inquired about all sorts of details of life in the town, expressing particular pleasure at the fact that there was no night club of any kind; then he let the poor hamster go — he was so frightened that by this time he was almost suffering from St Vitus's dance — and went in search of suitable premises.

Once more fortune smiled on him and before night fell he had managed to rent a nice little shop with a room adjoining and several side chambers, all of which had their own exit.

The days and weeks passed peacefully. The townsfolk had long since forgotten their fear and once more the streets were filled with cheerful chatter from morn till eve.

A board had been fixed above the new shop. On it was written, in a neat round hand:

> Ties — All Colours and Styles
> Prop. Amadeus Knödlseder
> (Green Shield Stamps)

The crowd gathered round to stare at the glories on display.

Previously the mood in the town had always been one of bitterness and despondency when the flocks of wild duck flew past — they were so puffed up with pride at the splendid shimmering green neckties nature had given them. How times had changed! Now everyone who was anyone had a top-quality tie, but much, much gaudier. There were red ones and blue ones, one favoured yellow, another checks and the burgomaster had such a long one his front paws kept getting tangled up in it when he scampered along.

Knödlseder Neckwear was on everyone's lips and the proprietor was considered a repository of civic virtues: thrifty, hardworking with an eye to profit and sober (he only drank lemonade).

During the day he served his customers in the front shop. Just occasionally he would take a particularly discriminating client through to the back, where he would stay for quite a while. Presumably he was bringing his ledgers up to date; at least at these times he was heard to belch, loudly and frequently, which, in businessmen such as he, always indicates strenuous intellectual activity.

That the customer in question never left the premises through the front shop was no cause for surprise — there were so many exits at the rear.

After closing time Amadeus Knödlseder loved nothing more than to sit on a precipitous cliff playing soulful melodies on his reed pipe until he saw the object of his secret affection — an ageing chamois, a spinster with horn-rimmed spectacles and a tartan shawl — come trotting along the narrow rocky ledge opposite. He would offer her a silent, respectful greeting and she would reply with a chaste bow of the head. There were already rumours going round that they would tie the knot and all those who knew about their mutual attachment could not get over their astonishment and kept saying how pleasing it was to see with their own eyes the beneficial effect of a well-ordered existence even on someone with such an unfortunate genetic inheritance as a bearded vulture must of necessity have.

Despite this, the mood among the inhabitants of the marmot town remained sombre, a circumstance that was solely due to the fact, as baffling as it was disturbing, that the size of the population was decreasing in a way that was both frightening and inexplicable, on a weekly basis, so to speak.

Hardly an hour passed without some family reporting a member 'missing'. They racked their brains as to what might have happened, they waited and waited, but none of those who had disappeared ever returned.

One day even the spinster chamois went missing! They found her smelling salts on the rocky ledge, she must have had an accident caused by an attack of vertigo.

Amadeus Knödlseder's grief knew no bounds.

Again and again he plunged, wings outspread, into the abyss — in order, as he said, to find the body of his beloved. In between he would perch on the edge of the gorge, chewing on a toothpick and staring fixedly down into the depths.

He completely neglected his neckwear business.

Then, one night, the horror was revealed. The owner of the house where the vulture lived — a grumpy old marmot — went to the police station and demanded his tenant's shop be compulsorily opened and the goods inside confiscated, since he was not willing to wait any longer for the rent he was owed.

'Hmm. Strange. Herr Knödlseder hasn't paid the rent, you say?' The officer could hardly believe it. Was Herr Knödlseder not at home? Surely, he said, all they had to do was to wake him?

'Him? At home? The old marmot gave a shrill laugh. 'Him? he never comes back before five in the morning — and then drunk as a bat!'

'Is that so? Drunk?' The officer gave his orders.

The first rays of the rising sun were already appearing and still the bailiffs were sweating away at the heavy padlock on the door leading to the rear part of the tie shop.

An agitated crowd was milling round in the market square. 'Fraudulent bankruptcy!' — 'No, speculation. With dud cheques!' went the cries from snout to snout.

'Fraudulent bankruptcy. Hah! I told you! Hah! What's that I keep hearing? Fraudulent bankruptcy?' said the ancient hamster, who had also turned up. It was the first time he'd appeared in public since his terrifying encounter with Knödlseder.

The general unease grew and grew.

Even the elegant marmottes, driving home from revelry and entertainment wrapped in their expensive furs, stopped their carriages and, craning their delicate necks, asked what was going on.

Suddenly there was a crash — the door had given way to the pressure. Grisly was the sight that greeted them.

A ghastly stench poured out of the store room and wherever they looked: spewed-up pellets, gnawed bones piled almost to the ceiling, bones on the tables, bones on the shelves, even in the drawers and the safe, bones upon bones.

The crowd was paralysed with horror. At once it was clear where all the missing marmots had gone. Knödlseder had eaten them up and taken back the goods they'd bought. Just like Cardillac, the jeweller in E. T. A. Hoffmann's *Fräulein von Scuderi!*

'Well now,' the hamster mocked, 'Fraudulent bankruptcy was it, eh?' They gathered round him, astonished that he'd had the foresight to keep himself and his family well away from any contact with the two-faced killer.

'But how could it be,' they all cried, 'that you were the only one to distrust him? The *obvious conclusion* was that he'd mended his ways and —'

'A bearded vulture mend his ways?!' the hamster cried scornfully. Pressing the tips of his thumb and fingers together, as if he were holding a pinch of salt between them and waving them expressively to and fro before his audience, he said, 'Once a vulture, always a vulture, right to —' But he got no further. Loud human voices could be heard. Tourists!

In a flash all the marmots had vanished.

The hamster too.

'Vunderfol! Charmink! Vot a sunrise! Aaach!' squealed a human voice. It belonged to a spinster with a pointed nose and idealistic views who followed it onto the plateau, leaning on her alpenstock, her bosom heaving for all it was worth, her guileless eyes round and wide, like two fried eggs. Only not so yellow! (Violet) 'Ach! Now, surrounded by ze charms of ze Natur, vich is soo beautiful, you cannot, Herr Klempke, say vot you said in ze valley below about ze Italian people. You vill see, ven ze var is over ze Italians vill be ze first to come and hold out zeir hand to us and say:

"Dear Chermany, forgive us, ve haf mended our vays." '

J. H. Obereit's Visit to the Time-Leeches

My grandfather was laid to rest in the graveyard of the sleepy little
town of Runkel. His gravestone is overgrown with thick, green
moss. It bears, below the eroded date and arranged round a cross,
four letters, the gold gleaming as fresh as if they had been carved
only yesterday:

V| I
V|O

Vivo — that is: 'I live' — was the word, I was told when I was still
a child and read the inscription for the first time. It has etched itself
deeply on my soul, as if the dead man himself had shouted it to me
from under the earth.

Vivo — I live: a strange motto for a gravestone.

It still echoes inside me and when I think of it, I feel as I did all
those years ago, standing beside the grave. In my mind's eye I see
my grandfather, whom I never knew in life, lying under the ground,
still intact, his hands together and his eyes, as clear and transparent
as glass, wide open and unmoving. Like someone who has remained
imperishable in the realm of decay and is quietly, patiently waiting
for the resurrection.

I have visited the cemeteries of quite a few towns and it was
always a faint, inexplicable desire to see the same word again on a
gravestone that drew me there, but I only found 'vivo' twice, once
in Denmark and once in Regensburg. In both cases the name on the
stone had been rubbed out by the finger of time; in both cases the
'vivo' shone fresh and bright, as if the word itself were full of life.

I had always accepted as true what people told me as a child,
namely that my grandfather had not left a single written word behind;

I was, therefore, all the more excited when, not long ago in a hidden compartment of my desk, an old family heirloom, I came upon a whole bundle of papers which had clearly been written by him.

They were in a folder on which were written the strange words: 'How can a person expect to escape death, unless he neither waits nor hopes.' Immediately the word 'vivo' blazed up inside me; like a bright light it has accompanied me my whole life through, only dying down for a while to flare up anew within me again and again, sometimes in my dreams, sometimes in my waking life. Although I occasionally thought that it was by chance that 'vivo' came to be on the gravestone — the choice of inscription having been left to the pastor — when I read the maxim on the cover of the folder I was immediately convinced it must have some deeper meaning, something that had perhaps filled my grandfather's whole life and being.

And what I read in his papers confirmed my view with every succeeding page.

There was too much of a private nature in it for me to reveal it to strangers; it must suffice if I briefly touch on that part alone which led to my acquaintance with Johann Hermann Obereit and is related to his visit to the time-leeches.

As became apparent from the papers, my grandfather was a member of the society of the Philadelphian Brethren, an order whose roots go back to ancient Egypt and which claims the legendary Hermes Trismegistos as its founder. The 'grips' and gestures, by which the members recognised each other, were also explained at length. The name Johann Hermann Obereit occurred frequently. He was a chemist, who seemed to have been a close friend of my grandfather and must have lived in Runkel. Since I was keen to learn more about my grandfather's life and the dark, otherworldly philosophy that informed every line of his writings, I determined to go to Runkel to see whether there were perhaps any descendants of the aforementioned Obereit and if so, whether there was a family chronicle.

It is impossible to imagine anywhere more like something out of a dream than that tiny little town that sits, a forgotten piece of the Middle Ages, quiet as the grave with its winding alleys and grass-grown cobbles, at the foot of the mountain castle of Runkelstein, the ancestral seat of the of the Princes of Wied, oblivious to the raucous noise of the modern world.

It was still early in the morning when I went out to the little graveyard and my childhood days came back to me as I walked from one flowery mound to another in the brilliant sunshine, mechanically reading off from the crosses the names of those who were sleeping in their coffins below. While still some distance away, I recognised my grandfather's gravestone from the glittering inscription.

A white-haired, clean-shaven old man with sharply defined features was sitting beside it, his chin resting on the ivory handle of his walking stick. He was regarding me with an oddly animated look, like someone in whom the similarity of a face has awakened all kinds of memories.

In his old-fashioned dress, almost going back to the early years of the last century, with its stand-up collar and broad, black silk cravat, he looked like an ancestral portrait from days long past. I was so astonished at the sight, so out-of-tune with the present, and had anyway become so bound up in everything I had read in my grandfather's papers that, almost without being aware of what I was doing, I softly said the name 'Obereit'.

'Yes, my name is Johann Hermann Obereit,' the old man said, without showing the least sign of surprise.

It almost took my breath away, and the things I learnt in the course of the conversation that followed were not calculated to reduce my amazement.

It is not an everyday experience to see a person before you who doesn't seem much older than you are yourself, but yet must have lived through a century and a half. As we walked along together and he told me about Napoleon and other historical figures he had known, in the way you talk about people who have only just died, I felt like a mere youth, despite my white hair.

'In the town they take me for my own grandson,' he said with a smile, pointing to a gravestone we were passing which bore the date 1798. 'By rights I ought to be buried here. I had the date of death carved on it because I didn't want the crowds gawping at me like some modern Methuselah. The word "vivo",' he went on, as if he could read my thoughts, 'will only be added once I am really dead.'

We quickly became close friends and he insisted I stayed with him.

A month must have passed. We often sat up together late into the night in animated conversation, but he always changed the subject whenever I asked him what the strange words: 'How can a person expect to escape death, unless he neither waits nor hopes' on my grandfather's folder might mean. However one evening, the last we spent together, the conversation came round to the old witch trials and when I expressed the view that the women would simply have been hysterics, he suddenly interrupted me and asked, 'So you don't believe someone can leave their body and go, let's say, to the Blocksberg for the witches' sabbath?'

I shook my head.

'Shall I show you how?' he asked, giving me a sharp look.

'I readily admit,' I said, 'that the so-called witches used drugs to put themselves in a trance and firmly believed they could fly through the air on their broomsticks.'

He thought for a while. 'Of course, you'll say I just imagined it,' he muttered and fell to pondering once more. Then he got up and fetched a notebook from the bookshelf. 'But perhaps you'll be interested in what I wrote down here when I made the experiment years ago. To start with, I must point out that at the time I was young and still full of hope' — I could see from his absent look that his mind was back in the past — 'and I believed in what people call life until I lost everything that was dear to me in quick succession: my wife, my children, everything. Then fate brought me together with your grandfather and he taught me to understand what desires are, what waiting, what hoping is, how they are all interwoven and how one can tear the masks off the faces of these ghosts. We called them the time-leeches because, just as leeches suck blood, they suck time, the true lifeblood, from our hearts. It was here in this room that he taught me how to take the first step on the path by which we can conquer time and crush the vipers of hope beneath our feet. And then,' he hesitated for a moment, 'yes, and then I became as wood, which cannot tell whether it is being stroked or sawn, thrown on the fire or into water. Since then I have been empty inside. I sought no more comfort. I needed none. Why should I have sought it? I know that I am and that only now do I live. There is a subtle difference between "I live" and "I live" '.

'You say all this so calmly, but it's terrible!' I exclaimed, deeply moved.

'That is only the way it seems,' he said with a smile. 'A feeling of happiness beyond your wildest dreams pours out from the motionlessness of the heart. This "I am" is like a sweet, eternal melody that can never die away once it has been born, neither when we sleep, nor when the outside world once more wakes in our senses, nor in death.

'Should I tell you why people die such premature deaths, instead of living for a thousand years, as it says about the patriarchs in the Bible? They are like the green suckers of a tree, they forget they belong to the trunk and die off in their first autumn. But I was going to tell you about the first time I left my body.

'There is an ancient occult doctrine, as old as the human race; it has been passed down by word of mouth until the present day, but only a few know of it. It shows us the way to cross the threshold of death without losing consciousness, and once we have done that, we are master over our own self. We have gained a new self and what until that point had appeared to be our "self" is now just an instrument, as our hands and feet are instruments.

'Our hearts and breathing stop, just like a corpse's, when our newly discovered spirit leaves our body — when we "journey like the children of Israel, leaving the fleshpots of Egypt behind and with the waters of the Red Sea a wall on either side." I had to practise it many times, suffering unspeakable torments, until I finally succeeded in freeing myself from my body. At first I felt myself floating in the air, as sometimes in our dreams we think we can fly, knees drawn up and light as a feather, but suddenly I was drifting down a black stream that flowed from south to north — we call it the Jordan flowing upwards — and its roar was like the pounding of blood in our ears. I could not see anyone, but I could hear lots of excited voices shouting out to me to turn back until I started to tremble. Gripped by some vague fear, I struck out for a rock that appeared in front of me. In the moonlight I saw a figure standing there, the height of a youth, naked and without the characteristics of either male or female sex. It had a third eye in its forehead, like Polyphemus, and was pointing motionlessly towards the interior of the country.'

Then I set off through a thicket along a smooth, white path, but I couldn't feel the ground under my feet and also when I tried to run my hand over the trees and bushes round me I found I couldn't touch the surface — there was always a thin layer of air my hand could not pass through. Everything was bathed in a pale light, as from rotten wood, so that vision was clear. The outlines of the things I could see appeared slack, with a mollusc-like squashiness and strangely enlarged. Young birds with no feathers and round, brazen eyes were sitting in a nest, fat and bloated like Christmas geese, squawking down at me, and a fawn, hardly able to walk but still almost as large as a full-grown animal, was stretched out wearily on the moss and ponderously turned its head towards me like an obese pug dog.

Every animal I saw was possessed of a toad-like lethargy.

It gradually dawned on me where I was. It was a country as real, as actual as our world, and yet only a reflection of it: the realm of ghostly doubles which feed on the marrow of their earthly originals and grow to monstrous size the more their earthly counterparts languish in vain hope and expectation of happiness and joy. When young animals on earth lose their mother and wait, confident in the belief that food will come, until they waste away in torment, a phantom image of them appears on this accursed island of ghosts and sucks up the life that is draining from those earthly creatures. And the life force of these creatures, dwindling through hope, here takes on form and the ground is manured with the fertilising breath of time lost in waiting.

As I walked on, I came to a town which was full of people. I knew many of them on earth and I recalled all their disappointed hopes and how they had become more and more bowed down with grief as the years passed and yet refused to tear the vampires — their own daemonic selves who were eating up their life and their time — out of their hearts. Here I saw them distended into puffy, bloated monsters, wobbling around with their blubber, eyes staring out glassily over fat, pudgy cheeks.

I saw a shop with the sign:

Wheel of Fortune Bureau de Change
Every Ticket Wins the Jackpot

Coming out was a grinning crowd, smacking their thick lips in satisfaction as they dragged sacks full of gold behind them — the spectres of all those wasting away on earth in their insatiable pursuit of a big win at the gambling table.

I entered a temple-like hall with columns that soared up to the sky. Sitting there on a throne of coagulated blood was a monster with a human body, four arms and the horrible snout of a hyena, slavering with venomous spittle: the war god to which superstitious savage African tribes made sacrifice, beseeching him to grant them victory over their enemies.

Terror-stricken, I fled the stench of decay filling the place. Back out in the street, I stopped in amazement at the sight of a palace more magnificent than anything I had ever seen. And yet every stone, every roof, every flight of steps seemed strangely familiar, as if I had built it myself in my imagination.

I mounted the wide marble steps as if I were the undisputed lord and master of the house. And there at the top I read on the doorplate — my own name:

Johann Hermann Obereit

I went in and saw myself in purple, sitting at a splendid table, served by a thousand female slaves, in whom I recognised all the women who had aroused my senses in life, if only for a brief moment.

I was overcome with a feeling of indescribable hatred, when I realised that my double here had been wallowing in luxury and gluttony since I had been alive and that it was I who had brought him into existence and given him all this wealth by allowing the magical power of my self to pour out of my soul in hoping, longing and waiting.

I was horrified to realise that my whole life had consisted of waiting, nothing but waiting in some form or other, of a kind of incessant draining of my lifeblood, and that the time left over which I could experience as *present* could be counted in hours. Everything I had so far thought of as the substance of my life burst like a bubble. I tell you, whatever we do here on earth, it gives rise to further waiting, further hoping; the whole universe is polluted with the foul stench of present time dying the moment it is born. Everyone has felt the enervating weakness that befalls us when we're sitting in a doctor's, a lawyer's, an official's waiting-room — what we call life is the waiting-room of death. Suddenly I understood what time is. We ourselves are formed out of time, we are bodies which appear to be made of material but are nothing other than frozen time. And our daily trudge along the road to death, what is it other than a reversion to time, and waiting and hoping mere accompanying phenomena, like the hiss of an ice cube reverting to water when it's placed on a stove?

As this insight came to me, I saw a quiver run through my double's body and its face contort with fear. Then I knew what I must do: fight to the death these spectres which suck us dry like vampires.

Oh, these parasites on our life know very well why they remain invisible to us, why they hide from our view; the devil's nastiest trick is to pretend he doesn't exist. Since then I have eradicated waiting and hoping for ever from my being.'

'I think I would collapse at the very first step, Herr Obereit,' I said, when the old man fell silent 'if I were to follow the terrible road you took. I can well imagine that one could deaden the feeling of waiting and hoping within oneself, if one worked hard enough at it, but still —'

'Yes, but only deaden!' Obereit broke in. 'Deep down inside "waiting" would still be alive. You have to take an axe to the root. Become like an automaton here on earth. Like a living corpse. Never put out your hand for a fruit, however attractive it looks, if it involves the least waiting; do nothing and it will fall, ripe, into your lap. At first it is like journeying through a dreary wasteland, often for a long time, but suddenly there will be a brightness all round you, and you will see all things, both beautiful and ugly, in a new, undreamt-of radiance. Then "important" and "unimportant" will not exist for you any more, everything that happens will be equally "important" or "unimportant". You will be as invulnerable as Siegfried after he had bathed in dragon's blood and you will be able to say: I am sailing out on the boundless sea of an eternal life with a snow-white sail.'

Those were the last words Johann Hermann Obereit spoke to me; I have never seen him since.

Many years have passed since that time. I have tried as hard as I can to follow his teaching, but waiting and hoping will not budge from my heart.

I am too weak now, to pull out the weeds, nor am I surprised any more that among the countless gravestones in the cemeteries I so rarely find one with the inscription:

$$\frac{V | I}{V | O}$$

Cardinal Napellus

We didn't know much about him apart from his name, Hieronymus Radspieller, and that he had lived for years in the tumbledown castle, where he had rented a whole floor for himself from the owner — a white-haired, surly Basque, the last servant of a noble family that had withered away in melancholia and solitude — and made it habitable with sumptuous antique furnishings.

It was a sharp, fantastic contrast when you went into his rooms from the completely overgrown wilderness outside, where never a bird sang and everything seemed devoid of life, apart from when the rotten, tangle-bearded yews groaned in terror at the force of the föhn wind or the dark green lake, like an eye staring up at the heavens, reflected the white clouds as they passed.

Hieronymus Radspieller spent almost the whole day in his boat, lowering an egg-shaped ball of glittering metal on long, fine silk threads into the still waters: a plumb-line to sound out the depths of the lake.

He must be working for some geographical society, we conjectured, as we sat together for a few hours in the evening after a fishing expedition. We were in Radspieller's library, which he had kindly put at our disposal.

'I happened to meet the old postwoman who brings the letters over the pass,' Mr Finch remarked, 'and she told me there's a rumour he was a monk in his younger days and used to flagellate himself until the blood came, night after night — they say his back and arms are covered in scars. Talking of Radspieller, where can he be tonight? It must be well past eleven.'

'It's the full moon,' said Giovanni Braccesco, pointing with his wrinkled, old man's hand out of the window at the shimmering path of light across the lake. 'We'll easily be able to see his boat if we keep a look-out.'

Then, after a while, we heard steps coming up the stairs, but it was only Eshcuid, the botanist, returning late from his excursions to join us in the room.

He was carrying a plant as tall as a man, with shining, steel-blue flowers.

'It's by far the largest example of this species that's even been found,' he said in expressionless tones, nodding to us. 'I never imagined monkshood would grow at this altitude.' Taking great care not to crush a single leaf or petal, he placed the plant on the windowledge.

He feels the same as we do, was the thought that came to me, and I sensed that at that moment Mr Finch and Giovanni Braccesco were thinking the same thing. 'He's an old man and he wanders restlessly over the earth, like someone looking for his grave without finding it. He gathers plants which are withered the next day. Why? What's the point? He doesn't think about it. He knows his activities are pointless, as we know ours are, but he will have presumably been worn down by the sad realisation that *everything* we undertake, great or small, is pointless, just as it has worn the rest of us down throughout our lives. Ever since we were young we've been like people who are dying, their fingers scrabbling fitfully at the coverlet, not knowing what to hold on to; like people who are dying and who realise death is in the room, so it makes no difference whether they fold their hands or clench their fists.

'Where are you heading for when the fishing season here is over?' Eshcuid asked, after he had checked his plant again and slowly come over to join us at the table.

Mr Finch ran his hand through his white hair, played with a fish-hook and, without looking up, shrugged his shoulders.

'I don't know,' said Giovanni Braccesco unconcernedly after a pause, as if the question had been directed at him.

After that an hour must have trickled away in such leaden, wordless silence that I could hear the blood pounding in my ears. Finally Radspieller's pale, beardless face appeared in the doorway.

As always, his expression had the composure of old age and his hand was steady as he poured himself a glass of wine and drank to us, but he brought an unaccustomed atmosphere of restrained excitement into the room which quickly transmitted itself to us.

His eyes were usually tired and indifferent, and had the strange characteristic that, as with people suffering from diseases of the spinal cord, the pupils never contracted or dilated and did not appear to react to light — Mr Finch used to say they were like matt-silk waistcoat buttons with a black dot on them — but today there was something feverish about them as his gaze flickered round the room, up and down the walls and over the shelves of books, apparently uncertain what to fix itself on.

Giovanni Braccesco tried to strike up a conversation by describing our unusual methods of catching the ancient, moss-grown giant catfish that lived in the permanent darkness of the unfathomable depths of the lake. They never came up to the light and spurned any natural bait; the only things that could get them to bite were the most bizarre forms anglers could think up: lures of shiny, silvery tin shaped like human hands which made swaying movements as they were pulled through the water, or others like bats made of red glass with cunningly concealed hooks on their wings.

Hieronymus Radspieller was not listening.

I could tell that his mind was elsewhere.

Suddenly the words came pouring out, as if for years he had doggedly kept some dangerous secret behind closed lips, only to release it with an abrupt cry: 'At last! Today my plumb-line touched bottom.'

We stared at him, uncomprehending.

I was so mesmerised by the strangely quivering tone of his voice that for a while I only listened with half an ear to his explanations of the process of measuring the depths of the ocean. There were many chasms down there, he said, thousands of fathoms deep, maelstroms whirling round which swept up every plumb-line and held it there, not letting it reach the bottom unless some fortunate chance intervened.

Then suddenly his voice erupted like a triumphal rocket as he declared: 'It's the deepest point on earth a human instrument has ever reached!' and the words burnt into my mind, striking me with a terror for which I could find no reason. There was some kind of eerie double meaning in them, as if there were an invisible presence standing behind him and speaking to me in veiled symbols through his lips.

I could not take my eyes off Radspieller's face. How shadowy, how unreal it had become all at once! If I closed my eyes for a second I could see little blue flames flaring up round it: 'Saint Elmo's fire of death' were the words that immediately came to mind and I had to force my lips to stay shut to stop myself shouting them out loud.

As if in a dream, my mind was filled with passages from books written by Radspieller and which I had read, full of amazement at his learning. They were passages blazing with hatred of religion, faith and hope, of everything the Bible has to say about promises.

It was, I somehow realised, the recoil from the fervent asceticism of a youth tormented by ardent longing that had sent his soul tumbling back down to earth: the pendulum of fate taking a man from light to darkness.

I pulled myself out of the benumbing daydream that had taken possession of my senses and forced myself to listen to Radspieller's story, the beginning of which still echoed in my mind, like distant, incomprehensible murmuring.

He had the copper weight from his plumb-line in his hand, twisting it to and fro so that it glittered like a piece of jewellery. He went on:

'You, as passionate anglers, call it exciting when you feel a sudden pull at the end of your line, which is only five hundred feet long, telling you that there is a large fish on the hook, that immediately a green monster will rise to the surface in a swirl of spray. Multiply that feeling by a thousand and you might perhaps understand what I felt when this lump of metal finally told me: You have touched bottom. I felt as if my hand had knocked at a door. It's the end of the work of decades,' he added softly. He was talking to himself and there was a note of apprehension in his voice. 'What … what will I do tomorrow?'

'It is a not unimportant discovery for science,' our botanist, Eshcuid, broke in, 'to have sounded out the deepest point on the earth's surface.'

'Science... for science,' Radspieller repeated absent-mindedly, looking round at each of us in turn questioningly, eventually exclaiming, 'What do I care for science!'

Then he hurriedly got to his feet.

Walked up and down the room a few times.

'Science is as much an irrelevance for you, Professor, as it is for me,' he said almost brusquely, suddenly turning to Eshcuid. 'Let us face facts: for us, science is just an excuse to do something, anything, it doesn't matter what it is. Life, ghastly, horrible life, has withered our soul, has stolen our innermost being, and to stop ourselves crying out all the time in our misery, we devote ourselves to childish fancies just so that we can forget what we have lost. Let us not deceive ourselves.'

We remained silent.

'But they have another meaning as well,' he said, suddenly overcome with agitation, 'our fancies, I mean. It only dawned on me very, very gradually. Some subtle spiritual instinct tells me that every act we perform has a double, magic meaning. We *cannot* do anything which is not magic. I know precisely *why* I have spent half my life plumbing the depths. I also know what it means that I have finally — finally — finally struck bottom and joined myself, right through all the swirls and eddies, by a long, fine thread to a world where no ray of this sun can penetrate, this hateful sun, whose only pleasure is to leave its children to die of thirst. What happened today is only a trivial, *external* event, but anyone who can see and can interpret what he sees is able to tell from the vague shadow on the wall who has walked in front of the lamp.' He gave me a bitter smile. 'I will tell you in a few words what the *inner* meaning of this external event is for me. I have found what I was searching for, from now on I am immune to those two poisonous snakes, faith and hope, which can only live in the light. I felt it from the the way it tugged at my heart today when I imposed my will and touched the bottom of the lake with my plumbline. A trivial external event has shown its inner face.'

'Have such terrible things happened to you in life? I mean when you were a priest?' Mr Finch asked. 'To make you so sore at heart?' he added, in a quiet aside.

Radspieller did not reply, he seemed to be seeing some image that must have appeared before him. Then he sat down at the table again and, staring fixedly at the moonlight outside, talked like a somnambulist, almost without drawing breath:

'I was never a priest, but even when I was young some dark, powerful urge turned me away from the things of this earth. There were times when, before my very eyes, the face of nature became a grotesque, grinning gargoyle which made me see the countryside, mountains, water and sky, even my own body, as the unyielding walls of a prison. No child, I imagine, feels anything when the shadow of a cloud crossing the sun falls on a meadow, but even then I was petrified with horror and, as if an invisible hand had torn a blindfold from my eyes, I found myself looking into the depths of a secret world full of the mortal agonies of millions of tiny creatures tearing each other apart in mute hatred among the roots and stalks of the grass.

'Perhaps it was hereditary — my father was suffering from religious mania when he died — but soon I could only see the world as a den of cut-throats awash with blood.

'Gradually my life became one long torment as my soul languished. I couldn't sleep, I couldn't think as day and night, without respite, my lips mechanically repeated the phrase from the Lord's Prayer, "Deliver us from evil" until I was so weak I fainted.

'In the valleys where I come from there is a religious sect called the Blue Brethren, whose adherents, when they feel death approaching, have themselves buried alive. Their monastery still stands with their stone coat of arms over the gateway: *Aconitum Napellus*, a poisonous plant with five blue petals, the top one of which looks like a monk's hood, which gives it its name.

'I was a young man when I sought refuge in the order and

approaching old age when I left.

'Behind the monastery walls is a garden where in the summer a bed full of these deadly plants blooms; the monks water it with the blood that runs down when they flagellate themselves. Whenever a new brother is admitted to the order, he has to plant such a flower, which is then given his Christian name, as if in baptism.

Mine was called Hieronymus and drank my *blood*, while I languished for years, vainly pleading for a miracle by which the "Invisible Gardener" would refresh the roots of my life with just one drop of *water*.

'The symbolic meaning of the strange ceremony of the baptism with blood is that we should plant our soul by magic in the garden of paradise and feed its growth with the blood of our desires.

'It is said that in one single night, at the full moon, a monkshood covered all over with flowers, shot up on the burial mound of the founder of the sect, the legendary Cardinal Napellus, and when the grave was opened the body had disappeared. The saint, so the story went, had changed into the plant, which was the first to appear on earth, and all the others are descended from it.

'When the flowers wither in the autumn, we collect the poisonous seeds, which look like little human hearts and, according to the esoteric tradition of the Blue Brethren, represent the "grains of mustard seed" of faith, of which it is written that whoever has it may remove mountains — and we ate them.

'Just as the terrible poison changes our hearts and puts us in a state between living and dying, so the essence of faith should transform our blood and become a miracle-working power in the hours we spend between mortal agony and ecstatic rapture.

'But with the plumbline of my insight, I ventured even deeper into these wondrous symbols and faced up to the question: what will happen to my blood, when it is finally impregnated with the poison of the blue flower? And the things all around me came alive, even the stones by the wayside cried out to me in a thousand voices, "It will be poured out, again and again, when spring comes, so that a new poisonous plant may grow bearing your own name."

'In that moment I had torn the mask from the vampire I had been feeding and I was seized with ineradicable hatred. I went out into the garden and crushed the plant that had stolen my name Hieronymus and grown fat on my life with my foot until not a fibre was left above ground.

'From then on my path through life seemed strewn with wondrous happenings. In the very same night a vision appeared to me: Cardinal Napellus, with his fingers in the position of someone carrying a lighted candle, bearing the blue aconite with the five-petalled flowers. His features were those of a corpse, only his eyes radiated life indestructible.

'He so resembled me that I thought I was seeing my own face. Horrified, I automatically felt my face, just as someone whose arm has been torn off by an explosion might feel for the wound with his other hand.

'Then I crept into the refectory and, burning with hate, broke open the casket that was supposed to contain the saint's relics, intending to destroy them.

'All I found was the globe you can see in that niche there.'

Radspieller stood up, took the globe down, placed it before us on the table and continued, 'I took it with me when I fled the monastery in order to destroy the last physical relic of the founder of the sect. Later I had the idea that I would show it more contempt by selling it and giving the money to a whore. And that is what I did at the earliest opportunity.

'Many years have passed since then, but I have not let a minute pass without searching for the invisible roots of that plant, which is the source of mankind's suffering, in order to banish them from my heart. Earlier I said that from the moment I saw the light, one "wonder" after another crossed my path, but I remained firm, no will-o-the-wisp has lured me into the mire.

'When I started collecting antiquities — all the things you can see in this room come from that time — there were some objects among them that recalled the dark rites of gnostic origin and the century of the Camisards. Even the sapphire ring here on my finger — strangely enough, its coat of arms bears a monkshood, the emblem of the blue monks — was a chance acquisition I came across rummaging through a hawker's tray, even that has not made me waver in my determination. And when one day a friend sent me this globe here as a present — the selfsame globe I had stolen from the monastery and sold — all I did was laugh at the childish threat from some stupid fate.

'No, the poison of belief and hope will not follow me up here in the thin, clear air of this world of snowy peaks; the blue monkshood cannot grow at this altitude.

'In me the old adage has become a new truth: If you would seek out the depths you must climb the mountains.

'That is why I will never go back down to the lowlands. I am healed. Even if the wonders of all the worlds of angels should fall into my lap, I would cast them away as so much dross. Let the aconite remain as a poisonous medicine for the weak and the sick at heart in the valleys, I intend to live and die up here in the face of the fixed, adamantine law of the unchanging exigences of nature which no daemonic spectres can break through. I will continue to plumb the depths, not aiming, not hoping for anything, happy as a child for whom the game is enough and who has not yet been polluted by the lie that life has a deeper purpose; I will continue to plumb the depths, but whenever I touch bottom I will cry out, as if in triumph, "It is only the earth I am touching, once again the earth and nothing but the earth, the same proud earth that coldly throws the hypocritical light of the sun back into space, the earth that remains true to itself, outside and in, just as this globe, the last miserable legacy of the great Cardinal Napellus, is and will ever be a piece of dead wood, outside and in.

'And each time the lake will tell me again: it is true that, generated by the sun, terrible poisons grow on the earth's crust, but inside, in its chasms and abysses, it is free of them and the depths are pure.' The intensity brought red blotches to Radspieller's face and his voice cracked with the emphasis he put on each word: 'If I could have just one wish' — he clenched his fists — 'it would be to let down my plumbline to the centre of the earth, so that I could shout out to the world, 'See: here, there, see: earth, nothing but earth!'

We looked up, taken by surprise when he suddenly fell silent.

He had gone over to the window.

Eshcuid, the botanist, took out his magnifying glass, bent over the globe and said out loud, in an attempt to cover the embarrassment caused by Radspieller's last words, 'This relic must be a fake. It must be from this century, the five continents' — he pointed to America — 'are all on the globe.' Matter-of-fact and normal though his observation was, it could not relieve the strained atmosphere which, for no obvious reason, began to take hold of us and gradually intensified until it was threatening to turn into fear.

Suddenly a sweet, overpowering smell, as of alder buckthorn or spurge laurel, seemed to fill the room.

I was trying to say, 'It's coming in from the park,' but Eshcuid forestalled my stuttering attempt to shake off the oppression that had taken hold of us. He stuck a needle in the globe and was muttering something about it being strange that even our lake, such a tiny point, was on the map, when Radspieller's voice started up again from beside the window and interrupted him in shrilly scornful tones:

'Why has the image of his Eminence, the great Lord Cardinal Napellus, stopped pursuing me, as it used to waking and sleeping? Is there not a prophecy concerning the neophyte in the Codex Nazareus, the book of the gnostic blue monks, written around 200 BC: "Whoever feeds the mystical plant to the very end with his blood will be faithfully guided by it to the gate of eternal life; the sinner who pulls it up, however, will see it face to face as death and his spirit will go out into the darkness until the new spring comes." Where are they, these words? Have they died? A two-thousand-year-old promise has been dashed to pieces on the rock that is me! Why does he not come, so that I may spit in his face, this Cardinal Nap—' Radspieller broke off with a gasp. I saw that he had noticed the blue plant that Eshcuid had placed on the windowledge when he came in and was staring at it.

I was about to jump up and hurry over to him when an exclamation from Giovanni Braccesco stopped me.

Eshcuid's needle had caused the yellowed parchment skin over the globe to split and come away, like the peel coming off an overripe fruit, leaving before us a large, shining glass ball.

Inside it was a wondrous work of art, enclosed in the ball in some way that was beyond our understanding: the figure of a cardinal in cloak and hat, standing and in his hand, his fingers in the position of someone carrying a lighted candle, a plant with steel-blue, five-petalled flowers.

Petrified with horror, I could hardly turn my head to look at Radspieller. Lips pale, his features those of a corpse, he was standing against the wall, upright and unmoving, like the statuette in the glass ball, and like it with the poisonous blue flower in his hand, staring across the table at the face of the Cardinal.

Only the light in his eyes told us he was still alive, but we knew that his spirit had disappeared for good in the black night of madness.

Eshcuid, Mr Finch, Giovanni Braccesco and I parted the next morning, almost without farewell. The horror of the last few hours of that night still held our tongues in thrall.

For years I have wandered the earth, alone and aimless, but I have never met any of them again. Just once, after many years, my path took me to that region. Of the castle only the walls were left, but as far as the eye could see there grew from among the fallen masonry, in serried ranks the height of a man in the scorching sun, a steel-blue bed of flowers: aconitum napellus.

The Four Moon Brethren
A Document

Who I am is quickly told. From the age of 25 to 60 I was valet to Count Chazal. Before that I had been a gardener's assistant in charge of the flowers in the monastery of Apuana, where I had also spent the dreary, monotonous days of my youth and had been taught to read and write thanks to the kindness of the abbot.

As I was a foundling, my godfather adopted me on the day of my confirmation and since then I have the legitimate name of Meyrink.

As far back as I can remember, I have always felt as if there were a band of iron round my head, constricting my brain and preventing the development of what is generally known as imagination. I could almost say I lack an inner sense, but to make up for it, my eyes and ears are as sharp as a savage's. When I close my eyes I still see with oppressive clarity the stiff black outlines of the cypresses that stood out against the crumbling monastery walls, still see the worn bricks on the floor of the cloisters, so distinct and clear I could count them — but all that is cold and mute, it doesn't speak to me, even though I have often read that things should speak to us.

I am being open, saying frankly the way things are with me, because I want to be believed. I take up my pen in the hope that what I write here will be seen by people who know more than I do and can, if they want and are allowed, shed light for me on what has been like a chain of insoluble mysteries accompanying me on my way through life.

If, contrary to all reasonable expectation, this pamphlet should fall into the hands of Dr Chrysophron Zagräus and Dr Sacrobosco Haselmayer, known as 'the Red Tanjur', the two friends of my late second master, the apothecary Peter Wirtzigh (who died and was buried at Wernstein am Inn in the year of the Great War, 1914), I trust they will bear in mind that it is not love of idle gossip, nor of poking my nose into other people's business, that has persuaded me to reveal something they have kept secret for perhaps thirty years. As an old man of seventy I have long since outgrown such childish nonsense; it is, rather, reasons of a spiritual nature that have compelled me to write this of which not the least is my heartfelt fear that after the death of my body I will become a — *machine* (the two gentlemen will understand what I mean).

But to return to my story. The first words Count Chazal spoke to me, when he took me into his service, were, 'Has a woman ever played a significant role in your life?'

When, with a clear conscience, I replied, 'No,' he seemed visibly content. Even today, the words burn me like fire, I cannot say why. Thirty-five years later my second employer, Herr Peter Wirtzigh, asked me the same question, down to the very last syllable, when I started work as his servant: 'Has a woman ever played a significant role in your life?'

Then, too, I had no hesitation in replying 'No', but for one terrifying moment I felt I was a lifeless machine when I said it, not a human being.

Whenever I ponder over it today, an awful suspicion creeps into my mind; I can't put it into words but — are there not plants which can never develop properly, which are always as yellow as wax, as if the sun never shone on them, and wither away because a poison sumach grows nearby and secretly feeds on their roots?

During the first months I felt very uncomfortable in the isolated castle that was inhabited solely by Count Chazal, his old housekeeper, Petronella and me, and was literally filled to bursting with strange, old-fashioned instruments, mechanisms and telescopes, especially as the Count had all kinds of odd habits. For example, although I could help him get dressed, he never allowed me to help him undress, and when I offered, he always used the excuse that he was going to read for a bit longer. In reality, I assume he must have been out in the dark, for in the morning his boots were often thickly coated with mud and marshy soil, even though he had not set foot outside the house during the previous day. And his appearance made me feel uneasy too. Small and slight, his body was out of proportion with his head; although well-formed, for a long time the Count gave me the impression he was a hunchback, though I could not say exactly why.

He had a sharp profile and his narrow, prominent chin with the pointed, grey beard jutting out in front gave him an oddly sickle-like appearance. He must have possessed a powerful vital force, for he hardly appeared to age at all during all the years I served him; at most the curious crescent-moon shape of his face seemed to grow sharper and slimmer.

There were all sorts of odd rumours about him going round the village: he didn't get wet when it rained, things like that; and: if he went past the houses at night, when people were in their beds, the clocks all stopped.

I ignored this idle gossip. The fact that from time to time the metal objects in the castle such as knives, scissors and rakes became magnetic, so that steel nibs, nails and other things stuck to them, is presumably a perfectly normal natural phenomenon; at least the Count explained it when I asked him. The castle stood on volcanic ground, he said; also such occurrences were connected with the full moon.

In fact the Count had an unusually high opinion of the moon, as I deduced from the incidents that follow.

I must first mention that every summer, on 21 July, an exceptionally bizarre guest came and always stayed for just twenty-four hours: the aforementioned Dr Haselmayer.

The Count always called him the 'Red Tanjur', why, I do not know, for Dr Haselmayer did not have red hair, in fact he did not have a hair on his head, not even eyebrows or lashes. Even in those days he gave me the impression of being an old man; maybe it was caused by the extremely old-fashioned clothes which he wore year in, year out: a dull, moss-green moleskin top hat, quite narrow, almost pointed at the top, a velvet doublet, buckled shoes and black silk knee-breeches on his alarmingly short, thin little legs. As I said, maybe it was only because of his dress that he looked so … so 'deceased', for his high, pleasant child's voice and his delicately curved girl's lips spoke against him being old.

On the other hand, I'm sure there were no eyes anywhere in the whole wide world that were as lifeless as his.

With all due respect, I have to add that he had a huge round head, which also seemed to be frighteningly soft, as soft as a boiled egg that's been shelled, and not just his pale, spherical face, but also the skull itself. At least, whenever he put his hat on, a kind of bloodless tube immediately swelled up all round under the brim, and when he took it off again, it was always a considerable time before his head returned to its original shape.

From the minute Dr Haselmayer arrived until the time he left, he and the Count used to talk — without a break, without a bite to eat, without sleeping or drinking — about the moon, and they did so with a puzzling ardour which I could not understand.

And they even, when the full moon fell on 21 July, went out during the night to the marshy little castle pond and spent hours staring at the silvery reflection of the moon in the water.

Once, as I happened to go past, I even saw the two gentlemen throwing lumps of some whitish substance — it will have been pieces of bread roll — into the pond, and when Dr Haselmayer realised I had seen them, he quickly said, 'We're feeding the moon ... er, sorry, I mean the ...er ... swan.' But there was no swan far and wide. Nor any fish, either.

The things I could not help overhearing later that night seemed to have some mysterious connection with that, which is why I memorised them, word for word, and immediately put them down on paper.

I was in my bedroom, still awake, when, in the library that was next door and never used, I suddenly heard the Count say, 'After what we have just seen in the water, my dear Dr Haselmayer, unless I am very much mistaken our cause is nearing fruition and the old Rosicrucian prophecy: *post centum viginti annos patebo* — after a hundred and twenty years I will be revealed — is turning out exactly as we would have wished. Truly, a most satisfactory centenary midsummer celebration! What we can say for certain is that in the last quarter of the previous century the machine was already rapidly taking over, and if things continue in the way we hope, in the twentieth mankind will hardly have time to see the light of day for all the work they will have cleaning, polishing, maintaining and repairing the ever more numerous machines.

'Today we can justifiably say that the machine has become a worthy twin of the Golden Calf of yore, for anyone who torments their child so badly that it dies will get at most fourteen days in prison, while anyone who damages a steam roller will get three years hard labour.

'But the production costs for such a piece of machinery are considerably higher,' Dr Haselmayer objected.

'That is in general true,' Count Chazal replied politely. 'But it is certainly not the only reason. I feel the essential fact is that, strictly speaking, man is merely a half-finished thing which is destined to become a mechanism at some point in the future. This view is clearly supported by the way certain instincts have already become automated — for example choosing the right spouse in order to improve the race. It is hardly surprising, then, that he sees the machine as his true offspring and his natural child as a changeling.

'If women were to start giving birth to bicycles, or revolvers you should see how people would start marrying for all they were worth. In the Golden Age, when mankind was less developed, they only believed what they could "think", but then the age gradually came when they only believed what they could eat; now, however, they have ascended the summit of perfection, that is, they only consider as real what they can sell.

'Because the Fifth Commandment says, "Honour thy father and thy mother etc.", they take it as a matter of course that the machines which they bring into the world and lubricate with the finest spindle-oil — while they themselves make do with margarine — will repay all the effort that went into nurturing them a thousand times over and bring them all kinds of happiness. What they completely forget is that machines can also be ungrateful children.

'They are so drunk on credulousness they are happy to accept the idea that machines are just lifeless things which have no effect on them and which they can throw away at will. Or so they think.

'Have you ever had a good look at a cannon, my friend? Is that a "lifeless" thing? I tell you, not even a general is given such loving care. A general can get a cold and no one would give a damn, but the cannons have aprons wrapped round them, so they don't get cold, and hats on to keep off the rain.

'All right, I agree that you could object that a cannon only roars when it's been primed with powder and the order to fire has been given. But doesn't a tenor only roar when the signal has been given and then only when he has been sufficiently filled with musical notes? I tell you, in the whole universe there is not a single thing that is truly lifeless.'

'But is not our home, the moon,' Dr Haselmayer objected shyly in dulcet tones, 'a dead planet, lifeless?'

'It is not dead,' the Count told him, 'it is just the face of death. It is — how shall I put it? — it is just the focusing lens which, like a magic lantern, reverses the effect of the life-giving rays of the accursed, show-off sun, draws all sorts of pictures out of the brains of the living, conjuring them up in what they call reality, and makes the poisonous force of death and decay germinate and breathe in the most diverse forms and expressions. It is exceedingly odd — do you not agree? — that, despite all this, humans love the moon above all heavenly bodies, that even their poets, who are looked upon as visionaries, sing its praises with sighs of rapture and ecstatic looks, and none of them pale with horror at the thought that, month after month, for millions of years, the earth has been orbited by a bloodless cosmic corpse. Truly, dogs are more sensible, especially black ones. They put their tails between their legs and howl at the moon.'

'Did you not write to me recently, my dear Count, that machines were directly created by the moon? How am I to understand that?' Dr Haselmayer asked.

'You have misunderstood me,' the Count replied. 'The moon merely *impregnated* men's brains with ideas through its poisonous breath and machines are the visible offspring.

'The sun has planted in the souls of mortals the desire for an abundance of joy, but also the curse of creating transitory works by the sweat of their brow and breaking them; but the moon, the secret source of earthly forms, confused them by giving this a deceptive lustre so that they were led astray into a false vision and transferred things they were meant to contemplate inwardly to the external, tangible world.

'The result is that machines have become the visible bodies of Titans, born of the brains of degenerate heroes.

'And just as to "comprehend" and to "create" something means nothing other than to allow the soul to take on the form of what one "sees" or "creates" and to become one with it, so men are now well on the way to turning themselves, as if by magic, into machines. They are helpless to do anything about it and will eventually end up as naked, never-resting, groaning, pounding mechanisms — as what they have always being trying to invent: a joyless perpetuum mobile.

'But then we, the Moon Brethren, will inherit the "eternal being", the sole, immutable consciousness that does not say, "I live" but "I am" and that knows: "even if the universe should collapse, I will remain."

'How could it be, if forms were not simply dreams, that we are able to exchange our body for another at will, to appear among men in human form, among phantoms as shades and among thoughts as ideas, and this by virtue of the secret of being able to divest ourselves of our forms as if they were mere toys chosen in a dream? In the same way as someone who is half asleep can suddenly become aware of their dream, shift that delusion, time, into a new present and set their dream moving in another, more desirable direction, jumping straight into a new body, so to speak, especially since the body is basically nothing more than a spasm, suffering from the delusion of denseness, of the all-pervading ether.'

'Excellently put,' Dr Haselmayer exulted in his sweet, girlish voice. 'But why do we not want to allow these earthlings to enjoy the blessing of transfiguration? Would that be such a bad thing?'

'Bad? It would be terrible! Incalculable!' the Count broke in shrilly. 'Just imagine: mankind with the power to spread their "culture" throughout the cosmos!

'What do you think the moon would look like after a fortnight of that? Velodromes in every crater and sewage farms all around. That is assuming they hadn't previously introduced the dramatic "art" and thus made the soil too acid for any kind of vegetation.

'Or do you want to see the planets linked by telephone during the hours of dealing on the stock exchange? And the double stars in the Milky Way compelled to produce official marriage certificates?

'No, no, my friend, the universe can manage with the old, easy-going routine for a while longer.

'But to come to a more rewarding topic, my dear Dr Haselmayer — by the way, it's high time you started to wane, I mean, depart; we'll meet again at Wirtzigh's, the apothecary's, in August 1914. That is the beginning of the end, the great end, and we want to celebrate that catastrophe for humanity in worthy fashion, don't we?'

Even before the Count had finished, I had slipped into my valet's livery to assist Dr Haselmayer in packing and accompany him to the carriage.

The next moment I was out in the corridor.

But what did I see? The Count came out of the library *alone*, carrying Dr Haselmayer's velvet doublet, silk knee-breeches and buckled shoes, as well a his green top hat, while Dr Haselmayer himself had disappeared. Without a glance in my direction, the Count returned to his bedroom and closed the door behind him.

As a well-trained servant, I considered it my duty not to be surprised at anything my master saw fit to do but I couldn't help shaking my head and it was a long time before I managed to get to sleep.

Now I must pass over many years.

They went by monotonously. In my memory they are like fragments of some old book that recorded confused events in elaborate script on yellowing, dusty paper, a book one had read and hardly understood at some time when one's mind was dulled by fever.

There is just one thing I am clear about. In the spring of 1914 the Count suddenly said to me, 'I shall soon be going away. To — Mauritius' (he gave me a quick glance) 'and I would like you to go to work for my friend Peter Wirtzigh, apothecary, in Wernstein am Inn. Is that clear, Gustav? I won't take no for an answer.'

I made a silent bow.

One fine morning the Count had left the castle without making any preparations. I deduced this from the fact that I did not see him again and a stranger was sleeping in the four-poster bed the Count had been in the habit of using when he slept.

It was, as I was later told in Wernstein, the apothecary, Herr Peter Wirtzigh.

Once I had arrived at Herr Wirtzigh's property, from which one could look down on the foaming River Inn, I immediately set about unpacking the suitcases and boxes I had brought with me to stow the contents away in the cupboards and chests.

I took out a highly unusual old lamp shaped like a transparent Japanese idol, sitting cross-legged (its head was a sphere of frosted glass); inside was a moving snake, operated by a clockwork mechanism, holding up the wick in its jaws. I was going to put it in a tall, Gothic cupboard, but when I opened it I saw, to my horror, the corpse of Herr Dr Haselmayer dangling there.

The shock almost made me drop the lamp, but fortunately I realised in time that it was only Dr Haselmayer's clothes and top hat, which had deluded me into thinking it was his body hanging in the cupboard.

Despite that, the experience made a profound impression, leaving me with a sense of premonition, of something menacing, ominous, which I could not shake off even though nothing particularly exciting happened during the months that followed.

Herr Wirtzigh treated me in a consistently kind and friendly fashion, but in many respects he was far too similar to Herr Dr Haselmayer, so that the incident with the cupboard kept coming back to mind whenever I looked at him. His face was perfectly round, like Dr Haselmayer's, only very dark, like that of a Moor — for years he had been suffering from the incurable effects of a complaint of the gall bladder, from melanosis. If you were only a few steps away from him and it wasn't very light in the room, you could often hardly distinguish his features and his narrow, silvery beard which, scarcely the width of a finger, went from underneath his chin up to his ears and stood out from his face like an eerie, dull radiance.

The oppressive strain kept me in its grip until August, when the news of the outbreak of a terrible world war hit everyone like a thunderbolt. I immediately recalled what I had heard Count Chazal say all those years ago about a catastrophe threatening mankind and so perhaps that was why I could not wholeheartedly join in the curses the villagers hurled at the enemy states; it seemed to me that the cause behind it was the dark influence of certain natural forces filled with hatred which use human beings like puppets.

Herr Wirtzigh was completely unmoved, as if he had long since foreseen it.

It was only on 4 September that he showed some slight agitation. He opened a door, which until then I had always found closed, and took me into a blue, vaulted chamber with a single, round window in the ceiling. Immediately below, so that the light fell directly on it, was a circular table of black quartz with a depression like a trough in the middle. Around it were golden, carved chairs.

'This trough,' Herr Wirtzigh said, 'is to be filled this evening, before the moon rises, with cold, clear water from the well. I'm expecting a visitor from Mauritius and when I call, you're to get the Japanese snake-lamp, light it — I hope the wick will only glow,' he added, half to himself — 'and stand, holding it like a torch, there, in that niche.'

Night had long since fallen, eleven o'clock, twelve o'clock struck and I was still waiting.

No one could have come in, I am sure of that. I would have noticed, because the door was closed and always creaked loudly when it was opened and I had heard no sound so far. There was a deathly silence all round and the pounding of the blood in my ears was gradually becoming a thunderous roar.

At last I heard Herr Wirtzigh calling me — as if from a great distance. As if it came to me from my own heart.

With the glowing lamp in my hand, almost dazed from an inexplicable drowsiness, such as I had never felt before, I felt my way through the dark rooms to the vaulted chamber and took up my position in the niche.

The mechanism hummed softly in the lamp and through the reddish stomach of the idol I could see the glowing wick glittering in the mouth of the snake as it slowly revolved, appearing to be creeping almost imperceptibly upwards in spirals.

The full moon must have been directly above the hole in the ceiling, for its reflection was like a motionless disc of silver with a pale green glow in the trough of water in the stone table.

For a long time I thought the golden chairs were empty, but eventually I could see that three were occupied. As they moved cautiously I recognised the men: in the north the apothecary, Herr Wirtzigh; in the east a stranger (Dr Chrysophron Zagräus, as I learnt from their later conversation); in the south, a wreath of poppies on his bald head, Dr Sacrobosco Haselmayer.

Only the chair in the west was empty.

My hearing must have gradually woken, for words were drifting over to me, some Latin, which I could not understand, and some German. I saw the stranger lean forward, kiss Dr Haselmayer on the forehead and say, 'beloved bride'. There followed a long sentence, but it was too softly spoken for me to be aware of it.

Then, suddenly, Herr Wirtzigh was in the middle of an apocalyptic speech:

'And before the throne there was a sea of glass like unto crystal: and in the midst of the throne and round about the throne were four beasts full of eyes before and behind. And I looked, and behold, a pale horse: and his name that sat on him was Death, and Hell followed with him. And power was given unto him to take away peace from the earth, that the inhabitants thereof should slaughter one another;

and to him was given a great sword.'

'A great sword,' came the echo from Dr Zagräus. Then he caught sight of me, paused and asked the others in a whisper if I could be trusted.

Herr Wirtzigh reassured him. 'He has long since become a lifeless mechanism in my hands. Our ritual demands that one who is dead for the world must hold the torch when we are gathered together. He is like a corpse. In his hand he carries his soul, in the belief that it is a smouldering lamp.'

His words were full of unbridled scorn and a sudden terror made my blood freeze when I felt that in truth I could not move a limb and had become as stiff as a dead man.

Once more Dr Zagräus spoke: 'Yes, the hymn of hatred is sounding throughout the world. I beheld him with my own eyes, the one on the pale horse, and behind him the myriad forms of the army of machines — our friends and allies. They have long since assumed power over themselves, but mankind remains blind, still thinking themselves their masters.

'Driverless locomotives, laden with boulders, come tearing along with mindless ferocity, fall on them and bury hundreds upon hundreds beneath the weight of their iron bodies.

'The nitrogen in the air condenses to produce terrible new explosives: Nature herself pushes forward, breathless in her haste to give up her best resources willingly in order to wipe out the white monster who, for millions of years, has dug scars in her face.

'Metal tendrils with terrible, sharp thorns grow out of the ground, catching their legs and tearing their bodies apart. And in mute triumph the telegraphs wink at each other: another hundred thousand of the hated race gone for good.

'Hidden behind trees and hills, the giant mortars lie in wait, their necks stretched up to the heavens, lumps of ore in their teeth, until the treacherous windmills give them secret signs with their arms to spew out death and destruction.

'Electric vipers dart along under the ground — there! a tiny greenish spark and an earthquake erupts with a roar, transforming the countryside into a mass grave!

'With the glowing eyes of predatory beasts the searchlights peer through the dark. More! More! More! Where are there more of them? And they come, swaying in their grey gravecoats, interminable hordes, their feet bleeding, their eyes lifeless, stumbling in their weariness, half asleep, lungs gasping, knees trembling — but quickly the drums bark out their fanatical fakir rhythm, whipping the benumbed brains into a fury until the howling, berserk frenzy breaks out and only stops when the showers of lead fall on nothing but dead bodies.

'From the east and the west, from America and Asia they come, the metal monsters with murder in their round mouths, to take part in the war dance.

'Sharks of steel creep round the coasts, suffocating in their bellies those who once gave life to them.

'But even those that stayed at home — the apparently "lukewarm" ones who for so long blew neither hot nor cold, who previously had only given birth to peaceable instruments — have awoken to play their part in the great death: tirelessly they belch out fiery breath into the sky day and night, and from their bodies pours forth a stream of sword blades and powder cartridges, lances, shells. None wants to sit there and sleep any more.

'More and more gigantic eagles are waiting to leave the nest to circle over the last hiding places of mankind; already thousands of iron spiders are rushing tirelessly to and fro to weave shining silvery wings for them.'

For a moment there was a pause and I saw that Count Chazal was suddenly there; he was standing behind the chair in the west, leaning on the back, arms crossed. He looked pale and emaciated.

With an emphatically insistent gesture, Dr Zagräus went on: 'And is that not a ghostly resurrection? The blood and fat of antediluvian dragons, long since decomposed and lying in underground caverns as mineral oil, is stirring, wants to come back to life. Simmered and distilled in fat-bellied cauldrons, it now flows as "petrol" into the veins of new, fantastic monsters of the air and sets them throbbing. Petrol and dragon's blood! Who can tell the difference? It is like the daemonic prelude to the Day of Judgment?'

The Count hastily broke in and I could sense a vague fear in his voice. 'Don't talk of the Day of Judgment, Zagräus,' he said, 'It sounds like a portent.'

The gentlemen stood up in surprise. 'A portent?'

'We wanted to meet today for a celebration,' the Count said, after having spent a long time looking for words, 'but until this moment my feet were kept firmly fixed in — Mauritius.' (I dimly understood that there was a hidden meaning behind the word and that the Count was not referring to the country.) 'I have long had my doubts whether what I saw in the reflection that floats up from the Earth to the Moon is correct. I fear, I fear — and icy shivers run over my skin at the terrible thought — that in the short term something unexpected might happen and snatch victory from us. What good is it that I realise there may be another secret meaning in the present war, that the world spirit intends to separate the nations from each other so that they stand alone, like the members of some future body; what use is that to me, if I cannot see the ultimate intention? It is the influences one cannot see that are the most powerful. I tell you:

'Something invisible is growing and growing and I cannot find its root.

'I have interpreted the signs in the heavens which do not lie. Yes, the demons from the depths are arming for battle and soon the Earth's skin will shudder, like the hide of a horse plagued by flies. Already the great ones of darkness, whose names are written in the Book of Hatred, have once more flung a comet out of the abyss of space, this time at the Earth, as they have so often thrown one at the Sun and missed the target so that it flew back to them, just as the boomerang of the Australian aborigines returns to the hunter's hand, when it has not struck its intended victim. But who, I asked myself, is behind this array of strength, when the fate of the human race seems already sealed by the army of machines?

'Then scales fell from my eyes, but I am still blind and can only feel my way.

'Can you also not feel the imponderable power, that death cannot touch, swelling up into a river compared with which the oceans are like a bucketful of dishwater?

'What a mysterious force it is that can sweep away overnight everything small and open up a beggar's heart until it is like that of an apostle! I saw a poor schoolmistress adopt an orphan and set no great store by it, and fear came over me.

'What has happened to the power of the machine in a world where mothers rejoice, when their sons fall, instead of tearing their hair? And could it be a prophetic rune that no one can read yet: a picture is displayed in the city stores, a cross in the Vosges with the wood shot away, but the Son of Man — *was left standing*?

'We hear the wings of the Angel of Death booming over the lands, but are you sure it is not the wings of another, and not those of death? One of those that can say "I" in every stone, every flower and every animal, both in and outside time and space?

'Nothing can be lost, it is said. But then whose hand is it that gathers this enthusiasm, released everywhere like a new force of nature, and to what will it give birth and who will inherit it?

'Is another about to come whose steps none can stay, as has happened again and again in the course of the millennia. I cannot get that thought out of my mind.'

'Let him come! As long as this time he comes clothed in flesh and blood again.' Herr Wirtzigh interrupted scornfully. 'They'll soon nail him with jokes. No one has ever defeated grinning laughter.'

'But he can come *without shape or form*,' Dr Zagräus muttered to himself, 'just as recently something uncanny befell the animals, so that overnight horses could count and dogs read and write. What if he should burst forth like a flame from human beings themselves?'

'Then we must deceive the light in humans with light,' Count Chazal broke in shrilly. 'From that point on we must inhabit their brains as the new, false brilliance of a deceptive, sober rationalism, until they confuse the sun and moon, and we must teach them to distrust everything that is light.'

I cannot remember what else the Count said. Suddenly the state of glass-like fixity, in which I had been held thus far, left me and I could move again. A voice inside me seemed to whisper that I should be afraid, but that was beyond me.

Despite that, I stretched out my arm with the lamp in front of me, as if to protect myself.

Whether a draught caught it or the snake had reached the space in the idol's head, making the glowing wick burst into flame, I could not say. All I know is that a blinding light suddenly burst my senses apart; again I heard my name being called, then a heavy object fell with a dull thud.

I presume it must have been my own body, for when I opened my eyes for a brief moment before I lost consciousness, I saw that I was lying on the floor and the full moon was shining above me. But the room was empty, the table and the gentlemen had disappeared.

For many weeks I lay in a coma and when I had eventually recovered, I was told — I forget by whom — that Herr Wirtzigh had died and had made me sole heir to his entire estate.

But I will have to keep to my bed for quite a while longer and that will give me time to reflect on what had happened and to write it down.

Just occasionally, at night, a very strange feeling comes over me as if there were an empty space yawning in my chest, stretching out endlessly to the east, south, north and west, and in the middle is the moon; it waxes to a shining disc, wanes, goes black, appears again as a slim crescent, and each time the phases are the faces of the four gentlemen as they sat at the round stone table the last time. Then, to take my mind off it, I listen to the boisterous sounds coming through the surrounding silence from the nearby robber's castle of the wild painter Kubin, who holds riotous orgies into the early hours of the morning with his seven sons. When day breaks Petronella, the old housekeeper, sometimes comes to my bed and says, 'How are we today, Herr Wirtzigh.' She keeps trying to tell me that, as the pastor knows very well, there has not been a Count Chazal since 1430, when the line died out, and that I was a somnambulist, who fell off the roof while sleepwalking and for years imagined I was my own valet. Naturally she denies that there is either a Dr Zagräus or a certain Sacrobosco Haselmayer.

'Of course, the Red Tanjur does exist,' she always says at the end, wagging her finger at me. 'It's over there on the stove. They tell me it's a Chinese book of magic. And we all know now what happens when a good Christian reads that kind of thing.'

I say nothing, for I know what I know. But every time the old woman goes out, I get up and open the Gothic cupboard just to confirm what I know. And naturally it's still there, the snake lamp and, hung up underneath it, the green top hat, doublet and silk knee-breeches of Herr Dr Haselmayer.

My Torments and Delights in the World Beyond Communicated by Spiritualist Table-Rapping

As is right and proper for a German writer, I recently — you will have read about it in the Munich newspapers, in the 'Culture' section, below the usual editorials on 'Foot and Mouth Disease in Bavaria' — died from unnatural causes.

Weary of contemplating, morning, noon and night, the ineluctable fate of the writer — a painful death smothered in gold at some point in the future — I decided to put an end to my suffering.

I hurried off through the blizzard — the city was wearing white for Whitsuntide — and entered one of those little stone buildings in which, as the inscription above the doors indicates, they insist on strict segregation of the sexes. Once inside I inserted a ten-pfennig piece, the dragon on sentry duty handed me a clean towel and I made a noose in it.

A choking sensation in my throat, masses of golden stars before my eyes, startled exclamations such as, 'What's going on here?', finally a jerk and my soul was free.

Immediately everything looked quite different but, thanks to the occult studies I had religiously pursued on earth and the fact that from a very early age I had kept my spiritual components in good working order, I had no problem orienting myself right away.

A female figure of unutterable beauteousness came gliding through the air and set about lavishing a series of ghostly caresses on me. The pungent smell of goat's milk she gave off told me she was already in an advanced state of purification but nevertheless — mindful of the Venusberg scene in Wagner's *Tannhäuser* — I extricated myself from her embrace. One second later she had cast off her mask and before me stood Mrs Pankhurst, the notorious maenadic leader of the Suffragettes, who was trying to impede my escape.

But already my fleet foot had taken me to the bank of a murky river where I boarded a boat propelled by the former president of the Charon Rowing Club himself.

The dress of my fellow passengers — chamois-leather trousers, tufts of hair on their hats and green, knee-length, footless stockings — as well as the fact that at regular intervals the gentlemen among them took out coloured phials, poured snuff into the hollow below the thumb and inhaled it with a noisy sniff, suggested to me they were the spectres of departed Bavarian notables.

My suspicion was confirmed by certain malicious references in verse form to my Protestantism. For example:

> Silly old Prod,
> You don't believe in God.
> Liar, Liar!
> You'll burn in hell fire.

Our journey took us past cypress groves in the Lake-Garda-Riviera style and we finally landed safely on a promontory that was teeming with departed souls. It was uncommonly busy, a real immigration port. Extremely interesting, I can tell you.

The formalities were rushed through hurriedly, the officials were already muttering about lunch. We were weighed and shooed along though the eye of a needle by a camel driver, though I was exempted from this later requirement, since I could demonstrate my status with a fat bundle of unpaid bills.

A few minutes later I was sitting on the box of a stagecoach crammed full of souls of all social classes. With a crack of the whip and the clatter of hooves, we set off for the Elysian Fields, as I — unfortunately mistakenly — assumed.

Limousines sped past us. 'Heading for Hell' I was told.

Eager to learn about my new surroundings, I turned to the coachman, a strapping Egyptian Anubis, whose goodwill I had secured by telling him a few risqué anecdotes. 'Tell me, my good man, what is that grey tower over there? There, between the two telegraph poles?'

'Ach,' the coachman, clearly a Bavarian Egyptian Anubis, said, shaking his head gloomily, 'yon's the weather-ninny, sir. The ane that's in charge o' the barometer stuff, ye ken, the ane that delivers the temperature differences for them as are still down there on earth. He's gettin' tae be an auld sourpuss, an' he's gaen' a wee bit saft in the heid, too, tae tell the truth.'

'I say, you there. Yes, you, coachman.' The shrill voice of a North German lady joined in. 'Aren't we going to stop soon? The horses need their gingerbread.' From the swimming movements of her podgy arms, her military bearing and her little, crooked parrot nose I had no difficulty recognising that it was the soul of the celebrated singer and extreme preventer of cruelty to animals, Lilli Kraut, speaking.

The Anubis turned round irritatedly, spat through his teeth and shot her down with a pun.

'Yon's genuine Elberfeld stallions. They dinnae eat nae fruitbread, they only eat square roots and they can find those themselves.'

Soon afterwards we stopped outside a long school building.

Shivers of horror ran down my spine: that could only be Purgatory! And yes, there was Herr Sassafrass, the headmaster. He came out, gave me a penetrating look and said, 'That's Meyrink, Gustav, who kicked against the pricks.' Taking hold of my ear, he led me into the classroom. Right at the back, in the last row, was Lessing. He was wearing short trousers, buttoned at the back, and was crying. He hadn't done his allotted task again, to recite the essays of Herr Deertick without faltering. He was a very poor pupil! Once he'd whispered the answer to Lenau and another time he'd tried to lick off an ink-blot.[1]

The teaching staff gathered at the front, muttering to each other and sending me dark looks.

Hölderlin, whom I had sat down next to in my despair, whispered

---

1 Meyrink's classmates in the purgatorial school-room are well-known figures from German literature: Gotthold Ephraim Lessing (1729-81), Enlightenment playwright and thinker; Nikolaus Lenau (1802-1850), poet; Friedrich Hölderlin (1770-1843), poet; Else Lasker Schüler (1869-1945), Expressionist poet; Otto Erich Hartleben (1864-1905), dramatist; Sassafrass, the headmaster, is a figure from Georg Weerth's (1822-1856) *Humoristische Skizzen aus dem deutschen Handelsleben*.

a warning: 'You'll get "The Song of the Honest Man".'[2]

'No, they're saving that for Lasker-Schüler,' Hartleben assured me in a quiet voice, 'I heard them discussing it in the staff room. you're going to get the "Sioux Lament for the Dead".'

The 'Sioux Lament for the Dead'! Automatically, lips trembling, I started to run through it in my head:

> Behold him sitting on the mat,
> Reposing there, upright,
> With the dignity he had
> When he still saw the light.

'Well, if I can imagine the sound of a barrel organ as I recite it,' I thought, to calm myself down, 'I might be able to survive.' But then things took a turn for the worse. With a loud crash, a trapdoor in the floor opened and — clean shaven, his hand tucked into his coat front, his missing sideburns suggested by laurel leaves — the immortal astral body of an actor stepped up onto the teacher's rostrum.

A terrified murmur went through the rows of my fellow sufferers: 'Oh no, he's been copying Ernst von Possart!'[3]

Dear Readers, I — I — I — er — no, no, I simply cannot bring myself to describe the ordeal I went through, the intense pain as the spiritual dross within me crumbled away during this course of treatment. I would scarcely have survived it, believe me, had not a timely miracle occurred. As the great actor paused for effect after the words 'The smoke from his pipe still blew/ To the Great Spirit in the sky', a hand tapped me on the shoulder and my lawyer, Dr Seidenberger from Munich, handed me a document. From the black gown he was wearing, I deduced that he had not gone the way of all flesh, but had simply come to visit me in his *kama rupa* as the Indians call it, the psychic body which, as is well known, allows

2 'Das Lied vom braven Mann' by Gottfried August Bürger (1747-94), a popular poem of 21 8-line stanzas; the 'Sioux Lament for the Dead' is by Schiller.
3 Ernst von Possart (1841-1921), actor, most famous for roles such as Richard III, Mephisto, Shylock, Iago; he was actor/director at the Munich Court Theatre while Meyrink's mother was engaged there (1869-1880).

mortals to leave their earthly frame while still alive.

'Quick, sign this letter of attorney for me,' he said, adding, as I obeyed with trembling fingers, 'By the way, I'm supposed to be sorting out your estate and I could only find two pfennigs!?'

'That must be a mistake, Dr Seidenberger,' I exclaimed, 'I've never possessed that much.' But he wasn't listening any more. He went up to the headmaster, presented the letter of attorney, and said, in matter-of-fact tones:

'In the name of my client I hereby raise an objection to the proceedings that have already been initiated, on the grounds that my client is of the Protestant religion and that therefore the section of the Penal Code concerning "Purgatory" does not apply to him, in consequence of which I demand that he be released forthwith, failing which we will be compelled, if necessary, to take our appeal right up to the Imperial Salt Office, the third and last court of appeal. The costs of the appeal ...' etcetera, etcetera. Upon which Dr Seidenberger bowed and disappeared.

The teaching staff retired in order to confer, returned immediately, put on their mortar boards and announced my release.

Vaulting over the desks, I was out of the room in no time at all and in the open countryside, that realm of the green veil of Persephone, of which Ovid sings, and which is a true reflection of our earthly meads and glades.

With zephyrs murmuring all around, I took a deep breath and set off for the Elysian Fields.

At a bend in the path, half hidden by drifts of jasmine, the figure of a bent old man appeared. I could hardly believe my eyes. Was that not Solomon Galitzenstein, my dear old business associate from my long-forgotten days at the Vienna stock exchange?

He immediately recognised me as well. 'Hello, Meyrinkleben, what's doin' with the bank shares?' were his words of greeting, and before I could reply, he had taken my arm and invited me to join him in a game of Kalabriasz in the Café Gehinnom.

Gehinnom? Gehinnom? I vaguely remembered that Gehenna is a kind of Israelite subdivision of hell. I deduced that my friend had lost his way and ended up in Hades.

'How's tricks, then?' I asked sympathetically. At once Galitzenstein became extremely agitated and grabbed me by the waistcoat button. 'Tricks? Tricks!! Tricks don't come into it. 'stead of the stock market operatin' in perpetuity, people spend all the time here wailing and gnashing their teeth. Of course, that's not good for business.' In explanation he turned his pockets inside out. 'I tell you, it was almost better back there in Vienna.'

'But now and then you can get out and enjoy nature, a breath of fresh air — as now, for example,' I said in an attempt to cheer him up.

'That's just a special punishment for me,' Galitzenstein retorted bitterly. 'I only have to see one o' them acracias' (he pointed angrily at a fir tree as he talked himself more and more into a fury) 'what don't belong to me and what's attached to the ground at the bottom, and it fairly makes my blood boil.'

Although short, my stay in Purgatory had purified me. I could clearly tell that from my rising revulsion at such a materialist attitude.

'Wait, wait a moment,' Solomon Galitzenstein said, grabbing me insistently. 'You want to go to Heaven, I can tell, fine, I know you always had these fancy ideas, but if you should happen to meet a couple of archangels there — that kind's bound to have ready cash lying around — you tell 'em they should let me play the market for 'em, in railway shares or with a few hundred sacks of sugar if they prefer. If the deal goes through, I'll pass the whole fee on to you and a half cut of the profits.'

Outraged, I exclaimed, 'Get thee behind me, accursed wretch!' girded up my loins and strode off.

The orb of the sun was already declining as I continued to wander through the meadows when the sight of a wondrous *fata Morgana* swept away the rest of my disgruntlement. It was the precise reflection of an earthly occurrence, only even more uplifting, if that were possible: Dr Schmuser,[4] the incorrigible prophet-in-ordinary

---

4 A satire on Rudolf Steiner.

and founder of the theosophical-anthroposophical-rosicruci-pneumatotherapeutic society was taking his constitutional in the clouds, correcting with the one hand the galley proofs of the Akashic records the foreman of the cosmic works had entrusted to him, whilst tirelessly waving the other in greeting to the gods. Behind him was his guard of honour: twelve exquisitely affluent old ladies. Once more, I realised, he was leading the faithful; presumably he was escorting them to nirvana, which, as is well known, he had definitively transferred from Munich to Basel.

In the last rays of the setting sun I finally reached my longed-for goal. My heart was at peace and celestial refreshment flooded through my weary limbs.

I was greeted by loud chants of 'Hosannah, hosannah': a procession of pilgrims from Florence on the Elbe[5] had just arrived. There was no doubt at all, I had reached the Protestant Elysian Fields.

A maiden — designed by Fidus[6] — came skipping towards me and asked, 'Won't you tend the little lamb? The little lamb so meek and mild?'[7] When I declined with thanks, she took my hand and led me to the little entrance gate.

At the desk was a woman with her hair in a tight bun, dressed entirely according to the principles of the Rational Dress Reform Society, wearing little boots in elasticated prunello with patent-leather toe-caps (to go by the scar on her neck, she may well have suffered mildly from rickets during her time on earth, but otherwise she exuded an indescribably chaste charm). She handed me a crocheted purse with 'For our dear Gustav' embroidered on it in glass beads.

'The nickel coins,' she told me, 'are for the pleasure-machines. Not everyone can be perfect right away,' she added with a roguish grin. She had, I realised, a fiendish sense of humour.

To my surprise I saw that she had sleeve-protectors over her wings. When I asked why, for God's sake, she wore them, she pointed out

---

5 Dresden; the 'hosannas' have a touch of Saxon dialect.

6 Fidus = Hugo Höppener (1868-1948), an *art nouveau* artist and illustrator; he was also a Theosophist and worked for the magazine *Simplicissimus* at the same time as Meyrink.

7 The opening lines of Schiller's poem 'The Alpine Huntsman'.

that other feathered angels even wore capes to stop them catching cold, especially as it was the time of the moult just then.

As you can see, dear readers, everything here in the Elysian Fields is quite, quite different from the way citizens who are still embroiled in the world of the senses would imagine. Everything is so simple, so plain and clear! So refreshing! You see, our realm is not a place, but a state built up from the sum total of the repressed longings of the entire German petty bourgeoisie which, once the shackles of the flesh have been broken, quite naturally and irresistibly reveal themselves in their full splendour to the eye of the participant.

I went straight to the machines, my curiosity having been aroused by the woman at the desk.

There was so much to see!

And everything uncommonly cheap.

Here a bowl of sterilised manna, there a glass of ersatz nectar, a mouthful of alcohol-free ambrosia, then a few drops of soul oil — as recommended by Prof. Dr Jaeger — on my handkerchief. And all for just *one* nickel!

The gramophone with the trumpet fanfare and the triple hallelujah — delivered by Caruso — is free, since it is only for those in a more advanced stage of purification.

It really does your heart good.

But there was *one* device that particularly attracted me and will, I am sure, also be of interest to you: the sensual-thrill machine. (Only for the older, more mature gentleman, who is still somewhat behind in purification.)

A man who had passed away peacefully a good while ago, a managing director with pink wing stubs already showing through, explained it to me.

'You see this hole here?' he asked with an ethereal smile. 'To the uninitiated it looks quite innocent. You just have to put your finger in, the machine does the rest.'

'Well?' he enquired with a sly wink once I had done that. I was too overcome to reply. I was about to put in another nickel but the commercial gentleman gently pushed my hand back, saying that was enough to be going on with. 'Let's go and have some locust and wild honey in the Happy Reformer Café.'

We hurried off, hand in hand.

Although I appreciated his kindness and felt attracted to him, I have to admit that, to my shame, I soon forgot him. I was distracted by the overwhelming impressions and the warmth with which I was welcomed everywhere as one of the family, the good souls tactfully passing over the fact that in my former life I had devoted myself to producing modern literature.

In its solidly respectable opulence the café, furnished in the familiar German Renaissance style, recalled the best middle-class ambience: Japanese paper parasols in the corners, raffia mats hanging below them, richly adorned with photographs, bouquets of dried flowers in elaborate papier-mâché vases, or a delightful Nibelung coat rack with imitation bison horns, ditto boar tusks and Teutonic spears artistically arranged and stigmatised — er, sorry signalised as objects of practical use by tiny coloured lights.

The only thing that reminded me now and then that I was in Heaven and not in some city of art was the way that whenever the door opened to admit another customer, the hinges emitted the delightful notes of the shawm.

Every detail revealed the attentive work of a woman's hand: the sweets and chocolates were set out on charming little velvet cushions, the glass covers had little crocheted caps, even the plaster bust of Alois the Simpleminded had a blue ribbon round its neck.

Is it not touching, dear readers, that here, after death, we still hold to the traditional customs of the good old days?

Once my eyes had become used to the splendour, I saw, sitting on the sofa, an ancient greybeard who was wearing a green cardboard eyeshade to protect him from the light. It was, I was told, good old Torquemada, who had come from the neighbouring section of paradise to visit us Protestants for a little chat. Although, as was well known, he had been blind on earth, my informant went on, his eyesight was now quite acceptable, which gave me great satisfaction to hear.

From time to time, perhaps to show that he had entirely abandoned his former fanatical way of thinking, he played all sorts of sweet Spanish airs on a — if you'll forgive the expression — Jew's harp and we listened breathlessly to the soft, mellifluous tones, while Lucrecia Borgia, his constant companion, who is devoted to him, danced an extremely discreet fandango, naturally in a dress buttoned up to the neck.

I could go on for hours, dear readers, telling you about all the glittering entertainments here that come one after the other, from the fancy-dress ball to the tombola, where every winner can steal a kiss from the managing director's wife, but above all I must hasten to assure you that we do not spend all our time indulging in such amusements. No, we are ever mindful of our charitable duty towards the poor damned souls down in hell; once a year — at Christmas — a chest is sent down to Hades full of unwanted clothes, worn-out shoes, tinfoil bottle-tops and such things that give pleasure to the famished souls.

I would have loved to describe our fields to you in detail, but unfortunately there is not enough time — the spiritualist table-rapping machine can only be used in exceptional circumstances — and, moreover, I have to confess that I would not like my telepathic communication with the newspaper to become public knowledge in paradisal society.

To sum up, then. Nature here does not for one minute leave the pilgrim without some edifying message. Hardly has your eye rested on a green leaf than you become aware of a pithy saying engraved on it which uplifts you and supports you on the path of righteousness. Anything and everything has its moral message. The violet says, 'I am modesty, won't you copy me?' To cut a long story short, nature and education are united in harmony. The stems of the rose bushes have velvet wrapped round them, so that the thorns will not hurt you, and there are reformed vultures sitting in the treetops singing joyfully with the starlings and warbling their song, 'Loyal and honest for ever we'll be.'

Yes, even the sloth has turned over a new leaf and knits and sews from morning to night.

All this is actually the field of Lilli Kraut, who now resides among us and has become my bosom friend. She has finally got the authorities to agree that in purgatory every cow gets a cup of chocolate in the morning.

She has mastered the language of the birds wonderfully and when we wander out into the countryside at break of day, she keeps calling, 'Tweet, tweet,' and that has cut the cuckoo to the heart so that already most of them no longer lay their eggs in other birds' nests, but only in their own.

So to conclude ... er, what was I going to say? Er ... oh yes, I almost forgot the most important thing. Listen carefully now. A new, unknown play by Schönherr[8] that far outshadows *Faith and Homeland* is to be put on here in the near future.

You simply *have* to be there! I'm sure you realise that. So quick, follow my example, string yourselves up, gentlemen, string yourselves up.

Before it's too late.

With a hurried hosannah

Yours most deceasedly

Gustav Meyrink

---

8 Karl Schönherr (1867-1943), Austrian dramatist.

Herr Kuno Hinrichsen, Businessman, and the Penitent, Lala Lajpat-Rai

Dark clouds were gathering on the distant horizon. With correspondingly agitated steps, Herr Kuno Hinrichsen, managing director of the firm: *General Charitable Works*, 'Wholesalers of fat, lard and oils', paced up and down his princely study. His right hand, richly adorned with splendid rings, casually crumpled up a brochure he had been sent in his capacity of newly elected honorary president of the 'non-profit-making philosophical association' *The Light of the East*, which he had recently founded. He had quickly leafed through the brochure, while he was being driven home from the factory, in order to prepare himself for the banquet with a few catchwords and a clear opinion of his own about the view of life created by the ancient Indian philosophers, which he could casually drop into the conversation with the other guests at appropriate points. He seldom failed, whenever the opportunity presented itself, to expound his high-minded ideals, on the other hand he was unwilling to let slip any opportunity of emphasising his own firmly held convictions on all important questions, not to mention ones of a scientific, or even philosophical, nature, in order, as he put it, to remain 'master of the situation'.

At times as he read the pamphlet, written by a specialist in the field, a superior smile had played about the managing director's forceful lips and at the persistently repeated assertion that the world was not actually real but merely a delusion of the senses, sarcastic exclamations could be heard, such as, 'Oh, come on,' or 'Nice chaps, those Indians, but no get-up-and-go.' Finally, after his hand had automatically patted his wallet, he murmured, 'Well, a bank account, that's definitely real,' thus freeing himself from the spell of theoretical ruminations and with one energetic gesture he made himself 'master of the situation' again by thrusting the brochure into his pocket.

Herr Hinrichsen had merely deigned to note — with a glassy eye, so to speak — the appendix to the leaflet, a story about an Indian penitent, or, as one might say, had graciously allowed it access to his subconscious, for a variety of more pleasant reflections had come to occupy his mind.

His eldest son, Fritz, had sent a telegram from Africa: 'Shot my fiftieth pachyderm today,' and, if that were not enough good news, a business communication from the South Australian branch of the *General Charitable Works* had arrived to say that they had succeeded in setting up a gigantic vat which could take 10,000 penguins at once and transform them into superb lubricating grease in a few hours.

This put the Honorary President in a most contented mood and, after he had regaled himself with a lavish dinner in his country retreat, he took out the pamphlet once more to read the comic passage about the unreality of the visible world to his lady wife, when he was suddenly called to the telephone and given the horrendous news that a junior clerk by the name of Meier had taken the sum of 3,50 marks from the petty cash, without providing sufficient documentation as to its use.

What incensed him even more than the fact itself was the outrageous attempt by the managing clerk to put in a good word for the embezzler by alluding to his desperate personal difficulties.

There was nothing that infuriated Herr Hinrichsen more — especially as he was on the committee of the *Association for the Improvement of National Morality* — as theft in any form. In this respect his conscience had become an objective symbol of unbesmirchability throughout the land.

No wonder, then, that when he heard the telephonic bad tidings he literally went pale and could scarcely utter the words, 'The police! Meier must be locked up right away.'

Fiery snakes flashed across the black sky, the thunder was already rumbling menacingly and, with a correspondingly dark expression, the Honorary President emptied the fizzy drink his wife had prepared with her own hands and cajoled him into drinking, saying, 'Please,

please, Charitable Works,' — tenderly addressing him by her pet name for him — 'a little sip, just for my sake.' When this had calmed his tattered nerves, she gently pushed him down in the armchair, carefully closed the windows and lowered the richly embroidered blinds, so the lightning could not strike in the room, and tiptoed out.

Gradually the soothing drink had its effect and Morpheus took Herr Hinrichsen's wounded heart in his arms.

Already the first heavy drops were falling and the harbingers of the approaching storm were howling and rattling at the costly rococo shutters, but the sleeper did not hear them.

Confused phrases from the pamphlet performed a disrespectful jig before his inner eye, carrying him off out of the dependable present and into the dubious realm of dreams. The story of the Indian penitent in the appendix to the brochure, that he had merely glanced over, hardly paying attention, was suddenly happening, right there inside his head. Herr Hinrichsen saw himself — not without some misgivings — transformed in the twinkling of an eye into an extremely scantily dressed, penniless Indian fakir, who he was, and then, on the other hand, was not.

No rings on his fingers any more, not to mention a tie-pin, just a staff in his hand and, where previously the heavy, respect-inspiring gold watch-chain used to dangle down, nothing but a grubby loincloth.

And so he staggered off, tousled black hair hanging down to his shoulders, in a desolate, sun-scorched wilderness, scouring the landscape in vain for his 60 hp car. Tough dried grasses cut excruciatingly into his naked soles (the dreaming Herr Hinrichsen automatically pushed off his left ankle boot with his right foot) and with every step one more bit of his dignity as head of the *General Charitable Works* disappeared.

Instead, he was filled with a new, unknown and highly disreputable sensation: a positively perverse thirst, stored up during years of aimless wandering across lonely, dreary steppes, for spiritual enlightenment and the wondrous, mysterious goal of becoming one with the God Shiva, the destroyer of earthly life.

The businessman-fakir desperately tried to find his way back to his familiar waking consciousness as a major industrialist by concentrating his thoughts on the splendid vat with the 10,000 penguins but in vain. A merciless, invisible goad drove him on until he was nothing but an Indian penitent, in whose poor, unfruitful brain the burning desire for God and a weary lifetime of waiting for spiritual redemption had been turned into the act of blind wandering, aimlessly exchanging one place for another, which consumed his now empty time like a clock, so that the words of the sacred Veda might come true:

'Make thy way alone, as the solitary rhinoceros roams.'

Hour after hour the businessman-fakir had struggled on towards a dazzlingly white point, which gradually grew bigger as he approached and eventually turned out to be a stone column surrounded by trees standing beside a babbling spring: one of those venerable lingams into which, it is said, the bodies of ascetics are transformed when their souls have reached the last stage of ecstasy and been sucked up by the breath of the universal spirit.

And when the businessman-fakir performed the sacrificial rites of the sannyasin and poured a few drops of water on the lingam, murmuring the mystical syllables '*Bhur — Hamsa Bhur*' in his navel, heart, throat and forehead, letters of light appeared on the lingam, telling him that previously it had been the body of the great yoga teacher, Matsyendra Paramahamsa, whom the God Shiva himself had instructed from his own lips in the mysteries of '*Tat tvam asi*' — of becoming one — and transformed from a mute fish into a human being.

And the lingam turned into a thatched hut, from which came a voice asking, 'Who are you and what is your name?'

'I seek the path to God, I am the penitent Lala Lajpat-Rai,' the fakir replied, before Herr Hinrichsen had the chance to say, 'Hello, *General Charitable Works* speaking.'

Nor, much to his chagrin, could Herr Hinrichsen prevent the penitent from throwing himself to the ground before the saint, as he came out, and begging him to be his guru, his spiritual guide, on the heartbreaking path to nirvana.

But with a smile the guru, Matsyendra, touched the fakir on the top of the head and said, 'Thus I form the chain and give you the exercise: Thou shalt not steal,' a commandment with which the businessman expressed his agreement by a grunt of approval.

The penitent probably thought to himself that he had never stolen anything in his whole life, but he went away obediently and only returned after many days of pondering and prayer.

And when the guru asked him what he had lived on during that time and he answered, 'On the milk of a cow grazing in the valley,' he was told that he had stolen because the cow belonged to a rich merchant.

Under normal conditions that would have been enough for Herr Hinrichsen to dissociate himself entirely from the fakir but unfortunately he was inescapably trapped in the net of the dream and bound to him.

After a long time the penitent, Lala Lajpat Rai, imagining himself free from the sin of stealing, once more went to his guru and reported that he had only drunk the foam that dripped down from the mouth of the calf as it suckled, but he was told he was still a thief, for he had reduced the food of the blind earthworms, which Vishnu, the great sustainer of all life, graciously accords them in the form of those drops.

So then, without complaining, the fakir ate only the sparse grass, like an animal, but even that the guru called theft, since it was the cow's food, intended to be transformed in her stomach into nourishing milk for her helpless child.

'Great!' Herr Hinrichsen murmured as he stretched into a more comfortable position in his armchair. The penitent, however, huddled up silently outside the stone lingam, his heart filled with unutterable sadness, because he was unable to free himself from the sin of stealing and appear pure while a living man before the exalted saint.

Staring straight ahead from morning to evening, from evening to morning, he quietly repeated one word, 'Hari' — the sacred name of Shiva, the god of death — like a boundless, humble prayer to take away his body, his eternally thirsty, hungry, ravening body.

And the consuming fire in his entrails, his despair and his torment at being a man, all that he compressed into the word 'Hari' until his whole body, his blood and his bones were saying it with him, so that it grew into a single, uninterrupted cry for deliverance, seeming to fill the invisible universe.

When, on the fortieth day, the sun once more stood blood-red in the sky, the fakir sensed from the thunder in his heart and the storm that was beginning to rage in his brain, that the end had come.

His tongue grew hard and could no longer speak the name 'Hari' and his eyes took on the terrible look of one in the throes of death; his body began to sway and was about to fall forward, when there suddenly appeared before him, as immense as the cosmos, with a thousand faces, Matsyendra, the saint, the perfected one, and the Milky Way of the firmament was but a white hair at his temple.

And regaled him with heavenly bread and wine. Bread for his body and wine for his spirit.

And entered into him and became — himself.

And he spoke to the penitent with the penitent's lips: 'Henceforth you *cannot* steal, even if you wanted to. Everything you see inside yourself and outside yourself: "*Tat tvam asi*" — you are all that yourself. The world has become your body: "*Tat tvam asi*" — you are all that. And if you kill your parents and eat the flesh of your own children, you are not a murderer: "*Tat tvam asi*" — you are they. How can anyone murder and steal who has become *Tat tvam asi*? His body has become the world.'

Gently roused from his sleep by his wife, who handed him a telegram, Herr Hinrichsen woke. He quickly felt his neck and brow and established that he was perspiring excessively.

Outside flurries of hail were rattling the windows and the apartment was plunged in deep darkness that was only occasionally lit by sulphurous yellow flashes of lighting.

Herr Hinrichsen opened the telegram, full of expectation, but hardly had he glanced at it than the colour drained from his forceful features and an unarticulated groan rising from his chest indicated that he had only just escaped a fainting fit which, given his imposing corpulence, could easily have had fatal consequences.

A terrible clap of thunder shook the magnificent villa to its foundations and 'bankrupt' was the single, pregnant word that escaped Herr Hinrichsen's lips. The telegram said that a panic on the stock exchange had wiped out almost his whole assets in a few minutes.

Unable to move a muscle, even less to think, Herr Hinrichsen stared into space, but then a miracle! There suddenly appeared a shining hand, clearly belonging to his soul, which wrote — as did the one that appeared to Belshazzar, the erstwhile king of Babylon — in letters of fire on the wall: ' "*Tat tvam asi*": you are everything. Does that tell you anything, *General Charitable Works*?' and disappeared.

At a stroke Herr Hinrichsen was overcome with immense enlightenment.

He had for years had sole charge, with unlimited power of attorney, of the administration of significant funds belonging to orphans and of the investments of trusting widowed relatives, whose financial protection had become second nature to him. All it needed, therefore, was for a few transactions to be backdated a little, a harmless bookkeeping operation, and the whole loss would be theirs.

'Of course! It's so clear a blind man could see it. "*Tat tvam asi!*" I'm the whole lot of 'em!' Herr Hinrichsen exclaimed jubilantly again and again. 'And the world isn't real, anyway. I'd never've thought there was so much in this Indian philosophy,' he added, rubbing his hands, ''specially that trick with the "*Tat tvam asi*" Capital! Capital!'

The horrible storm outside had passed as quickly as it had come, the cheerful golden face of the sun pierced the last veil of cloud, and a luminous rainbow adorned a world refreshed as a jaunty Herr Hinrichsen commanded the servant, who had come rushing in, 'Put a magnum of champagne on ice for a toast to old Matsyendra.'

From then on Herr Kuno Hinrichsen, businessman, was 'master'

of even the most difficult situations and a convinced follower of the
Indian doctrine of the Vedanta to the end of his days.

The Clockmaker

'This clock? Mend it? So it'll go again?' the owner of the antiques
shop asked in surprise, pushing his glasses up onto his forehead and
giving me a somewhat bewildered look. 'Why do you want it to go
again? It only has one hand, and not a single number on the dial,'
he added, lost in thought as he examined the clock in the harsh light
of the lamp, 'just flower faces, animal and demon heads instead
of the hours.' He started to count and looked at me questioningly.
'Fourteen? But we divide the day into twelve parts. I've never seen
such a strange clock. My advice is to leave it as it is. Twelve hours
are enough to have to put up with in a day. Read the correct time off
this dial? Who'd bother nowadays? Only a fool.'

I couldn't bring myself to tell him that I had been such a fool
all my life, had never possessed another clock and perhaps for that
reason had often arrived too early, when I should have waited a little,
so I remained silent.

The antiques dealer interpreted this as meaning I stuck by my
desire to see it go again. He shook his head, picked up a little ivory
knife and carefully opened the housing that was decorated with jewels
and a fabulous beast in enamel standing in a four-horse chariot: a
man with female breasts, two snakes instead of legs, a cock's head
and the sun in his right hand, a whip in his left.

'I expect it's an old family heirloom?' the antiques dealer said.
'Did you not say just now that it stopped last night? At two o'clock?
Presumably the little red buffalo's head with two horns indicates the
second hour?'

I was not aware that I had said anything of the kind, but the clock
had indeed stopped at two o'clock that morning. Perhaps I had
mentioned it, but I couldn't remember and I still felt too exhausted
— at exactly the same time I had had a severe spasm of the heart

and thought I was going to die. As I felt I was losing consciousness I clung on to the thought: if only the clock doesn't stop. With the fading of my senses I must have confused my heart and the clock. Perhaps that happens to dying people. Perhaps that's why clocks so often stop at the moment their owners die? We do not know what magical power a thought can sometimes possess.

'Now that is remarkable,' said the antiques dealer after a while. He held his magnifying glass close to the lamp, so that the blindingly bright focal point fell sharply on the clock, and indicated the letters inscribed on the inside of the gold cover.

I read: *Summa Scientia Nihil Scire*.

'Remarkable,' he repeated. 'This clock was made by the "Madman". It was made in this town, I am sure about that. There are only very few such pieces. I never thought they could actually go, I assumed they were just an amusement. And — one of his little quirks — the same motto is in all his clocks: Supreme knowledge is to know nothing.'

I didn't understand what he was saying. Who could the madman he had mentioned be? The clock was very old, it came from my grandfather, but the way the clockmaker had talked, it sounded as if the madman who was supposed to have made it was still alive today.

Before I could ask, I saw in my mind's eye — but clearer and sharper, as if he were walking through the room — a man striding across a winter landscape, an old man, slim and tall, hatless, his full, snow-white hair blowing in the wind. His head was strangely small in contrast to his towering figure, his sharp-featured face was beardless, his eyes black, close together and with a fanatical look in them, like those of a bird of prey. He strode on in a long, threadbare velvet coat, such as the Nuremberg patricians used to wear.

'Quite right,' the antiques dealer muttered, with an absent-minded nod, 'quite right, the "Madman".'

Why did he say 'Quite right', I wondered. It must be a coincidence I immediately told myself, they're nothing but empty words. I never opened my mouth. He just said 'Quite right' the way you often do to emphasise something you've just said. It has no connection with the old man that I saw in my memory, no connection with his madman.

When I was still a little boy, on my way to school I had to go past a long, bare wall the height of a man which went round a park with elm trees. Day after day for several years, I broke into a run when I had to go along it, for every time I was gripped by a vague fear. Perhaps — I no longer know — it was because I imagined, or had been told, that a madman lived there, a clockmaker who claimed his clocks were living beings. Or was I wrong? If it was a memory of an experience from my schooldays, how could it be that something I must have felt a thousand times had slept in my memory until this day to suddenly burst out in such vivid detail? Of course, forty years must have passed since then, but was that an explanation?

'Perhaps I experienced it during the two hours more than an ordinary clock that my clock shows,' I said, amused.

The antiques dealer seemed taken aback at this and stared at me, uncomprehending.

I thought about it and eventually felt certain that the wall round the park is still standing today. Who could have wanted to pull it down? It was said to be the foundation wall of a church that was to be completed later. You don't destroy something like that. Perhaps the clockmaker was still alive? He would certainly be able to mend my clock, which I was so attached to. If only I knew when and where I had met him. It could not have been recently, for it was summer now and when, a few moments ago, I had remembered him, I had seen him in my mind's eye in a winter landscape.

The antiques dealer had suddenly become talkative and was telling a long story, but I was too deep in thought to follow it. I only heard a few disjointed sentences now and then, they came roaring towards me, then fell away, only to return, like breakers on the shore. Between them there was the buzzing in my ears, the pounding of the blood that people hear as they grow old and listen for it, only forgetting it in the noise of the day, the constant, menacing, distant beat of the wings of Death, the vulture slowly approaching from the abyss of time …

I could hardly tell who it was talking to me. Was it the man standing before me with the clock in his hand, or was it that being inside me that sometimes wakes in a lonely heart when one touches the locked caskets that secretly guard our forgotten memories so that they do not crumble to dust? Sometimes I caught myself nodding to the antiques dealer and I realised he had said something that was familiar to me, but if I tried to think about what he had said, his words didn't, as words you hear usually do, slip down into the recent past, from where I could have recovered them and pored over them with understanding; no, scarcely had their sound died away than they turned into rigid, lifeless figures, alien and incomprehensible to the ear. They had strayed from the realm of time into the realm of space and stood round me, dead masks.

In my torment I said, 'If only my clock would go again!' interrupting the dealer in the middle of his story.

I meant my heart, for I could feel that it was about to forget to beat and I was filled with horror at the thought that the hands of my life's clock could suddenly stop at a fantastic flower, the face of an animal or a demon, as the hands on the dial with the fourteen hours had. I would be condemned to spend eternity in congealed time.

The antiques dealer gave me the clock back. He must have thought that was what I was talking about.

As I walked along the deserted nocturnal streets — straight ahead, then this way and that, across sleeping squares, past dreaming houses, guided by flickering lamps and yet sure of where I was going — I was convinced the antiques dealer must have told me where the nameless clockmaker lived, where I could find him and where the wall round the park with the elms was. Had he not said that the old man could make my clock well again? How else would I have known?

He must also have described how to get to his house, and even if I hadn't paid attention myself, my feet seemed to know the way exactly. They took me out of the town and onto the white road which ran, between meadows redolent with the breath of summer, on into infinity.

Sticking to my heels, the black snakes the moon had lured out of the earth glided along behind me. Was it they who were sending me the poisoned thought: 'You will never find him, he died a hundred years ago'?

In order to escape them, I turned off sharp left onto a side-path and at once my shadow popped out of the ground and swallowed them up. I realised that it had come to guide me and it was a great comfort to see it striding along so unwaveringly; I kept on looking at it, glad not to have to look where I was going. Gradually I was overcome with that indescribably strange feeling I used to have as a child, playing by myself at walking along with my eyes closed, not caring whether I fell or not. It is like releasing your body from all earthly fear, like a cry of joy from your inner being, like once more finding your immortal self that knows: nothing can happen to me.

At such times the Arch-Enemy that we carry inside us — cold, clear reason — would leave me in peace and with it my last doubts as to whether I would find the man I was seeking.

Then, after walking for a long time, my shadow hurried towards a wide, deep ditch running alongside the road and disappeared into it, leaving me alone, and I knew I had reached my goal. Why else would it have left me?

My clock in my hand, I was standing in the room of the man whom I knew was the only one who could make it work again.

He was sitting at a little maple-wood table, motionless, staring through a magnifying glass held in front of his eye by a headband at a tiny glittering object on the light-grained wood. On the white wall behind him, the ornate letters in a circle like a large clock-dial, was the sentence:

Summa Scientia Nihil Scire.

I sighed with relief. I had come to the right place. The words were a spell banishing all compulsion to think, all demands for explanations: How did you get in? Through the wall? Across the park?

On a shelf covered in red velvet are clocks — there must be a hundred, in blue, green, yellow enamel, decorated with jewels, engraved, fluted, smooth or grooved, some flat, some rounded like eggs. I can't hear them, they're chirping too softly, but the air above them must be alive from the imperceptible noise they're producing. Perhaps there's a storm raging in some dwarf realm there.

On a stand is a small piece of flesh-coloured felspar, veined, with colourful flowers of semi-precious stones growing on it; in the middle of them, all innocent, the Grim Reaper with his scythe is waiting to cut them down: like a *memento mori* clock from the romantic Middle Ages. When he mows, the handle of his scythe hits the thin glass bell beside him, a cross between a soap bubble and the cap of a large fairy-tale mushroom.

The dial underneath it is the entrance to a cavern full of wheels.

Right up to the ceiling of the room the walls are covered with clocks. Old ones with proudly chased faces, precious and rich; calmly swinging their pendulum, they declaim their soothing tick-tock in a deep bass.

In the corner there is one in a glass coffin. Snow White, standing up, is pretending she's asleep, but a quiet, rhythmical twitching together with the minute hand shows she's keeping her eye on the time. Others, nervous rococo demoiselles — with a beauty spot for the keyhole — are overloaded with decoration and quite out of breath, as they each trip along, trying to take precedence over the others and get ahead of the seconds. Beside them are tiny pages, giggling and urging them on: tick, tick, tick.

Then a long row, gleaming with steel, silver and gold. Like knights in full armour; they seem to be drunk and asleep, for sometimes they snore loudly or rattle their chains, as if they had a mind to break a lance with Cronos himself once they wake and have sobered up.

On a windowledge a woodman with mahogany trousers and a glittering copper nose is sawing time to sawdust …

The old man spoke, rousing me from my contemplation. 'They've all been ill, I've made them all well again.' I had so completely forgotten him that at first I thought it was a clock striking.

The magnifying glass on the headband had been pushed up and was now in the middle of his forehead — like the third eye of Shiva — with a glow in it, the reflection of the light on the ceiling.

He nodded to me, keeping his eyes fixed on mine. 'Yes,' he said, 'they've been ill; they thought they could change their destiny by going faster or slower. In their arrogance they saw themselves as the lords of time and that cost them their contentment. I freed them from that delusion and gave their lives its calm again. From time to time on moonlit nights a person will find his way out of the town to me in his sleep, as you have, and bring me his sick clock, lamenting and begging me to mend it. But the next morning it is all forgotten, including my medicine.

'Only those who understand the meaning of my motto,' he pointed over his shoulder to the words on the wall, 'only they leave their clocks here for me to look after.'

I had a vague sense that the words on the wall concealed a further secret. I was going to ask, but the old man raised a warning hand. 'Do not seek to know. Living knowledge comes of its own accord. The motto has twenty-three letters; they are the numbers on the great dial of the invisible clock, which has one hour less than mortals' clocks, whose closed circle allows no escape. That is why people who "know" mock me. "Look," they say, "isn't it crazy?!" They scoff, they do not see the warning: Do not let yourself be caught in the noose of "time"!' They let themselves be guided by the insidious clock-hand of "reason", which is always promising new hours, but only gives them old disappointments.'

The old man fell silent. With a mute appeal I handed him my dead clock. He took it in his beautiful slim white hand and gave an almost imperceptible smile when he opened it and glanced inside. Cautiously examining the works with a needle, he pulled the magnifying glass down. I felt that a kindly eye was peering into my heart.

Musing, I observed his reposeful face. How could I have been so afraid of him as a child, I wondered.

Then I was suddenly gripped by a terrible fear: this man, in whom I have put my trust, my hope, is not real — now — now he's going to disappear! No, thank goodness. It was just the candle in the lamp flickering and trying to deceive my eyes.

Again I stared at him, pondering. Is this the first time I've seen him? That can't be true. Surely we've known each other since ...?

Then memory struck me like a flash of lightning: I had never run past a white wall as a schoolboy, I had never been afraid of a mad clockmaker who was said to live behind it. It was the word 'mad', to me an empty and incomprehensible word, that had frightened me when I was a little child and people had threatened 'that' was what I would become if I didn't listen to reason.

But this old man, sitting here in front of me, who was he? I thought I knew that as well: an image, just an image, not a person. What else could it be?! An image, a shadow-bud of my soul that had secretly formed inside me; a seed, it had taken root when I was lying in my bed at the beginning of my life, with the old nurse holding my hand and her monotonous murmuring that had carried me over into sleep. What was it she had been saying? What was it she had been saying?

A bitter taste came up in my throat, the sting of sorrow: so everything around me here was nothing but a shifting illusion! Perhaps in another minute I would be standing outside in the moonlight, a sleepwalker who has woken and must return home to the town, back to the world of the living, busy and obsessed with reason — no, to the dead!

What was it my nurse had murmured? I was desperate to know … and slowly, slowly it appeared inside me, syllable by syllable:

> If your heart should stop in pain,
> To him it take
> For he can make
> Any clock to go again.

'And she was quite right,' the clockmaker said calmly, putting down the needle. Immediately my dark thoughts vanished.

He stood up and held the clock to my ear. I could hear it going with a regular beat, precisely in time with the pulse of my blood.

I tried to thank him, but could not find the words, so great was my joy — and shame at having doubted him.

'Don't worry about that,' he said to comfort me, 'it wasn't your fault. I've taken out a little wheel and put it back again. Clocks like these are very sensitive, sometimes they can't stand the Second Hour. There you are. Take it back, but don't tell anyone it's going. They'll only mock and try to harm you. It's belonged to you since you were a child and you believed in the hours it shows, fourteen instead of one to — midnight, seven instead of six, Sunday instead of weekday, pictures instead of dead numbers. Stay true to it, but don't tell anyone. There's nothing more stupid than insisting on being a martyr. Keep it hidden by your heart and in your pocket have one of the ordinary watches, the officially calibrated ones with a respectable black-and-white dial, so that you can always see what time it is for other people. And don't let yourself be poisoned by the miasma of the "Second Hour". It's deadly, just like its eleven sisters. It starts off red, like a promising sunrise, but quickly turns red as a blazing fire, red as blood. The "Hour of the Ox" the old people of the East used to call it. The centuries go by and it passes in peace: the ox is ploughing. But suddenly, overnight, the oxen turn into roaring buffaloes, driven by the demon with the bull's head and trample the fields flat in their blind, animal fury; after that they learn to till the soil again. Ordinary clocks keep going in the same old way, but their hands don't show the way out of the orbit of humans' time either. All their hours are pregnant — each with a different ideal — but what they give birth to is an abortion.

'Your clock stopped at two, at the hour of destruction. Fortunately it passed over that. Others die from it and stray into the realm of death, yours found its way to me — to the one whose hands fashioned it. It is you it has to thank for that. It could only do that because you have lovingly guarded it your whole life through and never taken offence because its time is not that of the Earth.

He showed me to the door, shook my hand and said, 'A while ago you were in doubt as to whether I am alive. Believe me, I am more alive than you. Now you know the way here, we'll soon see each other again. Perhaps I can teach you how to make sick clocks well. Then' — he pointed to his motto on the wall — 'then the motto may be completed for you:'

Nihil scire — omnia posse.
To know nothing — to be able to do everything.

The City with the Secret Heartbeat

The city I am talking about is old *Prague*. Fate, the Pilot, brought me to this strange city from foggy Hamburg forty-five years ago. On the very first day, when I took a long walk through the unknown streets, I was dazzled by the bright, scorching sun brooding over the ancient buildings with its sweltering heat, a sun which seemed quite different from the cheerfully shining skies I remembered from my childhood in bright, carefree Bavaria. …

Even then, as I walked over the ancient Stone Bridge which crosses the calm waters of the Moldau to the hill with its dark castle exuding the arrogance of ancient generations of Habsburgs, I was overcome with a profound sense of horror, for which I could find no explanation. Since that day this feeling of apprehension never left me for a moment during all the time — the length of a whole generation — I lived in Prague, the city with the secret heartbeat. It has never entirely left me, even today it comes over me when I think back to Prague or dream of it at night. Everything I ever experienced I can call up in my mind's eye as if it were there before me, bursting with life. If, however, I summon up Prague, it appears more clearly than anything else, so clearly, in fact, that it no longer seems real, but ghostly. Every person I knew there turns into a ghost, an inhabitant of a realm that does not know death.

Puppets do not die when they leave the stage; and all the beings the city with the secret heartbeat holds together are puppets. Other cities, however old they may be, seem to me to be in the power of their people. Prague, as if disinfected by germicidal acids, shapes and manipulates its inhabitants like a puppeteer from their first to their last breath. Just as volcanoes spew forth fire out of the earth, so this eerie city spews war and revolution out into the world and it may well not be a delusion when the few people who keep their eyes open say that it secretly set off the first sparks of the last war!

On the Town Hall in the Old Town Square there is a huge astronomical clock with the signs of the zodiac, wreathed in legend. On the stroke of midday a little door opens and the twelve Apostles come out one after the other, only to silently disappear again, as if satisfied that the time for which they have been waiting patiently has not yet come, pursued by a thirteenth figure, Death with hourglass and scythe. He goes as well, with the cock of the far-off resurrection crowing above, like a prophecy of the apocalypse. It gives the sign and the hundred towers of the city join in, howling to drown out the mocking cockcrow that claims to know of the future collapse of all human time. I wonder if the long dead constructor of the clock had such an announcement in mind when he made it? He is supposed to have been mad. Perhaps madmen are closer to the last things than 'normal' people with their common sense. And one way or the other most of the puppets in Prague are mad, with a secret and concealed madness. Or obsessed with some bizarre idea.

Every year on 16 May, thousands — mostly peasant women with colourful headscarves and girls with hot, dark eyes — come in pilgrimage from the villages of Bohemia to the statue of St Nepomuk on the edge of the Stone Bridge. On such spring nights, surrounded by the glow of the five ruby-red lamps, it seems to hang in the air, shimmering in the silvery mist and looking to the south with the face of Jan Hus. In fact it never was St. John Nepomuk, it is the bronze statue of Jan Hus, only the people have forgotten, have swapped the names — the secret heartbeat of the city washes away all names, creating legend upon legend.

Often, on brightly moonlit nights, I wandered round the Lesser Town — the quarter on the other side of the Moldau, the very heart of Prague — and every time I got lost: an ancient town house where you feel it is impossible anyone can have lived there for decades, so thick are the layers of dust and verdigris on the doorknob; beside it a baroque building with opalescent windows which gleam like the glass of antique Roman tear-bottles; then a fifteen-foot-high wall, stretching out into infinity, with crumbling stucco on which the city's ghostly hand has drawn fantastic animal heads and staring faces that seem unmoving and yet have changed their expression every time you look at them. An overpowering fragrance of jasmine or elderflowers comes drifting down through the air and you sense: somewhere there are gardens, huge parks where perhaps no one has set foot since time immemorial. A vision steals over you: across the wall is a house where, in a mouldering room, is a dead woman, her worm-eaten body lying in a bed that has long since crumbled to dust. Or is it a monastery, a convent, the wall surrounds? With monks or nuns who prayed and chastised themselves until they were dead to the outside world. But if you look for it in broad daylight, you look in vain. Instead of the wall, there's a street with a house, three stories high, at the end; you look up at the roof — and there's another house on top of the first! A hallucination? No, the street takes a sharp turn, like a bent elbow, rising steeply, and high up there's another house. A queer man lives there, short, beardless, he looks like Napoleon and tells people's fortunes from a huge tome written in Hebrew letters. I once went to visit him and as I crossed the threshold into his room I heard him saying to a stranger in broken German, 'The drumming you heard during the night by the wall at the last street-lamp doesn't come from the soldiers, it comes from Žižka's drum. Before he died, he gave orders for his skin to be removed after his death and made into a drumskin so that his voice could be heard even though he was dead.'

'What did you mean by that?' I asked when we were alone. He looked astonished. He genuinely was astonished and denied ever having said anything like that. Some time afterwards I was told that he forgot everything he had said almost immediately after saying it. He was moonstruck, even by daylight.

Later, when the great war broke out, I was reminded of the drum of Jan Žižka, the one-eyed Hussite leader. I somehow felt there was some kind of shadowy connection. Or was it just coincidence? I don't think so — the city with the secret heartbeat has a strange way of speaking through the lips of its puppets.

The Pilot

Tomorrow is the fortieth anniversary of that day, the feast of the Assumption of the Virgin. I was sitting at my desk in my bachelor apartment in Prague. I had just put my farewell letter to my mother in the envelope and picked up the revolver, which lay in front of me, for I intended to set out on the journey across the Styx, to cast away a life that seemed shallow, worthless and with little promise of consolation in the future.

At that moment the 'Pilot wearing the cloak of invisibility', as I have since called him, boarded my ship of life and turned the helm. I heard a rustling at the door leading out into the hallway and when I turned round I saw something white being pushed under the door into the room. It was a printed brochure. The fact that I put my revolver down, picked up the brochure and read the title came neither from a feeling of curiosity nor from a secret desire to put off death — my heart was empty.

I read: 'On Life after Death.'

'Strange coincidence!' was the thought that tried to form inside me, but it hardly managed to get the first word onto my lips. Since then I have never believed in coincidence, I believe in the Pilot.

With trembling hand — it had not trembled for a moment before, neither when I wrote the farewell letter to my mother, nor when I picked up the revolver — I lit the lamp, for night had fallen, and read the brochure, which had obviously been delivered by my bookseller's messenger boy, from beginning to end, my pulse racing. It was all about spiritualism, above all describing the experiences the important scientists investigating this area — William Crookes, Professor Zöllner, Professor Fechner and others — had had with the mediums Slade, Eglinstone, Home etc.

I sat through the whole night until dawn started to break, with burning thoughts, which until then had been alien to me, going round and round inside my head; could such outstanding scholars as these have been mistaken? Hardly imaginable. But then what strange, incomprehensible laws of nature, flying in the face of all known principles of physics, had been at work?

In that night the ardent desire to see such things with my own eyes, touch them with my own hands, investigate their genuineness and understand the secrets that must lie behind them blazed up inside me to a scorching intensity which has remained with me ever since.

I took the gun — temporarily superfluous to requirement — and locked it in the drawer. I still have it: it has died of rust and the cylinder will not revolve, will never revolve again.

Then I went to bed and slept, a long, deep, dreamless sleep. Dreamless? Dreamless only in the sense that I saw no images or scenes I was involved in. But there are other, more profound experiences in deep sleep than dreaming in forms and figures; it is word and speech coming alive in some curious way when there is no mouth to speak apart from one's own. It is a dialogue in which two separate persons speak and hear, and yet are one and the same. When we wake after such a dialogue, we have always forgotten the words themselves, but in the course of the day their meaning will appear in our consciousness in the form of thoughts that suddenly occur to us, behaving as if they had just emerged from the womb of our brain.

That day I woke with the feeling that someone in the room had just said something out loud; the next moment, however, it became clear to me that it was I myself who had spoken in my sleep and for a fraction of a second I caught my lips murmuring — along with incomprehensible things that sounded as if they were in a foreign language — 'That is not the way to cross the Styx.'

For many years I was convinced that it was the Pilot who had said that to me and I developed many theories: false, semi-false, three-quarters true, spiritualist, superstitious and religious (the most dangerous of all) theories about who the Pilot might be. It takes a long time, a terribly long time before one realises what powers can disguise themselves as a pilot, it is an agonising journey through swamps full of will-o'-the-wisps.

'The solution is very simple,' say those 'profound thinkers' who know nothing at all. 'Schizophrenia,' say those who like juggling with words such as psychoanalysis, hysteria, mysticism, soul, magic, seeking God, spiritual rebirth, inner life — and cannot distinguish between growth and decline.

'Jesus Christ' is the 'Pilot' say others, the 'devout' Christians who have to let go of God's hand when they want to light a cigarette.

'The control spirit is the Pilot,' say the spiritualists, who have to ask a table when they want to know what things are like on the other side instead of learning how to cross over themselves.

When I woke from the deep sleep I called 'dreamless', I was overcome by an obsession which sometimes seemed childish. In the first two years I was driven solely by the compulsion to experience spiritualist phenomena. Any crank, fortune-teller or fool running round in Bohemia attracted me as an electric rod attracts scraps of paper. I invited dozens of mediums to my apartment and at least three times a week spent half the night in sessions with them and a group of friends I had infected with my monomania.

I continued this labour of Sisyphus tirelessly for seven years. All in vain. Either the mediums failed or they turned out to be deliberate or unconscious swindlers. But I was never fooled, not even one single time.

Even after the first two years I was beginning to have doubts, which grew stronger and stronger: could all the famous investigators in this area be wrong after all?

I could not believe that. The Pilot kept whispering to me when I was fast asleep not to give up the search. It was as if, night after night, I felt the lash of the whip from an invisible hand driving me on through new swamps full of strange will-o'-the-wisps. I bought any books on mediumism and similar topics that appeared: English, American, French and German books. One mirage after another appeared before me. Many, many times I decided to rid myself of this urge to seek out the unfathomable, by force if necessary, but every time I realised after only a few hours that it was too late, it was no longer possible. I was horrified, and yet secretly glad.

My brow grew more and more fevered, I was tormented by all sorts of ambitions; a lust for life, such as I can hardly understand today, flooded my whole being. But when I woke late in the morning after a night of wild excess (strangely enough such bouts of riotous living often followed immediately on spiritualist sessions, as if I had been plugged in to psychic batteries of the worst kind) I was never affected by the dreariness of the day, neither by disgust nor remorse — during the hours of sleep the mysterious bellows of the underworld of the soul had fanned the yearning for the world beyond the Styx to renewed ardour.

With the frivolity of youth I probably believed it would continue like that my whole life through. I had no idea that I was being torn apart. My destiny began to move at a gallop and I didn't notice. I did not notice that my whole being had gradually lost sight of any grey, that soon all it saw was bright white and deep black, all it could do was love to the point of self-abandon and hate utterly. I didn't hate people because they did me harm — for no reason at all I often felt them to be friends — nor did I love others, even though they were good to me; whole types of people literally made my hair stand on end just to think of them; it wasn't racial difference that awoke the hatred in me, it was above all that category of people who somehow remind one of the serene detachment that expresses itself outwardly through hair combed down over the ears or through a well groomed full beard and a 'dependable' expression. A psychoanalyst would say, 'The type of which it says in Revelations, "I will spue thee out of my mouth." This clearly must have its origin in a psychological complex and experience from earliest childhood that has been erased from your memory.' Perhaps he's right. But I do not think so. I suspect it is rather a warning from the Pilot, a warning of some event that will happen in the distant future, perhaps even in another — incarnation. Perhaps the devil will appear to me then, so that, in the habit of a pastor, I can *not* throw the inkwell at him.

This division into black and white grew stronger with the years, which was striking enough, since with increasing age the opposite usually happens: the contrasts blur in that banal grey that poets praise as the golden mean.

I have said that for a long time I did not realise that I was being torn apart. I did see, with growing fear, my ship of life being drawn into treacherous whirlpools from which it looked as if it would soon be impossible to escape. I won't describe them; given the calamitous situation under which everyone is suffering today[9] they would seem petty. 'Is that all? I wish I had those worries,' people would say. All I will say about the whirlpools and cyclones I was drifting towards is that at the time whenever I read in the newspaper that someone had been found in the woods, starved to death, or had hanged himself, I would say to myself, 'Is that all? Suicide — what an easy way out!'

Whenever I could see no way out in my everyday life, I would think, 'The Pilot, who is guiding me across the Styx in his special way, will help me.' And the more fervent my hopes, the more certain they were to be dashed. That was the most awful part of it.

People who had experienced a severe earthquake told me there was nothing more terrifying, more spine-chilling, than to feel the ground, which from earliest childhood you have believed to be absolutely unshakeable, shifting under your feet.

No! There is something even more terrible: to see one's last hope fade.

But at last I thought I had found what I had so long been looking for: an association of people, Europeans and Orientals, in central India, who claimed to possess the true secret of yoga, that ancient Asian system that shows the way to the steps that take us far above everything that is weak, incomplete, everything that is mere powerless humanity …

---

9 Probably 1915.

The Transformation of Blood

For thousands of years mankind has directed its efforts towards escaping our earthly suffering by finding and understanding the laws of nature in order to make use of them. The discoveries and inventions that have been made in this area are extraordinary; even more astonishing is the loss in everything connected with our instincts. The Germans in particular seem determined to become the nation most lacking in instinct, they showed it before the War, during the War and after the War. Unfortunately! Anyone nowadays who prefers to obey the voice of instinct, instead of listening solely to that of reason, and does not stick faithfully to the conventions derived from previous experience, which are often no longer valid, is dismissed as a fanciful dreamer at the mercy of chance. Humans are relying more and more on their reason gland and since that does not tell them anything connected with magic and other hidden powers of the soul, they imagine such things do not exist, or are of little value. It is an old misapprehension to assume a person guided by feeling is more or less the same as one who follows the guidance of their soul — proof of how shallow our knowledge of the soul has become! That explains the open contempt of the cold, rational person when others talk about 'soul'. The emotional type, he tells himself, is not up to the demands life makes on us and therefore has no right to exist. Perhaps in many cases he is right. 'My kingdom is not of this world,' the other will reply; but he is only saying it, inside he would very much like to do as well in this world as the rational type. He is, therefore, deceiving himself, the worst thing anyone can do. What both have in common is that they delude themselves that it is activity in the outside world that will let them prosper. Their hopes are vain, they are like a fool who thinks he can get rid of the shadow on the wall by covering it with whitewash. It is good fortune and a kindly fate alone that bring success; a superficial person, who sees only immediate causes, never those in the innermost depths of our being, is mistaken when he assumes that competence and efficiency are the sole key to success. Anyone who has learnt to observe life with a sharp eye and is not blinded by vanity knows that you cannot just grab competence like an object whenever you want if it is not already there in your blood; it is not even something you can acquire by training, it is a piece of good fortune that brings further good fortune, perhaps inherited in some cases or, as believers in the Asiatic doctrine of reincarnation say, a reward for things you have done in an earlier existence.

It is astonishing how indifferent this generation, so greedy for invention, is to the question of whether we can consciously become master over chance, fortune and misfortune, directing them at will. 'Because it is impossible,' comes the answer from millions of mouths.

Have you tried? Have you ever tried, tried and tried again to defeat even minor bodily illnesses and pain? Not by stuffing yourself full of medicine and following the advice of the doctor, whose science often fails? Embarrassed silence, a contemptuous smile; and they continue busily whitewashing the shadow on the wall. Any attempt to change oneself heart and soul into a person who is master not only of illnesses and minor trials and tribulations, but of chance and misfortune, is looked on as utter madness. Especially by those who proudly insist they are masters of their own will, but are in reality the most miserable slaves of an alien will-power, which secretly directs all their doings without them having the least suspicion it is so — they especially refuse even to try. They are slaves of the demiurge, which they look on as their god, as the one who determines their fate. And for them he does. Anyone who relies on others, even if those others are gods, is lost.

Philosophical knowledge alone can save us from the treadmill our life has become, and probably always has been from the very beginning — thus say those of the human race who possess understanding. But have our philosophers escaped the treadmill?

Was Kant able to rid himself of so much as a toothache? One could object that he didn't try. I do not believe that. I am sure that at one time or another he will have thought: how odd that *I know* so much, yet am no farther forward in the *ability to do* things. And even if the idea did not occur to him, it must have to the man of 'sound common sense'. Our European philosophers have thought up incredibly profound theories about life, existence and the phenomena of the visible world, and they have demonstrated the correctness of their discoveries logically, with mathematical precision even; but they have not shown how to become master over fate. Their insights have remained kiwis: flightless birds. There is a yawning gap separating theories from practice, they are like women who have no children. Simply transposing knowledge does not produce a change in destiny. You cannot think away the shadow on the wall; to change it you must change the position of the object between the light and the wall. Anyone who can do that — figuratively speaking— will become master of their fate. Of course it is possible that it will only make the 'shadow' uglier than it was before, but that is the fault of the person, who performed the operation wrongly. The deed must be preceded by knowledge.

Is there such knowledge? It is there, proof against rust like gold; rare and covered in filth, it still comes to light again and again, seemingly worthless to those who have eyes yet cannot see. Glittering mica it is for those who are alive yet know not why; foolishness for the numberless herd of humanity which, mindless and indifferent to everything that has not been drummed into it or secretly poured into its ears as the poison of the snake from the Garden of Eden, forever follow the same dreary road towards the realm of the dead, in a never-ending stream, like the migration of the eels down the river to their spawning grounds and into the fishermen's nets. This behaviour, in both eels and men, would be incomprehensible if their stoic equanimity did not rest on the inner assurance, secretly gleaming beneath the threshold of consciousness in both man and beast: 'I will not die, death is an empty phantom.' That is the only possible explanation why, if a person falls in the water, dozens of others risk their own lives and jump in to save them. If, on the other hand, they could save them by handing over money they wouldn't do it! Bürger's 'Song of the Honest Man' who refused payment for his bravery, has never been true. People fear life, only they don't realise it!

Many decent people delude themselves into thinking we humans are all, without exception, doomed to perdition unless we 'search our soul', repent, put the world behind us and all the other admonitions of pious zealots. The result? Many listened to them, beat their breast, then went off and spilt the blood of those who didn't believe in the same things as they did. Later, customs became less violent, but not because people had become better — just more indolent, less fanatical. They go to their churches on Sunday, behave as if they were taking to heart the things some well-meaning man reproaches them with from eleven to twelve, then they go back home, hang up their Sunday suit in the wardrobe and the Code of Civil Law continues to take precedence over the Book of books. Not least because it's got a flexible binding. And it's always the same in the Tragedy of History: each act ends with Bolshevism, the 'religion' of despair; followed by the interval, a new act, which you'd say was exactly the same again if the actors weren't wearing different costumes. And, as always, knowledge, the true knowledge that really matters, remains behind the scenes, ignored. It's not allowed on stage, the actors won't let it appear, they're afraid it might steal their applause.

It is thirty-six years since I first had an inkling of the mysterious Masked Figure behind the scenes of life. It only gave me mute signs, which for a long time I did not understand. I was still too young to comprehend what the figure was trying to tell me, I was still too captivated by the play being acted out on the stage. I imagined the play was important and had been written specially for me. Then, when I wanted to take part myself but found the role assigned to me unsatisfying, I was overcome with a furious, unbridled hatred for the players in their make-up. I saw their 'soulful' eyes, which in reality were trying to spot where their neighbour kept his purse, realised that the marvellous set was not a real palace, just painted cardboard, and poured out my fanatical hatred of all these histrionics in satires, or whatever you might call them.

The Masked Figure had only given me brief hints, but they were like an inspiration; they were enough to turn a businessman into a writer overnight. I will describe how that was possible in more detail later on. It happened through the transformation of the blood. A few quick, mute signs from the Masked Figure brought it about. For a long time I was convinced that all those beside me and around me in their make-up and costume were professional actors, until I gradually realised that some of them were so firmly convinced of the genuineness of the character they were playing that they had turned into it without being aware of it. They play their role, having forgotten that they were sent to join the actors against their will, that a hypocritical gang of directors engaged them when they were very young. Then my hatred began to fade, especially when I saw that they only just managed to attain their goals and very often they were other goals than the ones I was aiming for. Then I started hinting, in novels and stories, at the Masked Figure behind the scenes. Many pricked up their ears, others shook their heads and muttered, 'What's he on about? There's no one behind the scenes.' Did those who pricked up their ears spend long enough staring into the darkness, where I told them they could see the Masked Figure standing? How can I know? Some will have lost patience and turned back to the colourful satyric drama on the stage of life with its bright, artificial lighting. 'Crazy!' is probably their assessment of me and those I once wounded with my hatred join in, saying, 'He lied deliberately! He's a hypocrite, he has no ideals.' In one way they are correct: their ideals are not mine, I have an absolute hatred of make-up and bombast.

From the very beginning I interpreted these brief hints from the Masked Figure correctly. The more important signs and signals I only came to understand slowly, for life placed other images before my eyes; it interposed itself as an interpreter between myself and the veiled figure when I proved incapable of understanding his gestures by digging deep within myself. I was faced with the poisoned heritage of all humans, the belief that we can only enrich ourselves from the knowledge of others, we can only drink our fill from mankind's past. The interpreter, standing between myself and the Masked Figure, spoke a different language from the one intended for me, lying and sometimes, so that I would not notice the lies, telling the truth. I clung on to just one absolutely clear hint from the Masked Figure, despite the interpreter's scornful expression: wherever and whenever I could, I pointed to the figure behind the scenes. Whether people I spoke to about it believed me or not, whether they laughed, listened attentively, suppressed a smile or made an effort to keep a straight face, it didn't bother me. Often, even today, perhaps today more than ever, I cannot stop myself thinking, 'What's the point? Let the eels continue on their merry way!'

But the Masked Figure had me completely in his power, his will was stronger than mine. For a while he disappeared from view or, to be more precise, changed his form; at such times it was as if I could see his 'face'. That lasted for years. During that time the interpreter, life, spoke to me through books which often came into my hands in such strange ways that I couldn't shake off the feeling that an invisible schoolmaster had taken charge of my education. And every time a book on yoga was sent to me, I thought I had finally found the key to the secrets I was longing for. It had very quickly become clear to me that yoga, that strange, profound educational system of the Asiatic peoples, and not the philosophical theories of the thinkers and sages, was the sole road to a superhuman existence. Chance — fate travelling incognito, as a Russian once called it — gave me books that said so. I also came into contact with people who seemed to know more about yoga than the scholars who were learned in Indian writing. Whenever I heard the name of someone who appeared to be an initiate in these matters, I wrote to them, I hunted for them as if they must possess the elixir of life. I was gripped by an obsession: find them, find them, find them. I could write volumes about my experiences with such 'initiates'. In order to find a certain Captain Searle of the Anglo-Indian Marine Survey who, I had been told, was the disciple of a hathayogi (fakir) and could calm typhoons by repeating certain mantras, I sent several dozen letters to Australia,

America, England, India and China. When one of them finally reached its goal, Captain Searle had died a week previously.

I joined the Theosophical Society, founded a lodge in Prague and went round roaring like a lion to recruit members; I gave talks to a small group from English *siftings* and *pamphlets*. The only lasting reward for all my efforts was that I eventually acquired an ability in what you might call sight-translation, so that today I can read out aloud from an English book as if it were in German. Annie Besant rewarded me for my zeal by accepting me into a certain inner circle, the centre of which is in Adyar in India. I received a number of letters from her with instructions about yoga. From that moment until my resignation from the Society some three months later I led the life of a man who was almost mad. I existed on nothing but vegetable matter, hardly slept at all, ate a tablespoon of gum arabic dissolved in soup twice a day (it had been most warmly recommended to me by a French occult order for the purpose of awakening astral clairvoyance) performed asana exercises (Asiatic sitting positions with crossed legs) for eight hours night after night, at the same time holding my breath until I was shaking fit to die. Then, at the new moon, I rode out in complete darkness to a hill well outside Prague, known as the Cave of St Procopius, tethered my horse to a tree, sat in the asana position and stared at a point in the sky until it began to grow light. The instructions for all this, insofar as they had not come from Annie Besant herself, I had extracted from books of Indian or medieval provenance. And whenever my faith was threatening to collapse and I was beginning to despair, some second-hand bookseller would send me a catalogue of books on yoga, magic and the like which I had not yet come across and which buoyed me up with more false hopes.

One winter's night, when the snow was so deep it was impossible to ride out to my hill, I was sitting on a bench by the Moldau. Behind me was an old bridge-tower with a large clock. I had already been sitting there for several hours, wrapped up in my fur coat, but still shivering with cold, staring at the greyish-black sky, trying everything possible to attain what Mrs Besant had described to me in a letter as inner vision. In vain. From earliest childhood I had been surprisingly devoid of the faculty many people possess of being able to close their eyes and imagine a picture or a familiar face. It was, for example, quite impossible for me to say whether one or other of my acquaintances had blue, brown or grey eyes, dark or brown hair, a straight or curved nose, if I had had not previously looked at it specifically to ascertain that. In other words, I used to think in words, not in images. I had sat down on this bench with the firm resolution of not getting up again until I had succeeded in opening up my inner vision. My model was Gautama Buddha who had once sat under the bo tree with a similar resolution. Of course, I only stuck it out for about five hours and not, like Him, for days and nights. Suddenly I wondered what time it was. Then, just at the moment when I was being torn from my contemplation, I saw, with a sharpness and clarity with which I could not remember ever having perceived any object before in my life, a huge clock shining brightly in the sky. The hands showed twelve minutes to two. It made such a profound impression that I clearly felt my heart — not miss a beat, no: beat extraordinarily slowly. As if a hand were gripping it tight. I turned round and looked at the tower clock, which until then had been behind me. It is completely out of the question that I should have turned round earlier and thus got some idea of what time it was, for I had sat on the bench for five hours motionless, as is the strict requirement for this kind of concentration exercise. The clock, just like the one I had seen in the sky in my vision, showed twelve minutes to two.

I was overjoyed. There was just one faint worry: would my 'inner eye' stay open? I started the exercise again. For a time the sky remained greyish-black and closed, as it had been before. It suddenly occurred to me to see if I could make my heart beat in as calm and controlled a manner as it had done of its own accord when I had had the vision, or possibly, most probably even, before the vision. This did not occur to me the way things usually do, rather it was like a dimly perceived deduction or instruction from the sense of one of the Buddha's sayings which came to me as if from the invisible lips of the 'Masked Figure'. The saying was, 'Things come from the heart, are born of the heart and subject to the heart.' In that night this saying penetrated deep into my blood. It is not just a beautiful axiom, which one can appreciate as such when reading it and let it go in one ear and out of the other, no, it is the essence of a whole philosophy: the realisation that everything we think we perceive here on earth and in the material cosmos as existing objectively outside us is not material, but a state of our own self. This saying is also the subtle key to true magic and does not consist merely of theoretical knowledge. Often in my life when I thought I was lost it has helped me, like a strong hand held out in support. When, many years later, I fell 1,000 feet from the Dent du Jaman, it came into my mind at the moment when I first hit the ground, with my left shoulder, and managed to twist my body and thus change the direction of my fall, with the result that I didn't eventually land in a quarry, but in a gully full of soft snow. Was it the Buddha's saying that saved me? Was it that that gave me the flash of inspiration: turn your body! Who could say for certain? But it does seem to me that that was the case.

I sat on the stone bench and stared at the sky again. Finally I managed to bring my heart to the state of calm it had previously been in. The result was immediate. It was as if a circular piece of the night sky were receding, as if it were coming away from the atmosphere and retreating into more and more immeasurable depths of space. As it was happening, I observed myself as clearly as I could and it soon became clear to me that the sole purpose was that I should make the line of vision of my two eyes *parallel*. At the same time I recalled reading that sleepwalkers in a state of trance always looked as if their gaze were fixed on the distance. It was not long before I had not only achieved a degree — a small degree, but still sufficient — of control over my heart, but also over the direction of my gaze and this was immediately followed by something I had never seen before in my life: geometrical shapes formed in the round hole in the sky. The first sign was the so-called in *hoc signo vinces*: a cross within a capital 'H'. I looked at it coolly, as if uninvolved, without a trace of conceit or anything like that. Which was quite natural, since even in those days I had very little time for Christian ecstasies. It was merely as an 'observer' that I was interested to see this particular time-honoured sigil leading out the procession of my visions. Then other geometrical figures made their appearance, some of them similar to the magic signs you see in medieval Faust books. All of them were colourless. It was only much later that I saw images, bright and colourful pictures, often Greek statues, for example Pallas Athene.

All these images had one main thing in common: they were so sharp, so bright and in such glorious colour that the things of this earth seemed pale and blurred. However difficult it might be to understand, sometimes I could see them from all sides at the same time, as if my inner eye were not a lens, but a circle drawn round the visionary image. Eventually my inner eye became so practised that I could conjure up my visionary faculty at will, even when my external self was not at rest at all, for example when I was involved in a trivial conversation with someone or other. One of my favourite exercises was to observe, while I was reading the newspaper in the coffee house, a large tangle of rope that often appeared to me and then to untangle it in my mind, knot by knot, as clearly as if it were really there before me, until finally it was neatly coiled up, like the anchor hawser on a ship. There is one fact which I consider very important, since for me it proves that it is not my external person alone that calls up these images, but something that lies deeper: even today I cannot conjure up at will any image I happen to want. It would be of no value if I could. It would have failed in its true purpose of communication to me; then it would just be my everyday consciousness speaking to me of things which I already know of in other words.

The faculty of inner vision which I acquired or opened up during that winter's night was, by the way, the first turning point in my destiny that changed me, at a stroke so to speak, from a businessman to a writer: my imagination became visual. Previously I had thought in words, from then on I could also think in images; in images which I saw as if they were really there before me; no, a hundred times more real, more immediate than any physical object. 'Vision' has become a hackneyed word on the lips of the many; few have actually experienced one but everyone 'knows' exactly what a vision is supposed to look like. I myself used to prattle on like that when my eyes were still blind. A writer is praised if he has a keen talent for the observation of nature and can put it on paper by means of ink. He's a wretched photographer, nothing more. That kind of thing has nothing to do with the art I am talking about. With the theatre, perhaps. Vision probably has the greatest influence on painting, provided that it does not take hold of the painter's eye and innermost feeling alone, but also his hand, enabling it to reproduce the image. I know many painters and have made great efforts to explain to them that they wouldn't need a model if they only knew how to open their inner eye. They listened, uncomprehending; none has tried to follow my advice. They prefer to make tracings of nature, bewitched by the stupid principle that nature (external nature, that is) is the teacher of all art.

When I wrote a long letter to Mrs Besant after my experience on the stone bench, she was silent for a long time. Then I received her answer: try to rend the veil. I did not understand what she meant and kept asking again and again. From the empty platitudes she sent me — at least that was what they seemed to me — I quickly came to the conclusion that Mrs Besant had no idea what to do with me. (A strange event, connected with further visions I had, eventually cut the tie binding me to the Theosophical Society.) I continued my researches into yoga and eventually came upon the area that in India is called bhakti yoga (yoga, practised through the search for God, devotional fervour and religious ecstasy). The Masked Figure — or should I call it a kindly fate? — saved me from being afflicted with and crushed or torn apart by ecstasies, as are all those unfortunates (or fortunates, if they reach the goal) who suffer schizophrenia, show stigmata or see the 'light', like Ruysbroeck, and 'unbecome' in it, imagining they have found God as an object, forgetting that the Only God they are always talking about can never be anything but a subject. To me they are like mothers who carry a child and die when they give birth. Who knows whether in this way changelings are not sometimes born in the invisible world of causes and then —

growing into Molochs — send that poison trickling into the brains of humanity which we call a spiritual epidemic, such as Bolshevism at present or the Children's Crusade in the past?

Before being accepted into the inner circle of the Theosophical Society, people are given (as I was) the stern warning: 'Anyone who does not hold firm until the end, will be exposed to unheard-of danger in the spiritual realm.' When I informed Mrs Besant that I was leaving the Society, her reply was brief: 'I know, the snakes of Mara (an Indian expression for the Tempter) are many.'

I shall indicate the nature of the main experience which persuaded me to leave the Theosophical Society. The real purpose of the three months probationary period before final acceptance into the 'Inner Circle' is for one to find one's 'guide'. A guide is a fundamental prerequisite and essential on the path of yoga and magic. Since I assumed the images that appeared to me would give me a hint or indication of how I might find a guide, I made constant efforts to draw out more and more new visions from inside me. (By calming my heartbeat and making the sightlines of my eyes parallel, as mentioned above.) One night, again at around two o'clock, I was sitting in my bachelor's room in the *padmasana* (lotus position) practising *pranayama* (controlled breathing) as prescribed by the *ham-ssa* which consists of drawing and expelling breath through the left then the right nostril alternately. A strange numbness in the head is the usual consequence of this exercise. At the time I did not know — fortunately did not know! — that the secret purpose of *hamssa-pranayama* is to induce a kind of self-hypnosis. (I was told that by a young Brahmin, whom I only met in 1914.) Instinctively I fought against the numbness; if I had not, I would today probably be an unhappy medium or suffer from some other kind of schizophrenia, perhaps even religious mania. As it was, I clung to a valuable piece of advice (advice which is a jewel in Buddhist doctrine): always remain conscious. Sitting motionless, I stared fixedly at a large black circle on the wall, which I always had hanging there for the purpose of these exercises. Suddenly the paper circle became bright; it was as if a shining disc had come in front of it. I was completely awake and my mind clear. Then a figure the size of a grown man appeared, dressed in white, but with no head! I had already read a large number of occult books by then and since I have an excellent memory — and already had as a young man — a passage from one of them immediately occurred to me. It said specifically: apparitions in human form without a head signify extreme danger for those who see them. A feeling of uneasiness crept over me, but I still continued to stare at the illuminated disc. Why is this happening to me, I asked myself, despite the fact that I do not take drugs, like morphine addicts who, as their final collapse approaches, have visions of people with their heads cut off? A face below a turban — separated from the body by a gap the width of a finger — then began to form and its features gradually became clear. It looked so old it would be difficult to find a comparison. The vision remained for a while, then disappeared all at once. But the impression stayed with me for almost a whole day, as if it had etched itself on my consciousness: I could not dismiss it, as I had other visions. It gave me an extremely unpleasant feeling, which only faded the following night, when — in the deserted street as I made my way home from a meeting of the lodge of the Theosophical Society I had founded — I once more immersed myself in meditation exercises connected with finding a guru. Again my heartbeat calmed down and, despite the fact that the street was well lit and I was walking fairly quickly, a greenish beam of light the thickness of a man shot down from the sky a few yards in front of me. Where it hit the ground it split into three parts, forming a three-pointed anchor. I stopped and observed the phenomenon coolly and calmly. Not for a second did I have the feeling it was anything other then a vision. Here once again my refusal to be disconcerted by visions proved its worth. I kept a tight hold on my heart — I could almost say by force — for I sensed that the beam of light wanted to have a stronger effect on me than had ever happened with any of my previous visions. I can very well imagine that if a person with no experience in this area had a similar experience, they would delude themselves into thinking they were having a so-called divine revelation and be swept away, with nothing to cling on to and no lifebelt, into the boundless sea of theistic delusion.

At this point I would like to state expressly that in my personal opinion everything — everything!— to do with theism is a will-o'-the-wisp that leads us astray. I am not saying this in order to shake or shatter anyone's pious faith. As I have said before, I do not believe those who stumble through life indifferent to everything connected with the occult and materialistic to the core are doomed to absolute perdition. Far be it from me to assume that the 'hot ones' — those with theistic convictions — will be spewed out from the mouth of life. If I were to declare my own belief, it would perhaps best be as follows: who is the Jacob of the old Testament, who wrestled with an angel of the Lord for a whole night until he prevailed over him? Answer: one who does not follow the thorny path of theistic faith!

Ramakrishna, the last Indian prophet — the English scholar, Max Müller, has emphasised his great importance — Ramakrishna, a bhakta yogi par excellence, once said, 'A person serves their God for a long time, following everything He says to them, doing everything He does, just for His sake and in His honour, being less to Him than a slave. But then one day God hands over all power to His loyal servant, whom He places on His own throne.' This, be it noted, for those (and it will not be that many!) who follow, or long to follow the path of the bhakta.

When the light stood before me as I described it, I asked myself, 'What can this mean? What is it supposed to be telling me?' It never for a moment occurred to me to immerse myself in it as an uplifting sight, as a religious person might have done. Immediately the answer came to me in a 'thought' — I call it a thought because I can think of no other expression, in fact it was almost like hearing a voice, which informed me, 'The anchor means holding fast or hoping; the three prongs mean three days.'

Three days later something happened that was so strange I can scarcely bring myself to write it down for fear people might think I am fabricating it and making fun of all those who are reading what I have written. Must I insist that that is not the case? You can believe me or not, as you like. On the third morning after that night, I went to my business, a bureau de change in Prague. The servant was just sweeping out the office; none of the other staff was there. I was a little surprised to see, despite the early hour, a gentleman sitting in the waiting room and so asked him what he wanted. He was well-dressed, middle-aged, wearing glasses and had a squint. In reply he muttered a few incomprehensible words then pulled himself together and said with somewhat forced determination, 'I want nothing from you. I thought you wanted something from me.' I immediately recalled: 'Wait three days,' the words that had come to mind when I saw the anchor. From the conversation with the stranger that quickly followed, I learnt that he was called O. K., that he had spent a long time as a professor or teacher of chemistry in Japan, that he had been living for some time now in Dresden and was a spiritualist. But not a spiritualist in the usual sense, rather a 'pious' man, a kind of Christian bhakta yogi. He had possessed the gift of automatic writing since he was a child, he told me; however, it wasn't 'spirits' that spoke through his writing but none other than Jesus Christ Himself. I listened patiently and soon realised that I wasn't dealing with a swindler, as had often been the case, but at worst with a religious fanatic. I must point out that, despite my young years, I was even then an uncommonly sharp judge of character and perfectly capable of distinguishing lies from truth. Which was hardly surprising. Anyone who, like me, has entered the banking profession at a young age very quickly learns to read other people like an open book.

I invited Professor K. to go with me to my apartment, since a bureau de change did not seem the right place for a discussion of the occult, yoga and prophecy. Once there, Herr K. told me that three days ago — the time corresponded exactly to that of my vision! —he had as usual been occupied with automatic writing when suddenly his hand had refused to finish the sentence he had begun and had instead written a new sentence: Go to Prague to see a banker by the name of M. (me, that is) so that you can be with him early on the morning of the third day.

K. assured me he had never heard my name before. He had travelled to Prague to see what he might find and had sought me out.

When I asked what he had to tell me, he said he didn't exactly know but he had the feeling I was in great danger and it was up to him to save me. He suspected I had fallen into the hands of 'Asiatic devils'. (Up to that point I had not even hinted to him that I practised yoga.) I spent the whole day with K. listening to his strange, I might almost say rapt, discourse. He said there was only one way to change oneself from a dull normal person into a spiritually more valuable one and that was the path of revelation, which was granted to a person if they followed certain instructions, apocryphal and pious in the Christian sense, which could be most appropriately described as Rosicrucian, since they were alien to both the Protestant and Catholic churches. He gave me some of these instructions. Since he had an incredible store of knowledge and was a scholar in the best sense of the word, I gradually — I was considerably younger than him and therefore less self-assured than I might have been — fell under his spell. Even today it doesn't surprise me; theism is in the blood of every person who has had a Christian upbringing. In people who do not concern themselves with spiritual matters in their later life, theism is replaced with something that looks like atheism. I suspect, however, that such atheism is seldom genuine; mostly it is theism that has been buried beneath other debris. As K. talked, the theism of my childhood years was aroused and became even more alive within me as the memory of the vision of the man with his head cut off suddenly seemed to take on a deeper meaning: it struck me as if it were a similar experience, if on a small scale, to that of St Paul on the road to Damascus.

K. told me of a number of books which would be particularly fruitful for me, above all, the works of a certain Jakob Lorber. I acquired them straight away and read them conscientiously. If ever a man felt sick, it was me reading those books. But, with a perseverance I cannot understand today, I managed to delude myself into believing that what was written there in sugary rosewater was the quintessence of salvation. But if my meeting with Professor K. had ended with nothing more than a recommendation to read the godly Jakob Lorber, the result would have been bearable. I would probably not have understood the meaning of the apparition of the 'headless' man later on, but I would have been spared years of suffering. Thirteen years of suffering to be precise. His visit finished as follows: K. had already boarded the afternoon train to Dresden when he suddenly turned round and said, 'Oh yes, I have just remembered the most important thing I have to tell you. There is a man, Herr X., who lives in Vienna. He and many other former Theosophists, Germans and English, even an Indian Brahmin called Babajee, are the disciples of a genuine Rosicrucian who is said to be a simple craftsman living somewhere in Hesse. He knows and teaches the true yoga, on which the New Testament is secretly based.'

It was like a sudden flash of revelation. The Herr X. in Vienna he mentioned had been a friend of mine for some time. Moreover I knew a certain Dr Franz Hartmann, whom K. had also mentioned in connection with X. and who, as I knew or, rather, had been told by the Theosophists, was among the most profoundly initiated of the 'initiates' in yoga. If he and X. and others, whose names I prefer not to mention here, were disciples of the Rosicrucian O. K. had talked of, then I had finally found my guru, as the prophecy of the 'Inner Circle' of the Th. S. had said I would! I immediately went to Vienna to see my friend. He had a guest staying with him, an Englishman called G. R. S Mead who, as I knew, was secretary of the Theosophical Society in Adyar in India. By a sign he gave with his hand he indicated that he, too, was a member of the 'Eastern School' (the 'Inner Circle'). I said I had recently had a certain experience and asked if I could speak openly before X. Mead nodded. I started by describing the apparition of the man with no head. Suddenly Mead asked whether the man had not been wearing a white Brahmin thread. I said yes. Had I noticed that it was tied in a knot? I closed my eyes, called up the image, immediately saw the knot clearly and described the way it was tied. Mead stood up, touched his forehead and said, 'T'was the Master.' I looked across at X. out of the corner of my eye; he appeared to be suppressing a mocking smile.

When I then started to describe my meeting with Prof. K., X. became more and more serious. When I mentioned his last words, his remarks about the Rosicrucian guru, he quickly placed his finger on his lips as a sign that I should stop speaking at once. I concluded the sentence with a few more words. Later he took me to one side and told me things about the Theosophical Society which horrified me. I believed them! The evasive answers Mrs Besant gave to my questions about yoga, the awful kitsch the Theosophical *siftings* sometimes contained — that and other things seemed to confirm my assumption that everything X. told me was true. On top of that I had, a short time before, received a letter from William Judge in New York (he was regarded as one who had been initiated directly by the so-called Mahatmas of Tibet), saying that the 'Masters' in no way recognised Mrs Besant as president of the Society and had specifically authorised him to inform all the members of the 'Eastern School' of that.

Everything I had so far believed now appeared uncertain. I spent the whole night in meditation exercises — no images appeared to give me a sign. The 'Masked Figure' seemed to have abandoned me. Professor K. had 'inoculated' me and the rash appeared: the next day I told my friend X. that I was prepared to recognise the 'Rosicrucian' (I was given his name) as my guide. X. listened very attentively to what I said, then showed me a telegram he claimed to have received shortly beforehand. It said that I had already been taken on by the guru a few days previously (the date coincided with that of my vision of the anchor). X. assured me that the Rosicrucian was clairvoyant in spiritual matters, sometimes in physical matters as well, and I could rest assured that the 'new disciple' meant me and no one else.

Full of rejoicing, I wrote to Annie Besant that, in accordance with the prophecy she had given me at the very start, I had found the man who must presumably be taken as the one behind the title of 'guru'. Mrs Besant's answer: 'The snakes of Mara are many'— which I have already mentioned — came straight back. I immediately thought of the man without a head. Who is this suspicious 'person' with no head? I asked myself. A symbol of course, what else! But what did the symbol want to tell me? That disaster was approaching, I sensed. But what was the point of the warning if it did not tell me the way to escape the danger? What was the masked guide of my destiny trying to warn me of by letting me see the apparition of the headless Brahmin? I asked myself over and over again. But couldn't find the answer. Was the 'Eastern School' the headless man? Was it the Rosicrucian guide I had just found? I wavered from one interpretation to another and back again. In the thirteen years of torment along the thorny path that followed I asked myself again and again. Asked without getting an answer, at least not the answer I wanted: a clear answer with no possibility of misunderstanding. I did of course get 'answers', but delphic ones, now they would say one thing, now the opposite.

Only today, years after these events, do I know precisely what the man with his head cut off meant. Anyone who thinks about it can easily work it out, but I am unwilling to spell it out myself. For reasons which anyone who has paid attention to what I have just written can guess.

A few weeks later I went to the place in Hesse where the Rosicrucian lived. He had been a weaver, could neither read nor write and had had strange experiences in the area of spiritualism, which he called the preparatory stage for acquiring true knowledge, which came solely from the heart, and nowhere else, when it began to speak. This speaking of the heart he called the 'inner word'; it awoke gradually, he said, and was granted through 'grace' in the Christian sense. He showed his numerous disciples the way to this by giving them phrases, which he said he received from his inner voice for each one individually, to murmur to themselves. This murmuring-to-oneself, he said, would arouse our own heart's ability to speak and, moreover, a certain alteration would take place in our bodies until at the end of the way Christ's immortal body would be instilled in the disciple and with it Life Immortal. In his opinion one had to start with the body. Piety in the ecclesiastical sense was something he had little or no time for if it was not accompanied by this alteration of the body. If the only thing I had learnt from this man was that the body must be included in the transformation of the person through yoga, he would have earned my lifelong gratitude for that insight alone. It was, he said, completely impossible to achieve this alteration of the body through one's own rational knowledge and by one's own efforts.

He was right about that as well. 'Something extra must come from above to bring about the change,' was the way he put it. By 'from above' he of course meant Jesus Christ, the risen Christ who had overcome death and was with us day by day, and not the crucified Christ. For anyone who constantly visualised the crucified Christ, as did Catholic monks, especially the Jesuits, and not the living, risen Lord, would 'have their bones broken' or they would remain hanging on the cross. As an example he most often gave Katharina Emmerich, the nun who died in 1824 and who was reported to display the stigmata every Friday. His teaching regarding the transformation of the body was uncommonly profound and strange; it often reminded me of the Gnostics and their claims. He said that one had to experience everything from Christ's life — baptism, the washing of His feet, the Last Supper, as well as the crucifixion — literally, in one's own body, in the exact way it was written in the Gospels, otherwise it would remain pure theory, things one had heard or read, and would be no more than Christian edification. I came to know many of his 54 disciples and there was not one of them, with the possible exception of an old lady, whom I could call exaggeratedly pious. Apart from a few ordinary artisans, they were mostly elegant, genteel people. None, neither the 'guide' nor any of his disciples, showed a trace of asceticism or anything like that. Even stranger was the fact that with time almost all of us experienced in ourselves the 'reactions' which 'J...' — as we all called our guide — considered so important. Not only in visions, or mostly in dreams, but also on our own bodies, and that even though no one knew what phenomena would occur, since we were all strictly forbidden to tell the others what we had experienced, in order to exclude the possibility of autosuggestion. I will describe just one such reaction here: it consisted of letters appearing on one's skin. (Medical science calls it 'dermography' and attributes it to hysteria, without of course knowing what hysteria actually is.) Each of these letters had a particular meaning and indicated the stage of development the person in question had reached.

A layman could easily incline to the superficial view that it was all just worthless religious emotionalism. That would be quite wrong! On the contrary, I can assure you that the 'guide's' teaching method aroused an inner life the richness and worth of which no one who has not experienced something similar themself can imagine. This period of apprenticeship also included the transformation of the blood which compelled me to become a writer, not to mention other transformations which I cannot go into here. The first 'loosening-up' of my inner being, however, was brought about by the 'eye-opening' experience on the bench by the Moldau in Prague.

Here is an incident to illustrate the effect murmuring a phrase can have on a person and how profoundly it can change their character. One day Dr Franz Hartmann, who is well known in the history of the Theosophical Society and who was one of my co-disciples, came to the guide and asked him to take on a young man as a disciple, saying that he had seldom met anyone who seemed more suited to receive his teaching. For years, he went on, he had lived the life of an ascetic following the strictest rule, withdrawn from the world like a saint. The guide thought for a while, apparently listening to his inner voice, and then said in very certain tones, 'You're wrong, Fränzle' — he was Swabian — 'the man isn't genuine, he just thinks he is.' Dr Hartmann assured him he knew the young man very well; it was wrong to say he wasn't genuine. 'Then I'll give him an exercise so you can see how things are in his heart of hearts,' J... replied. Six months later Hartmann encountered the young man in a city, transformed into an elegant dandy. Greatly astonished, he asked what had happened. 'Oh, I had only done the exercise you gave me from that Swabian fool for a few days,' he said with a beaming smile, 'when I had a kind of revelation and ditched all that mystical nonsense.' A few months later he died from syphilis. 'You see,' J... said reflectively, when Hartmann told him, 'he's been revealed. Pity I couldn't help him.'

Of the numerous disciples the guide had, only two experienced as good as no reactions. One was my friend L. — and the other myself. L. has now died, at a grand old age and with the composure of a saint. It will remain a mystery to me why he, who was a devout Christian, never experienced anything of that kind, even though the guide always called him his favourite disciple. As far as I was concerned, it is fairly understandable for, despite the crazy efforts I made to to feel at home, to delude myself into thinking I felt at home with J…'s ideas, I was never transformed from a Saul into a Paul.

For thirteen years I spent eight hours every day, without leaving out a single one — how often I put off the most important actions external life demanded of me! — repeating the mantras. Not a single reaction occurred. Whenever I poured out my distress to my 'guide', he gave me a long, earnest look and said, 'You must be patient.' The only thing I experienced were strange, piercing sensations in the palms of my hands and soles of my feet, the first, mild signs of stigmata. In others they were much clearer, some even had the marks, circular red spots. 'The pains of crucifixion,' our 'guide' called them, signs of the change of the blood. None of my co-disciples experienced states of ecstasy; if they had, our guide would have expressed extreme disapproval, for the main point of his teaching was that our waking consciousness should be sharpened and neither split nor weakened. And this remaining in one's body, in contrast to 'going out of oneself', as was taught in the mysteries of the Ancient Greeks, is a further foundation stone, which is of greater value on the road to true yoga than anything else; by laying it inside me, the 'guide' gave me a jewel to take with me through my whole life. The fact is that there is a particular method of 'leaving one's body while still alive' (a standard expression among trained occultists, though the process strikes me as different, not so coarsely sensual) and it is regarded as an initiation; in reality, it is the worst kind of schizophrenia imaginable. Sooner or later it results in mediumism — incurable schizophrenia. Thus, strange as it may sound, in their mysteries the Ancient Greeks were no other than victims of an illness. The exceptions are those who were able to leap over the chasm of: 'My God, why hast thou forsaken me?' The teaching of that simple man from Hesse culminated in the assertion that a person's soul does not live in their body in order to leave it, in the way someone will turn back when they realise they are in a cul de sac, but in order to transform its physical matter. In many of his experiences he resembled Jakob Böhme, whom every educated person today knows as a wonderful man; as a clairvoyant he was superior to him in some degree, but he was far, far superior to him in this insight that it is wrong to turn away from the world, however sublime withdrawal from the world might seem.

Those who are interested in mysticism (the others, of course, will not even have bothered to repress the usual grins) will object that all mystics recorded in history, even Buddha Gautama, preached and taught: turn away from the world. The Buddha, for example, called it a house on fire which truth, common sense and reason would demand we flee as quickly as possible. I am aware of that, but everything within me cries, wrong, wrong, wrong. There is a certain truth in their teaching, but it can, indeed I am convinced it *must*, be interpreted quite differently. At least for a person of the present day. In this respect I beg to differ from the eminent models of the past. The past is always a poison when it is understood as dogma.

As I have already mentioned, of all the disciples of the man in Hesse I, along with my friend L., was the only one who did not experience the transformation of the body in the way that corresponded to the intentions of our 'guide' and to what, at the time, were also mine. His reassurance that I only needed to wait in patience kept me languishing in fervent hope for thirteen years. Later, after his death — which knocked more than a few holes in his prophecies and those of his disciples — L. told me that our 'guide' had confided in him that the fact that I did not melt in the furnace of the exercises was because deep down inside I was aiming for a quite different goal from the Christian one he taught. He saw his task, he said, as bringing me onto the 'right' road. I was astonished when my friend told me that. I had never revealed, not even by vague hints, how alien to me not only the Christianity of the church was and remained, but also the Rosicrucian-Gnostic variant of our 'guide'. 'Semitic superstition' Schopenhauer once said, when he acknowledged the importance of the book *The Oupknethat* (containing the wisdom of the Vedic Upanishads). Even when I read them as a youth Schopenhauer's words affected me like invigorating rays of light.

It is naturally not my intention to denigrate Christianity in any way in saying that; on the contrary, I am convinced the world would be a wonderful place if there were more (genuine) Christians. I simply wanted to confess that, despite the most fervent efforts, I have never managed to make the Christian faith my own, even though I was brought up in it from childhood. That kind of thing may well be child's play for the lukewarm.

I called the thirteen years I was a disciple of that 'guide' a thorny path. And that it was truly, not only spiritually but also physically. It may sound strange, but all exercises, not only the ones I have described here but all yoga exercises, whether they are right or wrong, not only change one's blood, they of necessity change our outward destiny as well. Naturally. You miss favourable opportunities and suchlike if you spend eight hours a day murmuring phrases to yourself instead of 'knuckling down' and 'getting on with it' (busy, busy, busy, eh!) — like the complete fool who's writing this stuff, the enlightened citizen will say, preening himself on his great cleverness. True, for a while yoga has these consequences for a person, but even those who devote their lives to outward things do not have control over 'chance'. Has mankind created anything really lasting? If we had, there ought to be gigantic remains surviving from primaeval times, unless your view is that in those days people went on all fours. The culture of an Atlantis has sunk, Egypt been destroyed, Niniveh laid waste, just as our creations will be swept away. Today people are saying that in the course of the last few decades the materialistic view of life has reached its end. Nonsense! If anything it has become even more crass, if that is possible. It has only been finished off in theory, and that only for the few who have followed the progress in epistemology or contributed to it. The rest have remained as blinkered as they always were. What do we hear if we tell a layman that our senses deceive us and that the things we perceive through them do not at all correspond to reality, which is not something that has only become known during the last few decades? Even people who have made such progress in 'culture' that they no longer eat

143

fish with two knives and thus imagine themselves uncommonly superior, even such people say, 'Ridiculous. If that were the case we wouldn't be able to photograph the world!' And, what is even more astonishing, even scientists, scholars and philosophers who believe the perceptible world is mere surface appearance and that everything is relative, even they rear up like a horse with the staggers when you ask them, 'If that is the case, why don't you admit the possibility of certain spiritualist phenomena, for example the materialisation of human and animal figures, the ability to pass through matter, the apport of objects from distant places? Such phenomena would be extremely easy to explain with the hypothesis — and I'm sure it's correct — which you gentlemen have put forward. Why do you insist on denying their possibility so obstinately? They simply demonstrate that things that don't happen every day do not have to be permanently excluded.' Professor Wilhelm Ostwald, one of the most prominent scientists of the materialist school, has put forward an explanation of what movement basically is; it is eminently suited to explaining spiritualist and magic phenomena. How baffling, then, to hear what Ostwald has to say about the *im*possibility of occult phenomena. If that is the way our scientific luminaries behave, then how can we be surprised that the philistines laugh when they hear people talk of philosophical values?

The facts teach us that it will never be possible to overthrow the materialist view of the world by means of theory; the eels cannot be converted and diverted from their path that easily. It has to happen in another way. The practical application of the doctrine of yoga could prove to be the means to that end. For a while it looked as if spiritualism would have the honour of making the first breach, but then the swindlers managed to bring it into disrepute, with the result that the laws which underlie it and could provide a key to spiritual values are as hidden from view as ever. And even assuming that we succeeded in getting spiritualist phenomena generally recognised, it would still be quite likely that materialism would turn it into a further triumph based on the discovery of a new, more rarified material side of nature. For example the invention of the distillation of alcohol from potatoes, that is of a volatile, subtle substance from a coarse one, did not manage to undermine the materialist view of the world. We will only have taken the first real step when we can prove that thoughts can produce physical changes in matter. But that will not remove the last obstacle, for science will say, perhaps even prove that, despite appearances to the contrary, thoughts belong to the field of physics or chemistry — say to the realm of electricity. The victory of the purely spiritual view will only come when people can demonstrate in practical terms to themselves and to others that matter as such does not exist at all but, as the Vedanta and other similar systems of knowledge teach, is an illusion of the senses, an idea that has coagulated into apparent materiality. The only way to come to such a conviction, which cannot be shaken by anything, is through yoga.

What is yoga?

Yoga encompasses all exercises involving the soul and the mind, a practical activity, that is, in which people today are hardly involved at all. I would put it this way: yoga is the leaven, theoretical knowledge merely flour and water.

Everything connected with yoga seems to come from Asia. Does that mean the Asians are masters in this area? It is possible that they had the knowledge in ages from which nothing has come down to us; legends claim that is the case. The undeniable fact is that there is no one with us today whom we could approach as a master of yoga. Theosophists and occultists maintain that the true yoga masters live in solitary seclusion, inaccessible to people who live ordinary lives, but that is naturally difficult to prove. We have little more than faith and trust to rely on. Who can guarantee that those you come across here and there in India who do practise yoga are not simply seekers? Does not almost everything suggest that the lofty path of yoga, leading to marvellous destinations, has been blocked since prehistoric times, to be replaced by schizophrenia, hysteria, mediumism and other pathological conditions, instead of the opposite: the perfection of mankind? Campbell Oman, the author of a remarkable book on the ascetics, mystics and saints of India, tells of a European by the name

145

of Charles de Russette, who had become a sadhu (a kind of penitent) and retired to a solitary existence in the vicinity of Simla. Russette told him he had seen Indian fakirs do the most wonderful things.

That kind of report can be read by the dozen; unfortunately most, when you look into them, turn out to be pure invention. When the British government was looking for a fakir who could perform one of the famous yogi miracles for the Wembley Exhibition, they could not find a single one! It is mostly travelling showmen who are wrongly seen as yogis — a result of the general ignorance as to what a yogi really is. Even an ascetic is not by any means a yogi, usually the opposite, in fact, namely someone who has taken piety to such an extreme that they have become schizophrenic. Yoga means something like 'union'. A bhakta yogi such as Ramakrishna or, to name a European, Ruysbroeck, claim that in their ecstasies they achieve union with God, but one could just as well say they were experiencing schizophrenia. The fact that Ramakrishna sometimes worked 'miracles', as his disciples unanimously assert, does not prove that schizophrenia is out of the question; similar things happen with spiritualist mediums and people who have been hypnotised.

The 'union' the yogi aims for is, rather, the indissoluble oneness of a person with himself. Such union with oneself is not present in ordinary people, as is generally assumed. Every person has split consciousness, as has every animal. One only realises this after one has practised yoga for some time. Which is rather strange, since it would take only a little power of observation for everyone to realise that their self-awareness is anything but unified. The way our heart and digestion work independently, our powerlessness to resist moods and thoughts, which 'occur' to us and do not let go of us for a long time, dreams, our inability to resist our need for sleep and many other things are clear proof that we are by no means masters in our own house. Schizophrenics, then, in the wider sense of the word! Myths, fairy tales and legends indicate these defects: the broken sword that Siegfried forges anew, which the 'dwarf' was unable to do, despite his cunning and inventiveness; Sleeping Beauty, who must be wakened with a kiss, the Fall in the Bible. These all bear witness to the state we are in at present, at the same time pointing to a possibility of becoming whole — to yoga! The religions — this word also means union! — of the advanced nations do not simply set up moral laws but also aim, for those who take them seriously, at union with God. Yoga has nothing to do with God; the Buddhists have not included any gods at all in their system and still practise yoga!

The union yoga is aiming for is the amalgamation of the subconscious — or superconscious, if you will allow that word — with our everyday consciousness. Coué, the French pharmacist who caused such a stir with his successful cures a while ago, tried to achieve something similar with his method of autosuggestion. In my opinion he made the same mistake as all dualists, even the religious ones: he addresses the inner person, that is the one we are unconscious of, as *tu*, the familiar 'you'! That only exacerbates the schizophrenia people are suffering from. I believe that anyone who follows Coué's method conscientiously will wake up one day to find himself a complete hysteric. They will pay dearly enough for any cure which they may have brought about through Coué's method.

The Christian Scientists are widely known today. The founder, the American Mrs Baker Eddy, claimed the Bible teaches that there are no illnesses, people just imagine they have them. The constant increase in the membership of the Church of Christ, Scientist, might suggest that actual cures sometimes occur when Mrs Eddy's instructions are followed. Looked at in the clear light of day, Mrs Eddy's theory is not much other than a deformed notion from the Vedanta. Coué made the mistake of addressing our subconscious as 'you' instead of as 'I' — if at all; Mrs Eddy, who, like all Anglo-Saxon females, remains tied to theism, calls on the Dear Lord as witness — as a strong-minded American she is naturally aware of all His intentions and in accordance with His will she preaches that one can conquer illness by thought. In a way, then, she addresses our subconscious as God. Once again we see the doctrine of yoga watered down! And the consequence? The method works for some and doesn't work for others. Depending on whether they are profoundly or mildly schizophrenic.

In my case it both worked and failed. In 1900, to celebrate the new century, so to speak, I was struck down with the most awful illness of the spinal cord. Today I still believe it was the result of J...'s exercises, which were so contrary to my inner nature. The doctors, including Krafft-Ebing and Professor Arnold Pick, in brief, the most renowned specialists for such diseases, diagnosed spinal paralysis in the lumbar region. Three years later the symptoms had moderated slightly, but I could still only walk with the help of two sticks, and that with difficulty. For a long time I had tried to follow the rules and instructions of the Christian Scientists to rid myself of my illness. In vain. Then, one night, I was making my way home to the apartment I had at the time in Žižkov in Prague. It was at the end of a steep street, which was covered in ice so that I could only climb it with great difficulty, step by step, keeping my shoulder against the walls of the buildings. I stopped, despairing of ever getting home in the darkness. Then I suddenly recalled the Christian Scientists' teaching of 'thinking away' an illness. I then performed the recommended exercise, with not the least hope that it would work, when I suddenly felt my feet, which for three years had been like numb lumps hanging from my ankles, come alive. One minute later I was completely well again, or so it seemed. Putting the two sticks under my arm, I literally sprinted up to my apartment, sliding on the ice like a schoolboy when the road flattened out. I went to bed, overjoyed at having recovered my health. When I tried to get up the next morning, I was as lame and ill as I had been before. However hard I tried, I could not regain the state I had been in the previous night. The doctor I told about this smiled to himself. I could tell what he was thinking: 'The man's a writer of fantasy, the story's just a product of his overactive imagination.' He explained: 'You have suffered a physical change to the membrane of the spinal cord. That cannot be reversed by autosuggestion; and even assuming that is what happened during that night, it is impossible that it should return to its former state within a few hours.'

That incident made me think long and hard. For almost thirty years now I have looked on life as a kind of conditioning to which some invisible being (I used the image of the Masked Figure at the beginning of this article) is subjecting me. If anything happened to me which many other people would have regarded as meaningless or malicious, I immediately asked myself, 'What is wanted of me?' If I had toothache, I didn't go straight to the dentist but tried for a few days to get rid of it by various methods of autosuggestion, for its 'message' seemed to be: 'Learn to master your recalcitrant body.' That miserable affliction, caused by nerves as thin as threads, seemed to me to be the ideal testing ground for me to practise the exercise of will-power. At the time I was, like everyone else I assume, under the delusion that the two little words: 'I will' could pull the stars down from the sky. In reality, they cannot even pull up a blade of grass. Since the effort of will always had the strange effect of making the toothache worse, I tried faith. Faith which, it is said, can move mountains. It turned out to be completely impotent, the nerve in my tooth took absolutely no notice of it whatsoever and did as it pleased. Didn't even get worse. At least the effort of will seemed to have annoyed it; faith, on the other hand, did no more than elicit a smile. Then I tried all kinds of crazy cures, especially those Paracelsus — God rest his soul! — serves up in his treatises on the so-called 'Mumia'. For example I took a little stick of wood, poked about on the nerve with it, then threw it into the fire thinking, 'Ha, pain, you nasty little beast, now you're getting burnt up. What do you say to that, eh?' Sometimes the effect was astonishing. The pain seemed to have taken a fright and held its breath. Not for long, unfortunately, it very quickly saw through the ruse and got its own back with a renewed outburst of fury.

It was only slowly, very slowly in the course of my life that I came to understand the apparently mysterious law at work here. I will go into it at a later point. It is the overcoming of our congenital schizophrenia which is the universal remedy — through the transformation of the blood. Naturally this transformation proceeds at snail's pace, for it is no mean feat to turn an ape-man into a perfected being. Nevertheless later on, when I had gone deeper and deeper into yoga, I managed almost every time to get rid of toothache by means of certain 'exercises', or whatever you might call them, and the effect was immediate and permanent, so that the dentist's diagnosis was 'arrested caries'.

The Asian yoga books appear to be very ancient. The Orientals obviously derive their knowledge from these books, especially from the *Yoga-sutras* of Patanjali, a legendary initiate. If the physiologists of today were to include this book in their investigations into the practical side, I do not doubt they would make discoveries in their own field which would astonish the world. Unfortunately it is only philologists and similar outsiders who have examined the book to determine its age and origins or to see how often the subjunctive is used, which is hardly designed to whet anyone's appetite to go into it more deeply. A second book, on the surface a miscellaneous collection of utter nonsense, is the *Hatha Yoga Pradipika*. The Hatha Yoga system is abhorred by so-called authorities in India for it teaches how to master one's own body and the Indians consider that stupid and contemptible since the be-all and end-all for them is to fly from reality and, connected with that, to leave everything that is crudely sensual behind them. Did not the venerable Sankaracharya, the founder of the Advaita school of philosophy and creator of the most sublime monism, teach that, 'Man is like someone riding through the water on a crocodile, thinking is it a piece of wood. At any moment the beast could drag him down into the depths. Therefore man should get off the crocodile (the body and everything connected with it).' In contrast to Hatha Yoga, Patanjali gives instructions in his Raja Yoga on how to master oneself by thought control.

As far as is possible for someone living now whom destiny compels to live in the world, I have tried out both systems in practice and have come to the conclusion that the two methods complement each other, though only if one does not follow them literally but grasps the meaning hidden behind the words. What the Kabbalah (esoteric Jewish doctrine) says about the Bible is also valid here: 'Damned is he who takes the scriptures literally.'

The following incident clearly shows that the Indian fakirs — in most cases at least — follow the *Hatha Yoga Pradipika* literally and are led astray by it (or at best, or worst, to mediumism): Colonel Olcott, one of the founders of the Theosophical Society, went on a study trip to the famous ruined city of Karli, an ancient place where fakirs and hatha yogis gather. An aged ascetic came up to him, threw himself to the ground at his feet and begged Olcott to take him to an initiate, for he had sought in vain for one his whole life through. Just imagine: he had been a fakir from his youth and asked a European for advice in an area which is supposed to be the jewel in India's crown!

What do we conclude from this? There are books and oral traditions in Asia, but only very few people can read, that is, understand them. I have already mentioned that joining J...'s spiritual school not only affected me inwardly but also changed my outward destiny. Of course, I cannot prove my life would not have followed the same course if I had not performed J...'s exercises; such a thing is impossible to prove! I am not alone in the opinion that yoga, performed seriously and fervently, will start a person's outward destiny moving at a rapid pace. Indians say that anyone who practises the Gavatri (hymn to the 'sun') every morning and is not pure and does not know the rite of the Rigveda exactly, will be torn to pieces. Many examples from history are quoted. What happened to me was similar. As if a horde of demons had been let loose on me, my life turned into a succession of misfortunes until I sometimes felt close to ultimate despair. The illness of the spinal cord I mentioned was one of the softest blows of fate. Just as that has finally disappeared almost entirely, all the rest turned out to be bluff on the part of fate. Pointless then? Oh no! Everything would have been pointless had I not kept on asking myself, again and again, 'Why?' Naturally a so-called clever person would say, 'If you had lived a nice quiet life as a respectable citizen and not as a crazy yogi and — admit it — as a bit of a rake, you'd have kept your health, acquired an imposing paunch and a three-foot long gold watch-chain to go with it and...' — and could ask yourself on your deathbed, 'What, actually, was the point of my life?' That, at least, would be my conclusion to his little speech.

Fortunately things turned out differently for me. I overcame the spinal illness, but that result was of secondary importance, the *way* I got rid of it through yoga, *that* was the key thing for me. I will describe later what the method I discovered consisted of so that one or other of you will be able to profit from it. That is the only reason why I am writing this. Some will feel I am taking up arms against religion and piety. I wouldn't dream of it! Without religion most people would stumble into an abyss and collapse like cripples whose crutches had been knocked away from under them. My book has been written solely for those who want to walk upright. Moreover, yoga is, as the word itself says, religion = union; union not with a god, however, but with something that is very 'godlike' (if you insist) — with the Being everyone ought to be; with the Being one actually is without realising, blinded and mutilated by schizophrenia as we are.

In order to get a thorough understanding — and to see the weaknesses — of the *Hatha Yoga Pradipika* I have mentioned, it is necessary to be familiar to a certain extent with the different Indian systems which it appears to bring together in an integrated unity. Superficial readers will get the impression that it was written by domineering priests, who want to maintain the respect in which their caste is held both here and in the world beyond by promises of earthly prosperity. It contains formulas for becoming master over the 'three worlds' or as beautiful as Indra and so on; they consist of precepts telling you how long you must hold your breath (at least two hours a day) and many other things that seem equally impossible in order to achieve this. I do not doubt for one moment that one can acquire all this by these methods, but other people will not notice the change in a person who has been thus transformed into a Croesus or an Apollo! No more than one can see the beautiful dreams of an opium smoker. Another flight from reality, then, is what is being taught, and the most stupid one possible into the bargain. If you read reports about certain occult phenomena performed by yogis and sanyassis, for example the levitation of the yogi Govinda Swami, of which Jakolliot talks, you do wonder whether the promises of the *Hatha Yoga Padipika* shouldn't be taken literally after all. But we should not let ourselves be deceived when there are sometimes phenomena associated with hathayogis which go beyond the realm of subjective perception and become visible for onlookers as well. It simply means that the fakir in question is nothing other than a spiritualist medium, as Govinda himself admitted when he said, 'I myself can do nothing, it is the spirits of the departed who do everything.' And it is beyond doubt that one can become mediumistic by staring uninterruptedly at the end of one's nose, as the instructions prescribe; after all the Scotsman, James Braid, proved that fixing one's gaze like that induces self-hypnosis. When the fakir Hari Das, who, as Dr Honigberger reported, was buried alive for months, was asked what he had felt while his body was under the earth, said, 'My soul roamed in wonderful regions.' That means that Hari Das contrived a 'leaving' of his body such as was taught, in my opinion, in the mysteries of the Ancient Greeks. Something similar can be observed in the howling dervishes of the Near East during their ecstasies (literally ecstasy means 'displacement'), although it is not so complete, for they retain a little of their waking consciousness and do not become corpselike, rigid and cold like Hari Das; a certain progress in my opinion, but far from ideal, for that would consist of being in possession of both one's waking and one's metaphysical consciousness at the same time, without heightening one at the expense of the other. A friend who had lived among the dervishes for a long time told me that certain Arab dervish sheikhs do achieve that. I have no means of checking whether it is true or not, but I imagine that even they will not achieve anything worthwhile in the sense I have always had in mind — that is having an effect here and not 'on the other side'. They are all theists, what they experience is a god and not themselves. Escape from reality via a kind of schizophrenia.

In order to have a clear awareness of this side and the other side at the same time, one would have to start by being clear about the process of normal sleep — that is what I told myself when I had read enough about yoga and reports of fakirs, yogis and dervishes. Suddenly sleep, such an everyday occurrence in the lives of all creatures, seemed extremely suspicious and significant. I decided to carry out some experiments. Making an effort of will to keep sleep at bay for a few nights led nowhere, as I soon realised. Moreover there are enough cases reported in the medical literature which prove that a long absence of sleep, brought about by an injury to some part of the brain, does not cause any significant change in people. Two remarkable experiments which were successful took me a few steps farther towards understanding that sleep can make it possible for someone to 'leave' their body, or at least to produce an effect at a distance without physical contact. They convinced me that the old claim of clairvoyants, that that is the case, was highly probable.

Once I read in an old tome on the occult: 'When the earthly person closes their eyes, the heavenly one opens them, and vice versa.' Also: 'Thoughts we take with us into sleep become realities.' I immediately tried it out. I had a friend, Artur von Rimay, whom I saw a lot at the time and who, like me, was keen to pursue metaphysical problems, and I went to bed with the firm intention of going to sleep and sending him a telekinetic sign by hitting a table in his apartment with a stick. In order to do this and the better to visualise the autosuggestion, I took a walking stick to bed with me, holding it tight while I tried to get to sleep. It is exceptionally difficult to fall asleep on command if you haven't practised it for a long time; your thoughts keep wandering, pushing aside the intention you have set yourself. It is my belief that the Stymphalian birds in the legend of Hercules symbolise thoughts — they can only be killed with an iron arrow. Contrary to expectation, however, and helped by a chance occurrence supported by the obedience of my heartbeat, I managed to fall asleep all at once. It was a short, deep, completely dreamless sleep that was almost like a faint. I woke up a few minutes later feeling as if my heart were standing still; at the same time I felt convinced my experiment had succeeded.

I could hardly wait for morning. As usual my friend came to see me at about ten. I waited to see if he would tell me anything. In vain. He spoke about all sorts of things except any kind of nocturnal happenings. After a while I asked him shyly 'Did you have any dreams last night, or something —'

'Was that you?' he broke in. I listened to his tale without interrupting him at all. He said, 'Last night, shortly before one' — the time corresponded to that of my experiment to the minute! — 'I suddenly woke up, startled by a noise in the next room, as if someone were hitting the table with a flail at regular intervals. When it got louder and louder, I jumped out of bed and hurried to the other room. The blows could clearly be heard to come from the large table in the middle of the room. But there was nothing to be seen. A few minutes later my mother and the old housekeeper in their nightdresses came dashing in, terrified. After a while the noise grew quieter and quieter and eventually died away completely. We just shook our heads and went back to bed.'

That was the story told by my friend, Artur von Rimay. (He is living in Vienna at present and can confirm that what I have written here is the absolute truth.) 'Why didn't you tell me all this straight away?' I asked. 'It really is strange enough.'

'The only explanation I can give,' he answered hesitantly, 'is that the strong impression the experience made on me faded while I slept afterwards. It seems so far away from me now I could almost say I just dreamt it — if I hadn't discussed it with my mother only a few hours ago. Tell me, did you really make it happen by telekinesis?' To prove it I handed him a piece of paper on which I had made notes during the night of everything I had done.

However strange the incident was in itself, what seemed more significant to me was the fact that it remained in the memory in a way that was disconcertingly different from, for example, an interesting natural, even an everyday experience. It would be more normal for something so exceptional to etch itself much more deeply on the memory. Would a mechanical membrane have recorded the noise of the blows on the table? Most people would say no, but I believe it would have. As far as I am concerned, similar observations much later — years later — in Levico in the South Tyrol, where I witnessed so-called ghostly manifestations, confirm that such happenings are objective and not simply subjective and certainly not peculiar hallucinations. The things I experienced in Levico — I will perhaps describe them in another place — were vivid, even fantastic, but I have to keep on visualising them in my mind's eye if I do not want them to vanish without trace from my memory. I could put it this way: it is as if I had experienced them a century ago, and not in this life. 'Quite, because they never actually happened,' the superficial doubting Thomas will object. No, they did happen! Not only are there many witnesses still alive, the events were put down in writing the following day. What eliminates all doubt is the fact that physical changes took place in objects, for example a wall in a room collapsed accompanied by a kind of explosion. The wall had to be rebuilt! One of the eye witnesses has the receipt for the work. (Clearer proof can hardly be necessary, even for a professor of science!)

Despite all this there is unquestionably a faint resemblance to what we call a hallucination in both cases. The only explanation I can find is that everything we beings experience through the senses is a hallucination, as the philosophy of the Indian Upanishads maintains; everything: the external world and dreams, feverish fancies, visions and the like. The fact that objects remain even when the person perceiving them dies or goes to sleep does not prove the contrary. Anyone who can think logically will easily work it out. What people call objective and what they call subjective are so intermingled in such subtle gradations that it will always give the impression that one thing is 'real' and another not. If the differences are small, in our amazement we allow ourselves to be confused.

My second experience of telekinesis took place in the following way: during the first stages of the spinal illness I have mentioned I was on a train between Dresden and Pirna around midday. I suddenly remembered to my horror that in a letter to my fiancée, now my wife, which I had already posted, I had forgotten to say something that was extremely important for our future. What it was I cannot say here, since it concerned a private matter, but it was a matter of decisive importance for us. Sending a telegram was out of the question for various reasons. What could I do? I broke out in a cold sweat. It was impossible to find any way to save the situation. Then I recalled the experiment I had done with my friend Artur von

Rimay. What had been successful once might work a second time. No, it simply *had* to work, it was a matter of all or nothing for us. So I told myself: you must appear to 'her', you must raise your hand in warning, must tell her by thought transference what it is about and what she must do. I therefore expressed my instructions in clear words which I visualised as written down. Then: fall asleep quickly, go in spirit to Prague and appear to her in a mirror. (I had assumed, mistakenly as it turned out, that there was a mirror in the room where she was at that moment.) The task I had set myself was so complicated, I thought it was impossible for it to succeed. The faith that was supposed to be so important was anything but present! And then, how was I supposed to fall asleep on command among all these loudly chattering passengers? I could feel my fear and despair growing, I could feel it in the way my heart was hammering wildly. Then I remembered the saying that had come to me on the stone bench by the Moldau: 'Things come from the heart, are born of the heart and subject to the heart' and had to suppress a cry of triumph. What need did I have of 'faith' and other recipes that sound as if they came from a cookery book: 'Take a hundred eggs...' ('Take', oh yes, but where from?) Calm my heart down, that was something I could do, it wasn't some heavenly soap bubble. I sent this cheerful thought down into my chest and after just a few minutes my pulse had slowed down so much that I put it at 40 beats a minute at most. I was overcome with a wonderful sense of calm which wasn't even disturbed when one of the other passengers asked me a question. I pretended to be asleep and shortly afterwards I fell into a genuine, deep sleep. A few minutes later I woke. As in the previous case, I had no memory of whether the experiment had succeeded or not. What I did have, however, was such a feeling of triumph that any further doubt or worry was impossible. I called up all sorts of doubts because I was interested to see if they would come. In that situation nothing would have been more natural than for them to fall on me like wild beasts. Strangely enough, it was as if they had been exterminated. There is an inner certainty which *cannot* be anything other than the consequence of something that has become irrevocable fact in one's sleep. This inner certainty we can call 'living' faith and everything one believes in that way will inevitably happen. It is, however, a most profound error to imagine it will work the other way round and one can make something happen through faith. Anyone who thinks that is confusing cause and effect!

As soon as I was back in Prague, I hurried off to see my fiancée. The thought transfer had worked perfectly. She told me, 'In the afternoon at the time you said, about half an hour after lunch, I had lain down on the divan and gone to sleep. Suddenly I felt I was being shaken and woke up. My eye fell on a polished cupboard beside the sofa. In its shiny surface I saw you standing there, a figure about eighteen inches high. You had your hand raised in warning. Immediately after that you'd vanished again. I racked my brains to work out what it was you wanted, but I couldn't. One hour later it occurred to me that I was to go down to the entrance hall and wait for the postman. When he came, I took a letter from him. I was just in time, otherwise it would have fallen into the hands of someone for whom it was not intended.'

There are two main aspects that make this case particularly interesting: there was no mirror in the room, so I appeared in the shiny polish of a piece of furniture; that meant I had thought about what I was doing and used my reason. If I had left my body, as a spiritualist would assume, such purposeful action would not have been that remarkable. However, that explanation does not seem very likely to me. One point against it is that as a reflection I wasn't dressed the same as in the train, I was wearing a white coat instead, the way ordinary people or children imagine ghosts. Moreover the Shabhavas, an Indian sect of very ancient origin who follow a meticulously designed method in order to be able to leave their bodies, say that when one really leaves one's body physically it results in rigor mortis and one's limbs turn icy cold. The body of the person concerned cannot come back to life on its own, someone else must do that by massaging their skin and placing some hot dough on the top of their head. Something of the kind happened with the fakir Hari Das, whom Dr Honigberger wrote about some 50 years ago.

Now it is absolutely out of the question that I should have fallen into a state of catalepsy on the train; my fellow passengers would have been bound to have noticed.

The second striking aspect is that my instructions were not transferred to my fiancée's thoughts in exactly the way I had intended. If that had been the case, it would have all gone wrong. Instead, she acted correctly, let us say from instinct; in a way she corrected my plan. Another oddity is that when she woke up on the sofa, she wasn't immediately aware of what she should do. It looks as if the thoughts that had been transferred were first of all processed inside her, below the threshold of consciousness. Does that not suggest that many of the things that 'occur' to us and impel us to act are completely alien in origin, while we imagine we are the ones who decide whether to act or not? In the magnificent Indian epic, the *Bhagavadgita*, that must go into greater detail about yoga than any other book, it says, 'Every deed that happens here, happens through nature's law. "I am the doer of this deed," is vain and idle prattle.' A pity the book is not read in school, young people would derive far more profit from it than what is intended by making them read the *Iliad*.

In my opinion the incident I have described is a case of telesuggestion similar to what happens in the physical realm with radiotelegraphy. It employed the contents of the imagination of the receiver, that is the belief, either hereditary or impressed on her since childhood, that an 'apparition' must always be clothed in white.

The process of thought transfer such as that described above presupposes the existence of an organ in human beings which enables the telegraphy to take place. Which organ is it? Are there in fact two organs, one the antenna and the other the receiver? Given our present state of knowledge, it is impossible to answer that question. The Theosophists say (they clearly picked the idea up somewhere, probably in India) that the pineal gland in the brain is the organ that performs both functions. I cannot help feeling that it is the heart that is the transmitter. Whenever in an experiment I succeeded in capturing thoughts that had been sent to me, I had the definite feeling the process was taking place in my brain and it was as if I were producing the thought myself. From that I concluded that the receiving organ must be the cerebral cortex and not the pineal gland. It has always seemed odd to me that in anatomy the cerebral cortex has the strange Latin name *pia mater*. I have still not managed to find who invented this term but it was obviously — or probably — the same person as the one who christened the lower section of the spinal cord the *sacral plexus*.[10] It would be worth getting to the bottom of this, as it could possibly be a key to the system and origin of the method of the abovementioned Shabhavas, which is closely connected with Hatha Yoga. The Shabhavas base their method on written records called Agamas, which are said to be much older than the Vedas, though our scholars maintain that the Agamas are a much later product of the human mind and show evidence of degeneration due to the 'superstition' they contain. I cannot get over the suspicion that such scholars are only too happy to present something — unchecked — as showing signs of degeneration simply because it contains things which they do not understand or which do not fit in with their ideas. To me the Agamas seem to be the ruins of ancient secret knowledge, long since distorted and half forgotten. It is indisputable that traces of the Agamas are contained in Mahayama Buddhism and it is possible that they derive from the ancient Tibetan Bhon religion and with that from Central China. From what I have heard, the latest research in this area confirms what I have always instinctively assumed.

The Agamas teach that there are seven centres of perception and receptivity to magic in the human organism. A particularly boneheaded Indian ass with a materialist outlook, the 'Reformer' Dayananda, refused to take that on trust and, determined to find out whether it was true or not himself, cut up a corpse with a butcher's knife. And, lo and behold, he found nothing. — Who's that laughing? Are there blockheads like that over here too? — These centres, which are called chakras or lotuses, are said to be situated in the

---

10 Meyrink is mistaken here. The *pia mater* is not the same as the cerebral cortex, but a soft membrane surrounding it. The name is translated from Arabic and means 'gentle mother' in contrast to the *dura mater* — 'hard mother'.

spinal cord, the lowest in the sacral plexus (!), the highest above the crown of the head (!!). (Dayananda, God rest his soul, did not find that either; he probably forgot to cut open the air above the corpse.) The Reverend Leadbeater, a highly dubious gentleman and current head of the Theosophical Society, brought the Agamas, which would hardly have been known over here until then, to Europe. Since he did not name the source, his unsuspecting disciples took them as Leadbeater's home-grown wisdom, which renewed their faith as adepts in him. Dr Rudolf Steiner, the founder of the Anthroposophical movement, brought them to Germany. Whether *he* knew the source, I could not say. The Shabhavas use the doctrine solely to leave their bodies. They do this by first of all concentrating their thoughts on the lowest nerve plexus, then, after they have had certain visions which tell them that the first stage is complete, they move up to the next chakra and so on until they break through the skull and are out in the open. As an outward sign of the final success of the experiment, the body falls into rigor mortis. Reading this, one cannot help thinking that it must be nothing more than a complicated, if probably also very practical method of initiating and carrying through a process of autosuggestion. The hatha yogis, who base themselves on the *Pradipika* and not on the Asama books, are also familiar with this process; they call it 'drawing up the kundalini' (power of the snake). It is probably through a superficial understanding of this word that the snake charmers of Asia and Egypt hit upon the idea of training vipers for public entertainment. The Buddha says somewhere, 'I draw a finer body out of my body, just as a child draws the juicy stalk out of the coarser exterior.' He too obviously knew and practised the procedure!

The Shabhavas claim one has different visions according to which chakra one is concentrating on. One of the first visions, they say, is to think one is riding up into paradise on a white horse. Since, as is well known, Mohammad also had the same experience, one could well assume that the corresponding chakra in his body — perhaps through a lesion of the spinal cord caused by a fall, possibly by the epilepsy he suffered from was 'brought to life'. A Shabhava would hardly have set himself up as a prophet if that had happened to him, but, of course, Mohammad had not been initiated in the Agamas, he was just a theist.

It does not sound very likely that purely external injuries to the spine could cause people to see visions and, looked at superficially, it is grist to the mill of those who incline to a mechanistic view of the world. But it does seem occasionally to be the case. A friend of mine, a keen footballer and a materialist to the point of absurdity, received such a violent kick in the back during a game in Birmingham that he was in severe pain for months. He told me — and he is an extremely truthful person — that soon afterwards he started to have strange hallucinations. Especially at night when he was walking through deserted streets, he saw female figures shrouded in white who were so clear he often wondered if they were people dressed up in costume. They blocked his way and most of the time he spread his arms and pushed himself into the walls of the buildings. When I asked him what had gone through his mind when he saw these apparitions, he gave the, for me, significant, answer: 'Nothing.' I suspect that it was not the physical injury that produced the visions, but a mental process. Anyone who has pain in one particular place in their body will automatically think of that place; that is, they will in a way be carrying out the same concentration of thought as a Shabhava does in a conscious and purposeful manner.

Therese Neumann from Konnersreuth, who has recently become widely known as a stigmatic, sustained curvature of the spine from carrying heavy loads and suffered from it for a long time, perhaps even still does, I couldn't say. One day the mysterious process of crucifixion began, repeating itself every Friday with blood coming from her eyes and the wounds on her hands. Moreover she has not taken any food for a long time, allegedly for a whole year. That kind of thing is said of Catholic saints. It is, of course, possible that one day Frau Neumann will be 'exposed' whether with good reason or not is neither here nor there, 'they' very often expose things that don't fit in with their ideas, but that doesn't mean the hundreds of authenticated cases of this type never happened. Devout people will see the 'Therese Neumann case' as a miracle, or even as proof that Jesus of Nazareth really was crucified. Someone who practises yoga will say it is a symptom of one or the other chakra being brought to life. He would even say — at least, I would say it, even though I am not a Shabhava: The deeper significance of the Biblical story of the crucifixion, no matter whether it actually took place or not, is similar to that of Mohammad riding to paradise on Berrak, the white horse. (Don't hesitate to accuse me of impiety, if you like. However, it is not impiety if I express my opinion so frankly.)

In the course of my extensive study of all kinds of books, which I pursued with particular assiduity in my younger years, I came across a volume entitled *Der Schlüssel zur Geisterwelt* (*The Key to the Spirit World*[11]) written in the middle of the last century by a man called Kerning. The writings of this man, whose real name was Krebs and who was a tenor and a Freemason, are completely unknown to scholars investigating the history of mysticism, even though he was a man of whom posterity will definitely take note. Kerning's books are deliberately written in such a way that the layman cannot but think the author was a child or weak in the head. Kerning's teaching or, to be more precise, hints, are so clearly reminiscent of the doctrine of the chakras, that one could believe he had studied the Agamas. In his day, however, that was completely impossible, since no one in the Western countries had even heard of the Agamas. Moreover Kerning himself gives his source: the Freemasons' ritual! Just as certain letters play an important, mysterious role in the doctrine of the chakras and their awakening, they do so in the ritual of the Freemasons as well. As far as I know, no one has ever given an interpretation of them, at least not an acceptable one. Kerning claims to have discovered how to use them in order to bring about what I call the 'transformation of the blood': one has to murmur them to oneself, like a litany! That is, he prescribes a similar way to my late guide, J...! Remarkable! J... could neither read nor write, knew nothing of Kerning when he

---

11 English translation: J Kerning: *Esoteric Education or the Unfoldment and Life of a Hero*, Kessinger Publishing, 2006 (originally: Esoteric Publishing Co, Boston, 1888); it appears to be the only work by Kerning to appear in English.

started out, and despite that hit upon the same system 'by himself'. This clearly contradicts the generally accepted explanation for such happenings, namely that knowledge can only be transmitted by word of mouth or by reading the records. Knowledge whose preservation is important for mankind and for its progress can perhaps lie hidden for a thousand years, but it cannot be erased. Some'where' and somehow the seed will be preserved and will sprout and flower when the time is come. Let militaristic fools and fanatics such as Calif Omar, who set fire to the library of Alexandria and destroyed it because: 'If the books say the same as the Koran, they are superfluous; if they say something different, they are pernicious', continue with their furious assaults on shadows on the wall. All they will do is leave a shameful memorial to themselves; the light cannot be extinguished, it lives on in our blood.

Among his many books, Kerning wrote one called *Testament*.[12] I edited it many years ago under the pseudonym of Kama, Arch Censor of the Royal Oriental Order of the Sat B'hai (a very interesting, but equally sterile occult secret order I belonged to at the time). Kerning had bequeathed the manuscript to the father of my late friend, Count Leiningen-Billighausen, who gave it to me. The content of this book is exceedingly significant and instructive for anyone with practical involvement in yoga, but also very dangerous. When I made it publicly available, I was not aware of this danger, otherwise I would never have had it printed. Fortunately it has more or less sunk without trace; I can't even remember who published it. Like the *Hatha Yoga Pradipika*, it teaches breathing exercises, only in a much more profound — and perhaps even completely wrong — way!

Since Kerning had no other source available than the Freemasons' ritual, it seems obvious that that must contain an ancient esoteric doctrine, which is a closed book to present-day Freemasons. Following that up might might yield some interesting results for a competent researcher. Even the most intensive searches for the origins of Freemasonry have not gone back more than a few hundred

---

12 Leipzig 1907; republished in *Rarissima 1. Seltenste Dokumente der Esoterik aus vier Jahrhunderten*, ed F.W. Schmitt, Sinzheim, 2003.

years. Up to the present the legend that it is immeasurably old has remained just that: a legend.

Kerning was a theist, but of a more subtle nature than other mystics. He was spared ecstasies and transports throughout his life. On the other hand he was a metaphysician through and through and regarded such things as clairvoyance as perfectly natural processes in which he was convinced one could train oneself. His system, which is almost always only hinted at and, probably intentionally, never clearly described, can be summarised in a few words roughly as follows: a person's innermost being (probably the 'other' Coué talks about) only speaks to the outer person through vague presentiments, a sense of approaching danger, instinct and so on. Never, or rarely and then only in people who have the gift from birth, through direct speech. The consequence is that we are often — mostly even — led astray, for we frequently experience a feeling of anxiety, brought on by physical discomfort, and then wrongly interpret it as a warning. Such 'deception' by feeling is, I am sure, the reason why over the centuries mankind has turned away from instinct, as if it were a will-o'-the'wisp leading us astray. Very much to our disadvantage! We have kept away from dangerous marshes but exchanged them for the arid, stony ground of an all-too-sober, unsatisfying rational life.

Kerning wanted to put an end to the uncertainty of vague feelings; he said this could only be done if one could create an infallible means of communication between the outer and the inner person (today we call this inner person the subconscious). This would develop spontaneously, he went on, if one murmured certain letters — eleven if I remember rightly — or, especially, the word 'I', to oneself for long enough. (In Vedic writings it says that anyone who has murmured the sacred syllable Om so many billion times will be rewarded with 'release'.) By this, Kerning says, our inner being will learn step by step to speak in words, removing the need for transfer by feeling and replacing it with a more reliable method. He called it 'the inner word' just like my former 'guide'.

His breathing exercises were aimed at achieving union with the cosmos; it would speak, he maintained, to anyone who had mastered the exercise.

The *Hatha Yoga Pradipika* discusses breathing, something our medical science has ignored to this day. In the *Pradipika* it says that as long as a person breathes alternately through the right and left nostril, he will remain an ordinary mortal subject to an inevitable karma; in that respect then, his will is not free! If, on the other hand, he succeeds in forcing his breath into the *susumna* — the spinal cord! — then he will become free, omniscient and a magician of high degree who can accomplish everything he wishes. (Since Raja Yoga expressly demands that every selfish wish must have been burnt long before, one might think such omnipotence must be pathetic. However, Raja Yoga clearly takes it for granted that there is a central 'I' that absorbs all the monads at the end of their way to Him, transforming every individual wish into a single one.) The present yogis of India and Tibet take this forcing of the breath into the spinal cord literally; they force themselves to hold their purely physical breath until they fall unconscious or, to put it more precisely, into a trance. Anyone can discover what a horrendous effort it takes to achieve this simply by trying it themself. First of all, I was told, sweat appears, then foam forms on one's skin and, finally, levitation occurs. I got as far as the formation of foam and no farther.

For many years I believed that *pranayama* (the technical Indian expression for breath control) was simply a recipe that had to be followed physically, word for word. Even today I do not doubt that used in that way it will produce astonishing results — in the mediumist, spiritualist area, I imagine, for observation of the mediums with whom I came into contact showed every time that their breathing was disturbed as soon as they fell into a trance. The way to true salvation is certainly not through simply holding one's breath. Trance is the separation or tearing apart of consciousness and not the 'union' indicated in the very word 'yoga'; it is a step in the wrong direction! In the Raja Yoga compendium, *Patanjali*, which I mentioned earlier, the path goes in the opposite direction, not starting out from breathing as the cause, but from mental concentration. Once that is profound enough *samadhi*, a state of rapt absorption, is attained and as a consequence breathing stops of its own accord.

In 1914 I was visited by a young Brahmin who knew a lot about yoga but had also received a European education having studied in Oxford. When I asked him what his opinion of *pranayama* was, I was surprised to hear him say that air from the atmosphere could, indeed, get into the spinal cord if it could find no way out of the tightly closed lungs. When I objected that that was an anatomical impossibility, he merely shrugged his shoulders. Even if he is right, I believe it can never be ordinary air; possibly the absorption of oxygen in the lungs leads to the release of one of the recently discovered noble gases, for example helium or argon or one still unknown, which then penetrates the spinal cord? That is just a guess, of course, though there is some possible support for my arbitrary assumption in the fact that the Indian word *prana* means not only breath but also 'life force'.

What Lall — that was the name of my Indian friend — said made such an impression on me, especially since he assured me it came from the lips of a genuine yogi, whom he had found after a long search, that I decided to take up the Hatha breathing exercises I had broken off in my youth. I found that I still could not manage to hold my breath for more than two and a half minutes. I was about to give up the exercises when one day I had a strange experience: I was already sweating from the incredible exertion of trying to keep holding my breath for three minutes when the horrific 'death shudder' started. Unable to hold my breath any longer, I tried to breathe out. For a moment I had a remarkable lightness of feeling and to my great astonishment I *could not* breathe out, but had to breathe in! The air in my chest had disappeared completely. As if it had been sucked in or absorbed by other organs. But my thorax had not sunk at all, as one would have expected, but was blown up or, rather, was pressing out as at the beginning. I was so astonished by the phenomenon that for a moment I almost lost control of my senses. Presumably as a result of this inner turmoil, nothing further happened, except that I breathed in, as if gripped by a convulsion, and thus somehow, in a way I was not aware of, released the bizarre tension in my thorax.

Once I had more or less got over my astonishment, I told myself that I had probably exhaled without realising. Later I repeated the experiment, determined to observe myself closely this time. For a long time I was unsuccessful, for to hold one's breath for two and a half, not to mention three minutes, it is essential — for me at least — not only to act on the lungs with one's physical muscles but also to 'stop one's thoughts' in a particular way. Now is it hardly possible to fix one's thoughts and observe oneself at the same time. Still, I believe I convinced myself, when the disappearance of the air from my lungs occurred once more, that I had indeed *not* breathed out. My friend Lall had expressly warned me against breathing exercises; they always ended in incurable disease, he said, or death before one's body was ready for it. Not knowing how to prepare my body, I decided, despite his warning, to try to find out through my own efforts whether I was ready. So I started off with the aforementioned exercises, just in case. However, I abruptly broke them off, for insistent warnings began to float in my consciousness in the form of unequivocal visionary images. They came a little too late. I immediately suffered from such a striking lack of imagination and of the ability to work as a writer, that I felt I had been mentally robbed. For a long time I couldn't write anything at all. I was so lethargic that for months I couldn't bring myself to leave the house; I sat in an armchair from morning to evening, brooding. I felt tired of life and it gnawed at me until I was almost in despair. In addition I felt unbearably thirsty. Diabetes? I asked myself. I didn't have the courage to have a medical examination. What despicable cowardliness we humans are capable of!

Then my wife urged me to go to the doctor. I didn't want to, so I went to the chemist. Blood sugar level 8%! A nice mess I'd got myself into! Especially for a hatha yogi who was supposed to become free of all illnesses. And 8%! The Reichsbank can afford such outrageous interest, but not a writer. There was nothing for it — surely destiny was making fun of me — but to eat humble pie and go to the doctor. For two years I followed his advice and lived on nothing but blotting paper, so to speak. True, the sugar stopped, but my weight dwindled too. You'll be able to levitate after all, I mocked myself. Just a few dozen kilograms less and it'll be easy. Should I start the breathing exercises again? I asked myself. Perhaps I gave up too soon? Once more a warning from my innermost being. I decided therefore at least to give some thought as to whether there might be a more profound meaning behind Hatha Yoga than the mechanical-seeming surface sense. Gradually it began to dawn on me: the breathing exercises must be seen in a completely different way. After a few months of trials I got to the real meaning.

Since then I believe I know how the strange positions the fakirs adopt are to be understood and how their effect is to be produced. It became clear to me that they proceed according to formulas that some blind imitator cobbled together in the dim and distant past from the genuine yogis he'd come across. All he'd copied was the outward show. Why does this or that fakir spend his whole life standing on one leg? Why does another hang, head downwards, from the branch of a tree and stay like that for days? Why does a third press his thumb into the palm of his hand until the fingernail grows through the flesh? I imagine I have found the key: standing motionless on one leg — the stylites did something similar (without knowing why, either!) — is a balance exercise. And why exercise balance? I didn't work out that final puzzle straight away. I solved it by performing the exercise. Naturally I wobbled this way and that, but then — initially it was scarcely noticeable — the sensation of a 'union' arose; it is difficult to describe, but I have no other word for it: of a union with myself! Soon I could produce this remarkable sensation without having to stand up. The memory alone reawakened it. And by awakening that strange feeling of union I finally managed to get my diabetes to start to disappear, so that today I can live almost the same life, with no special diet, as a healthy person.

To be quite honest, I have to mention that shortly before I was cured I happened to take a medicine which was not aimed at the diabetes itself — and it has so far never been prescribed for that purpose — but for a tedious side effect of my diabetes. (If any diabetic would like to try it, it is called Nujol.) It could be that this medicine contributed to my cure, but I do not really believe that myself. The immensely beneficial effect of the balance exercise in all respects — in every last respect, and that is putting it mildly — is so extraordinary that I cannot bring myself to describe it here for fear of weakening the effect of my general remarks in advance. Getting rid of an illness is the least I believe the exercise is capable of.

How a simple balancing exercise can produce such great effect is the question that will spring to mind. An experienced rock climber with a good head for heights also has a true sense of balance and yet he will get ill at times. Of course, if it were only a matter of balance, the objection would be justified. But it isn't that simple. Something additional must come 'from above', as my late 'guide' used to say. Not 'grace', no, certainly not that. Destiny doesn't go in for favouritism. I would like to put it figuratively: our inner person — the Masked Figure hidden, separated from us, alien, totally alien to us in our everyday consciousness — stands upright inside us; it is the spinal cord, the *susumna*, which is what yoga is all about. Our outer person is separated from it because it is standing askew, 'askew' in some sense or other to our inner person. That is why they do not coincide. To put it another way: the broken sword, that is the person with their consciousness limited to earthly things, is not broken crosswise, but lengthwise. (Is there a version of the legend in which Siegfried's sword is broken *lengthwise*?) I realised that the purpose of *my* life was to achieve union, both consciously and instinctively, with the Masked Figure: 'the Pilot wearing the cloak of invisibility' I once called it in a story. Whether that is the purpose of everyone's life, I would not venture to say; it looks as if most people are, *for the moment*, quite content to head mindlessly for the sea to spawn, like the eels. I can only guess at how my union with the Masked Figure will develop. Such processes move at a very slow pace, stage by stage, and they last for years and years. No one should deceive themself into thinking they have been successful until they have spent a long time testing out the things I have given as examples. Nor would I insist that my experiment is the only hint as to how to go about it. On the contrary, I believe everyone should find out for themselves what the right method is for them. Everyone is 'ill' and split in their consciousness in a different way.

Dreams can often give a hint as to how each individual should proceed in this. Before I got the exercise of finding my balance so that it suited me, I had a significant dream, which was repeated for several nights and for that reason attracted my attention. Dreams are nothing other than visions the sleeping person has; visions that I had and still have are waking dreams and nothing else. In both the sightlines of the eyes shift! Humans and animals have their eyeballs turned upwards when they sleep. Dreams and visions are pointless if we do not learn to train ourselves so that they become our guides. Life itself is pointless if it does not teach us in which direction we should steer the ship of our existence. It is easier than many people think to train yourself to have dreams that are full of meaning. It just takes perseverance, a refusal to give up, a firm, once-and-for-all decision not to stop, 'even if it should take a million years'. You have to go to bed with the obstinate question in your mind: what meaning will the dream I am expecting have? Children go to bed wanting to dream something nice and their mothers might well encourage this sentimental approach. If you do as I advise, the usual confused tangle of dreams will probably continue for a while, but then order will be established: the Masked Figure is beginning to speak. Mostly in symbols, sometimes however, if a person has a special talent for it, in clear, unmistakable images or even words. If the words are spoken by a figure you see in your dream then you must be extremely wary! It could be a case of a mediumist phenomenon, as deceptive as everything of that kind. Words and acoustic communications in dreams must, if they are to be trusted, sound as if you were saying them to yourself. Anyone who is on the right path to 'union' will never see the Masked Figure; how could one see something that is, basically, oneself? It is true that people have sometimes seen their own double — Goethe for example — but a double like that is not the Masked Figure, it is something quite different, which I have no reason to go into in more detail here.

I dreamt, then, that I was standing on the top of a mountain, the summit of which was just a few square metres of wet, slippery grass.

I had an unpleasant feeling of dizziness and had gone down on all fours, like an animal, for fear of losing my footing. I didn't dare stand up. This dream was repeated several times. Its message was clear, but for a long time I could not see the practical application. I took it in a much too superficial manner, thought it was a trivial warning about how to behave in everyday life. It was that as well, for at that time I was in a situation where I didn't quite know how to behave. However, the deeper meaning of the dream was: practise in your waking life what you see shown here figuratively. It will take you one step closer to union with your innermost being, which stands eternally upright. Such instructions alone are of genuine value. Anyone who interprets them in too shallow a manner should consider the fairy tale of the soldier who first of all found copper coins in the cave, then silver and finally gold. The more often the dream was repeated, the greater the efforts I made to stand up on the slippery peak, but I just could not manage it.

Then the dream changed: I was in a room with only one exit, which was directly opposite me. I wanted to go to the door but to do so I would have had to go past a tall pedestal with a huge, venomous snake on it, curled up and ready to strike the moment I came near. This dream was also repeated several times and, as with the first, I could not conquer my fear. There are myths, especially of Oriental origin and in their content occult in the best sense of the word, which say that people are gripped by an unconquerable feeling of fear when a particular stage of their inner development is approaching — like the fear I felt in the dream of the snake. It eventually started to affect my waking consciousness as well and so badly that I decided to try the exercise of getting my heart to stand still, since all the rational methods I employed to calm myself down failed completely. ('Aha!' the doctor would say, 'the side effects of diabetes,' but he would only be half right.) In this case making my heart stand still produced no effect either. Only when I did the balancing exercise did the feeling of anxiety disappear. Whenever the exercise was successful I monitored my heartbeat — every time it slowed down of its own accord! I felt I had taken a significant step forward, had moved one level higher on the path to the control and transformation of the blood. Strangely enough, this was accompanied by positive changes in my external life: agreeable (instead of the previous disagreeable) developments occurred, as if by chance. By chance! It was a chain of events fitting in with each other in such a remarkable way that the word 'chance' seems a cowardly disparagement to please the sceptic. It confirmed the suspicion I had always had that one could change one's destiny if one only had the right key. I had long since learnt to doubt whether the key was work — work in the sense the layman understands it. Throughout my life I have achieved as good as nothing through work; even though I would not say I was lazy, indolent or incompetent, any advance I made was always through good fortune alone. The only true key to happiness, well-being, health and the like is union with the Masked Figure. *That* is the one we call providence. *That* is the one who helps us when our need is greatest. Not some god on his throne above the clouds. Why does the help always come at the last moment? (Everyone has probably had the strange experience that it is always 'at the last moment' that 'something happens' because we have the wrong (!) kind of self-assurance and not the right kind that comes naturally from becoming one with the Masked Figure. The *wrong* self-assurance must first of all be pushed aside if the right kind is to appear. This pushing aside is done by our desperate need, unfortunately seldom with lasting effect, for our old self-assurance soon returns. To interpret a story from the Bible symbolically: Christ is asleep in the boat and his disciples wake him when they see the waves are getting alarmingly high.

There is a German saying that adversity teaches you how to pray; a person who has grasped yoga can add: even greater adversity teaches you to forget prayer. Anyone who is pleading for something will have the same experience as I did in my dream of the summit and the snake. I will recount an incident, that happened to me, which proves that dreams can at times speak clearly and not only in symbols. In 1922 I bought an old car. As often happens, the seller assured me the vehicle was in perfect order; not even his conscience was in perfect order. The car looked horrible and I decided to have the bodywork redone; until then it stayed in a garage to be checked over. When that was done I was going to drive it to a repair shop. Then my wife dreamt that we were driving there and the car suddenly overturned in the ditch on the right; our daughter was dead, she and our son hurt and I seriously injured. Exactly the same the dream was repeated six or seven times. I got my wife to go over the situation in the dream in detail. She described the landscape: 'And we're on a steep slope, with trees on either side, you're driving, our son beside you, my daughter and me in the back when suddenly the car tips, falls down to the right, overturns and we're all underneath.'

I found the matter more and more disturbing and didn't know what to do. The day was approaching when I was to drive the car to the repair shop. I thought it over and had a harebrained idea: I would trick fate. I decided to change things from the way my wife had seen them in her dream. I rang an acquaintance and asked if he would be good enough to drive my car to Garmisch the next day, there were various reasons why I was unwilling to do it myself. My thinking was that if I wasn't at the wheel myself I was in a way circumventing the prophecy in the dream. (Pretty stupid, the reader will say.) For the same reason I also decided not to take my daughter with us. My acquaintance was happy to do me the favour and it was all agreed.

At six next morning my acquaintance rang to say that unfortunately he had to call off: during the night a boil had appeared on his neck which was so painful he couldn't come. I scratched my head: so fate was determined to be right, was it, playing a game of chess with me and thwarting my cunning scheme? In that case we definitely are going to drive there! We'll see who comes out on top, my friend! I telephoned the repair shop in Garmisch and asked the owner to send his driver. After a lot of shilly-shallying — the man couldn't come, that kind of thing — I got what I wanted and was promised the driver would arrive in Starnberg by the next train. I went straight to the garage where the car was kept and asked the mechanic to check everything over again.

'Everything's okay,' he replied.

'Please have a look at the nearside wheels,' I asked him, telling him my wife had dreamt the car had toppled over to the right; perhaps there was a fault in the wheels on that side.

Very reluctantly the mechanic obeyed and removed the rear nearside wheel. 'What's this!' he suddenly exclaimed. 'The axle stub's broken. How on earth could I have overlooked that? I could bet it wasn't like that before.'

'Could that make the car crash?' I asked. 'Could the wheel fall off?'

'No, it would never fall off,' he replied, 'but it could suddenly lock; if you happened to be driving fast, you could lose control of the steering and naturally you would skid and crash.'

Just at that moment the driver from Garmisch arrived; I showed him the fault and asked whether he was still prepared to drive us. After a long discussion with the mechanic, he said yes, he was. I sat next to him, on the left, my son and wife in the back, thus going against the dream image. We set off at snail's pace. One hour later we were approaching Weilheim when my wife suddenly tapped me on the shoulder and whispered, 'We're coming to the area I dreamt of.'

There it was: a downward slope, trees on both sides. 'Go even more slowly', I told the driver.

'Why? We're going slowly enough as it is, 25 kilometres an hours at most.'

I insisted: 'No. Ten at the most, please.'

The car was just crawling along. Suddenly the driver whispered to me, 'Can you hear something? What's that grinding noise at the back?'

The next moment the car slumped down with a jolt. The driver slammed on the brakes and the car stopped, tilted to the right. A miracle that it hadn't overturned! Close by on the right-hand side was a deep ditch.

We got out. The wheel had not come off the axle, but the rim had detached itself — a fault no one would have expected — and, with the tyre and tube still on, was disappearing down the road like a goblin, until it rolled into the ditch.

Could one not truly say: We outwitted fate?

If one does not simply take a superficial view of this incident but looks at what is behind it, it becomes so interesting one could erect a whole system of philosophy on it. Even the way destiny insisted on trying to get its own way by — to put it crudely — 'making' my acquaintance ill during the night before the journey, so that I would have to drive myself, etc. I am sure destiny has been similarly thwarted at other times over the centuries, causing a stir. No wonder, then, that the belief arose that malign but stupid beings interfere in our lives. Perhaps, who knows, those who support such 'superstition' are not entirely wrong. Incidentally, the car had a strange fate. It was burnt in a fire that broke out in the repair shop in Garmisch so that only part of it was still usable.

In 1896 I had an experience, the inner workings and causes of which are so difficult to see that one would have to construct a far-reaching system to explain it completely. It is not connected with the dreams I have been discussing, but more with commands that one takes with one into one's deep sleep — rather like the case where I appeared to my wife by telepathy. I will describe it here simply because it was so odd.

At the time I was in regular correspondence with an Indian swami who lived in Mayavati in the Himalaya area and edited a little newspaper — *Prabudha Bharata* — devoted to the Ramakrishna movement. In the course of our correspondence the swami described a Tibetan method, involving magic, of compelling a thief by telepathy to return a stolen object. The method consisted of drawing a certain geometrical figure on paper before going to bed, imagining a vision of the desired object in the middle of it until one could see it clearly in one's mind's eye, then burning the piece of paper, imagining that would send the geometrical figure into the astral realm, where it would capture, so to speak, the stolen or lost object.

When the swami's letter reached me, I had just lost a meerschaum cigar holder; I suspected it had been stolen by my office messenger. In the way that we often become obsessed with recovering things of no value, I spent six weeks desperately looking for the cigar holder. Out of interest I followed the instructions the Indian had sent me. I did not in the least believe it would work, it was basically curiosity that led me to follow the instructions carefully. A few days passed — I had long since forgotten the matter — and, as usual, I set off home at lunchtime. It was my habit to do this at one o'clock, but that day I didn't leave until two, without there being any reason for the delay. Also on that day I did not take my usual short cut, a public passage through a building, but chose to go by a very busy, wide street, even though it was farther. I had no thought of the meerschaum holder. I could not go particularly quickly because of the crowd, so I walked along behind two men who were in lively conversation. I wasn't listening and, anyway, they were speaking Czech, so I wouldn't have understood. Suddenly one of them stopped, forcing me to stop for a moment. He took an object out of his pocket and held it out to the other. It was a black leather case that seemed strangely familiar. He opened it and the other looked inside. To my immense astonishment, I saw that it was my cigar holder. I wondered what to do. By this time the two had separated. I followed one of them, wrongly assuming he had taken the case. When we reached a deserted street corner, I stopped him and told him I had lost the cigar holder and since I was fond of it, I would like to buy it back from him. I assured the man, who was fairly shabbily dressed, that I wouldn't dream of demanding it back for nothing. As I handed him a tip, the man insisted I was mistaken, the other had put the case back in his pocket. Still, he told me he would get the holder for me quickly since the other man had offered to sell it to him. They were going to meet that afternoon at four, the man having offered to sell him other things, in the courtyard of an inn and he suggested I should be there too. Naturally I was there punctually. The two of them arrived a few minutes later. With an apparently innocent conversation the shabbily clad one got the other to show him the cigar holder again. When the man took it out of his pocket, I pounced like a hawk. There was a short exchange, but when the 'finder' realised I had no intention of taking him to the police, as he might have feared, he became extremely friendly, pocketed the money I offered with a satisfied grin and told me he had found it six weeks ago in a box of the concert hall of the Grand

Hotel, where he worked as a waiter. Since no one had reported it as lost, he thought he was justified in keeping it.

Since I would have liked to find out what circumstances had made the man go along Obststrasse at two that afternoon, I asked him all sorts of questions relating to that. Naturally the waiter found that strange, perhaps even dubious; whatever the case, he became very suspicious and eventually somewhat tart, at which I took my leave of him. But at least I had recovered my cigar holder in this bizarre way. Should I take it as the effect of the Tibetan magic diagram? I wondered. It could have been a coincidence. I decided to do a second experiment. For a long time I had not been able to find a walking stick I had which was shaped like a golf club and assumed I'd left it somewhere. Once more I drew the geometrical figure and imagined the golf-club walking stick in the middle of it. The next morning the stick was lying across a chair in my apartment. The maid swore she had not put it there and no one else could tell me anything either. But of course the stick could not have been lying for weeks on the chair I used every day.

This time it could hardly have been a coincidence. I decided to try it out a third time and waited for an opportunity where a successful outcome would be almost definitely out of the question. One soon presented itself. At that time I lived close by the Moldau, in a house built onto a mill. The eastern wall was washed by a raging arm of the river which shot out from the millrace there. When pruning a pot plant one day the scissors — a very old family heirloom of curious design which came from my grandfather — fell out of the open window into the river.

This time, I thought, the Tibetan magic is surely going to fail, but I still went through with the experiment, just to see. What then happened was incredible, a sheer impossibility! I was literally shattered. One morning the scissors were back on my desk! For a moment I thought I must be going out of my mind. Then I told myself: it's probably your memory that's at fault and you dropped a quite different pair of scissors out of the window. I immediately went to the kitchen and asked the maid, 'Did you put this pair of scissors on my desk'

'Yes, sir.'

'When?'

'Yesterday evening, when you were out, sir.'

'Where did you find them?

'Johann, the miller's apprentice, brought them. He said we'd probably dropped them in the river.'

'But how could the fellow have got them out of the deep millrace. Was he fishing there and if so, why?'

'No, the millrace was drained yesterday and is dry; the miller closed the sluice gate because there's something broken on the wheel,' the girl explained. 'That's probably when Jan found the scissors. I could ask him.'

I looked out of the window: there was no water in the millrace; it was full of tins and broken glass.

All that was mere chance? Impossible! Out of the question. I was so excited that on that same day I told all my friends what had happened. They as good as laughed in my face. They were naturally convinced I'd made it up. My assurances made no difference, people prefer to believe someone's lying than to accept baffling events — the conclusions they would be compelled to draw are too uncomfortable for them.

Even today I have no real explanation of what things might have played a part in these experiences. There are possible explanations in the case of the cigar holder: telepathic vibrations could have brought the waiter and myself together at the same moment in the crowded street; remarkable enough, but still possible. In the case of the scissors that seems to be out of the question. One can hardly assume that I broke a millwheel by unconsciously using magic! And if the wheel hadn't been broken, the miller wouldn't have drained the millrace.

When, years later, I told my friend Lall about these experiences, he said that it had all been done by certain elemental beings. Tibetan diagrams such as the one I had been given forced them to obey. 'Superstition, of course,' the enlightened European will say. Call it superstition if you like, but how can it produce such astonishing effects? Naturally I tried out the method lots more times — and it always failed! Lall explained that this was because I had told other people about it, especially hostile sceptics, which I should never have done. That restored freedom to the elemental beings and the diagram lost its magic. Incidentally, the scissors suffered the same sad fate as the car: they were burnt. That is, one day they fell into the kitchen stove fire and were no longer usable. Presumably the 'elementals' are strict about venting their anger on objects they have been involved with.

To return to the second fakir I mentioned, the one hanging head down from a tree that I had seen in an illustration in Campbell Oman's book. There was a picture of the fakir standing on one leg in Schmidt's book on fakirism and, as I have said, it helped me to develop the balance exercise. It was not so easy to copy the man hanging head down and I do not think the exercise would have produced any significant effect, it was just a piece of manifest nonsense for public consumption. I can only guess at what it is meant to say but, using hints from Indian books, I would put it this way: in the course of their development through yoga a person gradually acquires a different polarity from ordinary people. Perhaps the word 'polarity' is inaccurate but how can I describe a process of which I know as good as nothing?

Today we have no idea whether the ancient Indians had any precise knowledge of the law of gravity, or whether Newton really was the first person to discover it. However, it is safe to assume that the old Orientals — the Chinese above all — will have wondered why all things are bound to the earth and only birds and insects can fly. Away from the ground and free! That will surely have been what they desired, at least the ascetics and yogis. And if there was then a case like that of the Catholic monk of San Vito who, it is reported, fell into a trance before thousands of people while praying and floated up to the dome of the church (there are reports of hundreds of similar cases!), then there is no doubt that primitive investigators would have pondered how something like that could be explained apart from through the intervention of a demon or a god. That will especially have been the case among the ancient Egyptians, since there the caste of priests were also the custodians of science.

It seems very likely that one or another of them would have had the idea of seeing whether hanging head down would produce results as far as levitation was concerned. Perhaps these experiments led to the popular belief that they were the real key to controlling the desired phenomena. I believe that if hanging upside down for a long time is to be successful, that will not happen through the purely mechanical execution but only if it is accompanied by spiritual notions, such as I observed in standing upright and keeping my balance. It is also possible that some fakirs practise hanging upside down to produce physiological changes caused by the rush of blood to the head. Certain other fakir exercises are aimed at increasing the flow of blood to the head, for example slowly inhaling followed by exhaling as violently as possible. It can presumably be taken as proven that these and similar violent methods serve the sole purpose of inducing trance. That is, they are steps in the opposite direction to the one someone should take if they want to go forward on the path of development.

To sum up briefly: development and advancement lie in the ever greater heightening of consciousness, not in interrupting, shifting or reducing it. Although yoga and everything that comes into that area may look like hothouse nurture, in my opinion such accelerated growth is not at all unnatural but rather the most important thing one can strive for as long as one is here on earth. 'The sole deed that is worth accomplishing,' as the Indian books say.

To move on to the third fakir, the one who spends his whole life with his thumb pressed into the palm of his hand until the nail grows through. Why? What did the one who first did the exercise have in mind? He certainly can't have done it off the top of his head! The following explanation suggests itself: In earlier times and still today among savages, and even among Muslims, a madman is regarded as holy. Hystero-epilepsy gives the impression a person suffering from it is mad. As is well known, Mohammad was an epileptic. When epileptics have a fit, they turn their thumbs inwards, but not only that, they also bend their tongue backwards into their gullet. Once when I saw that happen, the question that immediately came to mind was: do fakirs also swallow their tongue? I tried to find out myself, but it was the swami in Myavati who eventually confirmed my suspicion. He wrote, 'I am very well acquainted with this fakir sect from my time in Amritsar; they constantly perform *Kechari Mudra* (swallowing the tongue).' So I was right, they copied the outward side-effects of epilepsy. I cannot say whether by that they manage to become epileptics but it is certainly not inconceivable, if one bears in mind that the opposite is possible, namely that one can bring an epileptic fit to an end by releasing the person's thumb and forcing their tongue back into its natural position.

Patanjali's rules for Raja Yoga indicate that even in ancient times they had discovered a law of nature which one could express roughly as follows: physiological effects can, if copied physically, create the causes which originally produced them; it is, then, possible to invert cause and effect. For example: taking slow, deep breaths results in calmness of thought; conversely, calmness of thought and concentrating one's attention automatically results in deep breathing. This example alone is a valuable key to practical magic, though a person lacking imagination will not put it in the lock, never mind turn it.

For a while I was satisfied with the explanation that the fakir sect turned their thumbs inwards simply in order to induce epilepsy, but then I asked myself why they held their thumbnail against the palm of their hand. Natural epileptics just hold their thumbs clenched in their fist. So there was a small difference! A primitive way of producing *stigmas*, was the thought that suddenly occurred to me and I suspect I was on the right track. Could the exercise be related to the Jesus legend? I immediately wrote to my friend in Myavati asking how old the thumb *mudra* might be and whether it arose about the time of the death of Christ. The answer came a few months later: 'I have made extensive enquiries; it was already known at the time of the Buddha and even then — several hundred years before Christ — was part of the hatha yogis' repertoire.' Is it then the stigmas the sect is trying to acquire and not just a state of epileptoid processes? Perhaps both. That stigmatics do not need food, neither liquid nor solid, to stay alive is something that has been established not only in the case of the present-day Therese Neumann of Konnersreuth, but also in very many earlier cases. An amazing phenomenon, for which doctors have found a very elaborate 'explanation', but still a phenomenon which none of those who starve themselves as a public show have been able to replicate. Their world record is 68 days fasting, but they all drank water. Clearly, therefore, with the stigmatics it must be spiritual factors that play the key role and produce that 'transformation of the blood'. It would be wrong to think that stopping taking bodily nourishment is the highest degree of physical change brought about as a result of spiritual processes. Leading English scientists established that when the famous Scottish medium, Daniel Douglas Home, was in a trance, his height reduced or increased by more than a foot. It is only the majority of people, who have no idea what matter really is, who find that strange. Stigmas, blood issuing from the eyes etc. are naturally only side effects of the ability to live without food and not its cause. I am also firmly convinced that the aetiology of this 'illness' has nothing to do with the drama on Golgotha. It is simply interpreted in that way by the Church, because there is a certain similarity. An experience I had when I was still a disciple of J... encourages me in this view. As I have already said, my co-disciples showed the beginnings of stigmas. Now at the same time a friend of mine, a doctor at the Prague lunatic asylum who was not a disciple of J..., was doing yoga exercises following Patanjali, thought concentration exercises that had nothing at all to do with the Jesus legend. And lo and behold, he too developed incipient stigmas! Is not the correct conclusion the assumption that stigmas are the outward sign of a change taking place in the body that appear when a particular stage of development has been reached? A stage similar to Mohammad's vision of the white horse. And if it really is a law of nature relating to physiology, it would explain at a stroke the point of the thumb exercise of the fakir sect: producing bodily changes

As I have said, it is futile to attempt to influence the wheel of fate by putting one's heart and soul into one's outward profession. Covering the shadow on the wall with whitewash, I called it. The value of such professional keenness is no greater than that of its opposite, the life of a tramp. Unless, that is, 'something extra comes from above'. If a manufacturer of braces makes his business more profitable by reducing his expenses, what, at best, will be the result? He will acquire a fortune which his son will inherit and his grandson squander, as is usual. What does the man get out of it? Nothing but chaff! But that doesn't just apply to people in the braces business, it applies to *everyone*! Differences in value are only outward show. Seen from above, a grassy plain and an alpine forest are just patches of green. If, however, something extra comes 'from above' — for the braces manufacturer as for Alexander the 'Great' — the picture immediately changes. What was previously worthless at once becomes meaningful, a way to the goal. What I call this 'from above' is learning to understand what the Masked Figure intends by imposing our fate on us. Anyone who does not acquire this kind of seeing and hearing is like a child that goes to school but does not realise it should pay attention. In such cases every day is wasted. It would be better to play truant and become a tramp!

The Alchemist's House

Chapter 3 from *The Alchemist's House*: Ismene

Ismene

A dull, bronze double call booms out from the great tower of the gothic cathedral and floats on vibrating wings through the damp chill of the dead night air, waking the bells of the other churches from their benumbed sleep so that, after an initial shudder under the impact of the wave of sound, they each join in like an echo with a 'Yeees — yeees' — quiet, loud, deep, high, distant, close.

The second hour after midnight, the witching hour of the Orientals.

Then the silent waiting starts up again: expectation, hope, fear: what will time bring?

Noiselessly, with white, glowing eyes shining afar, a monster, a dolphin head with almost no body, sweeps past the line of lamps up the hill: a limousine, streamlined, with the alien shape of some mythical antediluvian beast. In each side of the grotesque head is a row of little lighted windows with white silk curtains showing the shadow of a woman's head in hazy outline, like a puff of black smoke.

In the front of the dragon's head is a large, ungainly figure with huge paws, which seem to come straight out of its chest, as if it had no arms, holding a wheel: the chauffeur in the driver's seat, wrapped up in shaggy furs.

The car turns off through a small, winter-dead wood with abandoned crow's nests in the bare branches, heading for Salnitergasse. The harsh light from its nostrils floods the road with a blinding glare before swallowing up the shimmering ribbon in its maw.

The massive dark cube of the house 'At the Sign of the Peacock' looms up.

Needles of fire are sticking out of the cracks in the wooden shutters, as if it were burning inside.

Dull, phosphorescent smoke is pouring up out of the glass roof into the sea of mist.

Slowly the car creeps round the house. It has lowered its two eyes; suddenly it opens a third, much brighter even than the two others were. It pierces the darkness, moves along the wall, up, down — jumps back from the abrupt glitter of the mosaic door, briefly knocks the mask of night from the peacock's grinning demon face, continues its search for an entrance.

Bare walls, no door, no window. The car goes round the corner.

The door of the clockmaker's shop is closed but a glimmer of light behind its opaque glass pane shows that the occupants are still awake.

The chauffeur, wrapped up like a grizzly bear, gets out and knocks. Frau Petronella comes to the door, her full, white hair gleaming like snow in the light of the peaceful glow of the car's headlamps.

Gustenhöver, the clockmaker, is sitting quietly at a little maplewood table, he doesn't even look up when he hears the question: 'Where is the entrance to Dr Steen's apartment?'

He is holding a magnifying glass up to his eye in his beautiful slim fingers and examining a small gold object, glittering with precious stones, with close attention and sympathy, as if it were a sick living being whose heartbeats he had to count. The expression on his face is one of childlike compassion: poor little thing, has your pulse not been able to keep up with the pitiless rush of time?

On a shelf covered in red velvet are clocks — there must be a hundred, in blue, green, yellow enamel, decorated with jewels, engraved, fluted, smooth or grooved, some flat, some rounded like eggs. They can't be heard, they're chirping too softly, but they can be sensed, the air above them must be alive from the imperceptible noise they're producing. Perhaps there's a storm raging in some dwarf realm there.

On a stand is a small piece of flesh-coloured felspar, veined, with colourful flowers of semi-precious stones growing on it; in the middle of them, all innocent, the Grim Reaper with his scythe is waiting to cut them down: like a *memento mori* clock from the romantic Middle Ages. The dial is the entrance to a cavern full of wheels. No hands, no numbers for the hours, just mysterious signs arranged in a circle: Death has his own time, he doesn't want us to know in advance when the harvest will begin. When he mows, the handle of his scythe hits the thin glass bell beside him, a cross between a soap bubble and the cap of a large fairy-tale mushroom.

Right up to the ceiling of the room the walls are covered with clocks. Old ones with proudly chased faces, precious and rich; calmly swinging their pendulums, they declaim their soothing tick-tock in a deep bass.

In the corner is one in a glass coffin. Snow White, standing up, is pretending she's asleep, but a quiet, rhythmical twitching together with the minute hand shows she's keeping her eye on the time. Others, nervous Rococo demoiselles — with a beauty spot for the keyhole — are overloaded with decoration and quite out of breath as they each trip along, trying to take precedence over the others and get ahead of the seconds. Beside them are tiny pages, giggling and urging them on: tick, tick, tick.

Then a long row, gleaming with steel, silver and gold. Like knights in full armour; they seem to be drunk and asleep, for sometimes they snore loudly or rattle their chains, as if they had a mind to break a lance with Cronos himself once they wake and have sobered up.

On a windowledge a woodman with mahogany trousers and a glittering copper nose is sawing time to sawdust.

Once they were ill, all of them. Hieronymus, the clock doctor, patient, concerned, has made them well again. And now they can once more make sure, each in his or her own way, that not a minute gets lost, that the present cannot slip away unobserved.

Just one — it's hanging close by the devoted doctor — an old maid from the days of the Baroque, her cheeks powdered pink, has stopped — oh God! — at one second to seven.

'She's dead,' the others think, but they're wrong. 'I'm right once a day,' she thinks to herself, 'but no one notices and I can't say it myself.' Secretly she hopes Professor Gustenhöver will take pity on her. 'He's not like other men, he'll examine me when no one's there, he'll take me by the hand and say, "Stand up and walk, my girl." Then I'll be like a bride and I'll be able to dance, dance, dance again.'

The chauffeur repeats his question: 'Excuse me, but where is the entrance to Dr Steen's apartment?'

'You have to drive to the eastern façade of the house,' — Frau Petronella points in that direction — 'and lift the latch of the garden gate, then the gatekeeper will open it.'

The chauffeur thanks her and leaves.

Hardly has he closed the door, than the Grim Reaper comes to life. He mows and mows, hitting the thin glass bell so that it sounds swift and soft, like the distant twittering of coal tits: singsingsingsingsing-sing-sing.

The clockmaker raises his head and looks at his wife and she looks at him. It hasn't made a sound since it's been here and now it's striking, he thinks. 'Could it be for him?' Frau Petronella asks after a while, glancing at the door.

The old man thinks, the expression on his face looking as if he were listening inside himself. He rocks his head from side to side uncertainly. 'Perhaps — perhaps for his employer,' he says softly and hesitantly.

A light comes swaying through the little avenue of yews, along the gravel path from the entrance to Dr Steen's apartment to the garden gate.

The Copt, Markus, unlocks the gilded grille, lifts up his lantern to light the face of the lady who, wearing a veil and a long fur coat, is out of the car before the chauffeur can help her.

She grasps the Copt's wrist and jerks it vigorously round so that the light is falling on him while she is in shadow. There is something brusque, imperious about her action. Perhaps it is intended as a rebuke, or is she accustomed to treat servants like slaves?

She has not given the chauffeur any instructions whether to wait or not.

The Copt raises his lip, makes his tiger face and bares his gleaming black teeth. It is something which frightens everyone the first time they see it, no one knows what it is meant to express: anger, fury, astonishment, surprise, defence, attack? Or does it not come from his psyche at all? Is it just a remnant, an unconscious memory in the inherited body cells from those times millions of years ago when primaeval man still faced beasts of prey without weapons.

His olive-yellow complexion and overlarge onyx eyes make the Copt seem even more alien and unreal than by day.

'What a strange racial type!' any other visitor would probably have thought. The lady pays him not the least attention, striding past him with the arrogant words, spoken to no one in particular, 'This is where Dr Steen lives.' The Copt asks no questions and follows in silence.

The arched entrance to the house is suddenly brightly lit, revealing a small vestibule with an inlay of colourful marble. An old valet in black silk knee-breeches bends low into the darkness.

The lady lifts her veil. 'I wish to speak to my... I wish to speak to Dr Steen.'

The old man's expression shows a brief flicker of surprise and delight. For a moment he raises his hands, as if he were about to clap them together in astonishment, but then, when he registers the indifferent tone in which she has spoken, he lowers them again and his expression hardens as something like sadness and disappointment flits across it.

He helps the lady out of her fur coat and ushers her up a narrow staircase to a cramped vestibule. Kirgiz weapons on the walls.

He opens the door to a room and, when the lady has entered, remains on the threshold, head bowed.

The lady looks slowly round the room. Her previous swift,

decisive manner has given way to a strange, almost rigid calm which there is nothing to explain. It is a calm that has a disconcerting effect, since it is in stark contrast to her youthfully slim figure, her strikingly beautiful face and wonderfully slim, restless hands.

There is a delicate, unusual smell in the air coming from the many — it must be thirty-six — wax candles diffusing their gentle light from a chandelier in the form of peacock heads of fragile old gold set on the rim of a shallow, amaranth-blue bowl.

The lady drops her white kid gloves on the wall-to-wall silk carpet of a thousand iridescent colours. The servant remains motionless, makes no attempt to pick them up. He seems to know from previous occasions that he is not allowed to; that he is not allowed to do anything unless it is expressly indicated or ordered.

The walls are covered in purple antique damask silk, places where it has worn thin with age only emphasising how precious it is. Inlaid chests of drawers from the time of Augustus the Strong, marked by use, stand below tapestries with scenes from the Old Testament — the Fall of Man.

In a corner niche, violently disrupting the calm elegance of the room, is a mother-of-pearl pedestal covered with crude silver objects — barbaric Russian art — and in the middle, like a focal point of Slav vulgarity, is an emerald the size of a child's fist, with a hole drilled through and a silk thread. It is in front of a gaudily painted earthenware bust of a Mongol with a drooping moustache and slit eyes, representing Genghis Khan.

In the middle of the room is a long desk with the strangest objects on it: little Japanese Shinto shrines, Chinese jade figures, a tiny monkey skull, Egyptian statuettes of Horus and Osiris, covered in a white, chalky substance and with inserted sapphire eyes, ancient Mongolian river deities made from the mud of the River Peiho, the carved wooden death mask of a samurai with hideously contorted features, horn corals growing out of a stone that look like wonderfully delicate, six-inch high bushes ruffled by the wind, thin, opalescent ancient Greek tear bottles, boxes of rock crystal, ivory, horn and jasper in the most peculiar shapes and, standing upright on a little column of smoky quartz, a red-gold coin almost the size of a man's hand with a gleaming inscription:

By Gustenhofere's Powder redde

To Gold I was transformed from Ledde.

above it, as a coat of arms, a peacock.

Along the edge of the table is a row of those bizarre Javanese marionettes, made of buffalo leather and painted red, green, black and gold, representing demons with quadruple-jointed spider's arms, pointed noses, star-shaped pupils and receding foreheads, crowned with golden flames that the Malays call *wayang purwa*.

'Dr Steen is not at home,' the lady suddenly says to a much-darkened picture by Velasquez.

Her words sound neither as if she is impatient, nor talking to herself, nor asking a question; they are completely expressionless.

'Herr Dr Steen…… is on the way, in his aeroplane,' the servant replies, pausing after the first part, as if he is required to ascertain first of all that he is allowed to reply.

When the lady says nothing, he goes on, 'Herr Dr Steen has been away for five hours.'

'Dr Steen is unavailable during the day?'

'Dr Steen is unavailable during the day.'

'Is Dr Steen here at that time?'

'Dr Steen is here at that time.'

'Always?'

'Always.'

'What is that babble of voices in the next room?'

'The babble of voices in the next room is caused by a band of dervishes; Dr Steen… wants them…' A questioning pause, then the servant immediately stops, since the lady gives no indication that she wishes to hear any more.

'When my — when Dr Steen arrives, it will not be necessary to announce me.'

The servant takes one step backwards, waits for a few seconds, closes the door and leaves.

Above the house a rattle and roar of engines, which abruptly stops — the giant steel bird has settled on its nest. Minutes pass, a brief jolt runs across the glass roof, continuing as a quiver down the walls, and Dr Steen's piercing voice can be heard: 'Markus, will you help the pilot to fasten the hawsers, please.'

From the film studio comes the dull sound of Arabic drums murmuring a greeting.

A crash of heavy bolts, the clatter of an iron trapdoor and cold air sinks into the room; the candles of the chandelier in the purple room flicker, making the face of Genghis Khan come alive with little twitching shadows.

The rungs of a ladder groan under the weight of rapid steps, the trapdoor slams shut: Dr Steen has gone down through the glass roof into his dressing room.

The lady waits.

'Thank God you're back, sir,' she hears the old servant say and a shadow of displeasure crosses her face.

'We were afraid something might have happened to you,' — a woman's voice with a foreign accent that sounds like the cooing of a dove.

'There's no need to worry about me, Leila,' Dr Steen replies.

The lady raises her eyebrows in distaste.

'Anything new, old fellow?'

His valet's reply is halting but swift: 'The sheikh has arrived with the dervishes, sir...' In compliance with her command, he doesn't mention that the lady is waiting.

The next moment Dr Steen enters the purple room, stops short when he sees the lady and slaps his forehead in astonishment.

'What? Is that you, Ismene? How can it be? Where did you come from? I didn't get a letter. I assumed you were God knows where in the Far East.'

The lady remains seated, leaning back in the armchair, smiles, even if it is a slightly forced smile, and holds out her hand to him.

'I arrived just a few hours ago. In our house down there they told me you were living up here now and hadn't been seen in the town for months. I expect to be setting off on my travels soon and since I heard you were only available in the evening, I drove straight up. Anyway, it's Sunday tomorrow and one doesn't go out on a Sunday. How you've changed, Ismael.'

'Twelve years is a long time, Ismene —' He is about to compliment her on her beauty, she realises and quickly interrupts him. 'You've become a great scholar since we last saw each other. There's hardly a newspaper you read abroad that doesn't have whole pages about you and your new theories. I only glanced at them, of course. I'm sorry, but these things don't interest me. Nor can I agree with your view that Bolshevism and other great movements of recent years do not have their origin in men themselves but —'

'But in a realm of "ghosts", to put it briefly,' Dr Steen breaks in with mild mockery.

'Yes, that's more or less how I was going to put it, Ismael. It's an idea that shocks me. There's something irreligious about it that I find outrageous. Among the English too this theory generally meets with opposition, if not vehement disapproval.'

'Among the English? Don't you mean among English women?'

'How do you mean?'

'Because they instinctively sense that they would have to look a little more closely at their Liberty-silk views of the dear Lord, if they were to think the matter through. That doesn't suit them because it might lead to their approving of the most outrageous atrocities, for example being allowed to play cards on Sundays, the mornings of which should be reserved for prayer, the afternoons for procreation. And to think something through? For heaven's sake, what would happen to the sacrosanct tradition of narrow-mindedness! But let's change the subject,' he added quickly when he saw Ismene flush with almost uncontrollable anger. 'Forgive me, I wasn't getting at you. I completely forgot that your mother was a hundred per cent English.'

'As was our father,' Ismene broke in, a sharp tone in her voice.

Dr Steen gives her a long, hard look, then an ironic smile, but remains silent as he turns to look at the statue of Genghis Khan.

Ismene follows his look. 'I know what you are going to say, Ismael. That you're proud that…'

'— that my mother was of Mongolian descent and could follow it back to the great destroyer, Genghis Khan, and that I am her true son,' Dr Steen says quickly, 'and…' He suddenly falls silent, closes his thin lips tight and bites back what he was going to say: 'want to wipe these white rats off the face of the earth.'

'Well?' Ismene asks, ready to pounce. 'And…?'

'Well… nothing more.' Dr Steen is a master at repressing his emotions, even the fury that now blazes up in his heart. His face suddenly has such a soft, affectionate expression that Ismene forgets her distrust, even though she has been observing him closely.

He takes her hand, almost tenderly. 'No, you tell me what you've been doing all this time. Your letters were so infrequent — and so short! Whenever I read them I automatically thought of that pretty, charming young girl that you were before they separated us and sent you to boarding school in England. One forgets that others also grow up and, as in your case, turn into a beautiful woman, a beauty who has no equal anywhere in the world. You cannot imagine how surprised I was just now.'

Ismene indignantly dismisses his compliments with a wave of the hand. She puts on an angry expression, but Dr Steen's sharp eyes see at once that the poisoned arrow has made its mark, if only a graze. 'And now I know how thick I can lay it on,' he tells himself and starts to think hard, though nothing in his expression gives the slightest clue as to what is going on inside him. He appears to be concentrating fully on what his stepsister is telling him.

Urged on by his eloquent gestures, Ismene becomes more and more lively in her account; she has no idea that in reality he is not listening at all and only looks up now and then to throw in an expression of agreement or an astonished-sounding question.

'Basically my life is empty, Ismael, unspeakably empty, despite all my interesting, often almost adventurous journeys to distant parts of the world; eventually it was just a haphazard rush from place to place. As if I were being chased by something I don't know, something that behaves as if it wanted to catch me but never tries to grab me and takes malicious pleasure in the fact that I can't find peace. That compels me to search, even though I don't want to search, don't want to find anything. Wherever I go I sense hatred. No car is fast enough for me; when I'm travelling, everything inside me keeps shouting, "Keep going, keep going!" No destination I'm heading for, the destination is always behind me. Wherever I've been, Ismael, and whatever I've seen — or not seen. Pity, I should have kept a diary. But what would there be in it today apart from the eternal "Keep going, keep going!" '

Dr Steen pricks up his ears and forces himself to pay attention. From the way she is starting to speak more slowly, he senses that she is coming to the end.

'Now I long to be back in England. I want to see people again.' She twists and tugs at her handkerchief. 'To see people and no more niggers, niggers, niggers. The whole world consists of niggers. Even Germany. Even if they look like Europeans, for me the Germans are niggers. I'd like to slash them all across the face with a whip, these niggers of all colours and races. Oh, I can sense their insolent arrogance. When will they finally realise that we are the master race of the world!' She has worked herself up into such a blind fury that she does not see the expression of quite diabolical hatred that flashes up in her stepbrother's eyes of for a second.

She falls silent, almost breathless. Dr Steen nods and smiles, as if he agreed whole-heartedly, and says in a quiet voice, with a sigh, 'I can understand you, Ismene. I wish I could go to England with you, with all my heart I wish I could. But there will come a time when... I will... be able... to have a good look... at the place.' At these last words such a mysterious, incomprehensible tremor comes into his voice that Ismene looks up in surprise, almost fright.

The eerie quality of what he is saying is intensified by a wild, howling crescendo from the dervish drums that suddenly rips through the calm of the room and equally suddenly dies away.

Dr Steen quickly has himself under control again and goes on in a steady, friendly voice: 'Unfortunately — most unfortunately — I have no time for travel at the moment. First I must bring a great project to completion. I could almost say that my mission is not yet ripe. And then, you know Ismene, I do not like to see sad scenes. As I hear, people in England are suffering very much. What a tragic fate! Out of the most profound sympathy with the French, despite the fact that they are only niggers, as you so rightly said, England declares war on Germany! And now? Now they're suffering for it. Oh, it's enough to make you doubt the dear Lord, if such a thing were possible.'

Ismene grows suspicious. Was that mockery in his voice?

But he is looking at her with such enthusiasm, almost radiance, and he stretches out his hands in a gesture so overflowing with warmth that she dismisses her distrust, feeling deeply ashamed. It is his father's blood speaking in him, she tells herself, delighted.

'How beautiful he is!' it suddenly occurs to her. 'What a fascinating, eerie beauty. A kind of beauty I've never seen in a man before.' She shudders, a chill suddenly runs down her spine, she couldn't say why, and she involuntarily looks up to the ceiling to see if the candles are flickering again. A thought leaps out at her from the depths of her soul: 'That's what Lucifer must look like,' and she recalls stories of witches coupling with the devil which she once heard when still almost a child. She tries to drive the thought away. As a diversion she stares at Gustenhöver's gold coin with the inscription and the peacock coat of arms. The light on it blinds her like a burning-glass and the thought refuses to go away, grows into the question, 'Who, who was it who told me the story of witches coupling with the devil?' and the answer comes with frightening clarity: 'Ismael told it to me down in the garden one spring night when there was a full moon; we weren't much more than children!' She can see the scene in her mind's eye, tiny because it is so far in the past, yet she feels it as present, immense and overpoweringly bright, so fearfully alive in the vivid light of her awakened imagination that she thinks she can see the scene with her open eyes as the focal point in the glittering gold of the coin. A memory of the sweet scent of daphne comes over her, she feels once more the intoxicating vibrations in her blood, the secret gnawing of forbidden desire. In that night she was not clear what it meant, she had merely sensed it.

Now she is in no doubt, but she still does not suspect the true poison it conceals. Her cheeks grow hot with the flush of shame at herself, for with the memory a dream also unfolds in her mind, a dream she had that same night in which Ismael was the devil and she the witch.

She lives through it again with such devastating clarity that she asks herself, horrified, 'Did I really only dream it that one time? Have I not dreamt it night after night since then and just forgotten it when I woke up? Is that what is driving me when by day I dash from place to place? Is that the reason for the emptiness in my heart? For the dreariness all round me?'

Now she also remembers that she had told Ismael her dream the next morning — she must have been lured into telling him by sultry, smouldering urges — and once more the same feeling sets her senses on fire, her whole being in turmoil. She fans herself with her handkerchief, as if the room were too hot and tries — in vain — to force her thoughts out of the maelstrom inside her, out of the vague fear they might be transferred to Ismael. And yet — that is what she secretly desires, however much she resists — or thinks she resists — the desire.

'He'll have forgotten it ages ago,' she tries to reassure herself. 'Hadn't I long since forgotten it myself.' But the torment continues. 'Then why did everything come back to mind so clearly just now? Am I perhaps the receiver? Was it the image in *his* memory that woke mine?'

Clenching her teeth, she tries to put on a distracted, bored air; she does it too quickly for it not to strike her stepbrother at once. She can tell by the way he gently bites his upper lip, turning his gaze inward as if he were pondering abstractedly, like someone racking their brains to find the solution to a mystery.

She vaguely remembers something connected with his theories that she read somewhere a few weeks ago: 'If you want to find out

197

other people's thoughts, you only have to look inside yourself. There you will see them as images.' And then, 'If the other person senses that and fears it might happen, it is already too late.'

And immediately she fears 'it might happen'. She tries to curb her fear, but it would have been easier to hold back a wild horse. A chill running through her veins, a shock of terror that numbs her limbs, tells her, 'It's all over. He knows everything. Even worse, he has guessed that I'm sensing that he knows everything. Now I am at his mercy.'

Weary and forlorn, she drops her hand. But however much she at first tries to fight it, the hot, searing feeling the dream sparked off in her after that spring night smoulders up again. She is horrified, but then the cage of false horror is torn apart by the other person inside her, the person she is herself without knowing, the unbridled primal urge of the human animal to do what is forbidden, which rears its head again and again, and all the more wildly the longer it has been dormant.

Her eyes have been fixed on the tapestry on the wall, but only now does she realise what she has been staring at: the Fall of Man.

The picture is hanging on the wall in dead, faded colours, but it is going round and round in her blood, more vibrant, more alive than life itself; her whole soul is transformed in it.

She turns her gaze on the bust of Genghis Khan in order to draw strength against her brother from the insult to her good taste. Her hatred of 'niggers' must help her recover her Anglo-Saxon pride. In vain. The primal beast is stronger than everything once it has woken.

'If only he would speak, just one word,' she wails to herself, 'perhaps that would break the spell.' As she thinks that, she senses that she has no desire to quench the fire of lust.

Ismael looks up, a harmless look, remarkably harmless.

'I was mistaken, thank God, it was just my imagination.' She gives a sigh of relief. 'No, no, I don't want to be mistaken.'

Dr Steen slowly gets up out of his chair. 'Would you mind if I lit a cigarette, Ismene? Oh? So you smoke as well?'

The words sound trivial, banal, but her heart misses a beat when she hears them. She is gripped by an undefined fear, as if a huge bird of prey were circling high, high above her, just waiting to swoop down. She is so afraid, it makes her gasp for breath, yet she longs for it too. Lust and fear at the same time.

He goes to a little wall-cupboard, opens the doors, takes out a cigarette box and — putting it down where Ismene can't see it — one of the many crystal scent bottles. Then he lights Ismene's cigarette and one for himself, letting a few drops from the bottle fall on the floor.

For a while both are silent, lost in thought as they listen to the soft murmur of the drums coming from outside the room.

'I never dream,' Dr Steen suddenly says in a loud, piercing voice. Ismene starts, immediately sensing that he's aiming at something. What is he after? Again she shivers at a strange chill.

'I never dream — never,' he repeats and there's something rhythmical about his words, as if they were in time with the drumbeats.

She says, 'I remember now; even as a child you never dreamt,' but then quickly breaks off as she realises — too late — that she is taking the conversation in a dangerous direction, that she acted against her will. 'Can he guide my thoughts,' she wonders with horror.

He nods, a look of vicious satisfaction in his eyes. 'No, I've never dreamt. I imagine there are very few people who can say that of themselves. I'm glad I'm one of them.'

She forces herself to adopt a mocking tone: 'You look on that as a piece of good fortune?'

'Certainly!There are two forces to which you must never submit, they are as dangerous as vipers, you have to draw their fangs. Only then can you make them dance to your own tune. One is called fear, the other dream.'

'Yet dreams are the most wonderful thing I...' quickly she shuts her lips tight.

He remains silent. As a ploy, or so it seems to her.

'Yes, yes, you're right, fear...' she goes on in a forced, overloud tone. 'Fear! That's the worst thing of all...' She's trying to steer the conversation into innocuous waters and only succeeds in falling into one trap after the other.

'... for it forces us to do things we want to avoid,' he says, taking up where she broke off. 'Fear inverts our will; it is an independent force in nature, one could almost say it was a being. Anyone who understands it can direct it, can project it outwards, can use it as a weapon, like a flame-thrower, can — if they know the magic gesture that all such forces obey — set both men and animals wailing and gnashing their teeth. People think fear comes uncalled; no, I say, nothing comes if it is not called, only people don't realise they're calling. And this 'calling' without intending to is something that people learn in dreams. Learn without intending. The great monster that rules the world and that people falsely think of as the dear Lord teaches it in our dreams, pours its poison into the sleeper's ear. It slumbers in our psyche, ready to awake at once, as the inexorable enemy of the self, when the call comes. And this call is: 'Help'. Anyone who calls for help — loudly, softly or so deep in their heart that they do not realise they are doing it — calls fear, goes down on their knees before it and worships it. Anyone who is afraid of falling ill has already sown the seed of illness; anyone who is afraid of vertigo will fall off; anyone who is afraid of the devil will couple with him —'

'Why are you telling me all this?' Ismene breaks in hastily. She feels a slight hope dawning that he could be a helpful doctor. A doctor even though she feels with dreadful certainty that his last words injected a poison that is eating away at her, a poison that means ecstasy and death. It takes a great effort to stop herself grasping his hand.

He leans back, away from her. 'Why am I telling you? You will come to understand that yourself, perhaps sooner, perhaps later, perhaps never. So to continue: anyone who fears memories will find they attach themselves to their heels like red-hot chains until they have burnt to ashes everything inside the person that is weaker than fire. A scent that is smelt can arouse such memories. Women in particular are often so sensitive that sometimes they think they can smell the scent of, say, a flower which arouses memories in them of which they are secretly afraid. Then the second viper I spoke of — dream — pounces and memory and dream and fear join to form a magic circle from which there is no escape, unless,' Dr Steen points to the alchemist's coin 'they are called to true life.'

Ismene has to fight to stop herself fainting: he spoke of the scent of a flower — alluding to the spring night, there's no doubt about that now — and the room is suddenly filled with the scent of daphne. 'He evoked an illusion and made it reality!' Even while he was speaking she thought she could smell the scent of flowers, as if it were rising from the carpet; now it has become so distinct that she presses her handkerchief to her face in horror, overcome with a terrified fear: 'My senses are no longer obeying me, the past has become present, I've lost control over myself! What is going to happen now?'

He pretends he cannot see what is going on inside her. He puts the scent bottle unobtrusively down on the table and calmly continues his explanations:

'Before, you said you weren't interested in my theories. Forgive me if, despite that, I start talking in abstractions. Please do stop me if what I have to say bores you. I can't get what you said earlier about 'niggers' out of my head. The conviction of the English that all other races are 'niggers' and only exist to serve them — in one form or another — appears to be a peculiarity of the Anglo-Saxon blood. I can understand that, after all, half the blood in my veins is English, the other half — 'nigger blood'. No, no need to apologise, Ismene, there's no point in politeness. I have clearly inherited from our English father the feeling that I am justified in treating creatures of any race which I regard as alien, as an inferior race according to English standards, in the way I see fit. The difference is that I act on this feeling not by trying to subjugate people whom I regard as inferior, but by exposing them, to put it in alchemical terms, to the magic influence of a psychological process of transmutation. To put it more clearly and in a way that will be more comprehensible for you: I am trying to make 'lead people' into 'gold people'.

'If I am successful, I will have done them a great service, I will have raised them from the status of creatures in thrall to death to candidates for eternal life. If I fail and they are destroyed in the experiment, then they weren't worth anything better, they were mere lead that had no seeds of gold in it. You could ask me how I can presume to decide over the life or death of others. Now I am not conceited enough to think that we humans possess free will. I leave it to the philosophers to defend such figments of the imagination. I feel too much as an Oriental to imagine I am an independent unit separate from the great cosmos. That man,' Dr Steen points to the statue of Genghis Khan, 'had the mission of sweeping across the face of the earth like a ravaging storm. He did it, but his soul remained free of the blot of self-willed action. What is said in the *Bhagavadgita*, in that greatest of hymns to the freedom from all guilt, applies to him:

Every deed that happens here, happens through nature's law.
'I am the doer of this deed,' is vain and idle prattle.

And because there is Asian blood in my body, *I* do nothing, I remain free from the recoil that comes from any action; I am the executor and nothing more. And because I do what I must do, I also know what will happen. I have overcome the English blood in me and its delusion that it can do or not do things of its own free will. For centuries the English have been lords of the world; they have fulfilled a mission, there is no doubt about that, but they did not know it was a mission. They say it was — it lets them play the innocent — but they never believed it, otherwise they would never have coined the word 'nigger'. The mission suited their purpose. Anyone who does not know that they have been assigned a mission, does not know it from the very beginning even before they have taken the first step, brands themself as the doer and all the guilt falls on them.'

'So you believe the decline of England is imminent?' Ismene has composed herself. On the one hand she is glad that he has gone on to another subject, on the other she is overcome with patriotic outrage. 'Since when have you felt you were German? What you are expressing is clearly German hatred. Is your hope that England is on the wane not the pious hope of the Germans in general which they keep prophesying in the newspapers? "May God punish England," oh yes,' she adds scornfully.

He raises his hand. 'What are the Germans to me? I don't hate them and I don't love them. I don't hate the English, either, though it might sound like that to you. What I do hate is this hypocritical white rabble, whichever nation they claim to belong to. Please don't interrupt. I know what you're going to say. You think Asians are no better than the whites. Of course they aren't. But the Asian soul is ready to ignite. The European soul is burnt out, what they call love is the heat of the rut, what they call hate is a flicker of anger, revenge or covert lust for money. They do not know that hate is something metaphysical. How could they know that hate is something sacred, an immortal force which makes those immortal who are consumed by it; that it is more than a force, it is a being who is no longer tied to a solid form. 'Hate is detestable' say those who are on the side of love. As if love were anything other than feeble, impotent hate! A load of nonsense. If there really were something like love, then it could only reveal itself if the flame of hate cannot burn it up or transform it into ashes. And when, since time began, did that ever happen? Since the very beginning the angel of hate, the great spiritual alchemist of the cosmos, has been searching for that mysterious elixir that bears the name of love and yet cannot be found. The whirlwind of his wingbeats fans the sparks of hate gleaming in the hearts of men into fire and the blaze is called destruction.

'Ismene' is the third of the three chapters Meyrink completed for his novel The Alchemist's House *(also sometimes referred to as 'The Peacock' or 'At the Sign of the Peacock'). The first two are devoted to setting the scene and are of little interest in themselves. Meyrink also wrote a lengthy synopsis of the plot.*

The main character is Dr Steen, 'an extremely elegant, very rich man' who, 'on a whim, has set up a film company... the various actresses are his harem. (The description of those episodes is kept free of very erotic touches!) His main field of interest is so-called psychoanalysis, only he does not use his knowledge for the benefit of his fellow men but, on the contrary, to arouse complexes in his victims. He is blasé to such a terrible degree that there is only one thing that excites him: thinking up more and more new, spiritually sadistic methods of sending people's souls plunging into the "void". That is the elixir of life for him. Women simply surrender to him without knowing why. He "dissolves" them, just as an alchemist would dissolve metals in nitric acid.'

Ismene is not mentioned in the synopsis. Her function is probably that of the Steen's lover who is called Irene there: 'Further passages show Irene, as the "complexes" that have been injected into her develop, committing crime after crime and, out of her insane love for Dr Steen, confessing to things which not she but he has done.'

Through the Persian, Mohammad Daryashkoh, another inhabitant of the House at the Sign of the Peacock who also appears in some of Meyrink's early stories,[13] he learns of a sect called the Yazidi who 'do not worship God as the creator of the world, but the "fallen angel Malak Ta'us"[14] who in a certain sense is the devil. But, contrary to the Christian and Jewish view, this "devil" will reunite with God at some point.'

Dr Steen sees a secret image of Malak Ta'us and discovers a remarkable similarity to himself. He then plans to produce a film with himself in the leading role as the fallen angel Malak. His aim is: 'To open up the "abyss" so that it will devour the soul of humanity... He wants to arouse a magic "psycho-analytical" complex in the whole of humanity by showing them in the cinema the face of the angel Malak, that until then had only been seen by initiated Yazidi. He hopes that, as a cinema image, it will impress itself on sensitive minds and make them accessible to demonic "promptings".'

The final chapter is the filming of the last scene. At the crucial moment Dr Steen is struck dumb, apparently dead. But 'the end of

13 See, for example, 'The Man on the Bottle' , 'The Preparation', and 'The Wax-works' in *The Opal (and other stories)*, tr. Maurice Raraty, Dedalus, 1994.
14 Peacock Angel.

the novel hints that Dr Steen remains alive.' The importance of the clockmaker, Gustenhöver, as a secondary figure and the fact that Dr Steen gave him an old watch to repair, suggests Dr Steen will be 'cured' in the same way as the protagonist in 'The Clockmaker'. This is backed up by parallels such as the description of the clocks in Gustenhöver's workshop which is almost word-for-word the same as that in 'The Clockmaker'.

Part 2

The Golem

Originally published in serial form in Die weissen Blätter, *1913-1914, Meyrink's first novel remains his best-known one. The unknown narrator puts on the wrong hat one night when leaving the inn and finds himself transformed into the amnesiac gem-cutter, Athnasius Pernath. Meyrink's novel does not tell the traditional legend of the Golem and Rabbi Loew of Prague; rather, the Golem is a kind of symbol of the Jewish ghetto, reappearing every 33 years. There is also a mysterious connection between Pernath and the Golem, which appears at several points, including the extract chosen. The Tarock/Tarot cards are part of the symbolic structure of the novel and Meyrink relates them to the Jewish mystical tradition of the Kabbala; near the end of the novel Pernath falls off a roof with a rope tied round one ankle, briefly appearing in the same position as the* Hanged Man *in the Tarot pack.*

Extract from Chapter 7 of *The Golem*: Ghosts

Ghosts

Charousek had left a long time ago but I still could not make up my mind to go to bed. A sense of unease was gnawing at me, making rest impossible. I felt there was still something I had to do, but what was it? What?

Make a plan of our next moves for Charousek? No, that alone wasn't enough. He wouldn't let the junk-dealer out of his sight for one second anyway, of that there was no doubt. I shuddered at the memory of the hatred emanating from his every word. What on earth could it be Wassertrum had done to him?

This strange sense of unease inside me was growing, driving me to distraction. There was something invisible calling me, something from the other side, and I could not understand it. I felt like a horse being broken in: it can feel the tug on the reins, but doesn't know which movement it's supposed to perform, cannot tell what is in its master's mind.

Go down to Shemaiah Hillel?

Every fibre in my body resisted the idea.

The vision I had had in the Cathedral, when Charousck's head had appeared on the monk's body in answer to my mute appeal for help, was indication enough that I should not reject vague feelings out of hand. For some time now hidden powers had been germinating within me, of that I was certain; the sense was so overpowering that I did not even try to deny it. To *feel* letters, not just read them with my eyes in books, to set up an interpreter within me to translate the things instinct whispers without the aid of words: that must be the key, I realised, that must be the way to establish a clear language of communication with my own inner being.

'They have eyes to see, and see not; they have ears to hear and hear not;' the passage from the Bible came to me like an explanation.

'Key ... key ... key ...' As my mind was teasing me with these strange ideas, I suddenly noticed that my lips were mechanically repeating that one word. 'Key ... key . . . ?' My eye fell on the wire hook which I had used to open the door to the loft, and immediately I was inflamed with the desire to see where the square trapdoor in the studio led. Without pause for thought, I went back into Savioli's studio and pulled the ring on the trapdoor until I had managed to raise it.

At first, nothing but darkness.

Then I saw steep, narrow steps descending into the blackness. I set off down them, but they seemed never-ending. I groped my way past alcoves damp with mould and mildew, round twists, turns and sharp corners, across passageways leading off ahead, to the left or the right, past the remains of an old wooden door, taking this fork or that, at random; and always the steps, steps and more steps, leading up and down, up and down, and over it all the heavy, stifling smell of soil and fungoid growth.

And still not a glimmer of light. If only I had brought Hillel's candle with me!

At last the ground became level. From the dull crunching sound of my footsteps I guessed I was walking on dry sand. It could only be one of those countless passages that run, without rhyme or reason, from the Ghetto down to the river. I was not in the least surprised; half the town had been built over this network of tunnels and since time immemorial the inhabitants of Prague had had good reason to shun the light of day.

Even though I seemed to have been walking for an eternity, the complete lack of sound from above my head told me that I must still be within the confines of the Ghetto, where a tomb-like silence reigns at night. Had I been below even moderately busy streets or squares, the clatter of carriages would have reached me.

For a second fear grabbed me by the throat: what if I was merely going round in circles? What if I should fall down some hole and injure myself, break a leg and be stuck down here?! What would happen to *her* letters then? They lay in my room, and Wassertrum was sure to get his hands on them.

Unbidden, the comforting presence of Shemaiah Hillel, whom I vaguely associated with the idea of help and guidance, flooded through my mind. To be on the safe side, however, I went more slowly, checking my foothold at each step and holding one arm above me so as not to knock my head against the roof if the passage should suddenly get lower. Occasionally, and then with increasing frequency, my hand hit the rock above me until eventually it was so low that I had to bend down to continue.

Suddenly there was empty space above my upraised arm. I stood still and stared up. Eventually I seemed to make out a scarcely perceptible shimmer of light coming from the ceiling. Could it be the opening of some shaft, perhaps from a cellar? I stretched up and felt around with both hands above head height. The opening was rectangular and lined with stone. Gradually I began to make out the shadowy outlines of a horizontal cross at the bottom of the opening and finally I managed to grasp the bars that formed it and pull myself up and through the gap between them.

Standing on the cross, I tried to get my bearings. If my fingers were not deceiving me, that must be the remains of an iron spiral staircase? I had to spend a long, long time groping in the darkness until I found the second step, then I started climbing. There were eight steps in all, each one at almost head height above the last.

Strange! At the top, the staircase came up against a kind of horizontal panelling which let through, in regular lines, the shimmer of light that I had seen from below. I bent down as far as I could to see if, from the extra distance, I could make out the pattern of the lines. To my astonishment I realised that they formed the precise shape of a sixpointed star, such as is found on synagogues.

What on earth could it be?

Suddenly it dawned on me: this, too, was a trapdoor, with the light seeping round the edges. A wooden trapdoor in the shape of a star. I put my shoulder against it and heaved; one second later I was standing in a room flooded with bright moonlight. It was fairly small and completely empty apart from a pile of rubbish in one corner. There was only one window, and that had strong iron bars. I checked the walls several times, but however carefully I searched I could find no door or other kind of entrance, apart from the one I had just used. The bars over the window were too close for me to put my head through, but from what I could see of the street outside, the room must have been roughly on a level with the third floor, as the houses opposite had only two storeys and were considerably lower.

The pavement on the other side of the street was just in view, but the dazzling moonlight that was shining full in my face formed deep shadows, rendering it impossible for me to make out any details. The street must be part of the Jewish Ghetto, for all the windows of the building opposite were bricked up and merely indicated by ledges projecting from the wall; nowhere else in the city do the houses turn their backs on each other in this odd fashion.

In vain I racked my brains to try to work out what this singular building in which I found myself might be. Could it perhaps be one of the abandoned side-towers of the Greek Church? Or did it somehow form part of the Old-New Synagogue?

The situation was all wrong for that.

Again I looked round the room: not the slightest clue. The walls and ceiling were bare, the whitewash and plaster had long since flaked off and there were neither nails nor holes to suggest the room had ever even been inhabited. The floor was ankle-deep in dust, as if no living being had been here for decades.

I shuddered at the idea of examining the rubbish in the corner. It was in deepest darkness and I could not make out what it consisted of. At first glance it appeared to be rags tied up in a bundle. Or was it a couple of old, black suitcases? I prodded it with my foot and managed to use my heel to drag part of it towards the ray of light the moon cast across the room. It looked like a broad, dark strip of material that was slowly unrolling.

What was that spot, glittering like an eye? A metal button perhaps?

It gradually resolved itself into the arm of some curiously old-fashioned coat hanging out of the bundle. And beneath it was a little white box, or something like that; under the pressure of my foot it gave way and crumbled into a mottled, layered heap. I gave it another poke with my foot and a piece of paper fluttered into the light.

A picture?

I bent down: a Juggler, the lowest trump in the game of *Tarock*. What I had taken for a white box was a pack of cards.

I picked it up. How grotesque, a pack of cards in this eerie place! The strange thing was, I had to force myself to smile as a faint shudder of horror crept up my spine. I tried to think of a simple explanation of how they came to be here, mechanically counting the pack as I did so. Seventy-eight cards, it was complete. Even as I was counting them I was struck by the fact that the cards felt like slivers of ice. They gave off a glacial cold, and I found that my fingers were so stiff that it was almost impossible to release the cards from their grip. Once more I looked for a rational explanation. My thin suit and the long walk without coat or hat through the underground passages, the bitter cold of the winter's night, the stone walls, the severe frost

213

that seemed to flow in through the window with the moonlight — if there was anything odd it was that I had only started to feel the cold now. The fever of excitement I was in must have made me insensible to it.

Fits of shivering rippled across my skin, penetrating deeper and deeper into my body. My skeleton seemed to be turning to ice and I was aware of each individual bone in my body as if it were a cold metal rod onto which my flesh was freezing fast. Walking round the room, stamping my feet on the ground, beating my arms against my sides — nothing helped. I clenched my teeth to stop them chattering.

It must be Death, I said to myself, laying his chill hand on my skull. And I fought like a madman against the numbing sleep in which the freezing cold was enveloping me like a stifling, soft woollen cloak.

The letters in my room, *her letters!* The words exploded in my brain like a howl of despair. They will be found if I die here! And she is relying on me, she is looking to me to save her! Help! — Help! — Help!

And I screamed out through the bars of the window, sending my cry echoing through the deserted street, 'Help! Help! Help!' I threw myself to the ground and immediately jumped up again. I mustn't die, I mustn't! For her sake, for her sake alone! I had to find warmth, even if it meant striking a spark from my own bones. Then I caught sight of the rags in the corner, and I rushed across to them and pulled them on over my own clothes with shaking hands. It was a threadbare suit of some thick, dark material in an ancient, curious style.

It gave off a smell of decay.

Then I huddled down in the opposite corner and felt my skin slowly, very slowly begin to grow warmer. But the gruesome awareness of the icy skeleton inside my body refused to leave. I sat there motionless, my eyes wandering round the room. The playing card I had noticed first — the Juggler — was still in the ray of light that ran across the middle of the room.

I stared at it, I could not tear my eyes away.

As far as I could tell from that distance, it seemed to be a crude picture, painted in watercolours by a child's hand, representing the Hebrew character Aleph in the form of a man in quaint, old-fashioned dress, with a short, pointed beard, and one hand raised whilst the other pointed downwards. I could feel a disturbing thought seeping its way into my mind: did the man's face not bear a strange resemblance to my own? That beard, it wasn't right for a Juggler. I crawled over to where the card lay and threw it into the corner with the rest of the jumble, just to rid myself of the tormenting sight.

There it was now, lying there and gleaming across at me through the gloom, a blurred, greyish-white smudge.

I forced myself to think about what I could do to get back to my room. Wait for morning, then call out from the window to passers-by to find a ladder and bring me some candles or a lantern! Without a light I would never manage to find my way back through the maze of tunnels, that was certain, horrifyingly certain. Or, if the window should be too high, perhaps someone could climb onto the roof and use a rope ...? My God! It struck me like a bolt of lightning. Now I knew where I was! *A room without an entrance*, with only a barred window, the ancient house in Altschulgasse that everyone avoided! Many years ago someone had let himself down by a rope to look in through the window and the rope had broken and ... Yes! *I was in the house where the ghostly figure of the Golem disappeared each time!*

I was overwhelmed with horror. I tried to resist, but in vain; even the memory of the letters was powerless against it. My mind was paralysed and my heart started to contract convulsively.

Hastily I told myself it was only the icy draught blowing from the corner over there. Lips numb with fear, I repeated it over to myself, faster and faster, my breath whistling, but it was no use: that smudge of white over there, the card, it was swelling into blistered lumps, feeling its way forward to the edge of the ray of moonlight and then creeping back into the darkness. The silence in the room was punctuated by dripping sounds, half imagined, half real ... outside me, all around me, and yet somewhere else at the same time ... deep within my heart and then out in the room once more; it was the sound a pair of compasses makes when it falls and the point sticks into a piece of wood.

And again and again, that smudge of white ... that smudge of white! 'It's a card, a miserable, stupid little playing card!' I sent the scream echoing round my skull, but in vain ... now it was ... was taking on human form ... the Juggler ... and was squatting in the corner and staring at me with vacant eyes out of *my own face!*

For hour after hour I sat there without moving, huddled up in my corner, a frozen skeleton in mouldy clothes that belonged to another. And across the room he sat, he ... I ... myself.

Mute and motionless, we stared into each other's eyes, the one a hideous mirror-image of the other. Can he see the moonbeam too, as it sucks its way across the floor as sluggishly as a snail, and crawls up the infinite spaces of the wall like the hand of some invisible clock, growing paler and paler as it rises?

I fixed him with my gaze, and it was no use his trying to dissolve in the half-light of morning which was coming in through the window to help him. I held him fast.

Step by step I wrestled with him for my life, for the life that is mine because it no longer belongs to me. He grew smaller and smaller, and as the day broke he crept back into the playing card. I stood up, walked across the room and put the Juggler in my pocket.

The street below was still completely deserted.

I rummaged through the things in the corner that were now revealed in the dull morning light: some broken pottery, there a rusty pan, here scraps of mouldy material, the neck of a bottle. Inanimate objects, and yet so remarkably familiar. And the walls too, how clear the lines and cracks were becoming! Now where had I seen them before?

I picked up the pack of cards and it began to dawn on me. Had I not painted them myself? As a child? A long, long time ago? It was an ancient set of *tarot* cards. With Hebrew signs. Number twelve must be the *Hanged Man*, I seemed to remember, hanging head downwards with his arms behind his back? I flicked through the pack. There! There he was!

Then another image, half dream, half certainty, appeared before my inner eye: *a blackened schoolhouse*, crooked, hunch-backed, a sullen witches' cottage, its left shoulder too high, the other merging into a neighbouring house. There are several of us, adolescent boys ... somewhere there is an abandoned cellar ...

Then I looked down at my body and was thrown into confusion once more. I did not recognise the old-fashioned suit at all ...

I started at the clatter of a cart on the cobbles, but when I looked down from the window there was not a soul to be seen, just a mastiff standing pensively by the corner of a house.

There! At last! Voices! Human voices! Two old women were trotting slowly down the street. I forced my head part-way through the bars and called out to them. Open-mouthed, they stared up, asking each other what it might be. But when they saw me they let out a piercing cry and fled. I realised they had taken me for the Golem.

I expected a crowd to gather so I would be able to explain my situation to them, but a good hour passed during which, now and then, a pale face would arrive below, peer up warily at me and immediately start back in mortal fear. Should I wait — perhaps for hours, perhaps even until tomorrow — for the police to arrive, those state-licensed crooks, as Zwakh calls them?

No, I would rather try to investigate the underground passages, to follow them a little way to see where they led. Perhaps now it was day a glimmer of light might come through cracks in the rock?

I clambered back down the spiral stairs and continued on the way I had been following yesterday, over whole mounds of broken bricks, through subterranean cellars, then up a ruined staircase — to find myself suddenly in the hallway of the *black schoolhouse* I had seen in my dream ..

Immediately I was engulfed in a tidal wave of memories: desks bespattered from top to bottom with ink, arithmetic jotters, songs bawled out at full voice, a boy setting a cockchafer loose in the class, readers with sandwiches squashed between the pages and smelling of orange peel. But I wasted no time in reflection and hurried home.

The first person I met — it was in Salnitergasse — was a misshapen old Jew with white side-locks. Scarcely had he caught sight of me than he covered his face with his hands and started to reel off Hebrew prayers in a loud howl. At the noise, many people must have rushed out of their hovels, for an incredible clamour broke out behind me. I turned round and saw a teeming throng of pale, terrorstruck faces surging down the alley behind me. I stood dumbfounded until I looked down at myself: I was still wearing the strange, medieval clothes from the night before over my suit; the people must think they were seeing the Golem. Quickly I hurried round the corner and hid in an entrance, tearing off the mouldy clothes.

A second later the crowd was pouring past me, waving sticks in the air and shouting abuse.

The Green Face

*First published in 1916, Meyrink's second novel is set in an Amsterdam
full of refugees after a great war, though the haunting atmosphere
he creates is very similar to the Prague of* The Golem. *The 'green
face' of the title is a variant of the myth of the Wandering Jew, which
Meyrink uses here in a symbolic function not dissimilar to his use of
the Golem in his first novel. It ends with the cataclysmic destruction
of Amsterdam, followed by the 'mystical marriage' between the hero,
Hauberrisser, and his love, Eva, who had been murdered.*

Extract from *The Green Face*: Conclusion

Conclusion

The hours crept by unbearably slowly, the night seemed unending.

Finally the sun rose; the sky remained inky black, but around the
horizon there was a vivid, sulphurous gleam, as if a dark bowl with
glowing edges had descended over the earth.

There was an all-pervading, matt half-light; the poplar outside
the window, the distant bushes and the towers of Amsterdam were
faintly illuminated, as if by dim floodlights. Beneath them lay the
plain like a huge, blind mirror.

Hauberrisser scanned the city with his binoculars; in the wan light
it stood out from the shadowy background as if frozen in fear and
expecting the death-blow at any moment.

A ringing of bells washed over the countryside in tremulous,
breathless waves and then came to an abrupt halt; a dull roar filled
the air and the poplar was bent groaning to the ground. Gusts of
wind swept over the meadows like the crack of a whip, flattening the
withered grass and tearing the sparse, low bushes up by the roots.

A few minutes later the whole landscape vanished in an immense dust-cloud, and when it reappeared it was scarcely recognisable: the ditches had been whipped into white foam, the windmills were transformed into blunt stumps squatting on the brown earth, as their torn-off sails whirled through the air high in the sky. The pauses between blasts became shorter and shorter, until eventually nothing could be heard but the constant roaring of the wind. Its fury redoubled by the second. The wiry poplar was bent at right angles a few feet above the ground; branches gone, it was little more than a smooth stem, fixed motionless in that position by the immense force of the mass of air rushing over it.

Only the apple tree stood still, as if protected by some unseen hand in a haven of stillness, not one leaf moving.

A never-ending shower of missiles flew past the window: beams and stones, clods of earth and tangles of brushwood, lumps of brickwork, even complete walls.

Then suddenly the sky turned light grey, and the darkness dissolved into a cold, silvery glitter.

Hauberrisser assumed the fury of the tornado was subsiding, then noticed to his horror that the bark of the poplar was being stripped off in fibrous scraps, which disappeared instantly. The next moment, before he could really grasp what was happening, the tall factory chimneys towering over the south-west part of the docks were snapped off at the roots and transformed into thin spears of white dust which the hurricane carried off at lightning speed. They were followed by one church tower after another: for a second they would appear as black shapes, whirled up in a vortex, the next they were lines on the horizon, then dots, then — nothing.

The vegetation torn up by the storm flew past the window at such a speed that soon all that could be seen through it was a pattern of horizontal lines. Even the graveyard must have been ripped open, for now tombstones, coffins, crosses and gravelamps flew past the house, never deviating, never rising, never falling, always horizontal, as if they were weightless.

Hauberrisser could hear the cross beams in the roof groaning, every moment he expected it to be torn apart; he was about to run downstairs to bolt the front door so that it would not be blown off its hinges but, with his hand on the knob of the bedroom door, he stopped, warned by an inner voice that if he opened it the draught would smash the windowpanes, allowing the storm that was sweeping past the front of the house to rush in and transform it into a maelstrom of rubble. It could only avoid destruction as long as the hill behind protected it from the full blast of the hurricane and the rooms remained shut off from each other, like cells in a honeycomb.

The air in the room had turned icy cold and thin, as if in a vacuum; a sheet of paper fluttered round the room, then pressed against the keyhole and stuck there, held fast by the suction.

Hauberrisser went back to look out of the window. The gale was blowing the water out of the ditches so that it splattered through the air like fine rain; the meadows gleamed like smooth grey velvet and where the poplar had stood there was now a stump crowned by a flapping shock of splinters.

The roar of the wind was so constant, so deafening, that Hauberrisser began to think that all around was shrouded in a deathly hush. It was only when he went to nail back the trembling shutters, so that they would not be blown against the glass, and found he could not hear the hammering, that he realised how great the din outside must be.

For a long time he did not dare look out again, for fear that he might see that St. Nicholas' had been blown away, and with it the nearby house on the Zeedijk harbouring Swammerdam and Pfeill; when he did risk a tentative glance, he saw it still towering up undamaged, but it was an island in a sea of rubble: the rest of the frieze of spires, roofs and gables had been almost completely flattened.

'How many cities are there left standing in Europe?' he wondered with a shudder. 'The whole of Amsterdam has been ground to dust like a crumbling rock; nothing left of a rotten civilisation but a scatter of rubbish.' He was gripped with awe as he suddenly comprehended the magnitude of the cataclysm. His experiences the previous day, his exhaustion and the sudden eruption of the storm had kept him in a state of constant numbness, from which he only now awoke to clear consciousness.

He clutched his forehead. 'Have I been sleeping?'

His glance fell on the apple tree: as if by a miracle, the splendour of its blossom was completely untouched. He remembered that yesterday he had buried the roll of papers by its roots; it seemed as if an eternity had passed since then. Had he not written in them that he had the ability to leave his body? Then why had he not done so — yesterday, through the night or this morning, when the storm had broken?

Why did he not do it now?

For a brief second, he managed it. He saw his body as a foreign, shadowy creature leaning at the window, but in spite of the devastation, the world outside was no longer the dead, ghostly landscape of his previous experiences: a new earth was spread out before him, quivering with life, spring hovered on the air, full of glory, like a visible manifestation of the future, his breast trembled with the presentiment of nameless raptures; the world around seemed to be a vision that was gradually taking on lasting clarity — and the apple tree in blossom, was that not Chidher, the 'ever green tree'?

The next moment Hauberrisser was back in his body gazing out on the howling storm, but he knew now that the picture of destruction concealed within it the promise of the new land that he had just seen with the eyes of his soul.

His heart beat in wild, joyous anticipation, he felt that he was on the threshold of the last, highest awakening, that the phoenix within him was stretching its wings for its flight into the ether. His sense of the approach of an event far beyond any earthly experience was so strong, that he almost choked with the intensity of emotion; it was almost the same as in the park in Hilversum, when he had kissed Eva, the same gust of icy air from the wings of the Angel of Death, but now it was permeated with the fragrance of flowers, like a presentiment of the approach of life imperishable. He heard the words of Chidher, 'For Eva's sake I will give you never-ending love,' as if it was the blossoming apple tree that was calling to him.

He thought of the countless dead who lay beneath the ruins of the destroyed city on the horizon, but he could not feel sorrow. 'They will rise again, if in a different form, until they find the last, the highest form, that of the "awakened man" who will die no more. Nature, too, is ever renewed, like the phoenix.'

He was suddenly gripped by an emotion so powerful, that he felt he must choke; was that not Eva standing close beside him? He had felt a breath on his cheek, and whose heart was beating so close to his, if not hers?

He felt new senses ripening within him to reveal the invisible realm that permeates our earthly world. Any second the last veil that kept it from his eyes might fall.

'Give me a sign that you are near, Eva,' he quietly implored. 'Let my faith that you will come to me not be disappointed.'

'It would be a poor love that could not overcome time and space,' he heard her voice whisper, and his scalp tingled at the intensity of his emotion. 'Here in this room I recovered from the torments of the earth and here I am waiting with you until the hour of your awakening has come.'

A quiet, peaceful calm settled over him. He looked around; the whole room was filled with the same joyful, patient expectancy, like the half-stifled call of spring; each object seemed about to undergo the miracle of a transformation beyond comprehension.

His heart beat audibly.

The room, the walls, the objects around him were, he sensed, only delusory, external forms for his earthly eyes, projecting into the world of bodies like shadows from an invisible realm; any minute the door might open behind which lay the land of the immortals.

He tried to imagine what it would be like when his spiritual senses were awakened. 'Will Eva be with me? Will I go to her and see her and talk to her? Will it be just as beings of this earth meet each other? Or will we become formless, colours or sounds that blend together? Will we be surrounded by objects, as we are here, will we be rays of light, soaring through the infinite cosmos, or will the material world be transformed and ourselves transformed along with it?' He surmised that, although it would be completely new and something he could not at the moment grasp, it would also be a quite natural process, perhaps not unlike the formation of the whirlwinds which he had seen yesterday arise from nothing — from thin air — and take on shapes perceptible to all the senses of the body; yet he still had no clear idea what it involved.

He was quivering with the presentiment of such indescribable rapture that he knew that the reality of the miraculous experience awaiting him would far surpass anything he could imagine.

The hours slipped by.

It seemed to be midday: high in the sky a gleaming disc hung in the haze.

Was the storm still raging?

Hauberrisser listened.

There was nothing by which he might tell: the ditches were empty, blown away; there was no water, no hint of any movement in them; no bushes as far as the eye could see; the grass flattened; not a single cloud crossing the sky — nothing but empty space.

He took the hammer and dropped it, heard it hit the floor with a crash and concluded that it was quiet outside.

Through his binoculars he could see that the city was still suffering the fury of the cyclone; huge blocks of stone were thrown up into the air, waterspouts appeared from the harbour, collapsed, towered up again and danced out towards the open sea.

And there! Was it a delusion? Were not the twin towers of St. Nicholas' swaying?

One collapsed suddenly; the other whirled up into the air and exploded like a rocket; for a moment the huge bell hovered free between heaven and earth. Then it plunged silently to the ground. Hauberrisser's heart stopped still. Swammerdam! Pfeill!

No, no, no, nothing could have happened to them. 'Chidher, the eternal tree of mankind, will shield them with his branches.' Had Swammerdam not prophesied he would outlive the church?

And were there not islands, like the blossoming apple tree there in its patch of green grass, where life was kept safe from destruction and preserved for the coming age?

Only now did the thunder from the crash of the bell reach the house. The walls vibrated under the impact of the airwaves on one single, terrifying note, a note so piercing that Hauberrisser felt as if the bones in his body had shattered like glass; for a brief moment he felt consciousness fade.

'The walls of Jericho have fallen,' he heard the quivering voice of Chidher Green say aloud in the room. 'He has awakened from the dead.'

A breathless hush...

Then the cry of a baby...

Hauberrisser looked around, disorientated.

Finally he found his bearings.

He clearly recognised the plain, bare walls of his room, and yet at the same time they were the walls of a temple decorated with a fresco of Egyptian deities. He was standing in the middle, and both were reality: he saw the wooden floorboards and at the same time they were the stone flags of the temple, two worlds that interpenetrated before his very eyes, fused together and yet separate. It was as if he were awake and dreaming in one and the same moment. He touched the whitewashed wall with his hand, could feel its rough surface and yet at the same time knew without mistake that his fingers were stroking a tall, gold statue, which he believed he recognised as the Goddess Isis sitting on a throne.

In addition to his previous, familiar human consciousness, he had acquired a new consciousness, which had enriched him with the perception of a new world, which touched the old world, enveloped and transformed it, and yet in some miraculous way let it continue the same.

Each sense awoke doubled within him, like blooms bursting from their buds.

Scales fell from his eyes. Like someone who for his whole life has only known two dimensions and suddenly finds he is seeing rounded forms, he could for a long time not grasp what had happened.

Gradually he realised that he had reached his goal, the end of the path that is the hidden purpose of every human being. His goal was to be an inhabitant of two worlds.

Once more a baby cried.

Had Eva not said she wanted to be a mother when she came to him again? The thought was a sudden shock to him.

Did not the Goddess Isis have a naked, living child in her arm?

He lifted his eyes to her and saw that she was smiling.

She moved.

The frescos were becoming sharper, clearer, more colourful, and all around were sacred vessels. Everything was so distinct that Hauberrisser forgot the sight of his room and only had eyes for the temple and the red and gold paintings round the walls.

Lost in thought, he gazed at the face of the goddess and slowly, slowly a dull memory rose to the surface: Eva! That was Eva and not a statue of the Egyptian goddess, the Mother of the World!

He pressed his hands against the sides of his head, he could not believe it.

'Eva! Eva!' he cried out loud.

Again the bare walls of his bedroom appeared through the temple walls; the goddess was still there on her throne, still smiling, but close in front of him was her earthly likeness, a young woman, the picture of living beauty.

'Eva! Eva!' with an ecstatic cry of boundless rapture, he clasped her to him and covered her face with kisses: 'Eva!'

For a long time they stood entwined at the window, looking out at the dead city.

He felt a thought speak within him, as if it were the voice of Chidher, 'You are united to help the generations to come, as I do, to build a new realm from the ruins of the old, so that the time may come when I, too, may smile.'

The room and the temple were equally distinct.

As if he had the double head of Janus, Hauberrisser could see both the earthly world and the world beyond at the same time, and clearly distinguish all details, all objects:

Mike Mitchell

He was a living man
Both here and beyond.

Walpurgisnacht

First published in 1917, Walpurgisnacht *is again set in Prague and, like* The Green Face, *at a time of cataclysmic events, which reflect those taking place on the battlefields of Europe at the time. The novel moves between the ossified Habsburg bureaucrats and aristocrats in the castle district, which towers above the left bank of the Moldau, and the nationalist and revolutionary elements in the city below. Ottokar Vondrejc is the unacknowledged illegitimate son of Countess Zahradka; when the revolution breaks out, urged on by a drum made from the skin of the Hussite leader, Jan Žižka, Ottokar becomes the symbol of the nationalist movement. He is seated on Wallenstein's stuffed horse and carried through the streets, only to be shot by his mother, Countess Zahradka.*

Extract from Chapter 3 of *Walpurgisnacht*: The Dalibor Tower

The Dalibor Tower

The shadows of the old lime trees were already slanting across the quiet, walled courtyard of the Dalibor Tower, the grey dungeon on the Hradschin. For a good hour now the tiny warden's cottage where the veteran soldier, Vondrejc, lived with his arthritic wife and his adopted son Ottokar, a nineteen-year old student at the conservatoire, had been enveloped in the cool afternoon shade.

The old man was sitting on a bench, counting copper and nickel coins and sorting them into piles on the rotting wood beside him. It was the tips that the day's visitors to the tower had given him. Every time he reached ten, he made a line in the sand with his wooden leg.

He finished with a discontented grunt and muttered, 'Two crowns, seventy-eight kreutzer,' to his adopted son, who was leaning against a tree, desperately trying to brush out the shiny patches on the knees of his black suit; then he shouted it out loud, like a military report, through the open window, so that his bedridden wife could hear it in the living room.

That accomplished, Vondrejc, wearing his field-grey sergeant's cap on his completely bald head, sank into a deathlike stupor, like a jumping jack whose string had broken, his half-blind eyes fixed on the fallen blossoms strewn over the ground like so many dead damsel flies.

He did not even move a muscle when his son picked up his violin-case from the bench, put on his velvet cap and made his way to the barrack-sized gate with its official yellow and black stripes. He did not even respond to his 'Goodbye'.

The violin student set off down the hill, towards Thungasse where Countess Zahradka lived in a narrow, dark town house. After a few seconds, however, he stopped, as if an idea had suddenly struck him, had a quick look at his scratched pocket-watch, then hurried back up the hill, cutting the corners of the path up out of the Stag Moat as much as possible, to the New World, where, without knocking, he went into the room of Lizzie the Czech.

The old woman was so wrapped up in the memories of her youth, that it was a long time before she understood what he wanted.

'The future? What do you mean: the future?' she mumbled absent-mindedly, only taking in the last word of what he said. 'The future? There's no such thing as the future!' Slowly she looked him up and down, obviously confused by his braided student's jacket. 'Why don't they have gold braid nowadays? He is the Lord Chamberlain, you know,' she said to the room at large in a low voice. 'Oh! It's Pan Vondrejc mladsi, young Mr. Vondrejc wants to know the future. So that's it.' Only now did she realise whom she was talking to.

Without another word, she went over to the sideboard and fished out from under it a plank covered with reddish modelling clay, placed it on the table and handed Ottokar a wooden stylus, saying, 'Now, Pane Vondrejc, prick it from right to left — but without counting! Just think of what you want to know. Do sixteen rows, one below the other.'

Ottokar took the stylus, knitted his brows and hesitated for a while, then suddenly went deathly pale with excitement and, his hand trembling, feverishly stabbed the soft clay full of tiny holes.

He watched her eagerly as she counted them up, wrote them down in columns on a board and then drew geometrical shapes in a quadrilateral divided up into a number of squares, chattering mechanically all the while as she did so.

'These are the mothers, the daughters, the nephews, the witnesses, the Red Man, the White Man and the Judge, the dragon's tail and the dragon's head, all just as they should be according to the good old Bohemian Art of the Dots. That's what we learned from the Saracens, before they were wiped out in the Battle on the White Mountain. Long before Queen Libussa. Yes, yes, the White Mountain is soaked in human blood. Bohemia is the source of all wars. It was this time and it always will be. Our leader Jan Žižka, Žižka the Blind.'

'What's that about Žižka?' Ottokar interrupted feverishly, 'Does it say anything about Žižka?'

She ignored his question. 'If the Moldau did not flow so fast it would still be red with blood, even today.' Then all at once she changed her tone, speaking as if in bitter amusement, 'Do you know, my son, why there are so many leeches in the Moldau? From the source until it flows into the Elbe, wherever you lift up a stone on the bank, you will always find little leeches underneath. That's because at one time it was a river of blood. And they are waiting because they know that the day will come when it will feed them again ... What is that?' With a cry of astonishment she dropped the chalk and looked from the figures on the board to the young man and back again. 'What's that? You want to become Emperor of the World?' She looked searchingly into his dark, flickering eyes.

He gave no answer, but she noticed that he was clutching the table to stop himself falling. 'Would it be because of that woman there?' she said, pointing to one of the geometrical figures. 'And I always thought you were sweet on that Božena from Baron Elsenwanger's?'

Ottokar gave a violent shake of the head.

'Is that so? It's all over is it, son? Don't worry, a real Czech girl never bears a grudge, even if she's pregnant. But you beware of her,' again she pointed to the shape, 'she's a bloodsucker. She's Czech as well, but she belongs to the old race, the dangerous race.'

'That's not true,' said Ottokar in a hoarse voice.

'She is of the blood of the Bořivoj, I tell you. And you,' she gave the young man's narrow, brown face a long, thoughtful look, 'you are of the Bořivoj line as well. Two such as you are drawn together like iron and magnet. There's no need to waste my time reading the signs,' and she wiped her arm over the board before Ottokar could stop her. 'Just you be careful it's not you that's the iron and she the magnet, otherwise you're lost, son. Among the Bořivoj murder and incest were standard practice. Remember good King Wenceslas!'

Ottokar tried to smile. 'Saint Wenceslas was no more from the line of Bořivoj than I am. My name is Vondrejc, Frau ... Frau Lisinka.'

'Don't keep on calling me Frau Lisinka!' In her fury the old woman thumped the table with her fist. 'I'm no Frau, I'm a whore!'

'What I would like to know ... er, Lisinka, is what you meant by "becoming Emperor of the World" and what you said about Jan Žižka?' asked Ottokar timidly.

A creaking noise from behind made him stop. He turned round to see the door slowly open and in the frame a man appeared with a large pair of dark spectacles on his face, an incredibly long coat, which had something carelessly stuffed between the shoulders to make him look like a hunchback, his nostrils flared wide from cotton wool that had been stuffed up them, and a carroty wig and whiskers which one could tell from a hundred yards were stuck on.

'Prosím. Milostpane. Milady.' The stranger addressed Lizzie the Czech in a voice that was obviously disguised. 'Do hexcuse me, Ma'am, for the disturbance, but would I be right in thinkin' that 'is Majesty's Physician, Doctor von 'Alberd was 'ere a while ago?'

The old woman twisted her mouth in a silent grin.

'Do hexcuse the hinterruption, but I did 'ear 'e was 'ere, Ma'am.'

Still nothing but the corpselike grin. The strange visitor was clearly perplexed.

'You see, I 'ave to hinform 'is Excellency —'

'I don't know of any Majesty's Physician,' Lizzie the Czech suddenly yelled at him. 'Get out, and make it quick, you pest.'

Like lightning, the door was shut, and the dripping sponge that the old woman had taken from the slate and hurled at her visitor fell to the floor with a damp thud.

'That was only Stefan Brabetz,' she said, anticipating Ottokar's question. 'He's an informer, works on his own account. He dresses up differently every time and thinks nobody knows who he is. If there's anything going on, he soon picks it up. Then he'd like to demand money, but he doesn't know how to go about it. He comes from down below. From Prague. They're all like that down there. I think it must be a result of the mysterious air that comes up out of the ground. They all become like him in time, some sooner, some later — unless they die first. Whenever they meet someone, they give a sly grin, so the other will believe they know something about them. Have you never noticed, son' — she became oddly uneasy and began to walk restlessly up and down the room — 'that everything is crazy in Prague? Crazy from all the secrecy? You're mad yourself, son, you just don't know it. Of course, up here on the Hradschin it's a different kind of madness. Quite different from down there. More a kind of ... of fossilised madness. Everything up here's turned into a fossil. But once the storm breaks, these giant fossils will come back to life and smash the city to smithereens ... At least,' her voice sank to a low murmur, 'that's what my grandmother used to tell me when I was a girl. Well, I suppose that Stefan Brabetz can smell that there's something in the air up here on the Hradschin. Something's going on.'

Ottokar went pale and gave a shy, involuntary glance at the door. 'How do you mean? What's supposed to be going on?'

Lizzie the Czech stared straight in front of her. 'Yes, believe me, sonny, you're mad already. Perhaps you really do want to become Emperor of the World.' She paused. 'And why should it not be possible? If there weren't so many madmen in Prague, how could all the wars start there?! Yes, you stay mad, son. In the end why shouldn't a madman rule the world? Why, I became the mistress of King Milan Obrenović, simply by believing it was possible. And how close I was to being Queen of Serbia!' It was as if she suddenly woke up. 'Why are you not in the war, son. Oh? A weak heart, is it? Hmm. And why do you think you are not a Bořivoj?' She gave him no time to answer. 'And where are you off to now, sonny, with your violin?'

'To Countess Zahradka's. I'm to play to her.'

The old woman gave him a surprised look and once more subjected his face to a long and detailed scrutiny, then, like someone who is now certain, she said, 'Hmm. Well. Bořivoj. And does she like you, Countess Zahradka?'

'She's my godmother.'

Lizzie the Czech laughed out loud. 'Godmother, hahaha, godmother!'

Ottokar did not know what to make of her laughter. He would have liked to ask his question about Jan Žižka again, but he saw there was no point.

He had known the old woman too long not to be aware that her impatient expression meant that she wanted the interview to end. With a shy mumble of thanks, he slipped out of the door.

He had scarcely caught sight of the old Capuchin Monastery dreaming in the glow of the setting sun, than he heard, just beside him as if in greeting, the ancient bells of the Loretto Church casting their spell over him like a magical orchestra of aeolian harps. The air, vibrant with melody and fragrant with the scent of the flowers in the nearby gardens, enfolded him in the gossamer caress of some invisible, ethereal realm. Enchanted, he stopped and listened, and seemed to hear the tones of an old hymn, sung by a thousand voices. And as he listened, he felt at times that it came from within him, then as if the notes were hovering round his head, to echo and die away in the clouds; sometimes it was so near, he thought he could recognise the Latin words of the psalm, at others, drowned by the sonorous boom of the bronze bells, it sounded like faint chords rising from underground cloisters.

Deep in thought, he crossed the Hradschin Square with its feast-day decoration of silver-birch twigs, passing in front of the Castle; the noise of the bells crashed in resounding waves against its rock-hewn ramparts, making his violin in its wooden case vibrate, like a body in a coffin coming back to life.

Then he was standing at the top of the New Castle Steps, looking down the balustrade-girt flight of two hundred granite steps onto a sea of sunlit roofs, from the depths of which, like a gigantic black caterpillar, a procession was crawling slowly up. It seemed to raise a silver head with purple-spotted feelers, searching for its way, as, under the white canopy carried by four priests in albs and stoles, the Prince-Archbishop, with the little red cap on his head, red silk shoes on his feet and gold-embroidered chasuble round his shoulders, led the singing crowd upwards, step by step.

In the warm, still evening air, the flames over the candles carried by the servers were almost invisible ovals trailing thin black threads of smoke through the bluish clouds from the swinging thuribles. The setting sun lay on the city, streaming over the long bridges in a blaze of crimson and flowing past the piers with the current, gold transformed into blood. It flared up in a thousand windows, as if the houses were on fire.

Ottokar stared at the scene; he could still hear the old woman's words, how she had said the Moldau once ran red with blood. And the magnificent spectacle of the procession coming ever closer up the Castle Steps! For a moment he was in a daze: that was how it would be, when his mad dream of being crowned emperor was fulfilled! He closed his eyes so as not to see the people who were standing beside him to watch the procession; for a few minutes more he wanted to block out the sight of the everyday world.

Then he turned round and passed through the Castle courtyards, in order to make his way to Thungasse by another, deserted route. As he came round the corner by the Provincial Diet he was surprised to see the huge gates of the Wallenstein Palace wide open. He hurried along, to try and catch a glimpse of the gloomy garden covered in ivy with branches as thick as a man's arm, and perhaps see the wonderful renaissance hall and the historic grotto behind it. As a child he had seen all these marvels from close to, and the memory was deeply engraved on his soul, as of a visit to a fairy kingdom.

Lackeys in silver-braided livery and with close-cropped whiskers and clean-shaven upper lips were silently dragging the stuffed horse, that had carried Wallenstein when it was alive, out into the street. He recognised it by the scarlet blanket and its staring yellow eyes, which, he suddenly remembered, had often appeared in his childhood sleep, as a mysterious omen which he had never been able to interpret.

Now the stallion stood before him in the golden-red rays of the setting sun, its hooves screwed to a dark-green board, like a gigantic toy sent from a dream-world to these prosaic times, to this age which has stolidly accepted the most terrible of all wars: the war of men against demonic machines, compared with which Wallenstein's battles seem no more than alehouse brawls.

Once again, as at the sight of the procession, an icy shiver ran down his spine when he saw the riderless horse that seemed only to be waiting for some determined man, some new master, to leap into the saddle. He did not hear the passers-by commenting disparagingly on its moth-eaten hide. The mocking question from one of the lackeys — 'Would it perhaps please my Lord Marshal to mount?' — made his bowels churn and his hair stand on end, as if it were the voice of destiny coming from the primal depths. He was impervious to the scorn behind the servant's words. Only an hour ago, the old woman had said to him, 'You're mad yourself, son, only you don't know it,' but had she not gone on to say, 'In the end, why shouldn't a madman rule the world?'

He could feel his heart beating in his throat with wild excitement; he tore himself away from his fantasies and raced to Thungasse.

When spring arrived, old Countess Zahradka used to move into the small, dark mansion of her late sister, Countess Morzin, whose rooms were never brightened by a single ray of light. She hated the sun and even more she hated the month of May, with its soft, voluptuous breath and the cheerful people in their Sunday best. At that time, her own house, close to the Premonstratensian monastery at the highest point of the city, was fast asleep behind closed shutters. The stairs Ottokar was rushing up were of bare brick, and led, directly and without passing through a hall, into the stone-cold corridor with marble flags onto which the doors of the various rooms opened.

There were rumours — though God only knows where they came from — that the house, which resembled nothing more than a county courthouse, was haunted and, moreover, concealed an immense treasure. They had probably been invented by some wag to emphasise the contempt for all romantic fancies which seemed to emanate from its every stone. Ottokar's daydreams certainly vanished from his mind the moment he set foot on the steps. He was filled with such a sense of his own poverty-stricken insignificance that he gave an involuntary bow before he knocked and entered.

The room in which Countess Zahradka, sitting in a chair covered entirely in grey hessian, was waiting for him, was the most uncomfortable imaginable: the stove of Meissen porcelain, the sofas, sideboards, chairs, the chandelier of Venetian glass, that must have had a hundred candles, a suit of armour, were all covered with sheets, as if awaiting an auction; even the countless miniatures, which covered the walls from ceiling to floor, were veiled in gauze; 'to keep the flies off', Ottokar remembered the Countess telling him when once, as a child, he had asked her about the reason for these bizarre protective covers. Or had he only dreamed it? The many times he had been here he could never remember having seen a single fly.

He had often wondered what might be outside the clouded window-panes, by which the old lady used to sit. Could it be a courtyard, a garden, a street? He had never attempted to ascertain what it was; to do so, he would have had to go past the Countess, and the very idea was unthinkable. The eternal sameness of the room stifled any resolutions he might have made. The moment he entered, he was transported back to the time when he had had to make his first visit here, and he felt as if he himself were sewn up in hessian and linen, to protect him against non-existent flies.

The only object that was not draped, or at least only partially so, was the one lifesize portrait among all the miniatures; a rectangular hole had been cut in the calico, which covered picture and frame, revealing the bald, pear-shaped head, the staring, watery-blue fish-eyes and flabby cheeks of the old lady's late husband, the Lord High Chamberlain.

Although he had long since forgotten who had told him, Ottokar Vondrejc had heard from somewhere that the Count had been cruel and harsh, pitiless not only towards the sufferings of others, but also towards his own. It was said that as a child he had hammered a nail through his foot into the floor, merely to amuse himself!

The house was full of cats, all of them old, slow, creeping creatures. Often Ottokar would see a dozen or so walking up and down the corridor, grey and quiet, as if they were witnesses waiting to be called into court. They never entered the room, however; if, by mistake, one did put its head round the door, it would immediately withdraw it in haste, as if it quite agreed it was not time for it to give evidence yet.

Countess Zahradka's attitude to Ottokar was strange. Sometimes he would detect in her look something of the tender caress of a mother's love, but it would only last for a few seconds; the next moment he would feel a wave of icy contempt, almost hatred.

Her love, if it was that, was never expressed in words, but often enough her cruel arrogance found eloquent expression, even if it was more in the tone of what she said than in the actual meaning of her words.

He had first been commanded to perform before her on the occasion of his first communion, playing the Czech folk-song 'Andulko, mé dítě, já vás mám rád' on his half-size violin. Later he had played other tunes, love songs and hymns until, as his playing and technique improved, he could perform Beethoven sonatas; but never, no matter whether his performance was good, bad or indifferent, had he seen the slightest sign of approval or disapproval on her face. Even now,

237

he had no idea whether she appreciated his playing.

Sometimes he had tried to appeal to her emotions by improvising, to see if he could sense, from the rapid fluctuations of her response, whether his music had found the key to her heart; but he often felt her love when he was playing out of tune, and hatred when he reached the heights of virtuosity.

Perhaps the unbounded arrogance of her blood responded to the perfection of his playing as to an intrusion on her aristocratic privileges and flared up in hatred; perhaps it was her Slav instinct only to love what was weak and feeble; perhaps it was merely chance, but there was always an insurmountable barrier between them, and he very soon gave up the idea of trying to remove it, just as it never occurred to him to push past her to look out of the windows.

He gave her a mute, respectful bow, opened his violin-case, tucked his instrument under his chin and raised the bow to the strings, which prompted her stock, offhand response, 'Well then, Pane Vondrejc, play your fiddle.' Perhaps it was the contrast between the excitement he had felt as he stood outside Wallenstein Palace and the feeling of being trapped in the past which overcame him in this grey room, that led him, without thinking, to play the silly, sentimental song from the days of his first communion, 'Andulko ...' As soon as he heard himself play the first few notes, he started in confusion, but the Countess looked neither surprised nor annoyed; she was merely staring into space, like the portrait of her husband.

Gradually he began to improvise on the tune, following the inspiration of the moment. He would regularly allow himself to be carried away by his own playing, which he then listened to in astonishment, as if it were another person playing, not himself, a different person who was inside him and yet not himself, a person of whom he knew nothing except that he guided the bow. Ottokar would be so carried away by his music that the walls about him disappeared and he would find himself wandering round a dreamworld filled with shimmering colours and sounds, where he plunged into uncharted depths and surfaced with mellifluous jewels. Then it would sometimes happen that the dull windows became crystal-clear, and he knew that beyond them was a glorious fairy realm, filled with the flutter of glistening white butterflies, living snowflakes in the middle of summer; and he would see himself walking down unending avenues of overarching jasmine, drunk with love, his spirit bathed with the scent from the skin of the young woman in bridal white whose warm shoulder was pressing in intimate embrace against his own.

Then, as so often happened, the grey linen masking the portrait of the dead Count would turn into a cascade of ash-blond hair beneath a sunny straw hat with a pale-blue ribbon, and he would see a girl's face with dark eyes and half-open lips gazing down at him.

Dreaming, waking, sleeping, he felt those features within him, as if they were his true heart; and every time he saw them come alive, the 'other person', who was inside him, seemed to obey a mysterious command, which came from 'her', and his music took on the dark tones of a wild, alien cruelty.

The door to the adjoining room was suddenly opened and the young girl who had been in his thoughts entered quietly.

Her face resembled the portrait of the young lady in the Rococo crinoline in Elsenwanger House, she was just as young and beautiful. Behind her a horde of cats peeked in.

Ottokar looked at her as calmly as if she had been there all the time. What was there to be surprised at? She had simply stepped out of his mind and appeared before him.

He played and played, self-absorbed, lost in his dreams. He saw himself standing with her in the deep darkness of the crypt of St. George's, the light from a candle carried by a monk flickering on a barely life-sized statue in black marble: the figure of a dead woman, half decayed, her dress in tatters over her breast, her eyes shrivelled and a snake with a horrible, flat, triangular head curled up inside her torn-open stomach in place of a child.

And the music of his violin changed into the words, as monotonous as a ghostly litany, which the monk in St. George's would repeat every day to visitors to the crypt:

'Many years ago, there was a sculptor in Prague who lived with his mistress without the blessing of the Church. And when he saw that she was with child, he no longer trusted her and, believing she had deceived him with another man, he strangled her and threw the body down into the Stag Moat. The worms had already gnawed at her when they found it. They locked the murderer in the crypt with the corpse and, as penance for his sin, compelled him to carve her likeness in stone before he was broken on the wheel.'

All at once Ottokar came to, and his fingers stopped on the strings as his waking eye suddenly caught sight of the girl standing behind the old Countess' chair and smiling at him. He froze, incapable of movement, the bow raised in his hand.

Countess Zahradka took up her lorgnette and slowly turned her head. 'Carry on playing, Ottokar. It's only my niece. Don't disturb him, Polyxena.'

Ottokar did not move, only his arm fell loosely to his side, as if under the effect of a heart spasm.

For a good minute there was complete silence in the room.

'Why have you stopped playing?' asked the Countess angrily.

Ottokar pulled himself together, scarcely knowing how to hide the fact that his hands were trembling; then, softly, shyly, the violin began to whimper:

> Andulko,
> My little child
> I do love you.

A purring laugh from Polyxena brought the melody to a halt. 'Won't you tell us, Herr Ottokar, what that marvellous tune was that you were playing before? Was it an improvisation? It — called — up,' after each word Polyxena paused meaningfully; her eyes were lowered, and she plucked at the fringes of the chair, apparently lost in thought, 'a — vivid — picture of — St. George's — crypt, Herr ... Herr ... Ottokar.'

The old Countess gave an almost imperceptible start. There was something about the tone in which her niece spoke the name Ottokar which aroused her suspicions.

The bewildered student stammered a few embarrassed words. There were two pairs of eyes fixed upon him, the one full of such consuming passion that they seemed to scorch his brain, the other penetrating, razor sharp, radiating suspicion and deadly hate at the same time. He could not look at either without either hurting the one deeply or revealing his innermost feelings to the other. 'Quick! Play! Just keep on playing!' screamed something inside him. Hastily he raised his bow. Beads of sweat were forming on his forehead. 'For God's sake, not that blasted "Andulko" again!' As he drew the bow across the strings he felt to his horror that it was inescapable ... everything began to go black ... then the sound of a hurdy-gurdy from the street outside came to his rescue and, with crazed, mindless haste, he rushed into the music-hall song with the chorus:

> Pale as the lily
> Never should marry,
> My mother said;
> Lips like the cherry,
> Rosy and merry,
> Kiss and soon wed.

After one verse, he stopped; the gust of hatred that came from Countess Zahradka almost knocked the bow out of his hand.

Through a veil of mist he saw Polyxena dart over to the grandfather clock by the door, pull the linen cover aside and push the finger round until it pointed to VIII. He realized it was a way of telling him the time for their rendezvous, but the joy froze in his throat at the fear that the Countess had seen through the stratagem.

He saw her long, skinny, old woman's fingers rummaging in the knitting bag hanging from the back of the chair and sensed that she was about to do something that would be unimaginably humiliating for him, something so terrible he dared not even guess what it might be.

'Capital music — Vondrejc — capital,' said the Countess,

spitting out each word separately, took two crumpled notes from the bag and handed them to him. 'There's — a tip — for you. And buy yourself — a pair of — better — trousers on my account before the next time, those are all worn and shiny.'

Ottokar's heart almost stopped beating with the shame. His last clear thought was that he had to take the money, if he did not want to give himself away. Before his eyes the whole room dissolved into a cloud of grey: Polyxena, the clock, the face of the late Chamberlain, the suit of armour, the armchair, only the dusty windows stood out, whitish rectangles bursting through the gloom. He realised that the Countess had drawn her own grey cover over him — 'as a protection against the flies' — and that he would never be able to rid himself of it until death.

He found himself out in the street, with no memory of how he had come down the stairs. Had he been in the upstairs room at all? A burning wound deep within him told him that he must have been. And he was still clutching the money in his hand. Unthinking, he thrust it into his pocket.

Then he remembered that Polyxena would come to him at eight o'clock; he heard the towers strike the quarter; a dog yapped, it struck him like a whiplash across his face: Did he really look so shabby that the dogs of the rich barked at him?

He clenched his teeth together, as if he could grind his thoughts into silence, and raced on trembling legs towards his home. At the next corner he stopped, swaying to and fro. 'No, not home. Away, far away from Prague.' He was consumed with shame, 'The best would be to throw myself into the river!' With the decisiveness of youth he immediately set off for the Moldau, but the 'other person' inside him slowed his steps, whispering that he would surely betray Polyxena, if he were to drown himself, and concealing from him the fact that it was the vital urge within that was holding him back from suicide.

'Oh God, my God, how can I look her in the face when she comes?' he sobbed to himself. 'No, no, she won't come, it's all over.' At that the pain in his breast sunk its fangs even more deeply into his soul: if she did not come to him any more, how could he go on living?

He went through the black and yellow striped gate into the courtyard of the Dalibor Tower, aware that the next hour would be an endless torment as he counted each minute. If Polyxena came he would shrivel before her with shame; if she did not come, then the night of madness would swallow him up.

He shuddered as he glanced over at the dungeon tower with its round, white hat, towering up from the Stag Moat behind the crumbling wall. He had a dim feeling that the tower was still alive: how many victims had already succumbed to madness in its stone belly, but still the Moloch was not satisfied; now, after a hundred years of deathlike sleep, it was awakening again.

For the first time since his childhood he saw it not as the work of human hands, but as a granite monster with fearsome entrails that could digest flesh and blood, just like those of some nocturnal predator. It had three stories with a round hole down the middle like a pipe from gullet to stomach. In the dreadful darkness of the top floor, year after lightless year had gnawed at the condemned prisoners, until they were let down by ropes into the middle room for their last loaf of bread and jug of water, after which they would die of thirst, unless, crazed by the reek of decay from below, they flung themselves through the hole to join the stinking cadavers.

The courtyard of limes breathed the dewy damp of the evening twilight, but the window of the keeper's cottage still stood open. Ottokar sat down on the bench, as quietly as possible so as not to disturb the old, gout-ridden woman who, so he believed, was sleeping on the other side of the wall. He wanted to clear his mind of all that had happened for a moment, before the torture of waiting began: a childish attempt to outwit his heart.

He was suddenly overcome with a feeling of weakness; it needed all his strength to hold back the sobs which gripped him by the throat and threatened to suffocate him. From inside the room, he heard a toneless voice, which sounded as if someone were speaking into a pillow, 'Ottokar?'

'Yes, mother?'

'Aren't you going to come in for your dinner?'

'No, mother. I'm not hungry; I — I've already had something to eat.'

For a while the voice was silent.

In the room the clock chimed a soft, metallic half past seven. Ottokar pressed his lips together and clenched his hands. 'What should I do? What should I do?!'

Again he heard the voice. 'Ottokar?'

He did not reply.

'Ottokar?'

'Yes, mother?'

'Why ... why are you crying, Ottokar?'

He gave a forced laugh. 'Me? Whatever are you thinking, mother! I'm not crying. Why ever should I cry?'

The voice fell silent, unbelieving.

Ottokar raised his eyes from the shadow-dappled courtyard. 'If only the bells would finally ring out and break this deathly silence!'

He stared at a crimson gash in the sky, and felt that he had to say something.

'Is father in there?'

'He's at the inn,' came the answer after a pause. He stood up quickly. 'Then I'll go and join him for an hour or so. Goodnight, mother.' He picked up his violin case and looked at the tower.

'Ottokar?'

'Yes? Should I close the window?'

'Ottokar! Ottokar, I know you're not going to the inn. You're going in the Tower, aren't you?'

'Yes ... well ... later. It ... it's the best place for practising. Goodnight.'

'Is she coming to the Tower again tonight?'

'Božena? Who knows. She might. If she's free she sometimes comes and we have a chat. Is there any message for father?'

The voice became even sadder, 'Do you think I don't know it's someone else? I can tell by her tread. No one who has been working hard all day would step so lightly and so quickly.'

'You do get funny ideas, mother!' He tried to laugh.

'Well, I've said my piece. And you're right, you'd better close the window. It's better like that, then I won't be able to hear those awful songs you always play when she's with you. I ... I wish I could help you, Ottokar.'

Ottokar held his hands over his ears, then he put the violin case under his arm, hurried across to the gap in the wall and ran up the crumbling stone steps and across the little wooden footbridge into the top floor of the Tower. The semicircular room where he was standing had a narrow window, really no more than an enlarged slit for bowmen to shoot through, in the three-foot thick wall; it looked out to the south and in it the silhouette of the cathedral hovered over the ancient castle. For the visitors who came to visit the Dalibor Tower during the day there were a few rough wooden chairs, a table with a jug of water on it and an old, faded sofa. In the darkness, they looked as if they were rooted to the ground. A small iron door with a crucifix on it led into the adjoining chamber where, two hundred years ago, a Countess Lambua, Polyxena's great-great-grandmother, had been imprisoned. She had poisoned her husband and before she died, in her madness she had bitten open the arteries of her wrist and painted his portrait in blood on the wall.

Behind it was a dark cell, scarcely six foot square, where, with a piece of iron, a prisoner had scratched a cavity in the stone blocks of the wall, deep enough for a man to squat inside. He had scraped away for thirty years; a handsbreadth more and he would have been free — free to throw himself into the Stag Moat below. But he had been discovered in time and moved to the middle of the tower, where he had starved to death.

Restless, Ottokar paced up and down, sat in the window, stood up again; one minute he was certain Polyxena would come, the next he was convinced he would never see her again; each possibility seemed more dreadful than the other, each contained his hopes and fears together.

Every night Polyxena's image accompanied him in his dreams, waking and sleeping it filled his life. He thought of her when he played the violin, when he was alone he held imaginary conversations with her. He had built the most fantastic castles in the air for her, but what did the future hold? In the boundless despair of youth, such as only a heart of nineteen years can feel, he saw it as an airless, lightless dungeon.

The idea that he might ever play on his violin again seemed an utter impossibility. There was a faint, scarcely audible voice inside him, telling him that everything would turn out quite differently from his imaginings, but he did not listen, refused to listen to it. Often pain can be so overpowering that comfort, even if it comes from within, only makes it burn all the more.

The gathering darkness in the deserted room only increased his agitation until it was unbearable. He kept on imagining he heard soft noises outside, and his heart stood still at the thought that it must be 'her'. Then he would count the seconds until, according to his calculation, she should have found her way in through the darkness, but every time his expectation was disappointed, and the thought that she might have turned back on the threshold drove him almost to distraction.

He had become acquainted with her only a few months ago. It seemed to him like a fairytale come true when he thought back to it. Two years before that he had seen her, but as a picture, as the portrait of a lady from the Rococo period with ash-blond hair, narrow, almost transparent cheeks and a strange, cruelly lascivious expression round her half-open lips, behind which glistened the white of tiny, bloodthirsty teeth. The picture hung in the portrait gallery of Elsenwanger House, and one evening, when he had been sent to play to the guests there, he had seen it looking down at him from that wall, and it had branded itself on his mind so that whenever he closed his eyes and thought of it, it appeared clearly before him. Gradually it had come to dominate his youthful yearning and so captured his whole being that it had gradually come to life, so that in the evenings, when he sat on the bench beneath the limes dreaming of her, he could feel it nestling against his breast like a creature of flesh and blood.

It was the portrait of a Countess Lambua, he had been told, and her first name was Polyxena.

From then on he invested that name with all the beauty, joy, glory, happiness and sensuality his youthful imagination could dream up, until it became a magic word, which he only needed to whisper for him to feel the presence of its bearer like a caress which scorched him to the marrow. In spite of his age, and the fact that until then he had enjoyed perfect health, he sensed that the heart condition that suddenly began to trouble him was incurable and that he was doomed to die young, a feeling that never filled him with sadness, but was more like a foretaste of the sweetness of death.

From his childhood on, the strange, unworldly setting of the Dalibor Tower with its gloomy stories and legends had encouraged him to build castles in the air, in contrast to which the world around, with its poverty and oppressive narrowness, seemed a hostile dungeon. It never occurred to him to try to connect his dreams and longings with his everyday reality. Time stretched ahead of him, empty of plans for the future.

He had had very little to do with children of his own age. For a long time his world had been bounded by the Dalibor Tower with its lonely courtyard, his taciturn foster-parents and the old tutor, who had taught him until well past childhood because the Countess, who paid for his upbringing, did not want him to attend school.

His cheerless existence, and his separation from the world of ambition, the race for fame and fortune, would probably have turned him, before his time, into one of those solitary eccentrics wrapped up in their own daydreams who were so common on the Hradschin, had not something happened which had turned his soul upside down, something so uncanny and yet at the same time so real, that with one blow it had demolished the wall separating his inner life from the world outside, turning him into a man who had moments of ecstasy in which even his wildest fantasies seemed within easy grasp.

It had happened in the cathedral. He was sitting among old women saying their rosaries; he had been staring at the tabernacle, oblivious to his surroundings, not noticing their comings and goings, until all at once he realised the church was empty apart from someone sitting beside him — the very image of Polyxena. It was the very same face he had been dreaming of all this time, right down to her delicately chiselled nostrils and the curve of her lips.

For a moment, the gap between dream and reality closed, but only for a moment; a second later he was fully aware that it was a living girl he could see beside him on the bench. But that single moment was enough to give fate the purchase it needs to prize a person's destiny for ever off its predetermined path of rational decision and to send it careering into that boundless world where faith can move mountains.

In the confused, sensual ecstasy of one who finds himself face to face with the idol of his yearning, he had flung his arms wide and thrown himself down before the physical incarnation of all his dreams, he had called out her name, embraced her knees, covered her hands with kisses; trembling with excitement, he had told her, in a tumbling cascade of words, what she meant to him, that he had known her for a long time, without ever having seen her in the flesh.

And there in the church, surrounded by the golden statues of the saints, they had both been seized by a wild, unnatural love, which had carried them away like a hellish whirlwind, raised by the sudden stirring of a ghostly line of depraved ancestors, who for centuries had been confined to the portrait gallery.

As if by some satanic miracle, the young girl, who entered the cathedral an innocent virgin, had, by the time she left, also been transformed into the spiritual likeness of her ancestress, who had borne the same name of Polyxena and whose portrait now hung in Baron Elsenwanger's town house.

Since that day, they had met whenever they had the opportunity, without prior arrangement and without ever not finding the other. It was as if there were some magic attraction in their passion that drew them together; they acted instinctively, like dumb animals on heat who do not need understanding, because they understand the call of the blood. Neither of them found it at all surprising when chance led to their paths crossing at the very moment when their lust for the other was at its strongest. For Ottokar, each time he saw that it was Polyxena, and not merely her image, in his arms, it was the constant renewal of a miracle, such as had been repeated but an hour ago.

When he heard her steps approaching the tower — this time it really was her — his torment had already disappeared, had faded away like the memory of some illness he had long since recovered from. When they were in each others' arms he was never sure: had she come through the door, or through the wall, like some apparition? She was with him and that was all that he knew, or wanted to know; anything that had happened before had been swallowed up in the abyss of time.

And that was how it was now.

He saw her straw hat with the pale-blue ribbon appear in the darkness of the room, then it was thrown carelessly into a corner, and everything else followed; her white dress was like a cloud of mist on the table, the rest of her clothes were scattered around the chairs; he felt her hot skin, her teeth biting into his neck, heard her groans of pleasure: everything happened too quickly for him to grasp, like a series of lightning images, each one displacing the last, each one more overwhelming. He was in an ecstasy of voluptuousness which blotted out all sense of time. Had she asked him to play his violin for her? He had no idea, could not recall her saying so.

All he knew was that he was standing upright before her, her arms embracing his loins; he could feel Death sucking the blood from his veins, could feel his hair stand on end, his skin freeze, his knees tremble. He was incapable of rational thought, at times he felt he was about to fall backwards, then, at that very moment, he would wake, as if she were holding him up, and hear a song from the strings that his bow and his hand must have been playing, but that also came from her, from her soul and not from his, a song in which lascivious desire was mingled with fear and horror.

Half unconscious, unable to resist, he listened to the story the music told: everything Polyxena imagined, in order to whip herself up into an even greater frenzy of lust, he saw as a series of vivid images; he felt her thoughts pass into his mind, watched them come to life and then read them in elaborate letters on a stone slab: it was the extract from an old chronicle on which the picture 'The Man Impaled' was based, just as it is inscribed in the Little Chapel on the Hradschin, in memory of the gruesome end of one who tried to seize the crown of Bohemia:

'Now one of the knights who had been impaled went by the name of Bořivoj Chlaveć, and his stake had come out by the pit of his arm, leaving his head unharmed. This Sir Bořivoj prayed most fervently until the evening, and during the night his stake broke off at his backside and he went, with the rest of the stake still inside him, up to the Hradschin and lay down upon a dung-heap. In the morning he went straight to the house that stands beside the Church of St. Benedict and sent for a priest from the castle clergy, in whose presence he most fervently confessed his sins before the Lord our God and told him that without confession and receipt of the Holy Sacrament of one kind, as ordered by the Church, he could not die; it had been his custom every day to say a short prayer in honour of Almighty God and an Ave Maria in honour of the Blessed Virgin, and it had ever been his assurance that through the power of this prayer and the intercession of the Blessed Virgin he would never die without first receiving the sacrament of Holy Communion.

The priest spake, "My son, tell me that prayer," and he began, saying, "Almighty God, I beseech Thee, grant me the intercession of Thy most holy martyr, Saint Barbara, that I shall not die a speedy death but shall receive the Holy Sacrament before mine end, that, protected from all enemies, both visible and invisible, and preserved from evil spirits, I may at the last be brought to eternal life, through Jesus Christ our Lord and Saviour, amen."

After these words, the priest administered the Holy Sacrament, and he died the same day, and there was much wailing among the people when he was buried in the Church of St. Benedict.'

Polyxena had gone, and the tower lay lifeless and grey beneath the glittering stars of the night sky; but in its stony breast beat a tiny human heart that was full to bursting with the oath it had sworn not to rest and rather to share a thousandfold the cruel torture of the impaled knight than to die before he had laid at his lover's feet the highest prize that human will can aspire to.

The White Dominican

*Set in a symbolic version of the Bavarian town of Wasserburg am
Inn,* The White Dominican, *first published in 1921, focuses on
Christopher Dovecote, the last scion of a noble house, whose destiny
is to ward off the threats of the Medusa and achieve transfiguration;
he is then united with his love, Ophelia, the daughter of a theatrical
couple who commits suicide rather than go on the stage as her
parents want.*

Extract from Chapter 3 of *The White Dominican*: The Nightwalk

The Nightwalk

That night I had a strange experience. Others would call it a dream,
for men have only that one, inadequate word to describe everything
that happens to them when their body is asleep.

As always before I went to sleep, I had folded my hands so that,
as the Baron put it, 'the left lay on the right'. It was only through
experience over several years that I came to realise what the purpose
of this measure was. It could be that any other position of the hands
would serve the same purpose as long as they result in the feeling
that 'the body is bound'.

Every time since that first evening in the Baron's house I had
lain down to sleep in this manner, and every morning I had woken
feeling as if I had walked a long way in my sleep, and every time
I was relieved to see that I was undressed and not wearing dusty
boots in bed and need not fear being beaten for it, as had happened
in the orphanage. But in the light of day I had never been able to
remember where I had walked in my dream. That night was the first
time the blindfold was taken from my eyes. The fact that earlier in
the evening Mutschelknaus had treated me in such a remarkable

way, like a grown-up, was probably the hidden reason why a self — perhaps my 'Christopher' — which had until then slept within me, now awoke to full consciousness and began to see and to hear.

I began by dreaming I had been buried alive and could not move my hands or my feet; but then I filled my lungs with mighty breaths and thus burst open the lid of the coffin; and I was walking along a white, lonely country road, which was more terrible than the grave I had escaped from, for I knew it would never come to an end. I longed to be back in my coffin, and there it was, lying across the road.

It felt soft, like flesh, and had arms and legs, hands and feet, like a corpse. As I climbed in, I noticed that I did not cast a shadow, and when I looked down to check, I had no body; then I felt for my eyes, but I had no eyes; when I tried to look at the hands that were feeling for them, I could see no hands. As the lid of the coffin slowly closed over me, I felt as if all my thoughts and feelings as I was wandering along the white road had been those of a very old, if still unbowed, man; then when the coffin lid closed, they disappeared, just as steam evaporates, leaving behind as a deposit the half blind, half unconscious thoughts which normally filled the head of the half-grown youth that I was, standing like a stranger in life.

As the lid snapped shut, I woke in my bed. That is, I thought I had woken up.

It was still dark, but I could tell by the intoxicating scent of elderflowers that came streaming in through the open window, that the earth was giving off the first breath of the coming morning and that it was high time for me to put out the lamps in the town.

I picked up my pole and felt my way down the stairs. When I had completed my task, I crossed the wooden bridge and climbed up a mountain; every stone on the path seemed familiar, and yet I could not remember ever having been there before. In the high meadows, still dark green in the glowing half-light and heavy with dew, alpine flowers were growing, snowy cotton grass and pungent spikenard.

Then the farthest edge of the sky split open, and the invigorating blood of the dawn poured into the clouds. Blue, shimmering beetles and huge flies with glassy wings suddenly rose from the earth with a buzzing sound and hovered motionless in the air at about head height, all with their heads turned towards the awakening sun.

When I saw, felt and comprehended this grandiose act of prayer from mute creation, a shiver of deepest emotion ran through my every limb. I turned round and went back towards the town. My shadow preceded me, gigantic, its feet inseparably attached to mine. Our shadow, the bond that ties us to the earth, the black ghost that emanates from us, revealing the death within us, when light strikes our bodies!

The streets were blindingly bright when I entered them. The children were making their noisy way to school.

'Why aren't they chanting, "Doo'cot, doo'cot, diddlediddle doo'cot" at me as usual?' was the thought that awoke in my mind. 'Can they not see me? Have I become such a stranger to them that they don't know me any more? I have always been a stranger to them,' I suddenly realised with a startlingly new awareness. 'I have never been a child! Not even in the orphanage when I was small. I have never played games as they do. At least whenever I did, it was only a mechanical motion of my body without my desire ever being involved; there is an old, old man living inside me and only my body seems to be young. The carpenter probably felt that yesterday, when he spoke to me as to a grown-up.'

It suddenly struck me, 'But yesterday was a winter evening, how can today be a summer morning? Am I asleep, am I walking in my sleep?' I looked at the street lamps: they were out, and who but I could have extinguished them? So I must have been physically present when I put them out. 'But perhaps I am dead now and being in a coffin was real and not just a dream?' I decided to carry out a test, and went up to one of the schoolboys and asked him, 'Do you know me?' He did not reply, and walked through me as through empty air.

'I must be dead then,' I concluded, unconcerned. 'Then I must take the pole back home quickly, before I start to decompose,' came the voice of duty, and I went upstairs to my foster-father. In his room I dropped the pole, making a loud noise. The Baron heard it — he was sitting in his armchair — turned round and said, 'Ah, there you are at last.'

I was glad that he could see me, and concluded that I could not have died.

The Baron looked as he always did, was wearing the same coat with the jabot of mulberry lace that he always wore on feast days, but there was something about him that made him seem indefinably different. Was it his goitre? No, that was no larger or smaller than usual. My eyes wandered round the room — no, that was unchanged, too. There was nothing missing, nothing had been added. Leonardo da Vinci's Last Supper, the only decoration in the room, was on the wall as usual; everything in its usual place. Just a moment! That green plaster bust of Dante with the severe, sharp, monkish features, was it not on the right-hand end of the shelf yesterday? Had someone moved it round? It was on the left now.

The Baron noticed me looking round and smiled. 'You have been on the mountain?' he said, pointing to the flowers in my pocket which I had picked on the way.

I mumbled some excuse but he waved it aside. 'I know; it's beautiful up there. I often go myself. You have often been there before, but you always forgot it afterwards. Young minds can't retain anything, their blood is still too hot; it washes the memory away. Did the walk make you tired?'

'Not on the mountain, but on ... on the white country road,' I said, unsure whether he knew about that too.

'Ah, yes, the white road,' he mused, 'there are not many who can stand that. Only someone who is born a wanderer. It was because I saw that in you, all those years ago in the orphanage, that I brought you to live with me. Most people fear the road more than they fear the grave. They get back into their coffins because they think that is death and that it will bring them peace; but in reality the coffin is life, is the flesh. Being born on earth is nothing other than being buried alive! It is better to learn to walk the white road. Only one must not think of the end of the road, for it has no end. It is infinite. The sun on the mountain is eternal. Eternity and infinity are two different things. The only person for whom infinity and eternity are the same is one who seeks eternity in infinity and not the "end". You must walk along the white road for the sake of the walk itself, for the pleasure of walking and not to exchange one transient resting place with another. Rest — not a resting place — can only be found in the sun on the mountain. It stands still and everything revolves round it. Even its herald, the dawn, radiates eternity, and that is why the insects and flies worship it and stay still in the air until then sun comes. And that is why you did not feel tired when you climbed the mountain.'

He suddenly gave me a close look. 'Did you see the sun?' he asked.

'No, father, I turned back before it rose.'

He gave a satisfied nod. 'That is good,' adding under his breath, 'otherwise we would have nothing more to do with each other. And your shadow went before you, down towards the valley?'

'Yes. Of course ...'

He ignored my surprise. 'Anyone who sees the sun,' he continued, 'seeks eternity alone. He is lost for the road. They are the saints of the church. When a saint crosses over, he is lost to this world, and to the next one too. But what is worse, the world has lost him; it is orphaned! You know what it means to be a foundling; do not consign others to the fate of having neither father nor mother. Walk the road. Light the lamps until the sun comes of its own accord.'

'Yes,' I stuttered, thinking with horror of the terrible white road.

'Do you know what it means that you got back into your coffin?'

'No, father.'

'It means that for yet a little while you will share the fate of those who are buried alive.'

'Do you mean Mutschelknaus, the carpenter?' I asked in my childish way.

'I know no carpenter of that name; he has not yet become visible.'

'Nor his wife and ... and Ophelia?' I asked, feeling myself blush.

No; nor Ophelia either.'

'Strange,' I thought. 'They live just across the road, and he must see them every day.' For a while we were both silent, and then I suddenly burst out sobbing, 'But that is horrible! To be buried alive!'

'Nothing is horrible, my child, that you do for the sake of your soul. I, too, have been buried alive at times. On earth I have often met people who are wretched and in great need and who rail bitterly at the injustice of fate. Many of them sought comfort in the doctrine that came to us from Asia, the doctrine of the Karma which maintains that no being suffers unless it has sown the seed within itself in a former existence. Others seek comfort in the dogma of the unfathomable nature of God's designs. They all seek comfort, but none have found it. I have lit a lamp for such people by inserting a thought' — his smile as he said that was almost grim, and yet at the same time as friendly as ever — 'in their minds, but so delicately that they believe it came of its own accord. I ask them this question: "Would you accept the agony of dreaming tonight, as clearly as if it were reality, that you lived through a thousand years of unimaginable poverty, if I assured you now that as a reward you would find a sack of gold outside your door when you woke in the morning?" "Yes! Of course!" is the answer every time. "Then do not bemoan your fate. Are you sure that you did not choose this tormenting dream called life on earth which, at the worst, lasts seventy years, of your own free will, in the hope of finding something much more glorious than a miserable bag of money when you woke? Of course, if you sow a 'God with unfathomable designs' you will one day reap him as a malevolent devil.

"Take life less seriously and dreams more so, then things will improve, then the dream can become your leader instead of, as now, going round as a garish clown in the motley shreds of our daytime memories." Listen, my child. There is no such thing as a vacuum. That sentence conceals the secret that everyone must unveil who wants to be transformed from a perishable animal to an immortal consciousness. Only you must not apply the words merely to external nature; you must use them like a key to open up the spiritual realm; you must transform their meaning. Look at it like this: someone wants to walk, but his feet are held fast in the earth; what will happen if his will to walk does not weaken? His creative spirit, the primal force that was breathed into him at the beginning, will find other paths for him to tread, and that force within him that can walk without feet, will walk in spite of the earth, in spite of the obstacle.

'The creative will, man's divine inheritance, is a force of suction; this suction — you must understand it in a metaphorical sense! — would of necessity create a vacuum in the realm of first causes, if the expression of the will were not eventually followed by its fulfilment. See: a man is ill and wants to get better; as long as he resorts to medicines, the power of the spirit, which can heal better and more quickly than any medicine, will be paralysed. It is as if someone wanted to learn to write with the left hand: if he always uses the right, he will never learn to do it with the left. Every event that occurs in our life has its purpose; nothing is pointless; an illness says to a man, "Drive me away with the power of the spirit so that the power of the spirit will be strengthened and once more be lord over the material world, as it was before the Fall." Anyone who does not do that and relies on medicines alone has not grasped the meaning of life; he will remain a little boy playing truant. But anyone who can command with the field marshall's baton of the spirit, scorning the coarser weapons that only the common soldier uses, will rise again and again; however often death strikes him down, he will yet be a king in the end. That is why men should never weaken on the path to the goal they have set themselves; just as sleep is only a brief rest, so is death. You do not begin a task in order to abandon it, but to complete it. A task, however unimportant it appears, once begun and left half finished, corrodes the will with its poison, just as an unburied corpse pollutes the air of the whole house.

'The purpose of our life is the perfection of the soul; if you keep that goal firmly in your sights, and in your mind and your heart every time you begin or decide something, then you will find yourself possessed by a strange, unknown calm, and your destiny will change in an incomprehensible way. Anyone who creates as if he were immortal — not for the sake of the object of his desires, that is a goal for the spiritually blind, but for the sake of the temple of his soul — will see the day come, even if it is after thousands of years, when he can say, "I will it" and what he commands will be there, will happen, without needing time to ripen slowly. Only then will the point be reached where the long road ends. Then you can look the sun in the face without it burning your eyes. Then you can say, "I have found a goal because I sought none." Then the saints will be poor in understanding compared with you, for they will not know what you know: that eternity and rest can be the same as the road and the infinite.'

These last words were far beyond my comprehension; it was only much later, when my blood was cool and my body manly, that they reappeared, clear and alive. But that morning I heard them with a deaf ear; I just looked at Baron Jöcher and, in a sudden flash of recognition, I realised what it was that had struck me as different about him, an odd thing, his goitre was on the right side of his neck, instead of the left as usual.

Today it sounds ridiculous, but I was seized with a nameless horror: the room, the Baron, the bust of Dante on the shelf, myself, for one brief second everything was transformed for me into ghosts, so spectral and unreal that my heart froze in mortal fear.

That was the end of my experience that night. Immediately afterwards I awoke in my bed, trembling with fear. The daylight was bright behind the curtains. I ran to the window: a clear winter's morning! I went into the next room; the Baron was sitting there in his usual working clothes at his desk reading.

'You've slept in late this morning, my lad,' he called to me with a laugh when he saw me by the door, still in my nightshirt, my teeth chattering with inner cold. 'I had to go and put out the lamps in the town instead of you. The first time for many years. But what's the matter with you?'

A quick glance at his neck and the last drops of fear trickled out of my blood: his goitre was back on its usual left side and the bust of Dante was in the same place as ever. Another second, and the earth had once more swallowed up the dreamworld; there was an echo fading in my ear, as if the lid of the coffin had fallen to, and then everything was forgotten.

With growing haste, I told my foster-father everything that had happened to me; the only thing I held back was my meeting with the old carpenter, Mutschelknaus. Only at one point I asked by the way, 'Do you know Herr Mutschelknaus?'

'Of course,' he answered cheerfully. 'He lives down below. A poor, poor wretch, by the way.'

'And his daughter ... Fräulein Ophelia?'

'Yes, I know ... Ophelia as well,' said the Baron, with a sudden earnest air. He gave me a long, sad look, 'Ophelia as well.'

Quickly I went back to the nightwalk, for I could feel a blush spreading over my cheeks. 'Papa, in my dream, why did you have your ... your left neck on the other side?'

The Baron thought for a long time. When he began to speak, he kept searching for the right word, as if he found it difficult to adapt what he had to say to my still undeveloped understanding: "To make that clear to you, my son, I would have to give you an exceptionally complicated lecture lasting a whole week, and even then you wouldn't understand it. You'll have to content yourself with a few random thoughts I'll throw at you. Will you catch them? True teaching can only come from life or, better still, dreams.

'Learning to dream is thus the first stage of wisdom. The world can give you cleverness; wisdom flows from your dreaming, whether it is a waking "dream" (in which case we say, "something just occurred to me" or, "it has just dawned on me"), or a sleeping dream, in which we are instructed through symbolic images. Likewise all true art comes from the realm of dreams. The gift of invention as well. Men speak in words, dreams in living images. The fact that they are taken from the happenings of the day has deceived many into thinking they are meaningless; which they are, of course, if you don't pay them any attention! In that case, the organ through which we dream will atrophy, just like a limb we do not use, and a valuable guide will fall silent: the bridge to another life, that is of much greater value than earthly life, will collapse in ruins. Dreaming is the footbridge between waking and sleeping; it is also the footbridge between life and death.

'You mustn't take me for a great sage, my boy, just because last night my double told you so much that might seem marvellous to you. I have not yet reached the stage when I can claim that he and I are one and the same person. It is true, however, that I am more at home in that dreamland than many other people. I have become visible over there and lasting, so to speak, but I still always have to shut my eyes here when I want to open them over there, and vice versa. There are people for whom that is no longer necessary, but very, very few.

'You remember that you could not see yourself, and had neither body, nor hands, nor eyes, when you lay down in the coffin again on the white road? But the schoolboy couldn't see you, either! He walked right through you, as if you were empty air! Do you know where that came from? You did not take the memory of the form of your earthly body over to the other side. Only someone who can do that — as I have learnt to — is visible to himself on the other side. He will create for himself a second body in dreamland, which will later on even become visible to others, however strange that might sound to you at the moment. In order to achieve that, there are methods' — with a grin he pointed at the print of Leonardo's Last Supper — 'which I will teach you when your body is mature and no longer needs to be bound. Anyone who knows them is capable of raising a ghost. With some people this "becoming visible in the other realm" happens of its own accord, completely without method, but almost always only one part of them comes alive, usually the hand. That then often performs the most pointless acts, for the head is absent, and people who observe the effect cross themselves and talk of fiendish phantoms. You are thinking, how can a hand do something without its owner being aware of it? Have you never seen the tail of a lizard break off and writhe in apparent agony while the lizard stands by, in complete indifference? It is something like that.

'The realm over there is just as real,' ('or unreal,' he added in an aside) 'as this earthly realm. Each on its own is only a half, only together do they form a whole. You know the story of Siegfried: his sword was broken in two pieces; the cunning dwarf Alberich could not forge it together, because he was a creature of the earth, but Siegfried could. Siegfried's sword is a symbol of that double life: the way to weld it together into one piece is a secret one must know, if one wants to be a knight.

'The realm beyond is in fact even more real than this earthly one. The one is a reflection of the other, or rather, the earthly one is a reflection of "beyond", not vice versa. Anything that is on the right over there' — he pointed to his goitre — 'is on the left here. Now do you understand?

'That other man was my double. What he said to you I have only just now heard from your lips. It did not come from his knowledge, much less from mine; it came from yours!

'Yes, yes, my lad, don't stare at me like that, it came from yours! Or rather,' he ran his hand caressingly through my hair, 'from the knowledge of the Christopher within you! Anything I can tell you, as one human animal to another, comes out of human lips and goes into a human ear, and is forgotten when the brain decays. The only talk you can learn from, is from talking to — yourself! When you were talking to my double, you were talking to yourself! Anything a human being can tell you is, on the one hand, too little, and, on the other, too much. Sometimes it comes too soon, at others too late, and always when your soul is asleep. And now, my son,' he turned back to his desk, 'it's time you got dressed. You're surely not going to run around in your nightshirt all day?'

The Angel of the West Window

There is argument as to how far Meyrink is the author of the whole of The Angel of the West Window, *first published in 1927, and how much was written by his friend, F. A. Schmid Noerr, but it is generally dealt with as part of Meyrink's oeuvre. The novel is based on the life of the Elizabethan mathematician and astrologer, John Dee, and his skryer, Edward Kelley. At times it uses John Dee's 'diary' (Dee did actually leave an account of his dealings with 'some spirits'), at times a modern descendant, who has received his papers, becomes John Dee. The book is set partly in England and partly in Prague, where Dee went hoping for patronage from the Emperor Rudolf II.*

Extract from *The Angel of the West Window*: The Conjuration of the Angel of the West Window

The Conjuration of the Angel of the West Window

O the night of the Feast of the Purification of the Blessed Virgin! How deeply it is engraved on the memorial of my soul! Now all those hours of waiting, of feverish expectation are behind me, past and forgotten. A miracle, an unbelieveable miracle has been vouchsafed me from the world beyond. I am dumbfounded with wonder and amazement at the might and power of the glorious, thrice blessed Angel. Deep within my heart I have made apology to Kelley that I ever thought ill of him and that I saw the mote in my brother's eye and not the beam in mine own. He is an instrument of providence, that I now know and I shudder at the thought of it.

The days that preceded the night were a torment to me. Every day, I sent servants to London to enquire of the craftsmen that had contracted to make, according to Kelley's precise instructions, the table around which the five of us — Jane, Talbot, Price, myself and Kelley — were to sit when we conjured the Angel. It had to be made of pieces of costly sandalwood and laurel and greenheart and in the form of a five-pointed star. In the middle there was to be a large hole in the shape of a regular pentagon. Set in the edges were cabbalistic signs, seals and names in polished malachite and brown cairngorm. Now I am ashamed to the depths of my soul when I think of my miserable, mean-minded concern at the thought of the enormous sum of money this table would consume. Today I would tear out my eyes and use them as jewels to decorate the table if it were necessary.

And always the servants would return from London saying, tomorrow, the day after tomorrow. The table was never ready, there seemed to be a spell on it; for no reason this or that journeyman would suddenly fall ill and whilst working on it three had already died a sudden, inexplicable death, as if seized by the ghost of the plague.

I strode restlessly round the rooms of the castle, counting the minutes until the morning of the 21 November broke, dull and grey.

Price and Talbot were sleeping like winter marmots, a strange, heavy, dreamless slumber, as they later told me. Jane, too, had been nigh impossible to wake and she shivered with inner cold, as if taken by a fever in her sleep. My eyes alone were unresting; heat, unbearable heat coursed through my veins.

Days before, Kelley too had been seized with a mysterious unease; like some shy animal he avoided the sight of men; I saw him wander round the park in the twilight and start like a guilty thing surprised when steps approached. During the day he sat brooding on the stone benches, now here, now there, murmuring absent-mindedly to himself or shouting in an unknown language at the empty air, as if someone were standing there. When he awoke from this state it was but for minutes, and then he would ask breathlessly if all were prepared at last; and when I told him, despairing, that it was not, then he began to berate me with curses, which he would suddenly interrupt to return to his soliloquy ...

Finally, shortly after midday — I had not been able to force even one mouthful down, so wrought was I with the impatience and unrest of the long wait — I saw, on the brow of a distant hill, the carts and waggons of the London craftsmen approaching. In a few hours the parts — for it would have been impossible to bring it through the doors in one piece — had been assembled in the room prepared for it in the castle tower. As Kelley had ordered, three of the windows — to the north south and east — had already been bricked up and only the high, arched west window, a good sixty feet above the ground, remained open. On my orders the walls of the circular chamber had been hung with the pictures of my ancestors, dark with age; chief among them was to have been a portrait of the legendary Hywel Dda, from the brush — and the imagination — of an unknown master, but we had had to remove it, as Kelley flew into a wild rage the moment he saw it.

In the niches of the walls stood my tall silver candelabra with sturdy wax candles in them in preparation for the solemn conjuration. Like an actor memorising his part, I had spent much time walking up and down in the park to commit to memory the enigmatic, incomprehensible formulae that were needed to call up the Angel. Kelley had given them to me one morning and told me they had been handed to him, scratched on a strip of parchment, by a disembodied hand lacking a thumb. My mind immediately saw the terrible Bartlett Greene as he bit off his thumb and spat it into Bishop Bonner's face in the Tower. The memory sent a cold shiver down my spine, but I shook it off: had I not burnt the outlaw's present, the polished coal skrying-glass, and thus broken all bonds between us ...?

After much toil, the words had finally seeped into my blood so that they would come automatically to my lips when I opened them to pronounce the conjuration.

The five of us sat in silence in the great hall as the bell in the spire of the parish church tolled the third quarter before two — excitement had so sharpened my ear that the noise was almost painful to it. Then we climbed up the tower. The five-pointed table that almost filled the chamber shone bright in the light of the candles as Kelley, tottering as if he were drunk, lit them one after the other. Then we sat in order in the high-backed chairs. Two of the points of the pentagram were directed towards the west, where the clear moonlight and the ice-cold night air poured in through the open window. Jane and Kelley sat at these two points; I myself was sitting with my back to the east and my eye was drawn out into the wooded landscape, deep in shadow, through which the frosty paths and roads flowed like rivulets of spilt milk. On either side of me sat Price and Talbot in mute expectation. The candle flames flickered in the air, as if they too were restless. The moon, high in the sky, was hidden from view, but its bright light fell in dazzling cataracts on the white stones of the window-sill. The five-sided hole in the table gaped before me like a dark well-shaft.

We sat as still as the dead, though each one could surely hear his own heart thumping in his breast.

All at once Kelley seemed to fall into a deep sleep, for suddenly we could hear a snoring sound as he breathed. His face began to twitch, but that may only have been the light of the candles flickering over his features. I did not know whether to begin the conjuration or not, for I had expected to hear an order from Kelley. I tried to pronounce the formulae, but each time it was as if an invisible finger were laid upon my lips ... Is it all Kelley's imagination? I asked myself and was beginning to fall prey to doubt once more, when my mouth began to speak as if of its own accord and in a voice so deep and resonant that it seemed foreign to me, uttered the words of the evocation.

An icy numbness filled the room. The candles were suddenly as still as death, their flames rigid and giving off no light: you could break them off from the candles, I thought, break them off like withered ears of corn ... The pictures of my ancestors on the walls had become black chasms, like the openings into dark dungeons, and the disappearance of the portraits made me feel as if I was cut off from those who were there to protect me.

In the deathly silence a child's voice rang out:

'My name is Madini; I am a little girl from a poor family. I am the second youngest of the children; at home my mother has a babe at her breast.'

At the same time I saw hovering in the open air outside the window the figure of a pretty little girl of seven to nine years old; her long hair hung in ringlets over her forehead; her dress shimmered red and green and looked as if it were made from flakes of the jewel alexandrite, which appears green by day and at night blood red. Charming as the child looked at first sight, its appearance made a terrifying impression: it hovered outside the window, fluttering like taut, smooth silk, a shape without any physical depth, its features as if painted — a phantom in two dimensions. Is that the promised angel? I wondered, and a bitter disappointment fell upon me which the miracle of this inexplicable apparition could do nothing to lessen. Then Talbot leant over to me and whispered in a choking voice:

'It is my child; I am sure I recognise it. She died not long after birth. Do the dead continue to grow?'

There was so little pain and sorrow in my friend's voice that I felt sure he was as terrified as I was. Could it be an image, deep within him, that had been projected out into the air, that has somehow been released from his soul and taken visible form? But I immediately abandoned the thought as the phantom was obscured by a pale green pillar of light which suddenly shot up like a geyser through the hole in the table and then moulded itself into a human shape which yet had nothing human about it. It congealed into an emerald form, as translucent as beryl, and as hard — a hardness which seemed to gather and concentrate at its centre more perceptibly than in any earthly material. Arms detached themselves from the stone, a head, a neck. — And hands! Those hands! There was something about them that I could not quite pin down. For a long time I could not take my eyes off them until I saw it: the thumb on the right hand pointed outwards, it was the left-hand thumb. I will not say that this terrified me — why should it? But this apparently trivial detail emphasised the otherness, the ahuman nature of the gigantic being rising up before me even more than its miraculous, inexplicably tangible emergence from the green pillar of light.

The face, its eyes without lashes and set wide apart, was fixed beyond description. There was something fearful, paralysing, deadening and yet shatteringly sublime in its gaze which froze me to the bone. I could not see Jane, she was blocked by the figure of the Angel, but Talbot and Price seemed corpses, so deathly white were their faces.

The lips of the Angel were red as rubies and formed into a strange smile, turned up at the corners, where they tapered to a delicate point. The child before had seemed unnatural in its flatness, this gigantic creature was stupefying in its corporeal presence, which surpassed all earthly measure: there was not the slightest shadow cast by its garments to give it emphasis or perspective. Yet in spite of — or perhaps because of — that, it made me feel that until that point I had in my whole life on earth seen nothing but flat surfaces, when compared with the sight of this being from another world.

Was I the one who asked, 'Who are you?' Or was it Price? I cannot say. Without opening its lips, the Angel said, in a cold, piercing voice that sounded as if it were an echo from deep within my own breast:

'I am Il, the messenger of the West Gate.'

Talbot wanted to ask a question, but all he could bring out was incoherent babbling. Price pulled himself up straight; he wanted to ask a question but all he could do was babble too! I gathered all my strength to raise my eyes to the Angel's countenance, but I had to let them drop; I sensed I would die if I insisted. My head bowed, I asked in a stuttering voice:

'Il, All-powerful Being, you know that which my soul longs for. Grant me the secret of the stone! I would give my heart, I would give my blood — so fervently do I desire the metamorphosis from a human animal into a King, into one that has risen from the dead both here and beyond. I would understand St. Dunstan's book and its secrets! Make me into the one that I ... was destined to be!'

Time passed — it seemed an eternity. Deep sleep threatened to overcome me but I fought it with all the strength of my longing. The room resounded with words, as if the floor and walls were joining in:

'It is good that thou hast sought in the West, in the Green Realm. I am well pleased. It is in my mind that I shall grant thee the Stone.'

'When?' I screamed, almost consumed in wild, nameless joy.

'The day after tomorrow!' came the answer, syllable by syllable.

'The day after tomorrow!' My heart leapt up. 'The day after tomorrow!'

'Dost thou know who thou art?' asked the Angel.

'I? — I ... am John Dee.'

'You are? You are ... John Dee?!' the apparition repeated. The Angel said it in a piercing voice, even more piercing than before. I felt ... I dare not even think it: ... as if. .. no, I will not let it pass my lips as long as I have power over them, nor will I let my quill write it down whilst I have the strength to control it.

'John Dee thou art, Lord of the Manor of Gladhill and Master of the Spear of Hywel Dda, oh, I know thee well!!' came a shrill, mocking voice from the window. I sensed it was the spectral child outside speaking.

'He who has the Spear is the Victor!' — the words echoed from the mouth of the Green Angel. 'He who has the spear is called and chosen. The Watchers at the four Gates are all subject to him. But thou, follow ever thy brother Kelley. He is my instrument here on earth, he is appointed to lead thee over the abyss of pride. Him thou shouldst obey, whatever he demands. Inasmuch as the least of these my brethren demand it, grant it him, for I am he and thou grantest it unto me. Then I can be with thee, in thee and around thee until the end of time.'

'That I solemnly swear to you, Blessed Angel!' I replied, struck to the very marrow and trembling in every limb. 'I raise my hand and swear to you, even should I thereby perish!'

'Should ... perish!' came the echo from the walls.

There was a deathly hush in the chamber. I felt as if my oath were resounding through the depths of the cosmos. The candles flared up; the flames were horizontal as if in a blast of wind.

An icy cold that froze my fingers came from the Angel. With numbed lips I asked:

'Il, hallowed spirit, when shall I see you again? How can I see you when you are far from me?'

'Thou canst always see me in the coal-glass, but I cannot speak through it.'

'I have burned the coal,' I stammered, and I regretted that I had destroyed the skrying crystal in the presence of Gardner, my cursed assistant, for craven fear of Bartlett Greene.

'Shall I return it to you? John Dee ... heir to ... Hywel Dda?'

'Give it to me, mighty Il!' I beseeched him.

'Put thy hands together in prayer. To pray is to receive if ... a man ... has learnt to pray!'

'That I have,' I rejoiced. I placed my hands together — an object swelled up between my palms, pushing them apart. When I opened them, there was the coal skrying-glass!

'Thou hast burnt it. Through that it lost its old life; now it has thy life in it, John Dee. It is reborn and risen from the dead. Just like men, things live on too.'

I stared at the thing, full of astonishment. How marvellous are the ways of the invisible world. Not even the devouring fire of earth can bring destruction!

'I ... thank you ... Il ... I thank you!' I was about to stammer, but I was so moved that I could not speak. My voice was choked with tears. Then it burst out of me like a spring tide:

'And the stone? That too ... ?!'

'The ... day ... after ... tomorrow,' the whisper came as if from a great distance. The Angel had become a faint wisp and the child at the window seemed to my eye translucent, like milky glass. It hung in the air, lifeless as a scrap of silk. Then it sank back into the landscape, floated as greenish, shimmering mist to the ground and became a patch of meadow.

That was my first meeting with the Angel of the West Window.

After such favour, can fate hold any torment in store for me? Blest be the night of the feast of the Purification of the Virgin Mary.

We sat together for a long time and talked ecstatically of the wondrous occurrence. As if it were the greatest treasure in the world, I clutched

Bartlett Greene's — no, no: the Angel's coal crystal as a constant reminder that I had been found worthy of a miracle. My heart was full to bursting when I remembered the Angel's promise: The day after tomorrow!

Kelley lay in a deep sleep until the dawn appeared in a sky flushed red, as if smeared with blood from wounded clouds. In silence, shuffling like a weary old man, he went down the stairs without one glance at the rest of us.

How wrong is the common cry: Beware of him who bears the brand! I felt this as I watched the man with the ears cut off disappear down the stairs. 'He is an instrument of providence and ... I took him, my brother, for ... a criminal — — — I will practise humility,' I resolved. Practise humility ... and be worthy of the stone! —

One strange fact I learnt from Jane: I had assumed the Angel had stood with its back to her. To my surprise she told me that the face had been turned towards her the whole time, just as it had been turned towards me. She had heard what it had said, just as I had. Price spent his time trying to fathom how the miracle of the return of the coal had happened and what were the hidden laws behind it. He thought things were probably different than we, with our dull senses, supposed; perhaps they were not physical objects but visible manifestations of some unknown force. I did not listen to him! My heart was too full.

Talbot was silent. Perhaps he was thinking of his dead child.

Petroleum, Petroleum

> In order to secure to myself the priority of
> prophecy, I must point out that this story
> was written in 1903.
>
> Gustav Meyrink

On Friday, at midday, Dr Kunibald Jessegrim poured the strychnine solution gently into the stream.

A fish rose to the surface, dead, floating belly upwards.

You'd be as dead as that, by now, said Jessegrim to himself, and stretched, glad that he had emptied away his suicidal thoughts along with the poison.

Three times in his life he had looked Death in the eye in this way, and each time he had been locked back into life by a vague premonition that there was still some great deed, one wild, grand act of revenge waiting for him.

The first time he had wanted to put an end to it all was when his invention had been stolen, and then again ten years later, when he had been hounded out of his job because he had never given up pursuing the thief in order to expose him, and now, because — because — Kunibald Jessegrim groaned aloud as thoughts of his overwhelming misery welled up once more.

Everything had gone, everything he had depended on, everything that had once been dear to him.

And it was that blind, narrow-minded, baseless hatred of the crowd, driven by slogans to oppose everything that did not conform to dull mediocrity, that had done this to him.

To think of all the things he had undertaken, had thought of and suggested!

He had scarcely got going before he had to stop in the face of a 'Chinese wall' — the generality of obstinate humanity, and the cry of 'but...'

'The Scourge of God' — yes, that's the solution, Dear God Almighty make me a destroyer, an Attila! and the fury blazed up in Jessegrim's heart.

Tamburlaine, Genghis-Khan limping across Asia, and devastating the fields of Europe with his Golden Mongol Horde, the Vandal Kings, who found peace only on the ruins of Roman art — all these were of his kind, powerful brothers in barbarism, born in the same eagle's nest.

A monstrous, limitless affection for these creatures of Shiva grew in him. He felt that their dead spirits would stand by him, and another type of existence flashed into his body.

If he had been able to look into a mirror at that moment these miracles of transfiguration would no longer have presented a mystery.

Thus it is that the dark powers of nature surge into our blood, profoundly, and of a sudden.

Dr. Jessegrim was possessed of extensive knowledge. He was a chemist, and he found it easy enough to succeed.

In America such people get on well. It is no surprise that he was soon making money — a lot of money.

He had established himself in Tampico in Mexico, and made millions out of a lively trade in mescal, a new anaesthetic and social drug, whose preparation he had developed.

He owned four square miles of estates around Tampico, and the huge reserves of oil beneath them promised to multiply his wealth beyond measure.

But that was not the object for which his heart yearned.

The new year was approaching.

'Tomorrow is January 1st 1951, and those lazy creoles will have yet another reason for spending three days on the binge and dancing their fandangoes,' thought Dr. Jessegrim, looking down from his balcony at the tranquil ocean below.

'And it'll be hardly any better in Europe. The papers will be coming out in Austria about now — twice as fat as usual, and four times as stupid. A picture of the new year as a naked boy; a new calendar full of women in diaphanous clothes and holding cornucopias; notable statistics: on Tuesday at 35 minutes and 16 seconds past 11 it will be exactly 9 thousand million seconds since the inventor of double entry bookkeeping went to his eternal (and well-deserved) rest — and so on.'

Dr. Jessegrim sat and went on staring at the glassy sea, shimmering so strangely in the starlight, until midnight struck.

Midnight!

He took out his watch and wound it slowly, until his fingertips felt the resistance of the winder. He pressed gently against it, and then more strongly ... there, a slight click and the spring was broken. The watch stopped.

Dr. Jessegrim laughed a mocking laugh. 'That's how I shall twist your springs too, you ...'

A frightful explosion rocked the town. It echoed from far away in the south; the old seafarers reckoned its source would be found somewhere near the great peninsula between Tampico and Vera Cruz.

Nobody had seen any signs of fire, nor was there any indication from the lighthouses.

Thunder? At this season? And under a clear sky? Impossible. Probably an earthquake therefore.

Everyone made the sign of the cross. Only the landlords of the shebeens fell to cursing, for all their customers had deserted the bars, and had run to the hills behind the town where they told each other fantastic tales of their escape.

Dr. Jessegrim took no notice: he went into his study humming a little tune: farewell, my land of Tyrol ...

He was in a superb frame of mind as he fetched a map from the drawer and pricked it off with a pair of dividers, referring to his notebook and taking pleasure in the way everything fell into place. As far as Omaha, possibly even further to the north the oil-fields stretched, there couldn't be any dispute about that any more, and he knew now that underground the oil must be present in great lakes, bigger even than Hudson Bay.

He *knew* it: he had worked it out, he had spent twelve whole years on the calculations.

According to his view the whole of Mexico lay across a series of caverns under the earth, which in large measure, at least in so far as they were full of petroleum, were all interconnected. His life's work had been gradually to blast away any remaining dividing walls. For years he had employed armies of men at the work: what a mint of money that had cost!

All those millions he had made in the medical business had gone into it.

And if just once he had struck oil it would all have been in vain. The government would have stopped him blasting — they didn't like it anyway.

Tonight was the night when the last walls were to go: those against the sea, on the peninsula, and further north near St. Louis Potosi. The explosion would be automatically controlled.

Dr. Kunibald Jessegrim pocketed his few remaining thousand dollar bills, and drove off to the station. The express to New York left at four in the morning.

What else was there left to do in Mexico?

He was right: there it was in all the papers — the verbatim telegram from along the Mexican Gulf coast, abbreviated according to the international cable code:

'EXPLOSION CALFBRAIN BERRYMUSH' which approximately translates as 'Seasurface completely covered in oil; cause unknown, everything stinks. State governor.'

This interested the Yankees enormously, as the occurrence was without a doubt bound to make a great impression on the stock exchange and to push up the value of petroleum shares. And property dealing is the best part of life, after all!

The bankers of Wall Street, when questioned by the government about whether the event would cause a rise or a fall in the exchange shrugged their shoulders and declined to make a prediction before the cause of the phenomenon should be discovered; and in any case if the market reacted contrary to reason there would undoubtedly be a great deal of money to be made.

The news made no particular impression on European sentiment. In the first place they were covered by protective tariffs, and in the second place they were in the process of bringing in new laws, which involved the planned introduction of voluntary triennial numeric enforcement, together with the abolition of men's proper names, which was intended to stimulate patriotism and encourage a better attitude towards military service.

Meanwhile the oil was busily spewing out of the subterranean Mexican Basin into the sea, just as Dr. Jessegrim had predicted, forming an opalescent layer on the surface that spread further and further, and which, carried by the Gulf Stream, soon seemed to cover the entire ocean.

The shores were devastated and populations withdrew inland. What a shame about those flourishing cities!

And the sea took on a fearfully beautiful quality: a smooth surface, extending into infinity, glinting and shimmering in all sorts of colours, red, green and violet, and then again a deep, deep black, like images from a fantastic starscape.

The oil was thicker than petroleum customarily is, and in its contact with the salt water seemed to undergo no other change than that it slowly lost its smell.

The expert opinion was that a precise investigation of the cause of this phenomenon would be of great scientific value, and since Dr. Jessegrim's reputation (at least as a specialist in Mexican petroleum reserves) was well established, they lost no time in seeking his opinion as well.

This was brief and to the point, even if it did not deal with its subject in quite the expected way.

'If the oil continues to flow at the present rate, the entire oceanic surface of the planet will, by my estimation, be covered in 27-29 weeks, leading to a total cessation of rainfall in the future, since there will no longer be any opportunity for evaporation. In the best case it will only rain petroleum.'

This frivolous forecast aroused violent disapprobation and yet it appeared with every succeeding day to gain in probability, and as the invisible springs showed no signs of drying up, but on the contrary seemed to be augmenting in quite extraordinary fashion, a panic terror began to overcome the whole of humanity.

Every hour brought new reports from the observatories of Europe and America — even the Prague Observatory, which had so far contented itself with taking photographs of the moon, gradually began to focus on these new and extraordinary phenomena.

In the Old World nobody was talking about the new military proposal any longer, and the author of the draft law, Major Dressel Ritter von Glubinger ab Zinkski auf Trottelgrün sank into oblivion.

As always in confused times, when the signs of disaster stand ominously in the sky, the voices of discontent, who are never satisfied with the status quo, could be heard as they dared to question hallowed institutions.

'Down with the army, wasting our money! Waste, waste waste! Build machines, think of ways to save mankind in its desperate plight from the threat of petroleum!'

'But that won't do,' warned the more circumspect. 'You can't simply put so many millions of people out of a job!'

'What do you mean, out of a job? The troops only need to be paid off. Everyone of them has learned something, even if it's only the most elementary trade,' came back the reply.

'Oh yes, that's all very well for the men — but what are we to do with the officers?'

Now that was a significant argument.

For a long time arguments swayed back and forth, with no party gaining the upper hand, until the encoded message came via cable from New York: 'HEDGEHOG POUNDWISE PERITONITIS AMERICA', meaning: 'Oil flow increasing, situation extremely dangerous. Wire by return whether the smell is as bad with you. Regards. America.'

That was the last straw.

A poular demagogue, a wild fanatic rose up, mighty as a rock against the breakers, hypnotic, spurring the people on to the most ill-considered actions by his oratory.

'Away with these games! Let the soldiers go, and make the officers useful for once. Give them new uniforms if it makes them feel better — bright green with red spots, if it's my choice. Send them down to the beaches with blotting paper to mop up the oil, while the rest of us think of a way out of this frightful mess.'

The crowds shouted assent.

The counter-suggestion that such measures could hardly have any effect, and that it would be better to use chemical means found no favour.

'We know, we know all that,' came the reply. 'But what are we going to do with all those redundant officers, eh?'

Blamol

In truth, without deceit,
I say to you surely
As it is below, so is it above.

Tabula Smaragdina

The old cuttlefish was resting on a thick Blue Book that had come from a vessel that had sunk, and was slowly taking in the printed characters.

Landlubbers have absolutely no idea how busy a cuttlefish is all day.

This one had devoted himself wholeheartedly to medicine, and all day long, from morning to night, two poor little starfish were obliged to help him turn the pages, because they owed him so much money.

Around his corpulence, just where other people keep their waists, he wore a golden pince-nez: another piece of marine loot. The lenses were forced wide apart on either side, giving anyone who might look through them a disagreeably dizzy sensation.

All around was quiet.

Suddenly an octopus came lunging up, its baggy snout pointing eagerly ahead, its arms trailing in its wake like nothing so much as a bundle of sticks. It settled down beside the book, and waited for the old fellow to look up before composing an elaborate greeting and unwrapping a tin box from amongst its arms. 'The violet polyp from Turbot Alley, I presume,' observed old Sepia graciously. 'Yes, that's right, I knew your mother well, née von Octopus, (I say, Perch, just fetch me the *Almanach de Gophalopoda*, will you.) Now, what can I do for you, young polyp?'

'The inscription—read what it says,' oozed the other, embarrassed, pointing to the tin box. He had a rather slimy way of saying things

The cuttlefish stared hard at the box, like a prosecuting counsel, his eyes popping out.

'What is this I see — Blamol? This is a priceless find. Surely it comes from the Christmas Steamer that ran aground? Blamol! The new miracle cure — the more you take, the healthier you get!

'This must be opened at once: Perch, just dart off to the two lobsters over there, will you — you know, Coral Bank, Second Branch, the Scissors brothers — and hurry!'

The green sea-lily, who resided nearby, rushed over the moment she heard about the new medicine — oh, she really would like to try some, really and truly, she'd give anything!

And she undulated her several hundred tentacles in captivatingly languorous fashion, riveting everyone's eye upon her.

Sharks alive, was she beautiful! A big mouth, for sure, but that's often what makes a lady so exciting.

They were all gaping at her, so they missed the arrival of the two lobsters who were already busy at the tin, chattering to each other in their harsh, outlandish dialect. With a final gentle tap the tin fell apart.

Like a shower of hail the white pills swirled out and, lighter than cork, shot upwards and vanished.

'Catch them, catch them!' came the cry, and they all fell over in their haste, but none was quick enough. Only the lily was lucky enough to secure a single pill and she hastily stuffed it into her mouth.

Indignation all round: the least the Scissors brothers deserved was a box on the ear.

'You, Perch, I suppose you couldn't manage to watch what was going on? What's the point of your being my assistant?'

Everyone was left to swear and argue — all except for the octopus who, speechless with rage, was hammering away at a mussel with its clenched tentacles, enough to make the pearls squeak.

Suddenly there was a general silence: look at the lily!

She must have suffered a stroke: rigid and quite unable to move, with her tentacles stiffly extended, she could be heard gently whimpering.

The cuttlefish pulsed importantly over to her and commenced his examination with a mysterious air. With the aid of a pebble he palpated a tentacle or two and then probed further in. (Hm, hm, — Babynski's Reaction: disruption of the Pyramidal Channels.) Then with the edge of his wing he stroked the lily a few times across her cup, his eyes taking on as he did so an intense and penetrating quality. Finally, puffing himself up, he said in a grave tone: 'Lateral Chord Sclerosis — the lady is paralysed.'

'Is there anything we can do? What is your opinion? Please just help her — I'll go to the chemist's,' cried the good-natured seahorse.

'Help? Are you mad? Do you think I studied medicine in order to effect cures?' The cuttlefish was getting angrier. 'It seems to me you think I'm a barber. Are you trying to make fun of me? Perch, my hat and stick, if you please!"

One after another they all dispersed. 'The things that can happen to you in this life. It's awful, don't you think?'

The place emptied, soon leaving the perch grumpily casting about, looking for anything the others might have lost or forgotten.

Night descended upon the seabed. The rays of light, of which none knew whence they came nor whither they went, shimmered in the green water like a veil, tired, as though at the limit of exhaustion.

The poor sea-lily lay immobile, gazing at them with a heart full of bitterness as they rose and vanished into the distance far above. Yesterday at this time she had been fast asleep, curled up safely into a ball, and now — to have to die on the street, like a mere ... animal! Little pearls of air beaded her brow. And tomorrow was Christmas!

She fell to thinking about her husband, gadding about somewhere far away. Three months it was now since she had become a seagrass-widow. Really, it would have been no surprise if she had been unfaithful to him.

Oh, if only the seahorse had stayed with her!

She was so afraid!

It was getting so dark you could hardly see your own feelers in front of you.

Broad-shouldered night crept out from behind the stones and algae, devouring the pale shadows of the coral banks. Black shapes glided out like ghosts, with eyes aflame and luminously violet fins. Fishes of the Night! Hideous rays and sea-devils, going about their nefarious business in the darkness, lying murderously in wait amidst the wreckage of ships.

Stealthily, shiftily, mussels beckon to the belated traveller, inviting him all unwary to join in some gruesome vice amidst the soft pillows that can be glimpsed between their gently parted shells.

In the distance a dogfish barks.

Suddenly, a bright light flashes through the algal ribbons: a shining medusa appears, guiding some drunken revellers homewards — a pair of slick eels, with a couple of moray sluts twined round their fins. Two young salmon, gaudy in silver, have stopped to gaze at this scene of depraved intoxication. A dissolute verse can be heard ...

> Down where the green weed grew
> I asked when I had met her
> Did she want me to screw
> Her? 'Yes, oh yes, you'd better.'
> So down she bent
> And off I went
> Right where the green weed grew ...

'Out of my way, bloody salmon!' roars one of the eels, interrupting the song. Silversides bridles: 'Shut your trap! You'd do well to watch your language. Just because you think you're the only lot who were born on the right side of the Danube ...'

'Shh, shh,' the medusa pleads, 'watch your tongues, look who's over there!' They all fall quiet and gaze with some awe at a small group of frail, colourless figures making prim progress along the way.

Mike Mitchell

'Lancelets' someone whispers.

'? ? ? ?'

'Oh, very hoity-toity they are, Counsellors, diplomats and the like. Born to it. Real marvels of nature — no brain, no backbone: quite spineless.'

There ensues a minute or two of silent amazement before everyone swims away, this time quite peaceably.

The noises die away. Absolute silence descends.

Time passes. Midnight, the witching hour. Did we hear voices? Not shrimps, surely, at this time of night?

It's the Night Patrol: police crabs! What a noise they make with their armoured legs as they crunch across the sand, dragging their captives off to a place of security.

Woe betide anyone who falls into their clutches: no crime escapes them, and their lies stand on oath before the law.

Even the electric ray turns pale at their approach.

Lily's heart misses a beat in terror: here she is, a defenceless lady, out in the open! What if they catch sight of her? They'll drag her up before the beak in front of that old perjurer of a crab, the biggest crook in the sea, and then ... and then ...

Here they come, getting closer — they're just a step away; the cruel talons of ruin and disgrace are on the point of encircling her waist with their iron grip.

Suddenly the dark water shivers, the coral branches creak and shake like seaweed and a pale glow illumines the scene from afar.

Crabs, rays, sea-devils dart and scatter across the sand, pieces of rock break away and swirl up in the current.

A bluish, smoothly moving wall as big as all the world comes flying through the waters.

Nearer and nearer comes the phosphorescent light, the gigantic glowing wing of Tintorera, the demon of annihilation, comes sweeping up, stirring fiery chasm-deep whirlpools in the foaming water.

Everything becomes caught up in the spinning eddies.

The lily flies vertiginously up and down again over a landscape of emerald froth. Where now are the crabs, where the shame and dread? Raging destruction has come storming through the world, a bacchanal of death, a glorious dance for the prize of a soul.

The senses expire like a smoking flame.

Then next a frightful shuddering jolt, the eddies stand in the water, but continue to spin faster and faster, flinging down on to the sea floor everything they had previously torn up.

Many a fine armoured piece meets its Waterloo there.

When at last the lily awoke from her fainting fall she found herself lying on a bed of soft algae.

The gentle seahorse (who had taken the day off from work) was bending over her.

A cool morning stream fanned her face, and she looked up. She could hear the cackling of goose-barnacles and the cheerful bleating of a lamprey.

'You are quite safe here in my little house in the country' replied the seahorse to her look of enquiry, and gazing deep into her eyes. 'Please rest a little more, dear lady, it will do you good.'

But she could not, for all she tried. An indescribable feeling of nausea overwhelmed her.

'What a storm that was last night — my head is still swimming from all the commotion,' went on the seahorse chattily. 'By the way, can I tempt you to a spot of blubber — a really nice fat piece of juicy sailor-blubber?'

At the mere mention of the word the lily felt so ill that she was obliged to clamp her lips tight shut. But it was no use. She began to retch (the seahorse turned his head discreetly to one side), and in a moment had brought up the Blamol pill which, quite undigested, floated and vanished upwards in a cloud of bubbles.

Thank God the seahorse hadn't seen it.

The invalid suddenly felt as right as rain again. She curled herself up with contentment.

Wonder of wonders! She could curl up again, could move her limbs about, as before.

Ecstasy upon ecstasy!

The seahorse could feel bubbles of joy pricking his eyes. 'Christmas, it's really Christmas today!' he rejoiced. 'I must tell the cuttlefish at once: in the meanwhile you must have a really good long sleep.'

'What do you find so remarkable about the lily's sudden recovery, my dear Seahorse?' asked the cuttlefish, with a condescending smile. 'You are an enthusiast, my young friend. As a matter of principle I don't usually discuss medical matters with non-professionals (bring up a chair, Perch, for the gentleman), but I'll make an exception this time, and endeavour to match my mode of expression to your level of understanding as far as I can. So, you consider Blamol to be a poison, and you attribute the paralysis to its effects. What a mistake! I might add, by the way, that Blamol is now altogether passé, it is yesterday's panacea; today we usually recommend Idiotine Chloride: medical science strides eternally onwards. That the illness should have coincided with swallowing the pill was pure coincidence — it's well known that everything that happens in the world is coincidence — for in the first place Lateral Chord Sclerosis has a quite different set of causes (though discretion forbids me to name them), and secondly, Blamol works, like all such agents, not when you take it, but only when you spit it out — and then of course it's bound to be beneficial in its effects.

'And finally, as far as the cure is concerned, well, here we have a clear case of autosuggestion. In reality, — and by 'reality' I mean what Kant called the *thing in itself* — in reality the lady is just as ill as she was yesterday: she just doesn't notice it. It is precisely in the case of those with inferior mental powers that autosuggestion works so effectively. Of course I'm not implying anything by saying this — you know how highly I esteem the little woman at home:

> 'Give all honour to the ladies,
> They plait and weave ...'

as Schiller puts it.

But now, my young friend, enough of this, it will simply upset you unnecessarily. A propos — you will of course do me the honour? It is Christmas and — I'm getting married.'

'Who is he marrying, then?' he asked the Perch on the way out. 'You don't say — the blue mussel? But why not, though — just another one in it for the money.'

When, that evening, the lily arrived, somewhat late but with a glowing complexion, and leaning on the seahorse's fin, the congratulations were without end. Everyone gave her a hug, and even the veiled snails and the cockles who were acting as bridesmaids put their maidenly timidity aside in the warmth of their hearts.

It was a magnificent occasion, as only the rich can provide — the blue mussel's parents had millions after all, and they had even organised some phosphorescent sea-fire.

Four long oyster-banks had been laid out and the feast had lasted well over an hour, yet still more dainty dishes appeared. The perch went on steadily circulating with a glittering decanter (upside down, of course) of hundred year-old air, recovered from the cabin of a sunken wreck.

Everyone had become a little tipsy, and the toasts being drunk to the blue mussel and her bridegroom were being drowned out by the popping and clicking of dead men's fingers and the clatter of razorshells.

The seahorse and the lily were sitting at the far end of the table, quite in the shadows, hardly noticing their surroundings. From time to time he would squeeze one or other of her tentacles, and in return she rewarded him with a glance full of ardour.

Towards the end of the meal the band struck up with a song:

A joke, a kiss
For a married Miss
Is utter bliss;
It's quite what's done

> When you're having fun
> But he's got to be young ...

And their table-companions exchanged a sly wink. It would have been impossible not to suppose that everyone had their own ideas about what sort of liaisons were being quietly arranged here.

Dr. Cinderella's Plants

Do you see the little blackened bronze statue over there between the two lamps? That has been the cause of all the weird experiences I have had in recent years.

These phantom perturbations which have so drained my energy are all links in a chain which, if I pursue it back into the past, comes back every time to the same starting point: the bronze.

If I pretend to myself that there may be other causes of my anxieties, the image nevertheless recurs to me, like another milestone along the road.

But where this road is leading me — to ultimate illumination or to ever-increasing horror — I have no desire to know, wishing only to cling on to those occasions when for a few days I feel relief from my doom and can sense freedom until I am overcome by the next shock.

I unearthed the thing in the desert sands of Thebes one day as I was prodding about with my stick, and from the very first moment, as I was examining it more closely, I was struck with a morbid curiosity to know what the image might signify — I have never wanted to know anything quite so urgently.

In the beginning I would ask every explorer I met, but without success. Only one old Arabian collector seemed to have some idea about what it meant.

'A representation of an Egyptian hieroglyph,' he proposed; the unusual position of the arms of the figure must indicate some kind of mysterious ecstatic state.

I took the bronze with me back to Europe, and hardly an evening went by without my falling into the most remarkable reveries about its mystery.

An uncanny feeling would come over me on these occasions as I brooded on some poisonous and malevolent presence which was threatening, with malicious relish, to break out of its lifeless cocoon in order to fasten itself leechlike upon me, and to remain, like some incurable disease, as the dark tyrant of my life. Then one day, as I was concerned with quite a different matter, the thought which made sense of the whole riddle struck me with such force, and so unexpectedly, that I staggered under its impact.

Such shafts of illumination strike into our souls like meteors. We know not whence they come: we witness only their white-hot gleam as they fall.

It is almost like a feeling of fear — then — a slight — as — as if some alien ... What am I trying to say?! I'm sorry, sometimes I get so forgetful, especially since I've had to drag this lame leg along. Yes, well, the answer to my brooding thoughts appeared suddenly stark in front of my eyes: *imitation!*

And as if the one word had demolished a wall, I was overcome by the flood-waves of a realisation that that alone must be the key to all the mysteries of our existence.

An uncanny, automatic act of imitation, unconscious, perpetual, the hidden guide of every creature!

An omnipotent, mysterious guide — a masked pilot, silently stepping on board the ship of life in the grey of the dawn. Rising up out of those measureless chasms into which our soul delights to descend when sleep has closed the gates of day! And perhaps down there in those abysses of disembodied existence there stands the brazen image of a demon willing us to be like him, to shape ourselves in his likeness.

And this word: 'imitate', this brief call from the ether became a road for me, and I set out on it at that same moment. I took up the pose, raised both arms above my head in imitation of the statue, and lowered my fingers until the nails just brushed my scalp.

Nothing happened.

No change, either within me or round about me.

So as to make no mistake in my pose I looked more closely at the figure, and saw that the eyes were closed, as if in sleep.

I decided that I had had enough, broke off the exercise, and put further action off until nightfall. When that came I stilled the ticking of the clocks and lay down, reassuming the position of my arms and hands.

A few minutes passed in this state, but I cannot believe that I could have fallen asleep.

Suddenly there seemed to come echoing out from somewhere inside me a sound, as of a huge stone rumbling down into the depths.

And as if my consciousness were tumbling after it down a monstrous staircase, bouncing two, four, then eight and ever more steps at a time, my memory leaped back through my life, and the spectre of apparent death cloaked itself about me.

What then happened I will not say: none can say it.

People laugh at the idea that the Egyptians and Chaldaeans are supposed to have possessed a magic secret, guarded by uraeus snakes, and never betrayed by anyone of the thousands of initiates.

There are no oaths which can possibly bind so securely, we think.

And I, too, thought this once; but in that instant I understood.

It is an event in no way connected with human experience, where perceptions lie as it were one behind another, and there is no oath that binds the tongue — the merest thought of a hint at these things, here on this side, and it is enough to alert the vipers of life into taking aim to strike at your very heart.

So the great secret stays hidden, for it conceals itself and will remain a secret for as long as the world lasts.

But all that is merely incidental to the searing blow which has struck me down for ever. Even someone's superficial fate may be shifted on to a new track if his consciousness can break through the barriers of earthly perception for just one moment.

A fact, of which I am a living example.

Since that night, when I had that out-of-body experience (I can describe it in no other way), the course of my life has changed, and my existence, previously so unhurried, now reels from one inexplicable, horrific experience to another, towards some dark, unfathomable goal.

It is as if a devil's hand is measuring out my periods of lucidity in ever-diminishing quantities, thrusting into my path images of terror which grow in awfulness from one occasion to the next, as if slowly and stealthily to create a new and unheard-of form of madness in me, a form imperceptible to an outsider, unsuspected, known only through the nameless torment of its victim.

In the course of the next few days after the experiment with the hieroglyph I began to experience sensations which I took at first to be hallucinations. In the midst of all the sights and sounds of everyday I would become suddenly aware of strange roaring noises or jarring undertones in my ears, or catch sight of shimmering colours which I had never seen before.

Bizarre figures would appear, unheard and unseen by anyone else, acting out incomprehensible and unfathomable plots in shadowy gloom. They would shift their shapes, lie suddenly still as death, then slither down along the gutters in viscous elongation, or squat stupid and exhausted in dark doorways, as if drained of existence.

This condition of hypersensitive awareness does not persist — it waxes and wanes like the moon.

The steady decline of my interest in others, whose desires and hopes impinge on me only as if from a distance, suggests to me that my soul is engaged upon some dark journey, far far away from the rest of humanity.

At first I allowed these whispering voices filling the edges of my consciousness to lead me along. Now, I am like a beast of burden, strapped firmly into its harness and obliged to follow exactly the path along which I am being driven.

And so one night I was again dragged awake and forced to wander aimlessly through the silent alleyways of the Kleinseite, just for the sake of the impression that the antiquated houses make upon me.

This part of Prague is uncanny, like nowhere else in the world.

The bright light of day never reaches down here, nor yet is it ever quite as dark as night.

A dim, gloomy illumination emanates from somewhere or other, seeping down from the Hradschin on to the roofs of the city below, like a phosphorescent haze. You turn into a narrow lane, and see nothing: only a deathly darkness, until suddenly a spectral ray of light stabs into your eyes from a chink in a shutter, like a long, malevolent needle.

Then a house looms out of the fog — with decayed, drooping shoulders it stares vacantly up into the night sky out of blank lights set into the receding forehead of its sloping roof, like some animal wounded unto death.

Next door, another building leans inquisitively forward, glimmering windows peering down, searching eagerly through the depths of the well down below for any trace of the goldsmith's daughter who drowned there a century ago. And if you walk further on across the uneven cobbles and then suddenly turn to look back, you'll very likely catch sight of a pale and bloated visage staring after you from the corner — not at shoulder height, no, but quite low down, at about the level where you might expect to meet the gaze of a large dog.

There was nobody out in the streets.

Deathly still.

The ancient entries held their lips firmly clamped shut. I turned into Thungasse, where Countess Morzin has her great house.

There in the mist crouched a narrow building, no more than two windows broad, a disagreeable wall with a hectic pallor; and here I was gripped spellbound as I felt my mood of hypersensitivity rising within me.

Under such conditions I act spontaneously, as if driven by another will, and I scarcely know what the next moment will make me do.

So, in this state, I pushed open the door which had been merely standing ajar, and, passing down a passage, descended the stairs to the cellar, all as if I really belonged in this house.

At the bottom, the invisible rein holding me in check was relaxed and I was left standing in the darkness, painfully aware that I had done something entirely without purpose.

Why had I gone down there? Why hadn't I even thought of putting a stop to such a pointless idea? I was ill, patently ill, and I took comfort in the fact that it could be nothing else: the mysterious, uncanny force had nothing to do with it.

But in the next moment I realised that I had opened the door, entered the house and gone down the stairs without once bumping into anything, like someone who knew every step of the way: my hope evaporated on the instant.

My eyes slowly became accustomed to the darkness, and I looked about me.

There on one of the steps of the cellar stairs someone was sitting, How could I have got past without touching him?

I could only see the crouched figure rather indistinctly in the darkness.

A black beard covered a bare chest; the arms were bare too.

Only the legs seemed to be encased in trousers or perhaps a loincloth. There was something fearful about the position of his hands — they were so extraordinarily bent back, almost at right angles to the joint.

I stared at the man for a long time.

He sat there with such corpse-like rigidity that I had the sense that his outline had somehow become etched into the dark background, and that this image would remain until the house itself fell into ruin.

A cold shiver overcame me, and I went on down the twisting passage.

At one point I reached out to touch the wall. My fingers closed upon a splintered wooden trellis, such as creepers are trained on. They seemed indeed to be growing there in great profusion, for I almost got caught up in a maze of stalky tendrils.

The odd thing was that these plants (or whatever they were) felt warm to the touch and full of life — altogether they seemed to have a certain animal quality.

I put my hand out once more, but immediately snatched it back again: this time I had touched a round ball about the size of a walnut, which felt cold and which shrank away on the instant. Was it a beetle?

Just then a light flickered on somewhere, and for a second the wall in front of me was lit up.

Everything I had known of fear and horror up until then was as nothing to this moment.

Every fibre of my being shrieked out in indescribable terror. My paralysed vocal chords gave vent to a silent scream, which struck through me like a shaft of ice.

The entire wall, right up to the ceiling, was festooned with a network of twisted veins, from which hundreds of bulbous berry-eyes gazed out.

The one I had just fingered was still snapping back and forth, giving me a glance full of suspicion.

I felt faint, and staggered on for two or three more steps into the darkness. A cloud of different smells engulfed me, heavy, earthy, reeking of fungus and ailanthus.

My knees gave way and I beat the air about me. A little glowing ring appeared in front of me — the last dying gleam of an oil-lamp which flickered fitfully for a moment.

I leaped towards it and with trembling fingers turned the wick up, just in time to save the tiny sooty flame.

Then I swung round, holding the lamp protectively in front of me.

The room was empty.

On the table, where the lamp had been, there lay a longish object, glittering in the light.

My hand reached out to it, as for a weapon.

But it was no more than a light, crudely-made thing that I picked up.

Nothing moved, and I breathed a sigh of relief. Carefully, so as not to extinguish the flame, I ran the light along the wall. Everywhere the same wooden trellis-work and, as I could now clearly see, overgrown with veins, evidently all patched together, in which blood was coursing.

In amongst them countless eyeballs glistened horribly, sprouting alternately with hideous warty nodules like blackberries, and following me slowly with their gaze as I passed. Eyes of all sizes and colours, from brightly shining irises to the light blue tone of the eye of a dead horse, fixed immovably upwards. Some, shrunken and black, looked like over-ripe nightshade berries. The main stems twisted their way out of jars filled with blood, drawing up their juice by means of some unfathomable process.

I stumbled on shallow dishes filled with whitish fatty lumps in which toadstools were growing covered in a glossy sheen; toadstools of red flesh, that shrank away at a touch.

And all seemed to be parts of living bodies, fitted together with indescribable art, robbed of any human soul, and reduced merely to vegetative organisms.

I could see clearly that they were alive by the way that the pupils in the eyes narrowed when I brought the lamp closer. But who could be the devilish gardener who had planted this horrible orchard?

I remembered the man on the cellar steps.

I reached instinctively into my pocket for a weapon — any weapon — and felt the sharp object I had previously found. It glittered, bleak and scaly: a pine cone assembled out of a multitude of pink human fingernails.

With a shudder I dropped it and clenched my teeth: I must get out, out — even if the thing on the stairs should wake up and set about me!

And I was already on my way past him, ready to thrust him aside, when I realised he was dead, yellow as wax.

From his contorted hands the nails had been wrenched, and incisions in his chest and temples indicated that he had been a subject of dissection. In pushing past him I must have brushed him with my hand — he seemed to slip down a couple of steps towards me and then stood upright, his arms bent upwards, hands touching his forehead

Just like the Egyptian figure: the same pose, the very same pose!

The lamp smashed to the floor and I knew only that I had flung the door open to the street as the brazen demon of spasmodic cramp closed his fingers round my twitching heart.

Then, half-awake, I realised that the man must have been suspended by cords attached to his elbows: only by that means could he have been brought upright by slipping down the steps; and then, then I felt someone shaking me. 'Come on, the Inspector wants to see you.'

I was taken to a poorly-lit room, tobacco pipes ranged along the wall, a uniform coat hanging on a stand. It was a police station.

An officer was holding me upright.

The Inspector at the table stared past me. 'Have you taken his details?' he murmured.

'He had some visiting cards on him. We've taken those.' I heard the policeman reply.

'What were you up to in Thungasse in front of an open street door?'

Long pause.

'Hey, you!' warned the policeman, giving me a nudge.

I stammered something about a murder in the cellar of the house in Thungasse.

The policeman left the room.

The Inspector, still not bothering to give me a glance, embarked on a long speech, of which I heard very little.

'What are you talking about? Dr. Cinderella is a great scientist — Egyptologist — he is cultivating all sorts of new carnivorous plants — Nepenthes, Droseras and suchlike, I think, I don't know. — You should stay indoors at night.'

A door opened behind me; I turned to face a tall figure with a long heron's bill — an Egyptian Anubis.

The world went black in front of me as Anubis bowed to the Inspector and went up to him, whispering to me as he passed: 'Dr. Cinderella.'

Doctor Cinderella!

At that moment something important from the past came back into my mind and then immediately vanished again.

When I looked at Anubis once again he had become nothing more than an ordinary clerk with something birdlike about his features. He gave me my own visiting cards back. On them was printed:

Dr. Cinderella.

The Inspector suddenly looked straight at me, and I could hear him saying: 'You're the Doctor himself. You should stay at home at night.'

And the clerk led me out. As I went I brushed against the coat hanging on the stand.

It subsided to the floor, leaving the arms hanging.

On the whitewashed wall behind, its shadow raised its arms aloft, as it attempted awkwardly to take up the pose of the Egyptian statuette.

You know, that was my last experience, three weeks ago. I've had a stroke since then: I have two separate sides to my face, and I have to drag my left leg along.

I have looked in vain for that narrow, fevered little house, and down at the station nobody admits to knowing anything about that night.

The Ring of Saturn

One step at a time they came, disciples feeling their way up the circular stair.

Inside the Observatory the darkness came billowing up into the round space, while from above starlight trickled down along the polished brass tubes of the telescope in thin cold streaks. If you turned your head slowly, allowing your gaze to traverse the darkness, you could see it flying off in showers of sparks from the metal pendulums suspended from the roof.

The blackness of the floor swallowed up the glittering drops as they slid off the smooth surface of the shining instruments.

'The Master's concentrating on Saturn today,' said Wijkander after a while, pointing to the great telescope that thrust through the open roof panel like the stiff, damp feeler of a vast golden snail from out of the night sky.

None of the disciples contradicted him: they weren't even surprised when they looked into the eyepiece and found his assertion confirmed.

'It's a complete mystery to me. How can anyone in this near-darkness possibly know what the instrument is pointed at, merely by looking at its position?' said one, bemused.

'How can you be so sure, Axel?'

'I can just sense that the room is filled with the suffocating influence of Saturn, Dr Mohini. Believe me, telescopes really do suck at the stars like leeches, funnelling their rays, visible and invisible, down into the whirling focus of their lenses.

'Whoever is prepared, as I have been for a long time now, to stay awake through the night, can learn to detect and to distinguish the fine and imperceptible breath of each star, to note its ebb and flow, and how it can silently insinuate itself into our brains, filling them with changeling intentions; will feel these treacherous forces wrestling in enmity with one another as they seek to command our ship of fortune ... He will learn, too, to dream while awake, and to observe how at certain times of the night the soulless shades of dead planets come sliding into the realm of visibility, eager for life, exchanging mysterious confidences among themselves by means of strangely tentative gestures, instilling an uncertain and indefinable horror into our souls. . .

But do turn the lights on — we may easily upset the instruments on the tables in the dark like this, and the Master has never allowed things to get out of place.'

One of the companions found his way to the wall and felt for the switch, his fingertips brushing gently but audibly against the sides of the recess. Then suddenly it was light and the brassy yellow lustre of the telescopes and pendant metal shouted aloud across the emptiness.

The night sky, which until that moment had lain in yielding satin embrace with the window-panes, suddenly leaped away and hid its face far, far above in the icy wastes behind the stars.

'There is the big, round flask, Doctor,' said Wijkander, 'which I spoke to you about yesterday, and which the Master has been using for his latest experiment. And these two metal terminals you see here on the wall supply the alternating current, or Hertz Waves, to envelop the flask in an electric field.

'You promised us, Doctor, to maintain an absolute discretion about anything you might witness, and to give us the benefit of your wisdom and experience as a doctor in the mad-house, as far as you can.

'Now, when the Master comes up he will suppose himself to be unobserved, and will begin those procedures which I hinted at but cannot explain in more detail. Do you really think that you will be able to remain unaffected by his actions and simply by means of silent observation of his overall behaviour be able to tell us whether madness is altogether out of the question?

'On the other hand will you be able to suppress your scientific

299

prejudices so far as to concede, if necessary, that here is a state of mind unknown to you, the condition of high intoxication known as a Turya Trance — something indeed that science has never seen, but which is certainly not madness?

'Will you have the courage openly to admit that, Doctor? You see, it is only our love for the Master and our desire to protect him from harm that has persuaded us to take the grave step of bringing you here and obliging you to witness events that perhaps have never been seen by the eye of an uninitiate.'

Doctor Mohini considered. 'I shall in all honesty do what I can, and be mindful of everything you told me and required of me yesterday, but when I think carefully about it all it puts my head in a spin — can there really be a whole branch of knowledge, a truly secret wisdom, which purports to have explored and conquered such an immeasurably vast field, yet of whose very existence we haven't even heard?

'You're speaking there not just about magic, black and white, but making mention also of the secrets of a hidden green realm, and of the invisible inhabitants of a violet world!

'You yourself, you say, are engaged in violet magic, — you say that you belong to an ancient fraternity that has preserved its secrets and arcana since the dawn of prehistory.

'And you speak of the "soul" as of something proven! As if it is supposed to be some kind of fine substantive vortex, possessing a precise consciousness!

'And not only that — your Master is supposed to have trapped such a soul in that glass jar there, by wrapping it round with your Hertzian oscillation?!

'I can't help it, but I find the whole thing, God knows, pure ...'

Axel Wijkander pushed his chair impatiently aside and strode across to the great telescope, where he applied his eye peevishly to the lens.

'But what more can we say, Dr Mohini?' responded one of the friends at last, with some hesitation. 'It is like that: the Master did keep a human soul isolated in the flask for a long time; he managed to strip off its constricting layers one at a time, like peeling the skins off an onion, so as to refine its powers, until one day it managed to seep through the glass past the electric field, and escaped!'

At that moment the speaker was interrupted by a loud exclamation, and they all looked up in surprise.

Wijkander gasped for breath: 'A ring — a *jagged* ring, whitish, with holes in it — it's unbelievable, unheard of!' he cried, 'A new ring of Saturn has appeared!'

One after another they looked in the glass with amazement.

Dr Mohini was not an astronomer, and knew neither how to interpret nor to assess the immense significance of such a phenomenon: the formation of a new ring around Saturn. He had scarcely begun to ask his questions when a heavy tread made itself heard ascending the spiral stair. 'For Heaven's sake, get to your places, — turn the light out, the Master's coming!' ordered Wijkander urgently. 'And you, doctor, stay in that alcove, whatever happens, do you hear? If the Master sees you, it's all up!'

A moment later the Observatory was once more dark and silent.

The steps came nearer and nearer, and a figure dressed in a white silk robe appeared and lit a tiny lamp. A bright little circle of light illuminated the table.

'It breaks my heart,' whispered Wijkander to his neighbour. 'Poor, poor Master. See how his face is twisted with sorrow!'

The old man made his way to the telescope where, having applied his eye to the glass, he stood, gazing intently. After a long interval he withdrew and shuffled unsteadily back to the table like a broken man.

'It's getting bigger by the hour!' he groaned, burying his face in his hands in his anguish. 'And now it's growing points: this is frightful!'

Thus he sat for what seemed an age, whilst his followers wept silently in their hiding-places.

Finally he roused himself, and with a movement of sudden decision got up and rolled the flask closer to the telescope. Beside it he placed three objects, whose precise nature it was impossible to define.

Then he kneeled stiffly in the middle of the room, and started to twist and turn, using his arms and torso, into all sorts of odd contorted shapes resembling geometrical figures and angles, while at the same time he started mumbling in a monotone, the most distinguishing feature of which was an occasional long-drawn-out wailing sound.

'Almighty God, have pity on his soul — it's the conjuration of Typhon,' gasped Wijkander in a horrified whisper. 'He's trying to force the escaped soul back from outer space. If he fails, it's suicide; come brothers, when I give the sign it's time to act. And hold on tight to your hearts — even the proximity of Typhon will burst your heart-ventricles!'

The adept was still on his knees, immobile, while the sounds grew ever louder and more plaintive.

The little flame on the table grew dull and began to smoke, glimmering through the room like a burning eye, and it seemed as if its light as it flickered almost imperceptibly was taking on a greenish-violet hue.

The magician ceased his muttering; only the long wails continued at regular intervals, enough to freeze the very marrow of one's bones. There was no other sound. Silence, fearful and portentous, like the gnawing anguish of death.

A change in the atmosphere became apparent, as if everything all round had collapsed into ashes, as if the whole room were hurtling downwards, but in an indefinable direction, ever deeper, down into the suffocating realm of the past.

Then suddenly there is an interruption: a sequence of slithery slapping sounds, as some invisible thing, dripping wet, patters muddily with short, quick steps across the room. Flat shapes of hands, shimmering with a violet glow, materialise on the floor, slipping uncertainly to and fro, searching for something, attempting to raise themselves out of their two-dimensional existence, to embody themselves, before flopping back, exhausted. Pale, shadowy beings, dreadful decerebrated remnants of the dead have detached themselves from the walls and slide about, mindless, purposeless, half conscious and with the stumbling, halting gait of idiotic cripples. They puff their cheeks out with manic, vacant grins — slowly, very slowly and furtively, as if trying to conceal some inexplicable but deadly purpose, or else they stare craftily into space before lunging forwards in a sudden movement, like snakes.

Bloated bodies come floating silently down from the ceiling and then uncoil and crawl away — these are the horrible white spider-forms that inhabit the spheres of suicides and which with mutilated cross-shapes spin the web of the past which grows unceasingly from hour to each succeeding hour.

An icy fear sweeps across the room — the intangible that lies beyond all thought and comprehension, the choking fear of death that has lost its root and origin and no longer rests on any cause, the formless mother of horror.

A dull thud echoes across the floor as Dr Mohini falls dead.

His face has been twisted round back to front; his mouth gapes wide open. Wijkander yells again: 'Keep a tight hold on your hearts, Typhon is ...' as all at once a cacophony of events erupts.

The great flask shatters into a thousand misshapen shards, and the walls begin to glow with an eerie phosphorescent light. Around the edges of the skylights and in the window-niches an odd form of decomposition has set in, converting the hard stone into a bloated, spongy mass, like the flesh of bloodless, decayed and toothless gums, and licking across the walls and ceilings with the rapidity of a spreading flame.

The adept staggers to his feet, and in his confusion has seized a sacrificial knife, plunging it into his chest. His acolytes manage to stay his hand, but the damage is done: the deep wound gapes open and life trickles away — they cannot close it up again.

The brilliance of the electric lights has once again taken possession of the circular compass of the Observatory: the spiders, the shadows and the corruption have vanished.

But the flask remains in shattered pieces, there are obvious scorch marks on the floor, and the Master still lies bleeding to death on a mat. They have sought in vain for the knife. Beneath the telescope, limbs contorted, lies the body of Mohini, chest down. His face, twisted upwards, grins grotesquely at the roof reflecting all the horror of death.

The disciples gather round the spot where the Master rests. He gently brushes aside their pleas to stay quiet: 'Let me speak, and do not grieve. No one can save me now, and my soul longs to complete that which was impossible while it was trapped in my corporeal state.

'Did you not see how the breath of corruption has touched this building? Another instant, and it would have become substance, as a fog solidifies into hoar-frost, and the whole Observatory and everything in it would have turned to mould and dust.

'Those burns there on the floor were caused by the denizens of the abyss, swollen with hate, desperately trying to reach my soul. And just as these marks you can see are burned into the wood and stone, their other actions would have become visible and permanent if you had not intervened so bravely.

'For everything on earth that is, as the fools would have it, "permanent", was once no more than mere shadow — a ghost, visible or invisible, and is now still nothing more than a *solidified* ghost.

'For that reason, everything, be it beautiful or ugly, sublime, good or evil, serene though with death in its heart or alternatively, sad though harbouring secret happiness — all these things have something spectral about them.

'It may be only a few who have the gift of detecting the ghostly quality of the world: it is there nevertheless, eternal and unchanging.

'Now, it is a basic doctrine of our brotherhood that we should try to scale the precipitous cliffs of life in order to reach that pinnacle where the Great Magician stands with all his mirrors, conjuring up the whole world below out of deceptive reflections.

'See, I have wrestled to achieve ultimate wisdom; I have sought out some human existence or other, to kill it in order to examine its soul. I wished to sacrifice some truly useless individual, so I went about among the people, men and women, thinking that such a one would be simple to find.

'With the joyous expectation of certainty I visited lawyers, doctors, soldiers — I nearly found one in the ranks of schoolteachers — so very nearly!

'But it was always only nearly — there was always some little mark, some tiny secret sign on them, which forced me to loosen my grip.

'Then came a moment when at last I found what I was looking for. But it was not an individual: it was a whole group.

'It was like uncovering an army of woodlice, sheltering underneath an old pot in the cellar.

'Clergywives!

'The very thing!

'I spied on a whole gaggle of clergywives, watching them as they busied themselves at their "good works", holding meetings in support of "education for the benighted classes" or knitting horrible warm stockings and protestant cotton gloves to aid the modesty of poor little piccaninnies, who might otherwise enjoy their God-given nakedness. And then just think how they pester us with their exhortations to save bottle-tops, old corks, paper, bent nails and that sort of rubbish — waste not, want not!

'And then when I saw that they were about to hatch out new schemes for yet more missionary societies, and to water down the mysteries of the scriptures with the scourings of their "moral" sewage, the cup of my fury ran over at last.

'One of them, a real flax-blonde "German" thing — in fact a genuine outgrowth of the rural Slavonic underbrush — was all ready for the chop when I realised that she was — "great with child" — and Moses' old law obliged me to desist.

'I caught another one — ten more — a hundred — and every one of them was in the same interesting condition!

'So then I put myself on the alert day and night, always ready to pounce, and at last I managed to lay my hands on one just at the right moment as she was coming out of the maternity ward.

'A real silky Saxon pussy that was, with great big blue goose-eyes.

'I kept her locked up for another nine months, to be on the safe side, just in case there was anything more to come in the way of parthenogenesis or perhaps budding, such as you get with deep-sea molluscs for instance.

'In those moments of her captivity when I was not directly watching her she wrote a great thick book: *Fond Thoughts for our German Daughters on the Occasion of their Reception into Adulthood*. But I managed to intercept it in time and incinerate it in the oxy-hydrogen compressor.

'I had at last succeeded in separating soul from body, and secured it in the flask, but my suspicions were aroused one day when I noticed an odd smell of goat's milk, and before I was able to readjust the Hertz Oscillator which had obviously stopped working for a few moments, the catastrophe had occurred and my *anima pastoris* had irrevocably escaped.

'I had immediate resort to the most powerful means of luring it back: I hung a pair of pink flannel knickers (Llama Brand) out on the window-sill, alongside an ivory backscratcher and a volume of poetry bound in cyanide-blue and embellished on the cover with golden knobs, but it was all in vain!

'I had recourse to the laws of occult telenergy — again it was to no avail!

'A distilled soul is hardly likely to allow itself to get caught! And now it's floating freely about in space, teaching the innocent souls of other planets the infernal secrets of female handicrafts: I found today that it had even managed *to crochet a new ring round Saturn*.

'That really was the last straw. I thought things through, and cudgelled my brain for a solution until I came up with two possibilities: either to use deliberate provocation, as in the case of Scylla, or to act in an opposite sense, like Charybdis.

'You are familiar with that brilliant statement by the great Johannes Müller: "When the retina of the eye is stimulated by light, pressure, heat, electricity or any other irritation, the corresponding sensations are not specifically those of light, pressure, heat, electricity etc., but merely sensations of *sight*; and when the skin is illuminated, pressed, bombarded with sound or electrified, only *feeling* and its concomitants are generated." This irrefutable law holds here too — for if you apply a stimulus to the clergywife's essential nucleus, no matter by what means, it *will start crocheting*; if however it is left undisturbed' — and here the Master's tones grew faint and hollow — '*it merely reproduces.*'

And with these words he sank back, lifeless.

Axel Wijkander clasped his hands together, deeply moved. 'Let us pray, brothers. He has passed on, on to the tranquil realm. May his soul rest in peace and joy for ever!'

Vivo: The Life of Gustav Meyrink

Extracts from Chapter 4 of *Vivo: The Life of Gustav Meyrink —* 'The Duel Affair' and 'Prison'

The Duel Affair

Duelling remained widespread in the Austro-Hungarian Empire up to the First World War, long after it had disappeared in Britain — and also long after it had been made illegal in Austria. Its illegality did not apply to duels between army officers, for whom it remained a 'sacred obligation', and the laws were not enforced if an officer was involved. An officer who killed a civilian was invariably pardoned by the Emperor. Duels were taken seriously and could result in the death of one party. Mark Twain commented: 'This pastime is as common in Austria today as it is in France. But with this difference — that here in the Austrian states the duel is dangerous, while in France it is not. Here it is tragedy, in France it is comedy.'[15]

All sources agree that Meyrink was a renowned duellist. As there appears to be no report of an actual duel, this presumably refers to his skill with the sabre. In the events referred to as the 'duel affair' he issued a challenge — or challenges; Strelka says he issued a public insult to the whole of the Prague officer corps and challenged any officer who sided with his opponents — but it was not accepted.

As with many aspects of Meyrink's life, there are conflicting accounts of this business. Documents in the Meyrinkiana archives in Munich suggest the following course of events.

The matter arose, Meyrink explained in a declaration of December 1901, 'because Doctor Bauer deeply insulted me behind my back, at a time when he knew I was dangerously ill and therefore thought I could not defend myself.' Bauer rejected Meyrink's challenge on

---

15 Mark Twain: *Europe and Elsewhere,* New York and London, 1923, p. 225.

the grounds that, being illegitimate, he was incapable of 'giving satisfaction'. Meyrink regarded that as a further insult and took the matter to the military tribunal dealing with matters of honour. The tribunal upheld Dr Bauer's interpretation and declared Meyrink 'incapable of giving satisfaction'. Meyrink produced a document from the police stating that 'nothing to his disadvantage was known to them' and accused the chairman of the tribunal, a Captain Budiner, of lying. At the same time he consulted the authors of the military code of honour, who declared the decision of the tribunal invalid (one of them later withdrew his statement). In the meantime Captain Budiner and another officer brought a case of libel against Meyrink, which they won. Meyrink was sentenced to fourteen days in prison, which was commuted to a fine. Meyrink, however, refused to accept this and appealed, claiming there had been collusion between Budiner and a policeman called Olic. Ten days later, on 18 January 1902, he was arrested on suspicion of fraud. He was kept in prison, awaiting trial, until 3 March; the arguments with the military honour tribunal continued for another year, until March 1903. Lube (182) states that Dr Bauer always said he could not attend because of work commitments, so that no conclusion was ever reached.

There is another version of the initial cause of the challenge that led to all the complications. According to Eduard Frank[16] it all started when a Herr Ganghofer, who belonged to the same rowing club as Meyrink, did not greet his wife when they met in the street. Meyrink remonstrated and eventually issued a challenge. From that point on the versions are the same. In another place Frank claims that Meyrink's future brother-in-law 'was his bitterest enemy'. He does not relate that directly to the duel affair, but others must have done so, since Meyrink's second wife felt it necessary to issue a denial, in a letter to van Buskirk, presumably in the 1950s: 'There is no truth in the stories of the insult to his first wife, an argument with my brother.'

---

16 In his afterword to *Fledermäuse*, p. 423; there is a further variant in: *Prager Pitaval* (Berlin, 1931, pp. 326-8) by the journalist Egon Erwin Kisch; a long extract is printed in *Fledermäuse*, pp. 442-4.

The Ganghofer story tends to degenerate into vague assertions and the documents indicate that Dr Bauer was the person involved in the 'honour tribunal' case. Frank does name Meyrink's seconds, a Count Resseguier and a Herr Kolischer, though they could have been his seconds against Bauer. What this whole affair does indicate is how touchy Meyrink was about his personal standing, presumably because of his illegitimate birth. His submissions on the matter, as in other cases, are detailed and emphatic, full of underlinings, suggesting an obsessive side to his nature. A newspaper report of his arrest said, not without a touch of schadenfreude, 'It has long been no secret for many people that Meyer, who is so touchy in certain respects, so determined in defence of his honour, is anything but a gentleman.'[17] Given Meyrink's prickliness, it is quite possible that there was another affair involving Ganghofer, which became confused in some minds with the real cause célèbre.

The duel affair was the beginning of the end of Meyrink's period in Prague and it does bring out a number of aspects of his life there: his dubious standing because of his illegitimacy and his consequent extreme sensitivity about his personal honour; the contradiction between his desire to be accepted by the upper reaches of society and his contempt for and deliberate flouting of certain elements within it; his reputation as an athlete, especially as a swordsman. There is even, in a story related by Ursula von Mangoldt, a connection between Meyrink's duelling and his dabbling in magic. Mocked for being a bastard, he would react aggressively with a challenge. Once an army officer lodged an official complaint and Meyrink was arrested (one of Meyrink's complaints to the honour tribunal was that an officer had reported a possible duel to the police, leading to him being warned and threatened with deportation). Shortly before being taken to prison he had buried an egg underneath an elder bush, an ancient form of magic. As it rotted, the egg was supposed to satisfy the demons of the world below and alter the balance between him and the officer at the place where the duel was to take place. Three days later, while he was waiting in his cell for the duel, the

17 *Bohemia*, 19.1.1902.

news came that the officer had been fatally wounded in another duel. Meyrink was released. When he dug up the egg, only the shell was left. The contents had not rotted, they had completely disappeared.[18]

---

18 Ursula von Mangoldt: *Auf der Schwelle zwischen Gestern und Morgen*, Weilheim, 1963, p. 97.

Prison

Although there is no actual documentary evidence, it seems probable and is generally assumed that Meyrink's arrest was instigated by the two army officers involved in the dispute, in collusion with a police officer. It was either an act of revenge on the part of the officers or a way of rendering Meyrink hors de combat — or both. It was greeted in some parts of the press with the kind of response that would lead to an expensive libel action today; a newspaper article of 1927 on the case even suggests that the rumours about Meyrink's actions were deliberately leaked to the press, presumably from official sources (see the reference to 'statements from the authorities' in one of the articles quoted below). The report in *Bohemia* quoted above continued:

> That Gustav Meyer's financial situation was not exactly sound was at least known to those who had to resort to distraint against him and only managed to recover their money with great difficulty or not at all. It happened more than once that Meyer, in order to conceal the fact that he did not even have a few stocks and shares, banknotes or coins for his window display, simply had the window repaired... He naturally needed large funds to finance his normal lifestyle and he was truly excellent at acquiring these, if not always by means of pure, honest banking business. Gustav Meyer was a 'spiritualist' and that explains why he had many women among his depositors. A horde of his agents travelled round Bohemia persuading credulous people to entrust their money to banker Meyer. They were told he was the son of a sovereign,

> his business was the leading Christian bank in Prague
> and his sole aim was to help the poor through skilful
> speculations... In all this Meyer was very cautious in
> his choice of customers; he sought them among the
> kind of people of whom he knew that for the sake of
> their name they would rather lose all their money than
> take legal action against him, in order to avoid trouble
> with the police and the courts.

All accounts name the key figure in the accusations that led to
Meyrink's imprisonment on suspicion of fraud as a senior police
officer called Olic. According to the writer and journalist, Egon Erwin
Kisch, who, together with Paul Leppin, is one of the main sources
for this, in his appeal against the decision in the libel case brought
by the two officers, Meyrink suggested there had been some kind of
collusion between one of the officers and Olic. In the libel trial there
had been suggestions that some of Meyrink's bank dealings were
rather dubious and Olic used this to instigate the investigation. Some
sources also claim that Olic fancied the woman who later became
Meyrink's second wife, Mena Bernt, who was appearing as a singer
in the café chantant of a Prague hotel. It is interesting, though entirely
irrelevant, that Guillaume Apollinaire, in a piece called 'Le passant
de Prague' (The Passer-by in Prague) set in March 1902, says that
'the ground floor of the hotel I had been told about was occupied by
a café chantant'.[19] Could he have observed Mena singing there?

Meyrink was kept in prison for the two and a half months the
investigation lasted. Kisch claims that three hundred witnesses were
heard. All sorts of accusations were made: people who had put their
money in Meyrink's bank could not get it back; he used his customers'
stocks and shares for his own speculations, and, of course, that he
used his occult powers to influence customers. Another accusation,
that he claimed to be the son of Ludwig II of Bavaria, led to a search
of his apartment.

---

19 Guillaume Apollinaire: 'Le passant de Prague' in: *L'Hérésiarque et Cie*, Paris,
1967, p. 11.

There are also stories of bribed witnesses. Leppin says a Hungarian was put forward to claim he had deposited a share certificate with Meyrink, but when he asked for it back, Meyrink claimed never to have had it. Another version is that it was a woman who had deposited a security with Meyrink, which had disappeared. When asked for the serial number, she could not remember it and when asked to describe the shape and colour of the document she realised the game was up and made herself scarce.

In the end Meyrink was cleared of all charges. Max Brod's father was one of those who examined the books of Meyrink's bank:

> Enemies... had accused him of dishonesty in his business affairs and reported him to the state prosecutor's office. Quite unjustly, as my father told me. And he ought to have known, for he was an accountant, at that time already deputy manager of a large bank; and he was one of those who had been charged with examining the books of the firm of Meyer. All the reports agreed: no impropriety had been found.[20]

There is a document in the Meyrinkiana confirming this:

> It is hereby officially confirmed that the preliminary investigation against Herr Gustav Meyer, former banker in Prague, on suspicion of fraud, which was opened on 18 January 1902, was abandoned on 2 April 1902 following a declaration from the state prosecutor's office that they found no reason to continue the investigation.

Meyrink was completely exonerated but ruined. During the investigation, his bank had been closed. It never reopened; after the scandal and sensational reports in the newspapers people were

20 *Brod, p.294*

not surprisingly no longer willing to entrust their money to him. In typical fashion he refused to accept that and made desperate attempts to re-establish his good name by asking the newspapers, who had been so quick to condemn him, to print a statement that his books had been found to be in order. Only a few printed a brief version; the response of some was scornful. One is said to have written:

> Outrageous. Gustav Meyer, the notorious owner of a bureau de change who, after a series of problems with the courts in January of this year, was arrested on account of various widely publicised financial dealings and released because at present the law has no precise provisions for such 'dealings' has, after having been fortunate enough to escape retribution by the skin of his teeth, had the impu — imprudence to threaten to take the editors of the newspapers, which reported on his doings on the basis of statements from the authorities, to court — for libel. One would imagine that this type of person, only just having avoided the sword of Damocles, would be happy to sink back discreetly into social obscurity.[21]

The investigation had ruined his business and the period in prison had aggravated his ill-health. According to Kisch it took one more misfortune to drive him out of Prague. The court hearing Meyrink's appeal in the libel case brought against him by the two officers upheld the decision of the original court and even insisted he should serve the prison sentence, rather than pay a fine. Meyrink gave up, though he did not move immediately, as Kisch implies. It was the next year, 1904, that he left Prague for Vienna.

The experience of prison made a deep mark on Meyrink. Soon after his release, or perhaps even while he was in prison, he wrote two short stories which express the wretchedness and despair of incarceration. The September 1902 number of *Simplicissimus*, after

21 *Politik*, 22.4.1902; quoted in *Prager Tagblatt*, 21.1.1927.

his release in April, carried a piece by him called 'Das ganze Sein ist flammend Leid' (The Whole of Existence is a Blaze of Suffering) the title is taken from a poetic translation of one of the sayings of the Buddha: 'Sorrowful are all composite things. He who perceives the truth of this gets disgusted with this world of suffering. This is the path to purity.' Old Jürgen's feelings in his cell presumably reflect Meyrink's closely:

> The warder went from door to door with his heavy bundle of keys, shone his torch one last time through the barred openings, as is his duty, and checked that the iron bars had been put across the doors. Finally the sound of his steps died away and the silence of misery descended on all the unfortunates who, robbed of their freedom, slept on their wooden benches in the dreary cells.
>
> . . .
>
> During the first weeks the feeling of outrage, of furious hatred at being locked up for so long when he was completely innocent had pursued him even in his dreams and often he had felt like screaming out loud in desperation.

The prisoner is released and makes a meagre living selling caged songbirds until one day a woman brings two nightingales back and asks him to put out their eyes so they will sing more often. The man releases all his caged birds and hangs himself.

Before that, less than three months after his release, 'Terror' appeared in *Simplicissimus*. In it a prisoner in the condemned cell sees the terror he feels at his approaching execution as

> a hideous worm . . . a gigantic leech. Dark yellow in colour, with black flecks, it sucks its way along the floor, past each cell in turn. Alternately growing fat and

then elongating, it gropes its way along, searching.'
(Opal, 42)

In his first novel, *The Golem*, the hero, Pernath, is also unjustly imprisoned due to the machinations of a police officer called Otschin, which has deliberate echoes of Olic.

Editor's Notes:

1-8. are from Meyrink's collection *Fledermäuse (Bats)*, first published in 1916; the one story from *Fledermäuse* that has been omitted here is 'Meister Leonhard' which was published as 'The Master' in *The Dedalus Book of Austrian Fantasy 1890-2000*.

9. 'The Clockmaker' was first published in *Simplicissimus*, vol. XXXI no. 1, 1926.

10. 'The City with the Secret Heartbeat' was first published in *Die Gartenlaube*, no. 44, 1928.

11. 'The Pilot' was unpublished in Meyrink's lifetime; it first appeared in *Mensch und Schicksal*, vol. VI, no. 18, 1. 12. 1952.

12. 'The Transformation of the Blood' was unpublished in Meyrink's lifetime; it first appeared in *Fledermäuse*, ed. Eduard Frank, Munich, 1981; some of the incidents it contains appear in shorter articles Meyrink published (e.g. 'Magie im Tiefschlaf', 1928); it is not clear exactly when it was written, but internal evidence suggests 1927 or 1928.

13. *The Alchemist's House* was unpublished in Meyrink's lifetime. The manuscript (now in the Bavarian State Library) was collated by Meyrink's grandson, Julius Gustav Böhler, and first appeared in *Das Haus zur letzten Lantern*, ed. Eduard Frank, Munich, 1973, which also contains 'The Clockmaker', 'The City with the Secret Heartbeat' and 'The Pilot'.

14. *The Golem*, tr. Mike Mitchell, Dedalus, 1995; pp.103-113.

15. *The Green Face*, tr. Mike Mitchell, Dedalus, 1992; pp. 209-216.

16. *Walpurgisnacht*, tr. Mike Mitchell, Dedalus, 1993; pp.46-69.

17. *The White Dominican*, tr. Mike Mitchell, Dedalus, 1994; pp. 36-47.

18. *The Angel of the West Window*, tr. Mike Mitchell, 1991; pp. 55-71, 82-94.

19-22. From: *The Opal (and other stories)*, tr. and intro. Maurice

Raraty, Dedalus, 1994.
23. Mike Mitchell: *Vivo: The Life of Gustav Meyrink*, Dedalus, 2008; pp. 77-86.